What the

About Lionheart:

"This is a fast paced action and erotic love story with unique twists…Though a futuristic adventure is the story's base, this is foremost an erotic love story about the relationship between Mara and Sander. The love scenes are very hot and could easily melt the pages of the book! … For readers of erotica, this book is highly recommended!" - *5 Roses from Kari Thomas, A Romance Review*

"I must add how happy I am that Ms. Douglas took the "romance" portion of the genre seriously and blessed Mara and Sander with a heaping helping of love! It adds a depth to their intimacies that is missing in many "erotic" romances." – *Celia, A Romance Review*

"…Brimming with desire, need, and fearless love, LIONHEART by Kate Douglas will leave readers breathless… Ms. Douglas does an excellent job of combining passionate interludes with suspense to create an unforgettable love story that spans the universe. If you're looking for a tale that is sure to overwhelm your senses and take you on a thrilling ride, don't miss LIONHEART by Kate Douglas." - *Courtney Bowden, Romance Reviews Today*

"Ms Douglas' vibrant characters are unlike any other. Her detail to description gives the reader the insight into the very soul of the alien Sander, and the earth woman he loves...you will be hanging on the edge of your seat until the very end. A tale of sensual seduction, and surrender, that is a must read for any true erotica fan." - *Tracy Few, Timeless Tales Reviews*

"The characters in this story really seem to stand out and take a life of their own, and the ending is definitely well-deserved by both. Overall, a good read and a sexy hero... even if he is a bit unconventional!" - Ann Leveille, Sensual Romance Reviews

About Night of the Cat:

"Hot, sexy, and just pure fun, don't miss NIGHT OF THE CAT by Kate Douglas, the exciting second book in the StarQuest series!" - *Courtney Bowden, Romance Reviews Today*

"*NIGHT OF THE CAT* is a warmly satisfying read that leaves you purring in delight..." - *Ann Leveille, Sensual Romance Reviews*

"He is also the sexiest thing in fur — if you've ever owned a cat and felt their tongues lick your skin, then just try and imagine a large tongue like that licking your body — *everywhere.* Now uncross your eyes and go buy this book!!! And watch out for more intoxicating literary catnip from this fascinating writer!" - *Celia, A Romance Review, Rating: 5 roses!*

"This love story steams and sizzles, and is passionately intimate and erotically stimulating! The plot evolves around Jenna and Garan's forbidden love, and has a reader fanning herself as she keeps turning those pages devouring a book that just isn't long enough! ... Highly recommended for those who love an enticing erotic love story." - *Five Roses, Kari Thomas, Loves Romances*

About Pride of Imar:

Winner of the 2003 Silver Chalice Award

4 Stars from Romantic Times Magazine:
"PRIDE OF IMAR follows Night of the Cat in the Mirat-Earth series. Upping the intensity of character and plot, Ms. Douglas delivers an emotionally charged story that entertains and challenges. Very explicit and graphic sexual situations..."

"Ms. Douglas has a gift for writing mystical stories and putting the right touch of love in her characters..." - *5 Stars from Karen Simpson, Simegen*

"Kate Douglas just gets better with each book in the StarQuest series... Ms. Douglas brilliantly portrays the love, respect, and need of two people deeply in love with each other and proves that love really is the best medicine of all." - *Brenda Gill, Timeless Tales*

"...Ms. Douglas has a way with the written word that leaves me speechless. PRIDE OF IMAR is an erotic romance, but it's also a story of healing and love. Order your copy today." - *Michelle Gann, The Word on Romance*

"Sexually charged and action-packed, PRIDE OF IMAR by Kate Douglas is an erotic love story that fans of the Star

Quest series will eagerly devour!" - *Courtney Bowden, Romance Reviews Today*

"A moving and deeply erotic romance novel, PRIDE OF IMAR is more than just an escape-from-captivity book... Sheyna and Malachi are hot, hot, hot together! The romance is tempestuous, but perfectly orchestrated... PRIDE OF IMAR is another triumphant offering by the very talented Ms. Douglas." - *Ann Leveille, Sensual Romance Reviews*

Discover for yourself why readers can't get enough of the multiple award-winning publisher Ellora's Cave. Whether you prefer e-books or paperbacks, be sure to visit EC on the web at www.ellorascave.com for an erotic reading experience that will leave you breathless.

www.ellorascave.com

STARQUEST
An Ellora's Cave publication, 2003
Ellora's Cave Publishing, Inc.
PO Box 787
Hudson, OH 44236-0787

ISBN # 1843607956

LIONHEART:
ISBN MS Reader (LIT) ISBN # 1-84360-096-X
NIGHT OF THE CAT:
ISBN MS Reader (LIT) ISBN # 1-84360-172-9
PRIDE OF IMAR:
ISBN MS Reader (LIT) ISBN # 1-84360-259-8
Other available formats (no ISBNs are assigned):
Adobe (PDF), Rocketbook (RB), Mobipocket (PRC) &
HTML

LIONHEART edited by Jennifer Martin.
NIGHT OF THE CAT edited by Cris Brashear.
PRIDE OF IMAR edited by Kari Berton.
Cover art by Darrell King.

STARQUEST

Lionheart

Night of the Cat

Pride of Imar

by Kate Douglas

LIONHEART

Kate Douglas

Chapter 1

"You've been contacted again?"

"Yes. For the past five nights, now. He's come to me each night at about the same time."

"Do you still believe his is a peaceful mission?"

"Yes, Director. I do." Carefully controlling her nerves, Mara Armand faced the eight members of the governing board of the Armand Institute. How effective were her mental shields against this talented group of Sensitives? She'd never had a reason to hide anything from them before.

"As I explained, he opens contact with a kiss. Not a particularly warlike greeting," she added dryly, chuckling along with the men and women of the board.

"What else have you learned?"

She smiled in Fred Haydon's direction. Haydon had been one of her father's oldest friends. He would always see her as a child, never as the Armand Institute's newly elected leader.

"His name is Sander. His people call themselves Explorers. Their mission is one of peaceful telepathic study without actual physical contact."

Right. Who needed physical contact? Certainly not Sander—not with the ability to send the kind of telepathic kiss he'd given her last night. After an experience like that, Mara couldn't help but think the physical act of kissing must be highly overrated.

She wasn't about to share that information with the men and women sitting around the table, however. Hiding her guilt along with her thoughts, Mara subtly reinforced her mental shields.

"You're an empath." Malachi Franklin, the Institute's physician, pinned Mara with a deceptively benign stare. Had he picked up her wayward thoughts? He was precog. Did he see something she should know? "You feel no threat from this contact, no sense of deception?"

"None." She met his level gaze with one of her own. She'd never tried this before, hiding feelings from someone she'd known all her life.

Since first coming to the Institute as a small child, Mara's life had been an open book.

She wasn't certain how she felt when she realized how easy it was to deceive them.. It wasn't as if she were hiding anything dangerous. She'd never do that, never put the Institute at risk. Even so, it was unsettling to realize Malachi suspected nothing. His approving smile spread to the rest of the group.

"Then I recommend you continue the contact and learn whatever you can from these visitors." He turned and addressed the other members of the board. "Dr. Armand would have been thrilled to learn of an entire race of telepathic beings."

"I agree." Fred Haydon grinned mischievously at Mara. "Although the idea of kissing an alien before you start your conversation wouldn't do much for me, even if it is all in your head." Quiet laughter followed Fred's joke as Mara once again took her seat at the head of the long, marble table.

"Keep records of all your contacts. Learn whatever you can. It's a unique opportunity we've got here. But remember, be suspicious and be careful." The director gave Mara an encouraging smile, then glanced at the stack of notes in front of him. "Next order of business?"

Mara's thoughts wandered as the long meeting dragged on. Always they returned to the kiss. What had begun as a ritual greeting just five nights ago had changed to something completely different last night.

He'd first come to her in her dreams—alien, probing, curious and open. After the first brief moment of fear at the unexpected intrusion into her mind, she'd welcomed him, thrilled by the unique opportunity of telepathic contact, the chance to actually know a sentient being from another world.

The first night she'd sensed a gentle kiss on either cheek, the second, the soft caress of lips against hers. Nothing sensual, nothing out of the ordinary, if contact with an alien creature could ever be considered ordinary.

But last night...last night everything had changed. As usual, he had entered her thoughts, establishing the mindtouch she'd learned to welcome, the subtle, non-threatening link of one open mind with the other.

Mara, I, Sander the Explorer, greet you in peace.

That was the only part of the night that had remained familiar.

Warm lips brushed her cheek, first one side then the other before finding her mouth. On other nights the kiss had ended quickly and their telepathic conversation had begun.

Until last night.

She'd sensed the difference almost immediately. The familiar ritual greeting held a question, a subtle plea for acquiescence.

The brief contact deepened, lips warm against her mouth, the first touch of a tongue stroking, tasting, inviting her to open in welcome. Without hesitation she had done exactly that...without any concern this sensual invasion could be anything but wonderful. She'd welcomed the mobile tongue, those soft and searching lips, drawing him into her mouth, tasting flavors alien and intoxicating, giving herself over to this newfound sensuality, this contact of the mind that so inflamed her body.

She'd reached for him, sensing his body warm and solid against hers, but she'd touched only air and the light blanket covering her. When the kiss finally ended, she'd felt strangely bereft, her body and mind blatantly aroused, dangling there, suspended in the night by a silken thread of hot and pulsing need. A tenuous thread that parted as the explorer's ship passed out of orbit and her nightly contact with the presence ended.

"Mara? The meeting's adjourned." Fred Haydon stood up, chuckling as Mara rapidly blinked her eyes and tried to refocus on the group at the table. "You must have dozed off. Don't let your alien date keep you up so late."

Mara smiled thinly, thankful she'd at least managed to keep her shields in place, then gathered her papers and rose from her seat. "I'll try to remember that, Fred." She turned to leave. Suddenly, she felt mired in a thick wash of emotion.

Malachi Franklin stared at her from across the room. "Be careful, Mara. Remember, he's alien. His mind is obviously very powerful and we only know what he allows you to know. *Mind control takes many forms.* Use caution. Above all, keep us informed."

What does he know? Not only was Malachi the Institute's healer, he was also a powerful precog. The future sometimes opened to him, unfolding like leaves from a many-paged book. Did he see something Mara had missed? Did he sense danger somewhere along her path? Mara resisted the urge to try and read his emotions and thoughts, an act that would open her own mind to the doctor's.

Damn! Keeping secrets was not something she did naturally. She could, however, make promises.

"Of course, Malachi. I'll have a complete report for our next meeting." Mara brushed past him on her way out the door, her shields tightly drawn. She'd never hidden anything from anyone before, never felt a need to raise her shields, even to Malachi.

Which, of course, was the reason their brief affair had never progressed beyond friendship and a one time sexual liaison. He'd known exactly how she felt about him. They'd both realized it wasn't enough.

But now, now she concealed something profound, an act unprecedented in her knowledge of telepathy.

The kiss. Why had she deceived the board members about the starship captain's kiss?

Had she simply been embarrassed by her unbelievable response to Sander's sensuality? Was the kiss so special she'd wanted to keep it to herself, or had it been something more, something sinister?

Mind control takes many forms.

An uneasy shiver lifted the hair at Mara's nape as she headed back to her bungalow and another night of contact with Sander the Explorer.

* * * * *

"He's been orbiting Earth for almost three months, Mara, yet the contact you describe is essentially unchanged? There's no chance of his people making actual contact, of conducting a landing on our planet?"

"That's correct, Director. His people are forbidden physical contact with the species of warlike planets. Earth, with its myriad factions struggling under the rule of the World Federation, can only be classified as warlike."

The director, an old friend of her father's, nodded his head in silent agreement. "As much as I hate to think of our world as anything but peaceful, I must concur with your visitor's perception. We've not known peace for many years."

Mara carefully placed a silver disk on the table. "I've learned much about his home world, Mirat, and his mission to the stars. It's all here in my report."

Another board member spoke up. She smiled and Mara grinned in return. Bette, with her flowing silver hair and fingers covered with rings, was the one true romantic in the group. She was also a powerful telekinetic. "Have you any idea of his appearance?" she asked. "Are his people at all, well, humanoid?" Bette's soft question reminded Mara how little she actually knew about her visitor.

"We've never discussed our physical attributes. He does refer to families and pair bonds, so there appears to be a similar social structure among his people. He mentions the rigors of space travel, the loneliness, how much he misses his world."

"But nothing about himself? You have no mental image of a visitor who has come to you nightly for three months, now?" Mara jerked around at the director's probing question. "Aren't you curious, Dr. Armand?"

Mara sensed his gentle rebuke and bowed her head. The director rarely used her title. "Yes, sir. Of course I'm curious. But no, I have no perception beyond our conversation, nothing that tells me what he looks like."

"Still getting that 'ritual kiss,' Mara? Maybe I should park outside your bungalow and play chaperone."

Everyone laughed at Fred's dry wit. Mara merely smiled, thankful for his interruption, then gathered her papers and went home.

Now she played the conversation over in her mind, shivering slightly as she shed her clothes and crawled into bed. Deception weighed heavily on her mind, though she'd not lied when she told the director she had no idea of Sander's physical appearance. She'd sensed hands and lips, a body warm against hers, a wet tongue stroking, a very hot penis filling her, bringing her to mind-stunning completion.

Still, everything she'd sensed had occurred within her mind, no matter how strong the physical sensations had been. The thoughts had been put there by Sander, but the sensations she felt might be merely her interpretation of his telepathic lovemaking.

It was odd, though, that she'd never felt compelled to ask him what he looked like. Mara sighed, scissoring her legs against the cool sheets. Did it really matter?

Of course it did...or it would have with any similar contact she might have made with a male of her own species. Malachi's insistent warning drifted, unwelcome, through Mara's thoughts.

Mind control takes many forms.

Was Sander controlling her innate sense of curiosity? Was his mind that powerful?

It doesn't matter. She blinked against the darkness. Not if only her mind was involved. She was never going to see her starship captain. He was, and would remain, a lover in thought only.

Mara realized his visits had taken on an aura of pure fantasy.

The most exciting sexual fantasy she'd ever known.

Once his study of Earth ended, Sander would return to Mirat without ever setting foot on her planet. How would she bear it when he was gone? She grimaced, thinking of Fred's joke about the "ritual kiss." The members of the board had no idea, none of them did, how much farther that kiss had progressed.

Maybe Fred was right. Maybe she did need a chaperone. *Just look at me,* she thought—lying here naked in her lonely bed, knees apart, moisture welling up between her thighs in anxious anticipation, waiting.

She'd never slept naked in her life, not until Sander had come to her on his nightly visits as his ship orbited the planet.

Mara let her thoughts drift. She gazed at the only light in the room, a small portrait lamp illuminating the subtle colors of the oil painting of African lions Daniel Armand had done many years ago. Willing her agitation to subside, she thoughtfully studied the familiar features of the King of Beasts. His golden eyes had watched over her since childhood, guarding and protecting her along with the pride of females and small cubs clustered about his broad paws.

A comforting presence in her tiny bedroom.

Until three months ago, the only presence.

Why didn't I tell them? She should have put it in her report, the way Sander made her feel, the power of his mental touch. But how could she? How could she stand there, in front of that group of men and women who'd known her all her life, one of whom had been her lover, and explain that only now, after three short months of the alien's mindtouch, did she finally understand what had been missing in her life?

Mind control takes many forms.

No. She absolutely refused to believe that. Her report had been as complete as it needed to be. She'd told the board members what she'd learned about Mirat, about the other sentient species Sander described, the other worlds he and his team of explorers had visited. She would not, could not, tell them everything. She had given her life to her father's dream, her every decision weighted in favor of his beloved Institute.

Disclosing the specific nature of Sander's nightly visits would throw the Armand Institute into turmoil. The ever-protective board members would insist she end the contact.

Impossible.

There was still so much more to learn.

Mara thought of her life before Sander. That naive young woman was an innocent, a girl completely oblivious to possibilities. Now Mara's body hummed with a new level of sensual awareness, with needs she'd never before recognized.

Needs she'd discovered through her contact with Sander.

Was he affecting her mind? Was his sensual assault on her body part of an ultimate plan, some insidious plot for control?

"Ridiculous." Malachi's paranoid warnings and Fred's teasing must be getting to her. There was no danger in Sander. The only danger she foresaw was to her heart.

That was a danger she would face on her own. Mara glanced at the switch to the hummer, a simple device occasionally used to block the interfering thoughts of the other sensitive minds within the compound. Trusting her neighbors' consideration for her privacy, she still wished she could turn it on and relax with the knowledge she was completely alone with her alien visitor.

Unfortunately, the silent emanations from the device would block Sander's thoughts as well. She would have to take the risk, trusting the innate discretion of her fellow Sensitives to ensure her privacy. Spying on one another was an unforgivable act.

Sighing, she willed her troubled spirit to relax. Naked beneath the light sheet, she waited. As patiently as the tawny lion watching over her, she waited.

Will he come? She opened her mind to his gentle touch and settled into the darkness. The details of the weekly board meeting faded along with her nagging sense of guilt. The subtle buzz and tremor of a hundred minds disappeared as Mara focused her thoughts on the alien ship orbiting above the Earth.

She recognized his mindtouch immediately, the gentle quest into her thoughts, the almost physical caress as their minds linked and renewed acquaintance. Sighing in greeting, she felt the familiar languor envelop her limbs.

"Sander." She whispered his name aloud, even though he heard only her thoughts.

She thought of that first contact, how difficult it had been to understand him. Even now, as much as she'd improved, much of his mental conversation was lost to her. But his touch! He'd awakened her, caressed a pleasure center of her brain in such a way that his touch was now a drug she craved.

Mind control takes many forms.

She closed her eyes in denial. She would know if Sander lied. An empath sensed deceit as a powerful emotion.

Giving her mind completely over to his had been difficult. Trusting the unknown, opening herself to his life-force — very difficult.

Even now, she knew he was there, hovering just outside her consciousness. At precisely the moment she'd begin to doubt his presence he would appear, finally, at the corners of her mind, his touch as light as a butterfly's wing.

There! Just as she'd expected. The fragile, fluttering whisper of contact, the softest of kisses on her waiting lips, followed a moment later by a roughened finger trailing across her throat. She exhaled a sigh of surrender.

His deep, sensual laugh filled her mind as the sensation of that single finger sketched a fiery path between her breasts, encircling the rounded contour of first one, then the other, finally pausing to tease the silky underside of each in its turn.

Liquid fire pooled between her thighs. She felt the deep pulse low in her abdomen, the prickling, tickling whisper of the cool night air against her flesh. She arched her back, sighing once again and expanding her chest with a deep, lung-filling breath, lifting her breasts closer to his hands, seeking more of his caress. Broad palms cupped her breasts, strong fingers pinched and rolled her sensitive nipples into hard kernels. Unseen lips tasted her belly, nuzzling and nipping with sharp little bites and moist kisses.

Gone now was the teasing, almost tentative touch. The power of the presence grew, filling her thoughts with pure, unfiltered sensation, dragging a muted cry from between her lips.

Mara clutched the sheets with trembling fingers. She'd tried before to touch him, to stroke the entity giving her so much pleasure.

The only body she'd touched had been her own.

The kisses grew more intimate, the hands fondling her breasts more demanding, tugging and rolling her turgid nipples until she cried out. His hot and greedy tongue laved her belly with long, wet strokes, before dropping lower to trace the narrow crease between thigh and groin.

She groaned, arching her back, begging for more. Her heels dug into the firm mattress, raising her hips completely off the bed. Again she heard his laughter in her mind, a deep, masculine chuckle of pure, intoxicating pleasure. His tongue moved, flicking across her once, twice, then lingered with teasing, feather-light licks, a taste here, a soft stroke there, so close she felt his hot breath lift the silken curls between her legs, but no more, neither touching nor easing the growing pressure.

Her muscles began their own rhythmic pulse, a mute plea for fulfillment. She parted her knees, silently begging for completion, aware Sander's touch was to her mind, not her body, a mental touch so powerful she clenched her vaginal walls against his illusory hot tongue as, finally, it entered her.

This was new, this intimate kiss, reaching deeper, stroking, filling her with heat, then lapping away the dewy moisture. Now his teeth, not his hands, gently nipped and teased, stinging little bites followed by lush, soothing kisses, a delicate balance of pleasure and pain, pain and pleasure until she cried out.

"Now," she demanded, her voice a harsh plea for release. "Please, now!"

Sensation stopped. His touch disappeared. Her flesh quivered, bereft. She drew a deep, shuddering breath. Had she angered him? Driven him away?

Never.

The single word filled her mind, his laughter filled her soul. He hadn't left her! He waited there, just outside her conscious mind, teasing her with his presence. Why was he taking so long? What if his ship orbited beyond their reach? What if he left her, writhing here in agony, inflamed and needy?

Her flesh pulsed; empty, bereft.

He took her with his mouth, suckling, drawing the engorged folds of hot flesh between his lips, driving into her with that incredible tongue. Once again his huge hands enveloped her breasts, his fingers none too gently rolling the taut nipples into fierce little knots.

She bucked beneath his assault, loving him, needing him, taking greedy pleasure from each new sensation he brought her. His tongue — no, it wasn't possible — but his tongue filled her, pulsed within her, searing her tender flesh, driving in and out then back again in a rhythm older than time. She hovered at the brink of ecstasy, her breath labored, her throat taut, the scream silent.

She felt his tongue slip free of her greedy folds and sweep the length of her, a fiery brand marking the valley between her legs from front to back and back again, parting her thighs, circling that tiny nubbin of pure sensation, driving her to the edge, to the end of oblivion and back until finally, with a last powerful sweep and swirl he filled her, plunging in then out, then in again. His blunt fingers wound about the tender tips of her breasts, his rapacious tongue suddenly stilled deep inside then quickly withdrew as his lips covered her clit, suckling, sucking her soul, her spirit, her self…drawing the last ounce of sanity from her tortured mind.

She screamed in pure, wanton pleasure, hurled from the precipice, a willing sacrifice, her mind filled with his blazing release along with her own.

Panting, exhausted, unbelievably sated, Mara sprawled across the tumbled sheets. The night air chilled the damp emptiness between her thighs. Her besieged and beleaguered flesh pulsed with the final tremors of orgasm. Her nipples ached, a deep throbbing ache linked directly to her clit.

Once again, she felt his mouth cover her, relieving the painful pressure with a gentle caress, first suckling one breast, then the other.

Sighing, Mara drifted into sleep as Sander's starship drifted on in space.

* * * * *

Later, much later, a scream woke her, a scream of untold anguish and pain. Bolting upright in the predawn darkness, Mara instinctively grabbed the keyboard by her bed. Coordinates filled her thoughts, senseless numbers she was compelled to type into her computer, meaningless figures flying into her mind.

Her fingers stilled but the painful barrage continued.

Words lost, specific thoughts too scrambled, too frightened. Only the emotions. Her lover's emotions.

The clearest of them all...regret.

Chapter 2

"Were there any survivors?"

"One. Barely. They're bringing him into the Institute now."

"Is he...?

"Humanoid? You should know that better than anyone, Doc. You've spent the last three months getting to know him. Besides, you're the mind reader."

"I've told you, Haydon. I'm not a mind reader. I'm a moderately competent telepath with strong empathic abilities. I read emotions, not minds."

"I guess I should be grateful for small favors," Haydon answered, laughing with his usual good humor. "Otherwise you might find out just how little I have in mine."

"That's not true, and we both know it." Mara smiled, reaching out to touch her old friend's callused hand. His swirling emotions instantly flowed into her: elation, curiosity, warmth...fear.

Fear? That shouldn't be surprising, even though Fred Haydon was probably the most fearless member of her elite staff.

It was typical of mankind to fear the unknown.

The otherworldly creature currently under transport to the Armand Institute's private hospital was still, after three months of telepathic contact, an unknown. Thank goodness, though, for the strong mental link Mara and Sander had established. Enough of a link to draw the disabled craft close enough for the Institute's people to recover.

"You didn't answer my question, Mr. Haydon." Mara tried to keep her tone light and teasing, disguising the distress she'd struggled to control since this morning's contact. It hadn't been easy, shielding her thoughts and worries from the other Sensitives, fighting the urge to broadcast an open search for Sander while opening her mind on a narrow band as a beacon to his ship.

She felt drained yet euphoric. It had worked! Beyond all expectations, the mental guide she projected had drawn Sander to safety.

Haydon's talent was telekinesis, thank goodness, not telepathy. He moved small objects with the power of his mind, but he couldn't read her stormy thoughts.

It had been a difficult three months, living within the walls of the Armand Institute, surrounded by an entire community of Sensitives well aware she'd made contact. All of them curious, wondering. Telepaths, healers, empaths like herself, telekinetics like Fred...even the precogs sensed when a person was out of balance.

Contact with Sander the Explorer had definitely upset more than Mara's balance. At first her weekly reports to the Institute's Board of Directors had been met with cautious optimism. As her involvement with Sander grew, she soon realized she was editing more and more of the nature of their contact.

Even now she wondered if she'd lied to protect herself or to protect her father's dream of someday utilizing the full extra-sensory powers of the human mind. The Armand Institute had lost much of its vitality since Daniel Armand's death. Once a safe haven for study and the pursuit of extra-sensory knowledge, it had degenerated into an insular, walled community offering safety for those with psychic abilities from the controlling dictates of the World Federation.

Contact with Sander offered a chance to revitalize the Institute. Mara had promised to learn all she could about the telepathic alien.

No one knew how far beyond mere scientific research their relationship had grown.

Now, in mere minutes, she would actually meet him. Mara stumbled over a crack in the sidewalk. Haydon reached out to steady her. "Thanks," she muttered, flashing a quick grin at the older man.

He looked away, his feelings carefully shielded.

Just as she had been shielding from Haydon, from all the men and women of the Institute Board. Men and women who had been surrogate parents to her since Daniel Armand first brought her into his home.

Always sensitive to the psychological and emotional pain endured by an empath, they had protected her, befriended her, loved her.

Babied her.

She'd studied, completed her education, learned to survive with her exceptional gifts, and still the men and women on the board, in the entire Institute, for that matter, saw her as a child.

As an empath, it had been easier for her to go along with their perception than risk hurting feelings, insulting dear friends.

She thought of Haydon's teasing over the past few months. Honest, loving concern disguised in humor. Concern, still the same, as if she were still a child.

Mara sighed as they drew closer to the clinic. At some point, she knew, she would have to remind Haydon and the others she was very much an adult.

In moments Mara would be faced with her own duplicity. She had lied to Haydon, she had lied to the board members and she'd lied to herself. She'd denied the depths of her feeling for the unseen alien as he'd drawn her deeper and deeper into his sensual world.

Now it was too late. An affair of the mind had become an affair of the heart. Everything she'd learned about him, his goals, his ideals, his fine sense of honor, had made her love him more. Always, though, it had been a safe love, their separation decreed by his planet's laws.

Now, everything had changed and the question remained—not only, to whom had she given her heart, but to what?

"Is he…is he humanoid?" She repeated the question, one scientist to another. The woman in her wondered at the answer.

Haydon sighed, then rubbed the back of his neck. "We don't know yet, Doc. The safety pod was badly damaged when it entered the atmosphere. Security was afraid to open it until they could get a clear reading on the chemical composition of the air. They decided to move the unit intact. I know you said he can survive in our atmosphere, but no one wants to take any chances. They'll open it once they reach the hospital."

Her expression was troubled. "You said he's barely hanging on. What if…?"

Haydon tapped a series of keys on the small computer attached to his coveralls. Within seconds, a printed message filled the screen. "Still unconscious, but vitals are strong. And, quite humanoid," he added, winking at Mara. "You said you read him from the escape pod. Any idea what happened? What was the last message you received?"

Mara shuddered, recalling Sander's sense of fear, of frustration, of almost mindless rage at the unfairness of fate.

Then nothing. Unconsciousness or death? She hadn't been certain, not until now, that he'd survived. "Just feelings, really." She shook her head, trying unsuccessfully to wipe Sander's anguish from her mind.

Sometimes the emotions of others enveloped her in an almost physical net of pain. Sander's last message still reverberated throughout her body.

Much like the final, clenching spasms of an orgasm.

She took a deep breath, steadied herself. "He was trying to control the pod, he didn't take the time to actually communicate. He was afraid of dying before…" Her voice trailed off. She couldn't complete the rest of the visitor's fear.

Before we could actually meet.

"You're awfully sure it's a he. Must be that nightly kiss." The teasing quality was back in Haydon's voice.

Mara flashed him a quick smile. "A woman knows these things," she said, pushing the dark thoughts out of her mind. "C'mon, we'd better hurry. I want to be at the hospital when they bring him in."

The outside air was crisp and clear, the lush foliage growing about the Armand Institute's walled grounds filled with the chatter of birds and squirrels. Mara had to stretch to keep up with Haydon's brisk stride.

"Too bad your father didn't live to see this day, eh Doc? An entire race of telepathic beings! He would have been in his glory."

"I like to think he knows," Mara murmured, fighting the quick sting of tears. The Institute's founder, her adoptive father, had been killed barely a year ago. An accident, according to the World Federation officer who had recovered Daniel Armand's body.

Murder, as far as most of the Institute staff members believed.

"You're probably right," Haydon said gently, slowing his pace just a bit. "I've never known a more powerful mind, nor a kinder man than Daniel. If it hadn't been for him…"

Mara nodded her head, understanding exactly what Fred Haydon left unspoken.

Daniel Armand had been a powerful telepath, a man able to communicate with, and in many cases control, the minds of others. He'd recognized the potential of the human mind for both good and evil and had built his Institute to study, and in many ways, protect, those individuals possessing unusual and extrasensory mental skills.

His friend Haydon among them.

He'd never married, never had children of his own, but when Mara was brought to the Armand Institute as a troubled and frightened four-year-old orphan, Daniel Armand had recognized her empathic abilities at once.

He'd adopted her and filled her life with love. Saving her from almost certain insanity, he'd taught Mara to control the onslaught of others' feelings, to reach inside her mind and develop the latent extrasensory skills she hadn't realized she had.

Skills that had allowed her to receive telepathic contact from the captain of an alien ship circling Earth.

A ship of such unique composition and design that all the advanced technology of the World Federation had been unable to detect its location.

Mara had achieved what had never before been done on Earth: peaceful contact with an alien species.

She shuddered, remembering the amorphous things that had attacked Earth almost twenty years ago. Protected in their armed vessels like oysters within their shells, the aliens had waged a brief but vicious war against humanity.

The desperate cooperation of humankind had eventually defeated the attackers. During that deadly period, the World Federation was born. Since that time, fear of alien contact had been drilled into every man, woman, and child on the planet.

Mara closed her eyes, remembering the warmth of Sander's thoughts, the feelings he'd shared, the fears, the need...and the passion.

But is he human?

This time her heart answered, *Does it matter?*

Haydon suddenly broke into a run. "Hurry up, Doc. Looks like they've already moved the pod into the security wing."

Adrenaline surged. Mara passed Haydon, running up the steps and through the heavy set of double doors leading to the secure sector of the hospital.

Down the long hallway, behind the locked steel doors at the far end, Sander waited.

* * * * *

He regained consciousness slowly, sliding from serene oblivion into guarded awareness. He blinked in a futile attempt to adjust leonine eyes to complete darkness. Praise the Mother, the pod had remained intact, even though its supposedly "fail-safe" systems were obviously out. No one relished the thought of burning up during entry.

Very few relished death in any form, no matter how inevitable. He thought sadly of his companions, now mere motes of incinerated dust circling Earth's atmosphere. Good scientists all, they had died in the line of duty.

As he had survived. Sander loosed the safety harness, working by touch in the unlighted pod. The unit was completely dead, no functioning lights, no navigational readouts to indicate how far he might be from the mysterious Institute.

How far from Mara.

He'd felt the latent strength of her mind, the powerful surge pulling his ship as it tumbled out of orbit, dragging it toward the quadrant where the Institute nestled in its desert enclave. Had she been strong enough to wrench the damaged vehicle from its spiral into World Federation territory?

He reached out with his mind, then groaned as waves of pain rolled through his skull. He'd have to wait out the aftereffects of reentry before searching for her.

Ah, Mara. I know you heard me...but can you help me?

Sander and his crew had monitored Earth's communications for a full quarter, enough time to realize the warlike nature of the people inhabiting the third world from the sun, enough time to learn of their fear and loathing of alien contact.

The only welcoming voice had come from Mara. Her mindlink had warmed him through the long, lonely nights while he drifted in orbit above the planet, her thoughts and dreams and sweet mental touch exciting him as a lover's might.

One sensitive, passionate female amid an entire planet of strangers, a female who had joined with him in the most intimate behavior. His deep growl of loss and anger echoed within the close confines of the pod.

If she'd lost contact during his fall to earth, how would they ever find one another? If WF soldiers reached him first, his and Mara's dreams of their worlds eventually learning to communicate in peace would be forever lost.

Along with my life, if I don't get moving.

Guilt swept him. He gave up a silent prayer to the Mother for his lost companions, and at the same time questioned Her wisdom for allowing a small but deadly piece of space debris to share the same orbit.

If he hadn't been servicing the escape pod when the ship exploded...

He bowed his head against the pain. Three lives lost. Months of irreplaceable data. Most devastating of all, gone forever the chance to return to his own planet, to once more kneel in Mirat's sweet fields, to look past her twin moons into the universe beyond.

Never again to search the stars.

A sharp spasm of pain knifed through his chest, an agony of loss beyond comprehension. He took a deep breath, fighting for control. There would be another time to grieve, another time to offer up prayers for his companions.

To do that, he must, himself, survive.

Sighing, Sander reached for the latch that would open the pod and finally give him access to this strange new world.

* * * * *

Mara deftly pressed her palm over the scanner, only to unprofessionally scamper past the guard on duty the moment the doors opened. She skidded to a halt in front of a relatively small hunk of indeterminate material, its shape and size reminiscent of an antique VW Beetle.

The escape pod.

It rested in the center of the room, its hull blackened and pockmarked, one side of the landing gear bent and folded in upon itself. Armed guards surrounded the vehicle, but Mara sensed excitement, not fear.

Thank goodness the Institute, not WF forces, had recovered their visitor. She took a deep breath, thankful for Fred Haydon's steady hand on her shoulder, and cast her thoughts into the damaged sphere.

"No, Mara." Fred gently turned her in the direction of an examination cubicle. "He's out. Can't you read him?"

Not if I'm not projecting. Please, Mara. Don't be afraid. Not after all we've shared.

Her eyes widened fractionally. Malachi Franklin blocked Mara's view of the examining table, but Sander's thoughts rang loud and clear in her mind.

"Sander?" She swallowed deeply as the young doctor, his expression totally unreadable, glanced at her and stepped aside.

The figure sitting upright on the table said nothing, as if awaiting Mara's judgment. No expression marred his feline face, no emotions telegraphed themselves to her open and waiting mind. The only sign of his possible nervousness was the regular twitching at the tip of the long, almost prehensile tail curled loosely about one lightly furred ankle.

Mara stepped closer, fascinated by this man/beast she feared she had grown to love. *I never dreamed...*

What, Mara? That I would look so different from you? Our thoughts are very much alike, our needs the same. Do you find my appearance offensive?

"Never, Sander. Not at all," she said, speaking aloud. She stepped closer, close enough to reach out and touch his hand, more human than pawlike, but tipped with strong, sharp nails the color of ebony.

Oblivious to all but the alien, she grasped his hand, turning it palm side up, rubbing the soft leathery surface with her thumb. His blunt fingers encircled hers and he raised her hand to his mouth. She almost giggled when, instead of the courtly kiss she'd somehow expected, he ran the rough tip of his tongue from the sensitive inner flesh of her wrist to the tips of her fingers.

A very familiar tongue. She blushed as hot memories of the night before filled her mind, then quickly shielded her thoughts.

"You are strangely beautiful," he said aloud. His voice was deep, raspy, as if from lack of use.

Malachi Franklin looked stunned. "You speak perfect English! But how...?

Still holding Mara's hand, Sander turned to face the doctor. "As you know, we've been studying your world for a quarter...three of your months. On our world we communicate telepathically most of the time, saving speech for ceremonial occasions. We learn audible languages by mentally downloading the thoughts of a sentient being, incorporating both sound and meaning into the language centers of our own brains. We knew we would have to communicate verbally once we made contact with your people. We never once thought we'd be so lucky as to make mental contact..." He glanced at Mara, his eyes huge and golden.

Lion's eyes, staring at her out of a face that could only belong to the King of Beasts.

Except Sander wasn't a beast. There was nothing beastlike in the proud set of his shoulders, the broad chest and muscled thighs. Even the thick mane of dark, rust-colored hair that fell away from his wide brow and lay heavy along his back was more regal than beastlike.

He was plainly dressed, his feet bare, his dark green skinsuit a style quite similar to the ones worn by members of the Institute staff.

Except for the opening for his tail!

Mara bit her lips to keep from smiling, then laughed aloud when she felt Sander's telepathic burst of laughter.

On our world, the length and breadth of a man's tail is indicative of other masculine attributes, he projected, laughing out loud when her gaze automatically flashed from his sizable tail to the noticeable bulge at his crotch.

"Mara?"

"It's okay, Fred." Blushing once again, Mara gently disengaged her hand from Sander's light grasp. "I'm merely discovering that men are very much alike the universe over."

She stepped back, pulling her cloak of leadership about her like a protective shield. "Dr. Franklin, I assume you've finished your scans and our guest is in good health? No injuries from his crash? No unusual viruses or other infectious agents?"

At the doctor's begrudging nod, she turned to the chief of security. "Major Tamura, does anyone outside the Institute know of Captain Sander's arrival?"

"World Federation radar might have picked up the explosion, but Captain Sander assures me, telepathically, I might add, and it is truly an honor, Captain, to be so addressed," he nodded in Sander's direction, "the ship was constructed of the same material as the escape pod. It's unusual stuff, Doctor Armand, and it won't show up on their system. Industrials can't wait to get their hands on it." He nodded in Sander's direction, "with your permission, Captain," he added, before turning again to Mara. "Thanks to your coordinates, we arrived at the crash site within minutes of contact. It's an isolated part of the desert. Other than a lizard or two, I don't think anyone saw us recover the pod."

She blew out a breath of relief. "Thank you, Major. Continue to monitor WF communications for any reference to our guest." Mara smiled her dismissal, then turned once again to Sander. He sat, as before, on the edge of the examining table, his emotions pulsing too potently to lock away.

Excitement, curiosity, expectation...longing. A deep, sexual longing, a need as strong as her own, unspoken, unfulfilled.

It took her breath away. She stared into his deep-set, amber eyes, into the depths of his desire and heard the silent words, the almost humble plea he sent her.

Take me to your home, Mara. Take me home with you.

Her decision was easier than it should have been and probably not very sensible. She'd have to consider the implications of that later. Right now, Sander needed the sanctuary she represented.

He needed her. Malachi's early warnings slipped from her mind, unheeded. Biting her lips, she turned away from Sander and faced the room filled with expectant scientists and doctors, all lifelong friends.

"I know all of you have a million questions to ask Captain Sander, but he has had a long and harrowing journey." She smiled, shielding her innermost thoughts from Sander as well as the men and women gathered about her. "I've been his main contact, the one he's most comfortable with, so I'm taking him home with me."

"You can't do that, Mara. You don't know a thing about him." Malachi Franklin nodded in Sander's direction as if he were nothing more than an insentient creature. "I don't scan any contagions on him, but what about his contact with us? Agents perfectly harmless to humans might be devastating to him."

Sander quietly interrupted the doctor. "I was completely decontaminated and cleansed of potentially harmful agents before boarding my ship. My companions and I, Goddess grant them peace, took care to inoculate ourselves against your harmful bacteria and viruses once we reached Earth orbit."

"But..."

"Malachi, please."

"Mara, please." Malachi's sarcastic reply echoed in the suddenly quiet room. "Don't forget what I told you," he said, grabbing Mara's arm and forcing her to look at him.

Mind control takes many forms.

She stared into his dark eyes for one, unguarded moment, then pulled her arm free of his grasp. Ignoring the shocked gasps of the others in the room, the doctor's furious glare, and the barrage of oddly jealous emotions he directed her way, she raised her hand to forestall further complaints. "Later, after Captain Sander has eaten and rested, and if he's willing, you'll have the opportunity to speak with him."

She turned her back on Malachi and glanced again at Sander. His expression appeared unchanged, but his mental sigh of relief reverberated through her mind, reinforcing her decision. "If that's all right with you, Captain?" she added for the benefit of the listening scientists.

"More than all right." His face remained impassive, but he added a mental boost to his spoken words, loading them down with enough sexual innuendo to curl Mara's toes. "I gratefully accept your generous hospitality, Dr. Armand."

Mara could have sworn he purred.

Chapter 3

The electric tram silently carried them across the Institute grounds to Mara's private quarters. Here, away from the curious eyes and probing minds of scientists and security forces, Sander's broad shoulders slumped and his intelligent face held a withdrawn, shuttered expression.

Mara absorbed his emotions, silently reading his utter exhaustion and deep sense of personal loss. "The scientists who died," she said, gently touching the back of Sander's broad hand. "They were good friends as well as co-workers. I'm sorry for your loss. But I'm very thankful you survived."

"Thank you." He raised his head, focusing on her with wide-spaced golden eyes. "I don't think I've quite assimilated all my losses yet. It's only just beginning to sink in that I can't return to Mirat...my home."

"I thought you could contact your base telepathically. Can't you just, you know, call home and request a rescue?"

"Only from orbit, or better yet, deep space. I'm unable to project my thoughts beyond earth's gravity. Unless the Institute has a space vehicle available...?"

Mara shook her head.

"Then whether you want me or not, Mara, I am, for all intents and purposes, your prisoner."

"We'll not hold you against your will." She snatched her hand away from his. "You're free to leave the Institute whenever you want."

"Where would I go, my sweet Mara? Remember, I've been studying your people for quite some time. The World Federation barely tolerates the existence of the Armand Institute and then only because they want your mental powers as weapons of destruction."

"We will never..."

"I know that. You use your abilities for peace, to help mankind. But don't you understand? If my presence is discovered by WF troops, not only is my life forfeit, I put your Institute at risk as well. If they learn you had aided me...you understand, don't you? I am well and truly a prisoner here and completely at your mercy."

"Is that so awful?" Mara cupped the side of his face in her hand, awed by the strength of his jaw, the silky texture of his tawny pelt. "Ah, Sander...I still can't believe you're here. I never thought I'd actually meet you." She projected a sense of warmth and caring, bathing Sander in a flood of emotional welcome. She'd make him want to stay. She had to. He must know she loved him, loved him enough—

"It won't work, my darling Mara." Regret spilled from Sander as he reached up to cover her hand with his. "My sense of reality is, unfortunately, much more powerful than your emotional fantasy. But thank you for trying." He smiled, baring sharp canines between slightly parted lips.

"I do love you, Sander." Here, beside him, her hand warmly cupped in his, her doubts fled. She opened her soul to him, let him see himself as she saw him, gave him access to her deepest thoughts and emotions.

His smile was gentle, understanding, and in Mara's estimation, somewhat patronizing.

"You want me, Mara." He lifted her hand away from his face and stroked her fingers. "That's not love. You're very young, not only in years, but experience as well. I've made you want me. All those nights, projecting my fantasies and needs across space, invading your heart along with your body. Love is very different from wanting."

Mara angrily disengaged her hand from his. She could accept she was little more than a figurehead as leader of her father's Institute, but she was tired of being patronized by everyone.

She glared at Sander. "Is wanting so bad?"

Before he could answer, the tram halted in front of a small bungalow almost completely hidden in a dense copse of trees and shrubbery. Mara climbed out, her back to Sander, her mental shields tightly in place.

Exhaustion swept over him as he grabbed his small personal kit, the only thing he'd salvaged from the escape pod, and followed her up the winding path to a gated entrance.

Is wanting so bad? He'd never really thought about it quite like that. Travel and exploration had, up until now, been his life's work, a choice he'd made without reservation. The chance to study alien worlds, to seek out the myriad linked species of the universe, meant a life outside the pack. No lifebond with a mate, no offspring, no relationships other than occasional emotionless physical gratification.

His contact with Mara had been unique and more than gratifying. He'd wanted her. He had taken her on many occasions in what had been, for Sander, the longest relationship he'd ever maintained. Explorers did not mate with others on their crew unless the expectation of a lifebond existed. Sander knew first hand how personal complications could prove disastrous on long journeys.

There'd been no such restriction with Mara. Since he'd never expected to take their intimacy beyond the realm of the mind, Sander'd had no qualms about linking with the human empath whenever he'd had the chance.

She'd complied, freely, without guile, opening her mind to him, projecting her own desires and sexual needs so completely that Sander had surprisingly experienced total satisfaction.

But love? No, he couldn't call it love.

Gratification. Fulfillment of desire. Even, at times, satiation. Not love. Not with an alien species so different from his own kind. No matter how attractive she might be.

He admired Mara's lithe form as she stepped through the open door into her residence. Exhausted, hurting from the shock of reentry and the loss of his companions, his mind badly bludgeoned by all the events of the day, Sander still felt a deep thrill of arousal as he studied her.

It stopped him short. Made him reconsider.

Maybe Mara was right. Wanting, and getting, might not be all that bad.

* * * * *

Mara paused in the hallway, arms loaded with extra blankets. Sander's home world was warmer than earth. She didn't want him to be cold or hungry…or alone.

The enormity of what she'd done, bringing him into her home in answer to his quiet plea, washed over her. *Oh God,* she thought, *I've got him…now what do I do with him?*

"Whatever you like." Sander stepped out of the bedroom that had once belonged to Daniel Armand. His golden-eyed gaze swept over her.

Devoured her.

"You startled me." Avoiding eye contact, Mara swept past him and tossed the extra blankets on the bed. After all the weeks of their intimate sharing of thoughts and emotions, why did his presence unnerve her so?

"Because suddenly the fantasies have become possibilities and they frighten you." Sander's husky voice purred along the nape of her neck, raising goosebumps across her spine. Her mind was an open book to him! She barely controlled a shudder as he gently cupped her shoulders in his broad hands.

His fingers tensed and his sudden emotional withdrawal startled her. "Are you okay?" she asked, spinning so quickly she literally tumbled into his embrace.

His nearness took her breath away. His beauty stunned her.

An onslaught of pain ripped through her mind.

"What is it?" Gasping with the brutal onslaught, she reached up to place comforting hands at his temples. "What's hurting you? I don't understand."

"You have inquisitive friends," he whispered. Still grasping her shoulders, he closed his eyes and bowed his head. "Their thoughts and questions have been hammering me since I arrived…I can't block them anymore…too tired, too…"

No wonder he'd asked her to take him home!

Stop it. Now! Her mental command had hardly been issued when she felt the tension in Sander relax. "I'm so sorry. The other telepaths…you're much too unique to resist."

His eyes flicked over her face. "Will you resist me?" he murmured.

I don't know. She opened her mind, hoping Sander would see and understand her confusion. He was much too close, embracing her lightly, gazing down on her with his beautiful amber eyes. His hands lightly massaged her shoulders, hers still caressed his broad skull.

Impossible emotions swirled between them, unreadable, intense. Drawing on an inner strength she hadn't been certain she possessed, Mara broke the contact. She pulled gently out of Sander's embrace and turned to flip the small lever on the wall. A discreet humming filled the air then faded into silence.

Mara took a deep, calming breath, erasing the emotional turmoil as much as possible. Sander couldn't know the simple process of flipping that tiny switch had been an act of blind faith. She was now totally isolated from everyone else at the Institute, alone with the alien.

When she turned back to Sander, he stood quietly, hands at his sides, his mental shields tightly drawn. "I'm sorry for my associates' intrusion. That lever controls the hummer, an automatic shield. No one can scan you or telepathically contact you from outside this building when it's on."

Or hear me if I call for help. She smiled, projecting a confidence she wasn't certain she felt. "I rarely use it. If I had, you and I wouldn't have been able to communicate."

"But we did." Sander grabbed Mara's hand and tugged gently, drawing her back to him. "Mara, you need not fear me."

"I didn't mean for you to hear that." She gazed up at him, guarding her thoughts as carefully as she knew how. Would her lack of trust anger him? It should, she thought. There can't be true love without trust.

Maybe he was right. Maybe she didn't truly understand love.

But she understood need.

Should she tell him he excited her, tell him the reality of him was far greater than any fantasy she'd ever conjured?

Was there something freakish about her, to feel so drawn to a creature not only of another species, but from another world? So attracted to him she'd disregarded the well-meant warnings of her own people? She'd fantasized making love with Sander without any idea what he looked like, much less if the mechanics of the act were even possible between them.

Now that she'd seen him, the fantasy had taken on substance. Now that she'd touched him, she wanted more than the mental caresses they'd shared. To combine their bodies, one with the other, not just minds and emotions, but flesh as well.

What would it be like? Did his kind grapple and stroke and taste, did the males fill their mates with heated thrusts, or was their mating a mere act of procreation?

No, it had to be much more, to have resulted in a creature as sensual as Sander.

She swallowed deeply, fighting the building curl of heat rising in her womb. Their telepathic communication had been limited to her relatively minor abilities...but her imagination, oh, her imagination had run so free!

"Don't shield your thoughts from me. Please, Mara. Let me into your soul again. You're all I have." He sighed, a deep sound that reverberated through his broad chest. "Maybe you're right. Maybe wanting isn't so bad. But love...?" He brushed her cheek gently with the back of one blunt finger. The thick fur covering felt soft as mink and so warm against her skin.

She opened her mind to Sander's despair, the emotional anguish of a man every bit as confused as she. How could Malachi have mistrusted his motives? If Sander were truly manipulating her, wouldn't he profess to love her? Wouldn't he make use of her infatuation? The alien's honest confusion over his feelings honored her trust.

Sighing, she relaxed and leaned against his broad chest, inhaling the unique musky odor that clung to him. He rumbled beneath her cheek and she realized he was laughing.

"I do stink, don't I? Three months in orbit without a decent bath and I..."

"You don't stink!"

"Your thoughts tell me otherwise."

"Pay attention, Captain. I was thinking your scent was unique, exciting. Like cinnamon and cloves, only different." She grinned, carefully wrapped her arms around his slim waist and pressed her face against the silky fabric of his skinsuit.

Just as carefully, he unwound her arms and held her away from him. "I would like to make use of the bathing facilities, if you don't mind. I see in your thoughts both a shower and a large tub. Do I see you sharing the shower with me? Ah, Mara. What a wonderful idea."

She blushed. "I don't know what made me think that. I hardly know you."

"How can you say that? We've known each other as intimately as..."

"Please." Her face burned beneath his gaze. "You were right. That wasn't real. It happened in our minds." She closed her eyes, remembering, feeling so much more.

"Don't go shy on me now. I like what you're thinking."

Her skin blushed a fiery red, something unique to her race, he decided. Something he liked. She was so fragile, her smooth, hairless body lean and supple beneath her lightweight skinsuit. Unlike the women of his world, her only hair appeared to be the thick, black mane covering her skull, curling lightly over her shoulders and down her back. That, and the bird wing slashes above her green eyes.

He knew the dark tip of his tail jerked uncontrollably. Did she recognize the signal, the fact he broadcast his frustration and sexual excitement with every twitch and quiver of that damned tuft of fur? Very much like her blush, he suddenly realized.

"Come." He grabbed her slender wrist, taking control of the situation. "You may help me bathe."

"What?" Wide-eyed, she stared at him.

"You will bathe me. It's a common courtesy on Mirat. You said you wanted to know our customs." So what if he invented a custom or two? he silently rumbled. It sounded extremely courteous as far as he was concerned.

Chuckling to himself, Sander dragged Mara along after him toward the tiled bathroom at the far end of the master suite.

Chapter 4

Shielding her thoughts wasn't easy, not the way they roiled about inside her skull. Sander held her wrist in a gentle but firm grip and Mara concentrated on the feel of his hand, the soft tawny fur covering the backs of his fingers, the smooth, leathery texture of his palm. She used the harmless thoughts to block her deeper desires.

In the bathroom he released her wrist and ran one finger along an invisible seam, peeling the skinsuit down the furred length of his body, stepping out of the clinging fabric and standing before her, naked, but not nearly so naked as a human would be.

Panthera leo, the Latin description for earth's African lion popped into her head, with the additive, *erectus*, tagged on the end. Erect lion, manbeast, upright and powerful, he stood before her, an almost quizzical expression on his face.

Posing before her, she suddenly realized.

He wanted her to look.

You are so beautiful, she thought, leaving her mind open to him. Tall, at least four inches over six feet, his shoulders broader, more powerful than the average human's, his hips lean and narrow, a swimmer's build. Except he was covered from head to foot with a sleek pelt of tawny fur that darkened where his sex remained sheathed and tight against his belly.

His testicles were large, rounder than a human male's, drawn tightly up between his powerful legs, covered in the same sleek fur that disguised his penis.

His legs were manlike, strong and sinewy, ending in long, broad feet tipped with retractable nails. His tail was long and thick, and though it wrapped loosely about his left ankle, the tip twitched violently. She thought of what he'd said about the length and breadth of a man's tail and her glance flashed once again to the bulging sheath above his balls. Blushing uncontrollably, she switched her perusal to his face, to the broad, leonine head cloaked in a heavy, dark mane.

He watched her, his expression unreadable, his amber eyes with their black pupils narrowed to slits studying her every bit as intently as she studied him.

The fawn-colored fur that covered his face was lustrous as silk, the stiff whiskers at each side of his nostrils a sable counterpoint. Though definitely leonine, Mara realized his skull was too broad, his ears too neatly shaped, his eyes set too far forward for him to look exactly like the earthly version.

His mouth, though slightly muzzle-shaped, was much too mobile, much too sensual to belong to an animal.

What would it be like, to kiss that mouth, to delve inside, to tangle and twist and spar with the raspy tongue she'd felt against her wrist? She licked her lips, imagining, remembering.

A deep growl rumbled up out of Sander's chest.

"Oh God, Sander, I'm so..." She'd forgotten her mental shields, had been broadcasting her observations and opinions as clearly as if she'd spoken aloud!

I want to see you. Please, Mara. His golden gaze bored into her until she felt his desire curl into that heated place between her legs.

Fingers trembling, Mara slid the fastener aside and stepped out of her skinsuit, kicking the fabric off her bare feet and standing before him completely naked.

Her nipples beaded immediately into hard little kernels. The urgent dampness between her legs signaled arousal. She no longer attempted to shield her thoughts even though she'd not been able to read Sander's while she looked at him. Throwing her mane of dark hair back over her shoulders, she stood silently as he studied her.

The sexual flush that covered her belly and spread across her breasts and collarbones was no longer a sign of embarrassment. Never before had any man looked at her like this. Never, before Sander, not in all her twenty-eight years, had her sensual nature truly awakened.

She thought briefly of Malachi, of the simple, undemanding sex they'd once shared. They'd been friends long before becoming lovers. He was a brilliant physician, a healer with strong precognitive abilities, but his lovemaking had left her feeling bereft, as if something just out of reach would remain forever untouchable.

That relationship had flickered briefly then died. Until Sander, it had been enough. She'd filled her life with study and the pursuit of her father's dream. After Daniel Armand's death, his Institute consumed her, leaving little time for socializing. She worked through the long nights when sleep was elusive and pleasured herself when the sexual frustration grew too intense.

She thought of that now, while Sander's burning gaze traveled over her body. Remembered the touch of her own hand between her legs, her slim fingers stroking, searching for that elusive, explosive moment of unbridled sensation and wondered how different it would be to have Sander there. She recalled the nights he'd joined their minds in pleasure, only now she had substance for her fantasies.

That impossible, probing, and plundering mobile tongue—she couldn't have properly imagined it before, nor could she fully appreciate the size of his cock. Now she visualized that rigid shaft unsheathed, hot and thrusting, forcing her hungry flesh aside, a demon unleashed, demanding her response.

Her fists clenched at her sides and she swayed slightly, her lids lowering as the fantasy deepened. Her lips parted and her breath exploded in short, sharp gasps.

"Mara."

His strangled moan snapped her back to reality. Blinking rapidly to clear her mind, Mara realized Sander had turned his back to her. His long tail twitched and jerked as he fumbled with the shower fixtures.

Blushing furiously, Mara reached around him and turned the water on. When she brushed against him, he shuddered, but his shields were drawn tight. She couldn't even pick up his emotions, much less his thoughts.

Confused, she adjusted the temperature of the water and stepped back, allowing Sander to step into the shower. He kept his back to her, but the rigid set of his shoulders and the rapid jerking of his long tail told her something was terribly wrong.

"Sander, what is it?" She stepped into the huge shower behind him. He had asked, no, demanded, she help him bathe, hadn't he?

"Sander, look at me." She grabbed his arm to turn him.

He groaned, then slowly pivoted.

Mara gasped. Where his sex had been tightly sheathed against his taut belly, completely hidden within its foreskin, it now stood full and rampant, unsheathed and pulsing an angry red.

"Oh, my."

"Oh, my, is right, my lovely Mara. Look what your expressive little mind has done to me." He gestured unnecessarily at himself then cupped her shoulders in his broad hands. The warm water beat against both of them, filling the bathroom with steam.

"I...I..." She spun out of his grasp and reached for a soft cloth. "I'll wash your back."

"That's probably a good idea." He didn't laugh aloud. He didn't have to. Mara's sensitive nature picked up a bemused mental chuckle as Sander turned and braced his palms against the tile wall. He leaned forward, bending slightly so Mara could reach his broad back and shoulders. His tail curled behind him, bobbing between her parted knees with a life of its own.

She willed her fingers to stop their trembling as she worked a good lather into the rag with a small soap capsule, then lightly scrubbed the muscled ridge along Sander's spine. He sighed and some of the rigid tension in his body eased. Mara relaxed as well. Humming to herself, she continued bathing him, concentrating on his sleek thighs, then working her way back up his spine into the thick mane covering his shoulders and skull.

She shielded her thoughts, projecting only compassion and concern, using her empathic abilities to wrap Sander in a warm cocoon of tranquillity. He took a deep breath then exhaled and more of the tension ebbed out of his rigid frame.

Without speaking, Mara guided Sander to a small bench set into the shower wall, then stepped in front of him to continue washing his mane. After a moment, Sander wrapped his thick arms loosely around her waist and rested his head against her belly, giving himself over to her touch.

As he settled his big body against her, desire flared, but she quickly banked her feelings without projecting them. In that one unguarded moment as his pod had fallen toward earth, he'd broadcast a frightening depth of need, a terrible longing. Mara thought of that now, of how she'd wanted to protect him. She felt that way again, like a mother lioness protecting her cub.

Sander's no cub.

No, but even the King of Beasts needed time off now and then.

She ran her fingers through his dark mane, massaging the taut scalp beneath. The warm water beat steadily against her side and along

Sander's back as she directed the stream to rinse the soap from his thick hair and pelt.

She sensed the moment when he accepted both her mental and physical touch as healer, not as mate, his reluctant acquiescence to her care. She rinsed him, humming tunes from her nearly forgotten childhood. She brushed her hand lightly across his broad shoulders, projecting warm and gentle thoughts into the dark shadows of his aroused, then troubled mind. Now, as she finished bathing him, a deep rumble vibrated against her belly. She glanced down and bit her lips to keep from giggling.

Sander's long tail had gone completely limp. It swirled along with the flow of water toward the drain, its tufted tip trailing in the disappearing stream of soap bubbles and water.

Another rumble tickled her middle.

Her starship captain, *Panthera leo erectus,* had fallen sound asleep.

Tenderly, Mara stroked his shoulders, awed by the broad sweep of muscled pelt, the thick tangle of russet mane.

Smiling, she thoroughly rinsed him, not easy with his broad head resting heavily against her belly. She managed to squeeze most of the water from his thick mane and dry his back and shoulders with a warm towel without waking him.

It would have to do.

Come, my sleepy starship captain. She grinned. These feelings of warmhearted, almost motherly tenderness toward such a huge beast were almost impossible to comprehend. Sander tried to snuggle closer to her, almost knocking her down in the process. She leaned over and slipped one slim shoulder beneath his heavy arm and helped him stand.

Mumbling, only marginally awake, Sander rose and stumbled along beside her. He tripped clumsily over the tiled edge of the shower and practically fell across the huge bed just outside the bathroom door.

His sodden pelt left a dark imprint on the deep burgundy-colored bedspread. He rolled over on his side, drew his knees up against his belly and tucked his broad hands beneath his cheek. A monotonous rumble rolled from deep within his chest and filled the room.

Like a big cat. A very sexy big cat.

Amused by the comparison, feeling compassion more than passion for her alien guest, Mara toweled Sander dry as thoroughly as she could, covered his huge body with a heavy quilt and turned out the light. She paused just outside the door, caught in a conflicting whisper of emotions, Sander's emotions, barely audible to her sensitive heart.

Even in sleep he shielded his innermost feelings. The implications startled her. What other secrets might he hide?

She thought of the Institute, of Malachi's warning and the fate of her father's people. Her people. So much rested on her shoulders. Sander's mental abilities surpassed anything Mara had known and yet she had allowed him complete access to her thoughts.

What if he had deceived her? What if this love she felt for him was of his making? Had he manipulated her thoughts along with her heart?

But for what reason?

She could barely comprehend the losses he'd faced today. Never seeing his home again, his family. Could she face leaving Earth, knowing it was impossible to return?

Sander had said he could never go home again. He would forever be alien, an oddity even among the Institute members where acceptance of the unusual was a way of life.

What if he had lied?

Mara glanced back over her shoulder. Sander was merely a dark lump in the middle of her father's bed, drifting deeper and deeper into exhausted sleep.

She stepped back into the room, drawn to him, to the vulnerability she sensed he rarely allowed past his shields. This unguarded moment might be a chance, her only chance, to learn more about him, his motives and intentions.

One step closer, another, and the emotional whisper grew in volume, became a shout, then a primal scream of unendurable pain.

Stifling a cry, she grasped her temples, buffeted by the hopeless fear his conscious mind had managed to contain. These weren't the thoughts of an invader, or someone intending harm.

Loneliness, yearning, a depth of sorrow incomprehensible in its despair enveloped her, spilled in painful waves from his sleeping mind.

Oh, Sander…why didn't you tell me? To think he'd carried this sorrowful burden alone!

Why had she doubted his sincerity?

Mara touched his shoulder, the thick fur damp and cooling in the evening chill, and almost recoiled as his emotional anguish assailed her.

He shuddered beneath her touch, then relaxed as she quickly projected healing thoughts into his sleeping mind.

"It's not enough, is it?" She stroked his arm, so intent on trying to heal him she barely noticed her own free-falling tears.

Helplessly, she sighed, then slipped quietly into the bed behind him. She drew the heavy quilt over their naked bodies and settled herself tightly against his back.

His exact thoughts remained hidden from her, the images behind his pain shadowed and indistinct, but as an empath she knew emotions could not lie. She also knew she had the skills to help him. Wrapping her arms around his waist Mara curled close so that his taut buttocks pressed firmly against her thighs.

She wondered what to do about his thick tail and finally wedged it tightly between her legs, out of the way. The black tuft at the end curled lightly about her ankle instead of his.

You're definitely not what I expected, she thought, smiling at the pair they made. He grunted in his sleep, as if in agreement, and she quickly shielded her thoughts. As strong as his telepathic abilities were, she wondered if her personal shields could actually withstand him if he ever chose to enter her unwilling mind.

Probably not.

Oh well...there wasn't much he didn't already know. He'd seduced her mind along with her body. She'd opened herself completely to him—so far, without regret.

But what if you're wrong? Mara pushed the whisper of guilt aside. Quietly, she composed her thoughts and let her serenity flow over Sander's tumultuous mind, relaxing him into a deep, healing sleep. Not until then, when his breathing slowed and his broad frame relaxed against her, did she realize she'd been shielding herself from the worst of Sander's pain.

Sighing, feeling more than a little unworthy, Mara wrapped her arms tightly about his still body and drifted off to sleep.

* * * * *

The contact was subtle at first, the ritual greeting she'd grown to welcome. Her heart quickened with the first stirrings of arousal—expectant, impatient.

His mindtouch was gentle but certain. Her breasts responded, swelling, tingling beneath an invisible caress so real she found it difficult to believe he could love her this thoroughly with merely his thoughts.

She moaned, arching against his solid heat, projecting her own sensual images. Moisture collected between her thighs. At his insistence, she reached down and touched herself, stroking the tender folds of flesh, opening her mind completely to the erotic images Sander wrapped about her.

Before, they'd been indistinct, without substance. This time Mara's mind filled with his presence. He'd watched her once before, in the bathroom when she'd imagined pleasuring herself. Now those vivid images returned and with them the same gut-wrenching excitement Sander had experienced.

She trailed her fingers through the slick moisture between her legs, groaning aloud as she touched herself. Her fingers stroked the hot and swollen labia, circled the tiny, sensitive nubbin at the apex, then dipped between the dewy lips, imagining, remembering. Her breath caught in her throat, the memory of Sander's hot tongue filling her, slipping deep inside, a virtual mind-fuck of the soul.

Sander's excitement built as well, filling her with his psychic pleasure until she thought she might explode with need.

Suddenly, a strong hand stilled her probing fingers and tugged them gently from their erotic exploration. Mara sighed. In this dreamlike state she had no choice but to accept the pulsating emptiness between her legs.

She caught her breath at a new sensation. Each of her fingers, one by one, slowly drawn into a hot mouth, licked and suckled clean between firm lips. The rhythmic pulsing between her legs increased with each finger, each swirling lick of a sandpaper tongue.

Smiling in the darkness, she wondered what else he would think of, what new and carnal fantasies awaited her tonight.

Sander's quiet chuckle entered her mind, an intimate, earthy sound that raised shivers along her spine. *I'm real, my lovely Mara. Not a fantasy lover orbiting your world…this is Sander, your lover if you'll have me. Open your eyes, Mara…see me. Know me. I want you. Not your mind, not your tender emotions…you.*

Her dreamlike state shattered. Trembling fully awake, Mara groaned and rubbed her fiery cheek against the sturdy forearm embracing her. *You're here, you're...*

"Yes, my love." His voice reverberated against her nape, his heated body pressed into her from behind. Vaguely she recalled falling asleep, nestled against his back like spoons in a drawer.

Somehow, during the night, their positions had shifted.

The thick shaft between her buttocks wasn't that mobile tail of his at all. It was him, Sander, his sex aroused and hard, sliding against her like a hot brand, rubbing slick and wet across her clit with each forward and backward stroke.

"Sander, yes, please." She gasped for air and clamped her thighs tightly around his rigid shaft.

"I don't want to hurt you." His voice rumbled from behind her, strained and passion-filled against her throat. His teeth nipped the tender flesh below her ear. He tightened his arms around her and still his hips continued their gentle buck and sway. "I'm much larger than you, my love. Much too large, I'm afraid..."

"You're not." She rode him as best she could without penetration, that fiery member sleek and solid between her thighs, his breath sweet and hot against her throat.

The pressure built, taking her close, so close she could almost grasp fulfillment. His broad hands caressed her breasts and she arched her back, trapped in need, her hands searching behind her to touch the taut muscles of his buttocks, then fluttering down between her legs and encircling the slick head of his cock, stroking his heated length as he slipped back and forth and back again.

He groaned aloud, a sound of need as desperate as her own. Why didn't he take her? Why didn't he make love to her and ease this terrible longing?

With the question came the answer. This had to be Mara's decision. The risk was hers as much as the pleasure.

Struggling out from beneath his massive weight, Mara arched against him, raising up on hands and knees to present herself as completely, as vulnerably, as she knew how.

"You won't hurt me." She practically moaned the words. "Not unless you stop." Opening her mind, she shared her desire, her desperate longing for fulfillment.

She almost collapsed against the onslaught of his need. His passion, his raging thirst for completion with her, with Mara, not a female of his own species, but Mara, as he saw her.

Sleek, naked, hot and wanting, an innocent wanton.

His hunger increased her own tenfold. "Now, Sander. I want you *now*," she demanded, begged of him.

He took her.

Gently at first, projecting almost impishly how difficult this was, this control of passion. He knelt behind her, grabbed her waist in his strong hands and pressed against her, probing slowly with his swollen cock, easing it carefully between the wet and ready folds.

He shuddered against her, his dark nails digging into the tender flesh of her hips.

Immediately the pressure eased. "I'm sorry, I forget…"

She smiled over her shoulder, saw him kneeling close behind her as a towering shadow in the darkness, light glinting eerily off his bared teeth.

"Now, Sander," she repeated, rubbing her bottom in slow, sensuous circles against him.

Groaning aloud, trembling with his struggle for control, he slid farther inside her, stretching her, preparing her…then withdrew before entering completely.

Crying out her frustration, Mara collapsed forward on her folded arms and buried her face in the tumbled blankets, opening herself even more to Sander's tender invasion.

His grasp tightened almost imperceptibly around her waist, his thighs tensed against the backs of her legs and once again he eased slightly into her, gently, so gently she wanted to scream. She felt him throbbing, pulsing within her.

Once again, he slowly withdrew.

The barely perceived motion of his hips against hers stilled, his huge member rested hot and slick and damp against her buttocks, branding her. She felt him shift his weight, then Sander reached around and touched her, teased the sensitive nubbin of flesh between her legs with the smooth curve of one rapier sharp nail. Mara gasped at his touch, her breath caught tightly in her chest as the slick hardness of Sander's claw was slowly, oh so slowly replaced by the rough pad of his fingertip. Smooth steel to sandpaper scratch, sliding with glacial speed across her raw nerve endings. Smooth once again, then the gentle abrasion, barely felt. Ruling her heart, forcing the blood to pulse in time with the *slick, rough, slick*.

Her breath, short puffs without substance, her world coalescing, tightening into one raw, sensitive pleasure-ripe nerve of need and desire. She cried out, the sound a plea, a moan...a prayer. He cupped her with his huge hand, fingers splayed across her mons, holding her in place, a willing prisoner.

Pressure building, he swelled against her, hinting at power barely held in check. Mara shuddered, sensed the explosive potential she and this huge beast shared. "God, now, Sander. Now." She bucked against him, crying out as he filled her.

Thrusting hard and deep, his guttural roar echoed off the walls, his careful restraint shattered. Sander's strong hands clutched at her sides, his hips thrust forward and he stretched and penetrated her slick passage with molten steel. Penetrated and filled her, molding flesh and heat and passion, two worlds colliding in pure, unadulterated lust.

A moment, a mere flash of panic burst into her mind, that this could not, would not work. Then suddenly, as if to mock her fears, Mara's body welcomed his powerful onslaught, shuddered beneath his force as she took him, all of him, more than she could have imagined, took him deep within herself until his unyielding shaft filled her body and his open mind filled her soul.

His fervent apology for causing her pain, no matter how brief, was swallowed in Mara's passion. Images, unfiltered, unshielded, erotic images of lust and need and something more, something tender and sweet saturated her thoughts, until she paused, suspended, hovering on the brink of emotional oblivion.

She cried out then, a guttural, unfamiliar sound, wrenched from some untouched level deep within her soul, a cry of rapture, of joy, of demand and desire.

He was huge, thick, hot, not human, so much more than human, taking her physically, mentally, emotionally. He thrust into her, again and again, his heavy balls slapping against her, his cock stretching the tender inner walls, filling her up, slick and hard and so perfect, so perfect she knew she might burst, might shatter beneath the onslaught.

Then she did shatter, crying out, baring her teeth and calling his name, while he plunged into her again, then once more. His deep-throated roar mingled with her mewling cries of pleasure, mingled and drifted into a shuddering sigh with one final, clenching spasm, all he could wring from her depleted body.

Chapter 5

She slept, finally, curled in his embrace. Sander rested his chin against the top of her head, stunned.

So this is desire? This powerful emotional morass nearly unmanned him. Desire, before Mara, had been the easy relief with a ready female. If one wasn't available, he'd pleasured himself.

Desire satisfied.

Would he ever know satisfaction again? Never. Not without Mara. All those sexual mind games with her. He'd been so in control. Control! He'd laugh if it weren't so painful. Only the Mother knew how little control he had.

Thank the Mother Mara slept. He felt so weak he probably couldn't shield his thoughts or emotions from a three-day-old cub, much less an empath with much more potential than even she imagined.

His cock twitched and he willed it to settle down. Not easy, since the damned thing still rested within her hot flesh.

He wanted her again, but it was too soon.

At her climax, as she'd crested within his embrace, her mind had opened completely.

She hadn't been exaggerating.

She did love him.

Unfortunately, the experience they'd just shared had shattered a few of Sander's illusions as well. *Wanting isn't enough. Getting isn't enough. Only love will ever satisfy completely.*

Impossible.

They were from different worlds, of different species. They couldn't even produce a viable offspring, not as mismatched as their genetic codes must be.

Even on Mara's world, a pair bond existed for procreation of the species. Anything else could only be considered a temporary match.

That's not acceptable. It might have been...before. Now, having tasted her, known her as he'd never known another female, Sander couldn't let her go. Couldn't imagine her in the arms of a male of her own species.

Malachi Franklin's image flashed into his mind. The doctor loved Mara. He hadn't attempted to hide his jealousy from Sander, although it was obvious that, empath though she might be, Mara was oblivious to the man's feelings.

That hadn't stopped the young physician from practically issuing a challenge to Sander, right there in the clinic. At the time, it hadn't really mattered. Now it did. Sander growled, a low, menacing sound of male possession. Mara stirred in his arms and he quickly brought his emotions under control.

She was his and he would hold her. She fascinated him, her ready wit, her quick mind. Her love for her associates, for the Institute her father had built. Her loyalty and vast capacity for sharing. He knew she'd taken his pain on her own small shoulders, had freed his anguished mind and allowed him the healing sleep of peace.

She risked everything, her friends, her beloved Institute, her own safety, to protect him, an alien explorer from another world. She'd tried to hide the guilt she felt, the fact she'd hidden the depth of their relationship from members of the Institute. He'd even felt her moments of distrust, her inner battle over loving him.

What better description of love, than to risk all for another? Mara was willing to give up everything to keep him safe. Could he do any less? Would he? So much had changed since knowing this most special female. Without her, Sander knew there would be no life. She ordered his, now, in all ways possible.

What else could he offer Mara? Even if he escaped her planet, somehow made it home to Mirat, what woman would willingly go into a life of permanent exile from her own kind?

It certainly wasn't a choice Sander would make for himself. To be an oddity, an aberration...forever alien. He didn't want it for himself, he could never ask it of Mara.

He wouldn't have to. He was stuck here.

Stuck here with Mara in my arms. Sighing, he nuzzled the damp skin between her shoulder and throat. It could be worse.

Sander? Is something wrong? Her inner muscles convulsed about him and he was suddenly hard again.

"No, sweet Mara." He whispered against her throat, struggling to bank his surging libido. "Nothing's wrong. Go back to sleep."

"What if I don't want to?"

He felt the smile behind her words, couldn't ignore the sensual sweep of her warm buttocks against his belly.

"You should obey me, woman. On Mirat, the female always bows to the male's desire."

"And if she doesn't?"

"Then suitable punishment is immediately forthcoming." He rolled over on his back, carrying Mara with him so that she faced the ceiling, still impaled on his hard cock.

He held her close against his body with long sure strokes of his broad hands, trailing his fingers along her thighs, then dipping them into the honeyed flesh between. She moaned, a low, animal sound. Her small hands reached behind her and she clasped his hips. She arched her back against him, digging her shoulders into his chest and forcing him even deeper inside her.

Her thick mane of hair covered the lower half of Sander's face, filling his nostrils with her fragrance. Blood coursed through his veins. Her fingers, clasped tightly in the short pelt covering his hips, seared him like ten fiery brands.

*If this is punishment…*Her laughing jibe filled his mind.

He surged into her, then just as quickly lifted her away, denying her fulfillment. "It is now." He chuckled when she whimpered in frustration.

Without warning, she laughed and rolled off of him, turning out of his grasp to quickly reverse her position and straddle his hips. "Let's talk punishment," she countered, her voice a low, seductive murmur. She rocked against his rigid shaft, trapping him between her strong thighs with long, slow sweeps guaranteed to drive him wild. His hips bucked beneath her and she laughed, then leaned forward and grabbed his shoulders, torturing him with her sensuous, teasing strokes.

As she moved over him, her hair swept along his chest, across his face, filling his nostrils once again with her scent. He bucked his hips to throw her — she clung to him. He tried a quick jab to enter her, but she pressed even tighter against him, flattening her small breasts into his furred chest.

It would be so simple just to grab her waist and lift her, to thrust into her exactly the way he wanted. She was tiny compared to him— fragile, hairless little thing that she was.

I heard that! I am not a hairless little thing! I'm tougher than you imagine.

"You understood my thoughts!" He clasped her waist to still her movements and grinned at her. "I wasn't projecting, just thinking, but you understood the words, the intent, not just the emotions. I told you your powers were greater than you thought."

She threw her head back and laughed aloud, childish delight at her newfound understanding written all over her face, filling his mind.

Overflowing into his heart.

"You may be tough, but you are practically..." he ran one blunt finger through the damp nest of curls at the apex of her thighs, "...hairless."

She trembled when he touched her.

"Will you let me in?" He gently lifted his hips and teased her again, stroking the tight little bud with the hard edge of one curved nail until she gasped.

"Never," she said, hissing through clenched teeth.

He circled her taut buttock with his left hand, trailing his fingers along the damp crease between her cheeks. The fingers of his right hand continued their rhythmic strokes, teasing, tantalizing.

She panted in short, erratic gasps, struggling to breathe. He watched her face, her green eyes hidden beneath lowered lids, her full lips slightly parted, the tiny pink tip of her tongue barely visible.

He continued stroking her with his blunt fingers, knowing exactly what pleased her, exactly where to touch—how firm, how deep, how soft. He wouldn't tell her she was broadcasting. For now, let her think he was an instinctively wonderful lover.

Perhaps later he'd explain how she'd directed each move he made with her soft mental pleas.

Praise the Mother, she'd shielded the bungalow, or every telepath in the Institute would be sharing her pleasure!

Carefully hiding his laughter, Sander repeated his question. "Will you let me in?"

It took her a moment to respond, and then her ragged whisper was barely audible. "I'm thinking about it." She groaned as he deepened his touch, then raked her fingers from his belly to his shoulders.

They left mussed ridges of tawny fur on their upward journey.

Sander groaned, caught completely in her passion. "Just thinking?" He clenched her bottom in one hand and dipped the fingers of his other deep inside her damp folds, stroking slowly, in and out, raising and lowering his hips in the same languorous rhythm. "Think harder."

She moaned in response, then trailed her fingers across his belly until they met at his engorged shaft. Lightly, tenderly, like the kiss of a butterfly's wing, her fingers trailed the length of him.

Once more, then again, surer this time. Her touch was fire, heat and liquid flame, those tiny fingers grasping and stroking him. He tried to think, to project some quip that might indicate he was in control, but he was lost.

She raised up on her knees and he grasped her tightly about the hips. Then slowly, so slowly he thought he might die with the wanting, she lowered herself on his rigid shaft.

Sander tightened his jaw, fighting for control of that huge member that suddenly had a life of its own. Mara was so tiny he didn't think it would work this way, but she carefully settled herself against him, taking him all the way inside.

She grinned triumphantly and he realized she'd been just as afraid as he.

Not any more.

Leaning forward, she brushed her long hair across his chest and moved, slowly at first, then faster as confidence and passion overtook her.

She felt so good, so unbelievably tight and hot. He grasped her hips, rotating his hands until he stroked her with his thumbs, just at the point where their bodies joined.

She moaned aloud, then flashed him a cheeky grin. Her thoughts, *I'm still thinking,* filled his mind like a challenge. Suddenly, she reached behind herself with both hands and gently squeezed his balls, deftly cradling and stroking them with her supple fingers.

His world went black.

He was spinning, spinning out of control, thrusting into her on his own quest for mindless pleasure, filling her with his seed, opening his mind and heart in one vast, unshielded burst of love.

Long moments later, when his gulping struggle for air had finally been reduced to shallow panting, when the thudding of his heart no longer deafened him, he wasn't even certain he'd taken her with him.

Oh, you did, Sander. Most definitely you did.

Her mental touch was strong and clear. He felt as weak as a day old kitten. "Somehow, I think our roles have reversed, little one," he said, barely able to open his eyes. She lay sprawled across his chest, her panting in cadence with his own shallow breaths.

Mmmmmmmm?

"These feelings I'm having with you, for you. They're all new to me. I'm not certain how to react."

"So far, you seem to be doing just fine." She brushed her hair back and lifted her head away from his chest, raising up just barely enough for him to see one sparkling green eye beneath the winged slash of a dark brow. "I heard your thoughts, Sander. You didn't shield your thoughts or emotions from me, not this time. You do love me, you know. Denying it won't make it go away."

"I'm not denying it," he said, searching for the right words. How could he explain to Mara what he barely understood himself? "I guess I'm just trying to figure how we'll make this work. We're...breaking new ground?"

"Is that what you call it? Groundbreaking?" She nuzzled her face in the thick fur covering his chest. His fingers ran lazy circles over her sleek back. "I prefer to think of it as earth shattering," she said. "Like rockets and fireworks. I think I saw stars. You showed me stars, Sander. If you can do that, you can do anything."

"Let's hope so, lovely Mara. Because I have a feeling this groundbreaking, earth shattering experience we've shared may not set well with your people."

She sighed in response, clinging to Sander's broad chest like a small, trusting kitten and faded into sleep. There was no real answer, not now.

Somehow he would protect her. Even if it meant giving her up, he would protect her.

But not tonight. Tonight this lovely female, these warm, new emotions, all of this, belonged to him. Forcing his whirling thoughts to relax, Sander wrapped his arms around Mara and willed sleep to come.

*****

At first she thought it was Sander's heartbeat, the pounding that seemed to reverberate throughout her entire body. Then she recognized Haydon's voice, frantic, calling her name.

"Wha...?"

"Mara, who is it?"

Sander's deep voice rumbled in her ear and suddenly Mara was wide awake, scrambling across the tumbled blankets, frantically searching for her robe. A faded afghan would have to suffice. She wrapped it tightly around her shoulders, completely covering herself.

"I'm coming," she yelled, then made the mistake of glancing back toward Sander. The burgundy quilt concealed his hips but he'd raised himself up on one elbow to watch her and the sight of that broad, furred chest and the rumpled mane of dark hair covering his shoulders was almost her undoing.

He winked at her, a very human gesture. "You're coming?" *Again?* He chuckled, a low, seductive sound that reawakened the slumbering fires within her.

"Mara, are you in there? Are you okay?"

"Yes, Haydon. Just a minute." *I'll get you for that*, she projected, then hurried out of the room before Sander could frame a reply.

She cast her thoughts toward the man on the other side of the stout door, then realized the hummer was still engaged, shielding the building. Clutching the afghan tightly around herself, Mara unlocked the door and opened it just enough to peer outside.

The storm of emotions almost knocked her flat. Rage, fear, anger, disgust, jealousy, concern, and overlying all of it, hate—a hatred so strong, so intense, she clutched her middle and gasped with the onslaught.

There was an almost audible click as the assembled knot of scientists and security forces simultaneously slammed their personal shields in place.

Haydon shoved at the door. Mara was certain he would have pushed her aside if Sander hadn't suddenly appeared at her shoulder. Completely dressed, his once-tousled mane swept neatly behind his shoulders, Sander exuded a quiet confidence that immediately calmed the crowd.

"What's wrong, Mara?" he asked aloud. She knew his calm question was more for the benefit of the milling group than herself.

"I was just going to ask Haydon," she said, frowning at her old friend. She'd never seen him so obviously distraught, nor known him to draw his shields so tightly around his emotions. "Haydon?" she prompted.

"No one could reach you," he said, glaring over her shoulder at Sander. "You never leave the hummer on all night. You hardly use it at all."

"Was there a reason you needed to get in touch with me?" She waited, her attention focused on Haydon, but she knew Sander scanned the dozen other minds in the group.

"Not me, personally," Haydon sputtered. "I was worried about you, alone here with that…"

"I told all of you there was no reason to be concerned about Captain Sander's presence in my home," she said firmly.

"Malachi said…"

"Yes, Haydon. What did Dr. Franklin have to say? Or maybe I should just ask Dr. Franklin." She peered over the heads of the men standing below Haydon on the steps, and saw Malachi half hidden at the back of the crowd. He at least had the decency to duck his head, though she felt his shame and embarrassment before he quickly banked his emotions.

"What's going on here?" Shing Tamura suddenly appeared at the end of the overgrown walkway.

"My friends were worried about me," Mara said, dismissing the swirling emotions that had buffeted her a few moments earlier. She had been less than honest with all of them. For all they knew, Sander could pose a threat to her safety.

Mind control takes many forms.

The strong warning seared her mind.

She glanced quickly in Malachi's direction, but he appeared to be concentrating on a whispered conversation with the man next to him. Was someone else trying to warn her?

She shook off a definite sense of unease. "I engaged the hummer for privacy because a few of our more curious residents were not allowing Captain Sander a much needed rest. They know now that everything's fine and they can all leave." She raised one eyebrow, directing her comment to her old friend. Grumbling, Haydon refused to make eye contact, but he did turn away and step off the porch.

"I'm sure the rest of you have work to do," Major Tamura added, moving aside to let the men depart. He waited until the last had gone, then nodded in Mara and Sander's direction.

"We need to talk," he said. Mara stepped aside to let him in. Tamura quietly entered then closed the door behind him, shutting out the lingering mental vibrations. "I picked up a transmission a couple of hours ago." He glanced at the hummer switch on the wall. "It's still engaged, isn't it?"

"Yes. I didn't have a chance to turn it off." Mara adjusted the afghan around her body and curled up in an overstuffed chair. Sander sat on an embroidered ottoman, his expression completely unreadable.

As was his mind. Mara felt momentarily shut out, then realized Sander wasn't intentionally blocking. All his attention was focused on the diminutive major.

"I'd like you to keep it on at all times." Major Tamura gestured once again at the switch. "I'll explain to the staff that it's to insure privacy for Captain Sander. I came here to tell you the World Federation picked up yesterday's explosion on their scanners and recovered a small portion of the mothership. No mention of bodies, only debris, but debris that's obviously not of this world. We need to keep our guard up and hope the WF doesn't trace anything here. The hummer's an extra precaution, in case the WF's got any Sensitives working for them."

"Thank you, Major," Sander answered before Mara could collect her scattered thoughts. She'd never considered the idea of a Sensitive choosing to work for the WF. The possibility was unnerving, to say the least.

"Major Tamura," Sander continued, still focusing on the security chief. "Would you tell the members of Mara's staff I'll come and talk to them later this morning, after we've eaten? I know they're curious about me, about my intentions. I don't mind answering their questions or explaining myself to them. I have nothing to hide from the people of the Institute."

"Thank you. That should help calm everyone down." The major turned to Mara. "I apologize, Dr. Armand, for the ruckus this morning. I should have expected this kind of reaction. Malachi and Fred and a few of the others spent a little too much time in the lounge last night. I didn't realize you and Dr. Franklin had been seeing each other," he added, leaving the comment open-ended.

"What happened between Malachi and me…that's been over for a long time. Really, Major, it meant nothing." Mara drew the afghan even tighter across her breasts. "I don't know. Malachi may have…" She glanced helplessly in Sander's direction.

A man would be a fool not to dream of you.

His deep, thoughtful gaze caught and held her. Immobilized by the hunger in his eyes, she could no more turn away than breathe. Only Major Tamura's subtle cough reminded her they were not alone.

"What time should I tell the staff to expect you?" The major stepped closer to the door and paused with one hand on the doorknob.

"A couple of hours. Dr. Armand has some work to take care of and we'd both like to break fast," Sander said, taking control of the conversation.

Mara could only nod in agreement.

"Good day, then. Doctor, Captain."

The door clicked shut behind him.

The room should have been completely silent. Mara couldn't tell, not over the rush of her blood and the pounding of her heart. She bit her lips, then smiled serenely at Sander. "What work is that, Captain?"

"Satisfying my needs," he growled, rising from the overstuffed stool and leaning over Mara. His big hands grasped the chair at either side of her head. She tucked her knees up tighter under her chin. Only her toes peeked out from under the faded throw.

"You have needs?" she asked, teasing. He was so close, his face only inches from hers as he hovered over her, his heat a palpable thing, warming her, arousing her once again as her body recalled its own needs.

"Oh, I have needs, Mara. Needs that, luckily, coincide very much with your own."

He gently parted her fingers where they clutched the blanket to her chest, and tugged the faded fabric loose. It fell away, exposing her legs from knees to toes, the rounded curve of her hip and thigh, the soft swell of her breast.

He surged hot and hard against the tight fabric of his skinsuit and welcomed the pressure. This time was for Mara, not himself. She'd been shaken by the forces at her threshold this morning, frightened by the swirling emotions directed her way.

Including the warning against him. He'd heard it, the brief message, so subtle even he had been unable to determine its origin. One of her associates, possibly all of them, mistrusted him, even feared him.

He'd sensed the inevitability of disaster in their minds. They would never accept him, not as Mara's mate. Possibly not even as a citizen of her Institute, no matter how open-minded they considered themselves.

He pushed the thoughts from his mind, easy enough with Mara's sweet flesh so close, with her heart so welcome and open. He sensed no mistrust in her this morning, not anymore. A deep growl born of desire filled him. He lifted her out of the chair, and with the afghan trailing behind them, carried her to the closest bedroom.

This room was smaller, more austere than the one where they'd spent the previous night, but he knew instinctively this was Mara's room. The room where he had first come to her, first touched her heart, her mind, her body.

With an unexpected sense of reverence, Sander gently placed her on the faded patchwork bedspread and sat beside her. She gazed up at him, eyes deep green and solemn, lips slightly parted, the pink tip of her tongue barely visible between her teeth.

He stroked her, running his hands slowly along her sleek sides and over her rounded breasts, smiling at the rosy blush that quickly heated her skin and puckered her dark nipples into tight little beads.

He leaned over her, brushing her breasts and belly with his coarse mane, laving her flesh with his tongue. She tasted of salt and sex and when he circled the tiny indentation in her belly, she groaned and raised her hips in blatant invitation.

"Sander, we can't do this," she whispered, all the while urging him on.

"Yes. We can." He ran his tongue along the tender flesh of her inner thigh, then barely flicked the damp folds between her legs. He paused a moment at the sweet flesh, then swept the ridges and valleys, carefully aware of the rough, sandpapery texture of his tongue and the sensitive nature of her sex.

The taste intrigued him, the salt/sweet combination of Mara's and his flavors. So many times they'd come together during the night, but not once had he taken the time to really taste. No, each time, at Mara's insistence, he'd carefully bathed her with a soft cloth before taking her with his mouth.

Not this time.

They'd fallen asleep in the pale light of dawn, his sex still tightly linked with hers, and not awakened until her associates had pounded on the door.

"Sander, I..." She reached out to push his head away and he knew exactly what concerned her.

"No, Mara." He rested his chin on her belly and smiled at her. "We're doing this my way." He projected his need, his desire and then the intoxicating essence of their flavors, the combination of man and woman, and almost laughed at the look of surprise on her lovely face.

Then he did laugh when she lay back down and parted her thighs for him.

He opened his mind completely, letting her taste what he tasted, feel what he felt, and at the same time she directed him, her mind subtly sharing her need so that he knew where to stroke, how deep to explore.

His tongue filled her and she remembered the night he'd first taken her like this. Then she hadn't known the sandpapery texture, hadn't been fully aware of size and strength, only of the sensation. Now his strong teeth pressed against her clit, his furred jaw rubbed the sensitive spot behind her sex and his lips suckled and teased the engorged folds of tissue.

His hands, broad, strong, thick-fingered, caressed her breasts with a supreme gentleness, rolling the taut nipples between soft finger-pads, cupping them and squeezing just enough, milking each drop of sensation from the sensitive mounds, gently raking her flesh with his dark nails.

Over and over again, that rough, impossible tongue filled her, stroking in time with the convulsive clenching of her muscles, flicking and circling her mound, then bringing her down with a gentle pressure against her clit until it was time to take her up again, almost to the edge, almost to fulfillment, almost...

"Sander, please," she begged, bucking her hips against him, pleading for release. He filled her mind with sensation, until she cried out. She shared the pleasure/pain of his massive erection, felt the taut restraint of his skinsuit against his taut flesh, knew the erotic, rhythmic pulse of her own muscles around his tongue.

Before he could stop her, she skimmed her shaking fingers along the seam of his skinsuit and tugged his hips close. Surprise filled her senses, Sander's surprise, as his swollen member sprang free of confinement and she took him in her mouth.

Overload.

She had no other way to describe it, no conscious method of dealing with the interplay of orgasmic pleasure filling her, a wrap of thoughts, hers to his and back again, spiraling deeper, higher, filling her heart and soul and body.

He groaned, a bestial roar of pleasure, then bucked against her and she tasted him in her mouth, the same salty/sweet flavors he'd found in her. She stretched her lips to encircle his size, circling the ridge along the bottom of his shaft with her tongue, cupping his taut balls in her hands, squeezing gently, raking him with her own small nails until he pulsed again, then once more before collapsing beside her.

She held him between her lips, drew his hot seed into her mouth, suckling the last drops from his body with each ebbing tremor. She cleansed him with her tongue, bathing the now pliable flesh that had moments before surged ramrod stiff and hard, so large her lips had barely circled its girth. Now she took him fully, gently, completely.

Seconds, hours, a lifetime later, she nuzzled the damp fur at his groin, kissed his unusually flaccid penis, then raised her eyes to look at him. His head rested heavily on her thighs and she could only describe his expression as "shell-shocked."

This time Mara laughed aloud.

A moment later, he joined her, laughing until his shoulders shook and tears dampened her legs. "Oh, Mara. Mara what you do to me."

She sensed the bittersweet pain that filled him and projected a sense of pure, unadulterated joy. How could she have possibly doubted him, doubted this?

"We have to break fast," she said, raising up on her elbows. "Then shower and go to that damned meeting you promised and show them exactly who and what you are. They will accept you, my starship captain. They must. Until then, we'll keep our shields locked down tight because I'm not willing to lose this, Sander. I'm not going to lose you."

Having made her pronouncement, she slipped from beneath him and headed for the shower.

Chapter 6

The recreation hall was filled to overflowing, the curious, seeking minds practically short-circuiting in their quest for contact with the alien. Shing Tamura leaned against the back wall, watching, absorbing, occasionally probing a particularly open mind.

He sensed fear, some confusion, a brief shaft of quickly shielded hatred that he tried to coordinate, but missed. He'd have to pay attention to that one.

He glanced at his timepiece, then up at the podium. Fred Haydon puttered about the stage, adjusting the microphone, checking the lights. He'd seriously thrown himself into the role of father figure when Daniel was killed. Shing searched the man's mind and came up against a blank wall.

Unusual for Haydon to block. Malachi, however, was a different story. The handsome young doctor sauntered across the stage, conferred briefly with the old man, then headed back to ground level. He grabbed a chair in the front row and plopped down, a morose expression on his face. Shing probed his mind briefly, knowing it would be a waste of time. Malachi'd kept his thoughts blocked ever since he'd decided he loved Mara.

About the time the alien arrived.

Shing had been surprised to learn Malachi and Mara had at one time been lovers. There'd been no outward sign of anything other than a professional relationship between the two. Mara said the affair had been brief and over long ago. Shing had a feeling Malachi had never quite gotten the message.

Or perhaps he sensed there was more between Mara and her alien than she'd admitted to the board.

It wasn't like Mara to hide anything from members of the Institute. Just today, Shing suddenly realized, he'd discovered she'd been hiding quite a bit.

After the brief conversation he'd had with Mara and the alien this morning, there was no denying those two, odd as it might sound, were lovers. The passion sizzling between them had practically glowed. That kind of attraction couldn't have developed in the bare twenty-four hours since Sander's arrival.

Maybe old Haydon was right when he'd asked Mara if she needed a chaperone. There must have been a hell of a lot more to that ritual kiss than she'd told the members of the board.

He studied the young doctor slouched insolently in his front row seat. Could Malachi possibly know about Mara and Sander?

That could be a problem. Jealousy was jealousy, no matter how it manifested itself. How would the rest of the Institute members react when they figured out what was going on? The security chief paused a moment, considering. It should have bothered him, the thought of Daniel Armand's daughter finding intimacy with an alien, especially one as beastlike as Sander.

It didn't, though. At their first encounter in the hospital lab, Sander had let Shing into his mind, had opened his thoughts completely in order to gain the major's trust.

It had worked.

Captain Sander, beast or human, was an honorable man. Someone worthy of respect and of Mara Armand's love. Still, Shing wondered, why had she felt it necessary to lie to the board members?

There was a subtle shift within the recreation center, a stirring, and then Sander stepped out on the stage, alone, regal and powerful. Shing glanced around the filled room and spotted Mara on the far side, leaning against the wall. Good, he thought. All attention will be on the alien.

Sander's presence filled the room, commanding, strong, open. Then, much to the surprise of the gathered throng, his thoughts filled their minds.

It is easier, he projected, *to show you my world than to describe it. And, selfishly, it gives me a great pleasure, since I may never see Mirat again.*

* * * * *

Mara watched from her place at the back, seeing the images Sander projected with part of her mind, observing her associates at the same time. She caught Shing Tamura's eye and he nodded in her direction. Good. He was watching as well.

Before long, Mara was as caught up in Sander's story as the rest of the audience. He told them how, as an Explorer, he searched the stars, unraveling the secrets of the diverse but connected species of the universe. On Earth, the primate ruled, on Sander's world, the cat. On another he'd met a sentient species similar to Earth's fox, on still another, the eagle. There was even a watery planet peopled with intelligent and civilized dolphins, creatures very close to developing their own specialized form of space travel.

The goal of the Explorer was to learn *why*? Why the uncanny coincidence of similar DNA among various species on different worlds? Why the common links among species throughout the universe? His people had been gifted with telepathy and the ability to communicate with all intelligent life forms. After their first alien contact many centuries ago, Explorers of Mirat had searched the heavens for answers.

With the Mother's blessing, someday, they would know. Unfortunately, he, Sander the Explorer, would not be among them.

"You're telepathic. Why can't you contact your people?" Malachi's question rang out as a challenge. Mara watched him closely.

"As I explained to Dr. Armand," Sander said, speaking aloud, "I cannot project beyond Earth's atmosphere or gravity. I can only project from space. There was no time to call out when my ship exploded."

"What about a kinetic mindlink?"

Mara searched the crowd. She didn't recognize the voice.

"Explain, please. I don't know what you mean." Sander leaned over the podium, an intent look on his beautiful, leonine face.

Tim Riley, a young man fairly new to the Institute, stood up. He glanced around nervously. "A kinetic mindlink. We've been working on it in class," he said, glancing in the direction of one of the older instructors, a telekinetic who had been one of the Institute's original members. "Dr. Antoon has us join minds to move objects. Even the ones who can't lift a thing by themselves can help move really big stuff when they work together. Maybe we could move a message the same way."

"It'll never work." Fred Haydon rose to his feet. "A successful kinetic mindlink requires everyone opening their minds, completely, I might add, with one another to reach a common goal. You got a secret...*wham,* the whole group knows it. No way are ya gonna get enough people willing to blend minds with each other, much less with him." He gestured toward Sander, then slumped back in his seat.

"I don't know, Fred. I think it's worth a try." Malachi Franklin stood up. "I, for one, would be more than willing to help Captain Sander go home."

"Thank you for your sincere offer." Mara recognized Sander's sarcasm and blushed when she realized he was answering Malachi as if the young doctor were a rival.

Before she had time to think much about it, she noticed Shing Tamura edge his way along the back wall and head out the door. Then the meeting grew livelier as the group debated the pros and cons of kinetic mindlinking, and she was soon drawn into the discussion.

✹ ✹ ✹ ✹ ✹

"Do you think they'll do it?" Mara snuggled against Sander's broad chest. He'd opened the top half of his skinsuit and she absentmindedly stroked the exposed patch of tawny fur. She needed this moment of quiet privacy, the two of them sprawled on the overstuffed couch at home after a long morning of questions and arguments over the proposed mindlink.

"I don't know, but Tim's idea sounds plausible. It's something we've never done on Mirat. Your Mr. Haydon is correct when he says the mindlink will require a complete sharing of thoughts for success." Sander swept a finger along the side of her jaw, repeating the same rhythm as Mara's.

Mara sensed the turbulence beneath his quiet words, as if he searched his own thoughts in readiness to open his mind to one and all. Any secrets, any subterfuge, any thoughts no matter how private, up to and including his love for Mara, would be part of the public domain.

"Not many of us are willing to open ourselves to others," he said, as if speaking to himself. "We naturally shield ourselves, protecting our innermost secrets. Protecting those we love."

Understanding his hesitancy, Mara pressed her lips against that place on his broad chest where his heart beat a steady rhythm. The same place, on her own slender form, where her heart beat in counterpoint. Telling him without word or thought that the decision was Sander's alone, that she would support whatever choice he made.

His broad hand swept her hair back from her eyes. His golden-eyed gaze caught her with its hypnotic light. "It should work," he said. "Combining the power of enough minds should send a message well beyond the gravitational pull of Earth. All I need to do is get Mirat's coordinates right, and…"

"And you'll leave," she whispered. "Sander, how can I let you go when I've only just found you?" Mara slipped out of his gentle grasp and knelt on the floor beside him.

"Come with me." He cupped her face in his huge hands, then nuzzled her cheek with his own. "Come with me, Mara. Come to Mirat and be my lifemate. We'll travel the stars together. You'll see things you never imagined."

"I can't, Sander. You know that. I can't leave the Institute. It was my father's dream. I have to carry on."

"But is it your dream?"

She hesitated. "You're my dream. The Institute is my responsibility. I have no choice." She wanted to weep with the pain of it, the thought of losing him forever when she'd only just found him, only now had discovered what had been missing for all her life.

"Come. I want to show you something." Sander lifted Mara in his arms and carried her into her own bedroom. He stood her in front of him so that both of them faced Daniel Armand's painting, and loosely wrapped his arms around her waist.

"I noticed your painting this morning, after we made love. I realized I was looking into the faces of my ancestors. Why do you have this particular portrait on your wall, Mara?"

"My father painted it for me. I was born in August and my astrological sign is Leo, the lion. Dad said the lion would protect me and always watch over me. That as long as I needed him, he would be there." She turned in Sander's arms and rubbed her face against the soft pelt covering his chest. "Are you that lion, Sander? Will you stay with me? Is that what you're trying to tell me?"

"No, Mara. I think that's what your father was trying to tell you." He grasped her arms, holding her away from him so that she had to look into his eyes. Golden amber, flashing with myriad fires and emotions, they mesmerized her.

"You said his powers were amazing." He pinned her with that powerful gaze. "You said his mind was more developed than any you'd known. That he had strong, precognitive abilities. Did he know, Mara? Did he give you that painting to prepare you for me? How else can you explain your acceptance of me as mate? As lover? On your planet I'm an animal, Mara, a vicious beast that once roamed the jungles and plains. An animal you keep in zoos, much as we keep our primates locked away. But you don't think of me as a beast, do you my love? You think of me as your protector, as your mate. Because that's what your father wanted you to think."

Her eyes widened. Was it true? Had her father known? She'd never questioned his dedication to the Institute. Nor had she questioned her own desire to continue his dream after his death.

Mind control takes many forms. Malachi's warning suddenly held new meaning. Did her father control her, even now? Had he programmed her future before his death? Her thoughts whirled madly, spinning out more questions than answers, but before she had time to sort her jumbled thoughts, a loud knock at the door shattered the silence.

Sander followed Mara into the front room. He stood with her as she opened the door.

"I'm sorry to intrude, Doctor, Captain, but Major Tamura sent me." The young officer on the front porch took a deep breath, swallowed, then continued. "We've intercepted a message from the World Federation. They know the Captain's here. They're on their way."

"But how?" Mara clutched Sander's sturdy arm. Thank God he stood beside her, or she would have fallen.

"According to Major Tamura, someone from the Institute…"

"What? One of our people?" *Oh God, Sander. They're my family!*

"That's what Major Tamura said. We have a traitor, Dr. Armand. Please, you and the Captain need to come with me. The Major's waiting for you at headquarters."

* * * * *

"Our Sensitives are reporting troop movements in this area and also some possible action over here." Major Tamura pointed at a large map of the southwestern segment of the North American continent.

"Your father chose this site well, Dr. Armand. We still have a few days before we need to worry about any kind of attack. The elevation and rugged terrain make it difficult for most aircraft, so they'll have to move troops in the old fashioned way—on foot and land vehicle."

"All well and good, Major, but what do you suggest when they arrive?" Mara folded her arms across her chest and struggled to shield her emotions. Broadcasting the fear and anger that coiled like steel springs along her spine could affect everyone in this room.

"Dr. Antoon has some suggestions." The major gestured to the lanky, gray-haired man seated on top of one of the scattered desks in the office.

"That I do, Major. Thank you. Ya'll remember the kinetic mindlink Tim mentioned this mornin'? I've been workin' with a number of the Institute's telekinetics and we've had some success with mindlinked manipulation of ferrous materials."

"You bend metal?" Sander's quiet comment was followed by the physicist's short bark of laughter.

"You got it, Captain. We bend big metal, in a big way. Tim." He signaled the young man by the open door. "Wouldja'll be so kind as to call in your, *ahem*, partners in crime?"

Tim Riley looked over his shoulder and waved to someone just outside the office. Fourteen young men and women trooped in, a scruffy looking bunch of pre through post-teens in ragged pants and purposefully tattered shirts. They stood self-consciously defiant, gathered closely around Dr. Antoon.

Mara glanced at Sander. *They're going to protect us?*

He grinned back. *I have a feeling we're in for a surprise.*

"Major, Dr. Armand, I wantcha'all to look out that window." Dr. Antoon gestured in the direction of an old storage shed across the yard. It sagged in the middle and tilted slightly to one side.

"It's all yours, kids." He stepped aside.

The transformation was instantaneous. As one, the fifteen young people, Tim Riley at their center, straightened, focused, and melded. When they linked hands, Mara felt the power of their minds. Amazed, she watched the shed lift free of its foundation, pivot, move across the uneven ground, then explode in a shimmering tangle of twisted shards of metal.

"Oh my." She looked at Sander, then at the beaming faces of Dr. Antoon and his equally pleased young telekinetics. "Oh my," she repeated, grinning. She'd had no idea anyone at the Institute was pursuing this kind of knowledge, especially this lanky Southerner and his ragtag army of teenagers. It was exactly the kind of study her father would have loved. She laughed aloud with a brief surge of hope. "Why haven't you told me about this before?"

"We didn't feel we were quite ready yet, Doc. There's always been that unwritten rule against using our minds as weapons, so we've kinda kept this, well, you know..." His voice trailed off, but it was obvious he couldn't hide his self-satisfied grin. "We still have some bugs to work out, but..."

"In the meantime, it's the best defense we've got. A damned good defense, Doctor. I am impressed." Major Tamura drummed his fingers on the table. "However, it doesn't solve Captain Sander's problem. Or the Institute's, in the long run. You realize, Dr. Armand..."

"Once the WF sees what Dr. Antoon's army can do, we will never be free of them. Even if we manage to help Sander get home..."

"They will still come after you," Sander interrupted. "I am sorry, all of you, for putting the Institute in this terrible trouble."

"It's not your fault." Mara reached out and touched Sander's hand, needing his strength, wanting to comfort. "It would have happened, sooner or later. They've been monitoring us for a long time."

"Even so..." Sander's golden gaze locked with hers. His thoughts filled her mind, his regret, his sadness, but most of all, his love.

Mara felt a tremor pass through his powerful hand, then a steely resolve that told her he had come to some private, final conclusion.

One she was certain she wasn't going to like.

"If I give myself up to the World Federation, it should buy you time, give all of you an opportunity to—"

"Never." Mara's abrupt denial was drowned out by the combined voices of the others in the room, each of them refusing the alien's offer.

"How can you, any of you, make this decision for the rest of your people? Mara, listen to me, all of you, hear me. I've brought this trouble upon you, failed a major directive of the Explorers' creed, not to interfere with other worlds. I cannot allow you to sacrifice—"

"Can it, Sander." Mara laughed aloud, suddenly ripe with a sense of freedom, of power she'd not felt in all her twenty-eight years. For the first time since her father's death she saw a future for the Armand Institute. A future that rested solidly in her hands. "We'll take this meeting to the Rec Center. I want everyone there. If the WF wants a fight, we'll give 'em a fight. And you," she pointed at Dr. Antoon, "are going to round up enough Sensitives willing to learn this mindlink of yours and somehow we'll get that message off to Sander's world."

She pulled her hand out of Sander's and stood alone in front of the small group she'd silently dubbed Antoon's Army. They were so young for such a terrible responsibility! She glanced at Shing Tamura and his security officers, then at the lanky, low-key Dr. Antoon.

"You are my family," she said, addressing each one of them. "When my father died, you helped me survive the loss, you kept the Institute alive for me until I was able to take over. But I'm not my father. The Institute, under my care, has become stagnant. If it weren't for people like you, Dr. Antoon, there would be no new steps taken, no new ideas explored. We've become a self-serving group of oddities, reaching inward, not out, not helping mankind explore the power of the mind, the potential that exists in every one of us. You've reminded me there is power here and it's time we let the World Federation know what we're about."

She turned to Sander, shutting out the curious minds of the others around her. She grabbed his two large hands in hers and held them against her heart. *If it weren't for you, I would never have known what I was missing. The other half of myself, Sander. You're right, I think my father did know. I'm certain he would approve of the choice I'm making. I love you. I will always love you, but I can't leave the Institute. That decision was made when I promised to carry on my father's dream. All I can do is give every man, woman, and child here a chance to determine their own destiny. That applies to you as well. It will be your choice to stay or leave.*

Still grasping Sander's hands, Mara carefully blocked his distress and faced the questioning faces of her friends. "I want everyone in the Rec Center in fifteen minutes. Every citizen of the Institute, Sensitive or not. Sander's right. This isn't a decision for any one of us to make alone. It's one we'll make together."

Chapter 7

This time, Mara stood at the podium, Sander beside her, Shing Tamura and Dr. Antoon waited in the wings. All the board members except for Malachi sat together to one side of the stage. The Rec Center was filled, the voices of the two hundred plus residents of the Institute babbling in heated discussion over this second unheard of call to meeting.

"We have some important decisions to make." Mara barely raised her voice but a sudden hush fell over the room.

All eyes were upon her, all minds searching. She felt the questions, the concern, and even the compassion of her friends and associates.

She also felt hatred, disgust, revulsion. But from whom? Later. She'd have to track those thoughts later. "Major Tamura has intercepted messages from the World Federation. They know Captain Sander is here and they are planning an attack."

"How'd they find out?" a voice called from the back. Mara couldn't immediately identify the speaker.

"One among us told them," she said, clutching the sides of the podium. "We have a traitor in this room."

The silence was as deafening as the earlier babble had been.

"Whoever it is has a powerful block in place. Neither Sander nor Major Tamura can locate this person. We must move quickly. Anyone willing to help project a message to Mirat, please meet with Major Tamura immediately. If you are telekinetic and want to work with Dr. Antoon to help protect the Institute, meet with him. The rest of you have one of two choices. Either prepare to fight when the time comes, or escape now, while you can. I don't know if we can hold this place, but we intend to try."

"There is another option." Sander glanced briefly at Mara, his thoughts tightly shielded, then stepped forward. All eyes focused on his, all minds opened to him. He glanced down at Mara, at the love not only for him but for her people shining so brightly on her face, and smiled. "I offered to turn myself over to the World Federation. Mara says it's a useless gesture. I can't leave that decision solely in her hands."

"It might buy us some time." Malachi Franklin stood and faced Sander from his place near the back wall. "You're the cause of our problem. They're attacking because you're here, aren't they?"

"Yes, they are." Sander glanced again at Mara. She glared across the room at Malachi and the image of a mother protecting her cub immediately came to mind.

He hadn't been a cub for a long time.

"They're attacking because they've wanted an excuse to control us for years." Mara's voice rang out across the room. "We all know they killed my father. They figured I'd be too weak to hold the Institute together. Unfortunately, they were almost right. But they didn't count on the power of this group when we work together. Sander can be their excuse to rule us, or he can be the incentive that makes us finally pull together and find out just what it is we're capable of. If you want out, Malachi, now's the time. Anyone else?"

"Your father would be ashamed." The anger in Fred Haydon's voice startled even Sander. Mara's face turned a sickly pale. Sander grabbed her shoulders from behind, supporting her. "You've been lying to us all along, you and your stories of peaceful alien contact," he spat. "You've made contact, all right. You've been intimate with that damned thing, haven't you, Doctor Armand? Rutting with an animal, that's what it is. It's against the laws of nature, against God's laws. You disgust me!"

The old man turned his back on the stunned faces of his fellow board members and stalked out of the room. Sander knew Mara would have crumpled if he hadn't held her. All eyes in the room turned as one away from Haydon, some in censure, others merely curious, to stare at the couple at the podium.

Sander opened his mouth, prepared to deny the accusation, to protect Mara. If he must return to Mirat without her…it was best this way. Before he could speak, she straightened, and he felt her gathering her defenses, felt the power in the thoughts she shielded even from him.

"Haydon's right," Mara said. Something in Sander deflated, died. "I freely admit I was not completely honest with the board." A shocked gasp filled the room at Mara's admission.

She smiled and shook her head. "It's not what you think. During the three months Captain Sander and I communicated telepathically, I was learning things about myself, things much too personal to share with you." She looked directly at the tight group of board members.

"Please understand." She smiled regretfully at the weathered faces of the men and women who had helped Daniel Armand develop the Institute from the very beginning. Men and women who'd loved and cared for her since her childhood.

"I reported everything to you I felt affected the Institute, but I couldn't tell you what was happening to me. You've watched over me as if I were your daughter and I love each and every one of you. There are some things, however, that an adult daughter doesn't tell her father, things she hides from her mother, no matter how much she loves them."

A short cough from the back of the room was the only sound to break the silence. Mara straightened her shoulders, her eyes still fixed on the distinguished group of elders. "I can assure you, I have done nothing to jeopardize the Institute, nor have I been, as Fred so succinctly put it, rutting with an animal."

She reached out for Sander's hand, grasping it tightly in her small one. "I've made love with Sander and he with me. He is not a beast. Though he's not human, he is a good and honorable man." She turned to him, still holding his hand in hers, and reached up to stroke his cheek. "I do love you, Sander. I'm not ashamed, nor afraid, for anyone to know it."

A chair clattered to the floor as Malachi Franklin exploded to his feet. "I knew it," he sneered, opening his thoughts and projecting his disgust so violently that many in the group turned away in shock. "I warned you about mind control, Mara. It's a dangerous weapon and he's adept at using it. Can't you tell he's controlling you? You're letting him destroy your father's dream. Why can't you see it?"

With a final, heated glare at Sander, the young doctor charged out of the room, leaving an uneasy silence in his wake. Mara stood as if carved in stone and stared blindly out over the sea of familiar faces. Sander gently cupped her chin and turned her face to his.

"Do you believe him? Do you really believe I've controlled your mind?"

She looked into his amber eyes, filled with compassion, brimming with love, and nodded her head. "At first I wondered if Malachi's warning made sense. My feelings for you were so intense. I wondered if all your first contacts were as intimate as ours. Not anymore. Oh, I know you've controlled me," she said, blinking away the sudden rush of tears. His grasp tightened almost imperceptibly. "With love, Sander. You've controlled me with your love. I've been your willing victim."

She covered his large hand with her smaller one. "My father's Institute must stand or fall on its own merit, Sander. Your arrival may have been the catalyst, but if not for you, the World Federation would have found another reason, eventually, to attack us. At least with you by our side, we have hope."

There was a subtle shift within the room as everyone listened to Mara's softly spoken answer. Whispers and comments spread among the Institute members, Sensitive and non-Sensitive alike, as they finally understood the implications of her words, the potential truth in Malachi's warning.

Mara stood quietly within Sander's strong embrace, awaiting judgment, knowing they had every right to judge her. She had lied to them and only her heart knew for certain Malachi's warnings were without merit.

A woman's voice broke through the uneasy mutterings, and the room fell silent. "Dr. Armand, I know what it's like to love someone who's a little bit different." Gentle laughter met Lucy Andrew's comment. Her husband, blind since birth and horribly disfigured, was a Locator, a man whose lack of vision and physical imperfections did not hinder his ability to find whatever was lost. They were the loving parents of beautiful telepathic twin girls. "I...we actually," she touched her husband's withered hand, "would be happy to do what we can to help. Count us in."

"Me too, Dr. Armand, Captain Sander." Billy Powell, a gentle giant of a man who could grow flowers in cement, if need be, stood up and looked around him. An expectant hush fell over the group. Then, as one, every person in the room stood, including the members of the board.

Mara clasped Sander's hands to her heart and sobbed.

Sander stood behind her, stunned by the outpouring of love and emotion filling the drafty old Rec Center. To think they loved this tiny woman so much! How could he even consider asking her to leave this place and come with him?

How could he not?

"I don't know how to thank you," he said, humbled by the response of people he didn't know, people of another species, willing to risk their lives to save his. "But there might be something I can offer. It's slim, but still a chance. If we successfully contact Mirat and if we can hold out against the World Federation long enough for a ship to arrive, any of you who wish to come to my world are welcome. It may not have to be a lifelong exile. I merely offer a safe haven to keep the Armand Institute, and all of you, alive."

Mara grew very still in his arms, but she'd drawn her shields tight, effectively blocking his questing mind. Would she agree?

"I've always wanted to travel, Captain." Shing Tamura pushed himself away from his spot at the side of the stage. He grinned. "I think I've got an idea how we can get that message to Mirat. Unfortunately, it's gonna really piss off the World Federation."

"You do have a wicked mind, Major Tamura." Sander laughed at the mental image Shing presented him, then explained it to the expectant group. "A kinetic mindlink might be enough to get a message to Mirat, but bouncing it off the brand new World Federation communications satellite gives it a much better chance of transmission."

"The only drawback," Shing added, stepping up to align himself with Sander, "is that the power of the link will most likely bounce the satellite out of orbit."

"What a shame," Mara said, laughing along with the rest of the crowd. She couldn't allow herself to think about losing Sander, not now. The fact her people were willing to work together for her alien lover guaranteed their willingness to combine forces to save the Institute.

Maybe there was a chance after all.

* * * * *

"How's it going?" Mara stepped aside and Sander walked into the house. "You look exhausted."

"Antoon's Army is amazing." Sander dropped into the overstuffed chair. "Dr. Antoon's got the telekinetics, maybe forty or so, working together like a well-tuned instrument. They actually picked up the tram and put it on top of the Rec Center and not one of them moved a muscle or broke a sweat." He reached for Mara and pulled her down onto his lap. "I can't wait to see them manipulate a few weapons or pick up armored vehicles. They'll drive the troopers nuts. How're the telepaths doing?"

Mara curled up in Sander's lap, idly running her fingers along the fastener of his skinsuit. "Shing's got them working together. That's a struggle in itself. He wants you to meet with them later tonight to try and send your message. With the power of your mind in gestalt with the others, he thinks it'll work."

"Then what, Mara? Will you come with me? Will you come home to Mirat?"

She ignored the question. "Has Shing figured out who our traitor is?"

Sander tilted his head so he could look directly into her dark green eyes. Her thoughts and emotions were still shielded. He didn't attempt to break through her carefully constructed mental wall. "He thinks it's Malachi. The man's obsessed with you. When you said you loved me, I swear I felt him snap."

"He's a healer and a precog, I'm an empath...but neither one of us had the slightest idea how the other really felt. I had no idea he loved me." She slipped her hand inside Sander's skinsuit, stretching her fingers wide to span that part of his chest just over his heart. There it was, thundering away where it belonged, where it would be in any human male. "I hope it's not Malachi, Sander. He's a dear friend and a good man. I do love him, though I'll never be in love with him."

"We may never find out. He seems to have disappeared. Shing has no idea where he's gone." Sander brushed the hair away from her eyes. "Love me, Mara. I need to feel you, to be inside of you." His fingers trembled against her cheek. That tiny evidence of vulnerability made her want to weep.

Without speaking, she uncurled herself from his lap and led him into her room. He stood still while she peeled his uniform off his broad shoulders, then rolled the shiny fabric down his torso and past his narrow hips. He slipped the softskin boots off his feet and helped her as she removed his skinsuit. The dark tip of his tail hung remarkably still. Mara couldn't help but compare its lack of motion to the wild jerking and twitching the first time she'd seen him.

Had it only been three days?

She removed her own skinsuit, and he gently lifted her in his arms and stretched her out on the bed.

"Will you ever open to me again, Mara?" He lay down beside her, and stroked her cheek with one strong, furred finger. His thoughts were there, open, clear, strong and unyielding. He loved her, he needed her.

It was her choice, to follow him to the stars, or to stay with her people. Then she wondered, would her people stay with her? Sander's offer of a safe haven was the main topic of discussion at the Institute, a topic Mara was unwilling to influence. It had to be their choice. As this had to be hers.

I don't know! A sob caught in her throat, then another. She wanted to bury her face against his broad chest and cry until there were no more tears. Instead, she cupped his face in her hands and dropped her mental shields, opened her mind and her heart.

Sander, please, look into my heart. Do you see why I'm so torn? I love you, but these people have supported me, loved me all my life. Haydon was my father's oldest and dearest friend. Malachi was there for me, every day after they found my father's body. My father brought all these special people together when he created the Institute. Do I have the right to ask them to leave the planet of their birth? Can I abandon them, abandon my father's dream?

"I don't know, Mara. I have no choice but to return to Mirat if it's possible. Not only does my continued presence here bring danger upon all of you, but I am a sworn Explorer. Only you can decide to come with me or stay. I love you and will abide by whatever decision you make." He kissed her then, a long, slow kiss that built into a spiraling curl of heat.

That doesn't mean I won't do everything in my power to influence your decision.

His mouth plundered hers, his tongue an impossible blend of sandpaper rough and gentle caress. He filled her mouth, suckling her tongue, exploring the tender flesh between her lips, all the while filling her mind with his love.

His hands swept along her sides until he found her breast. He kneaded the soft flesh and she saw in his mind that on his world, the women's breasts were not so full, nor as sensitive to touch.

He liked the difference, she knew. Liked it very much. He played with the smooth nipple, taking great pains to touch and tease the rosy bit of flesh into a throbbing kernel of need. Obviously satisfied with the results, he proceeded on to her other breast.

His lips and tongue moved to her throat, along her collarbones, one side to the other, then across her sensitive breasts, bathing her like the big cat he was, stroking every inch of her skin with that hot, sandpapery tongue.

He traced the contours of her hip and taut buttock, the slightly rounded swell of her belly, the long stretch of smooth thigh and muscled calf, leaving each bit of flesh damp and tingling.

She grasped the blanket beneath her, absorbing each sensation, each hot stroke of his tongue. Her toes were not ignored, each carefully circled and stroked, and he held her ankles when he licked the soles of her feet, ignoring her shrieks and pleas for mercy.

Finally, when she thought she might die, when she'd begged and practically wept for the wanting, he parted her knees and knelt between them, then stretched her arms out to her sides and held her wrists firmly to the bed.

He hadn't touched her sex. Her entire body tingled from his ministrations, but not once had he gone near that hot, needy part of her. She arched her back, begging, beguiling, but all he did was lean forward and blow hot little puffs of air against her.

She moaned, incapable of speech, unable to project any thoughts beyond *need,* and *want* and *now.*

He was so close, that huge, swollen member thrusting out from its furred sheath, the tiny drops of liquid at its tip telling her he was as desperate as she.

His thick tail, moments before drooping impassively, now jutted out behind him, the dark tuft at the tip twitching and jerking hypnotically.

Still he waited and still he teased, a flick of his tongue against her belly, a hot breath of air just near her clit. She dug her heels into the bed and raised her hips, coming to within a hairsbreadth of contact with his erection.

He pulled back and laughed.

"What do you want from me?"

"All of you, Mara. That's all I want." He leaned over and lightly rubbed the fiery tip of his penis against her clit, then backed away again.

She gasped at the shock of contact, then moaned in frustration.

"Again, Mara?" This time he slipped between her tender folds for merely an instant, then pulled away.

"No, Sander, damn you," she cried. "You know it's not enough. I need you. Now."

"Only now, Mara?" His gaze was pensive, filled with longing.

She glared at him, wishing she could be angry, wanting to tell him to go away and never come back.

But that's exactly what she'd been planning to do, wasn't it? Send him back to Mirat, alone? A sudden chill swept over her body, the reality of life without Sander, without his love.

Impossible.

What had she been thinking?

"Forever, Sander." A sob welled up in her throat, then another. She looked into his eyes, cat's eyes, golden and luminous, filled with the wisdom of the ages, brimming over with love. "I don't know how it'll work, but it has to be forever. I love you too much to let you go."

His growl as he entered her could only be called victorious. Her answering cry, one of desperate fulfillment.

He thrust once, twice, then shuddered in her arms as she convulsed around him. Grasping her legs, he wrapped them about his waist and she clung to him, her wrists crossed behind his neck, her helpless sobs wracking her body. He lifted her, falling back on his haunches and cradling her against his chest.

"It'll work, my love. It has to. There can be no other choice." He nuzzled the damp crease between her neck and shoulder, then kissed the hot tears that spilled across her cheeks.

"Sander, how? I'm not strong enough to give you up, but I can't abandon my people. What if they're not willing to leave Earth? What if your ship doesn't come? There's so much uncertainty." Her tears fell faster, soaking the thick pelt that covered his chest.

He would do anything to ease her torment. "Somehow, my love," he whispered, "we'll find a way." Mara shuddered in his arms, losing the struggle against the convulsive sobs shaking her entire body. Silently, Sander rocked her as he would a kitten in distress. His lips moved against her dark hair in a silent plea, a prayer for an answer to all her questions.

Praise the Mother, there must be an answer.

Chapter 8

"What happened?" Mara grabbed Sander's arm and tugged frantically. Surrounded by the other telepaths, he stood there shaking his head, a bemused expression on his face.

Had the message gone through? Was a rescue ship coming? "Sander, are you all right?" Why hadn't he let her help? She'd offered, hadn't she?

"I don't believe it." The usually unflappable Shing Tamura slapped his thigh and grinned. "I absolutely goddamned don't believe it!"

"KaPow!" Tim Riley clapped his hands together. "Well, Major, you said we'd piss 'em off."

"That you did, Major." Sander grabbed Mara and swung her into his arms. "And yes, my love, I think the message went through. I pray to the Mother we were successful, but we won't know for certain until a rescue ship arrives. Unfortunately..." He kissed her full on the mouth, "the message didn't just nudge the WF satellite out of orbit."

"Nope." Major Tamura slapped Sander on the shoulder. "In fact, it blew that piece of high-tech spy junk into about a zillion tiny little pieces. Good thing the bastards don't know who did it! They'd be here in a heartbeat, cannons ready!"

"Should make for a right purty meteor shower." Dr. Antoon's dry comment was met with cheers and laughter.

Sander hugged Mara once again, then dropped her legs so that she stood beside him, still wrapped in his arms. He bowed his head a moment, as if gathering his thoughts. "I have put every one of you in terrible danger and yet you have risked all to help me." He gazed solemnly out at the room filled with telepaths. "Return with me to Mirat. Please, for the sake of your Institute, for your lives." He smiled tenderly at Mara. "Please. Come with me."

"It's something to consider." Major Tamura straightened and stretched, arms over head. "Right now, though, we all need to rest. I've got a pounding headache from that exercise in mass communication."

"If our message made it, how long before the ship arrives?" Tim Riley's question was obviously on every mind in the room.

"Depends," Sander said, rubbing the back of his neck. "Our method of travel is actually a form of telekinesis, literally moving the ship from coordinate to coordinate with the power of the mind. It took me about seven of your days to reach Earth from Mirat, but with the combined mental energy of a full crew, this ship should travel somewhat faster." He turned to Major Tamura. "Can we hold the WF troops off four, maybe five days? If the ship's not here within a week, we'll know the message failed."

"The way Antoon's Army's been training new recruits, I'd say we have a chance." He touched Sander's arm, a gesture Mara had noticed many of her friends making. They wanted, no needed, to touch him, to make physical contact with him, now that they had linked their minds with his.

She felt oddly bereft, isolated from the group. Why hadn't Sander wanted her to join the mindlink? She had freely admitted she'd once doubted him; she still hadn't agreed to return with him to Mirat. Maybe Sander no longer trusted her.

"We've got a few days to prepare," she said, choking back the hurt and turning away from Sander to encompass the room full of Sensitives. "Go home. Take time to consider Captain Sander's offer of refuge. Discuss it with your loved ones. Rest. That's an order."

* * * * *

Mara crawled into bed beside him and snuggled up against his chest like a warm and willing kitten, but he knew her heart was uneasy, steeped in its own silent misery. He waited patiently for her to gather her thoughts.

Finally, her words, suffused with heartache and sadness, filtered sorrowfully into his mind.

Why wouldn't you allow me to join the mindlink?

He nuzzled her raven hair, knowing she deserved the truth, wondering how to frame his answer so as not to cause her more pain.

"There was much danger," he finally said, answering her aloud so that he might hide his deeper thoughts. "The risk of that powerful burst of energy deflecting back on the combined minds, the possibility of the traitor joining the link in order to sabotage our projection, any number of risks I'm not willing to let you take."

"I make my own decisions, Sander." Her body stiffened in his embrace.

She deserved the truth. "There is also the question of your indecision," he said, deeply regretting the need for honesty. He knew his words would bring her more pain. "Mindlink is a literal melding of minds, a complete subjugation of self. Your turmoil over whether or not to choose exile with me would be part of the group knowledge. If you can't share your feelings with me, the man you profess to love, how could I expect you to share them with the group?"

She gasped at his harsh condemnation, a shattered denial of what he knew to be the truth. He grabbed her shoulders and forced her to look at him, forced her to see the tormented love in his eyes. "You would have blocked, Mara." He struggled for control, knew his ragged voice frightened her, but she had to know the truth. "Do you understand what I'm saying? Your indecision would have doomed the link to failure, possibly injured or even killed the participants. Is that a risk you're willing to take?"

He snarled and turned away, unable to meet her shocked and horrified eyes. "Well, I'm not, Mara. Do you know why? Not because of your damned Institute, not because of your friends. I'm not willing to risk you, Mara." He sighed heavily, hating himself for frightening her. "But I guess I've already done that, haven't I?"

Her touch was tentative, a mere whisper of trembling fingers on his rigid shoulder, but when he turned back to her, she threw herself into his arms. Without hesitation, he drew her into his embrace, once again tucking her head beneath his chin.

"Oh, Sander, I love you so much. You're right I am uncertain. I don't know what to do. I didn't think of the danger. All I could think of was you and the fact you shared yourself with everyone but me. I'm sorry. How stupid...I've been so selfish." Harsh sobs wracked her body, her guilt-ridden mind projected shame and remorse and indescribable disgrace.

"Oh Mara, Mara, no, my love. Listen to me!" He sat up, shoving the tangled sheets aside, cupping her tear-streaked face between his hands, forcing her to meet him, eye to eye. "You've failed no one, my love. I'm the one who's selfish. I'll do whatever I can to hold you."

Her lips trembled and the pain in her emerald eyes was almost his undoing. He fought an unbearable urge to kiss her tears away, knowing, once he tasted her, he would be lost.

"You are still responsible for the members of this Institute, Dr. Armand. You are their leader. You've not failed anyone, including me. Yes, I want you to come with me, but you'll make your decision when the time is right, not before, and you'll make it for the right reasons. Remember, a general sends his troops to battle, he rarely takes up the sword himself. There was no way for you to know about the danger with the mindlink. I should have explained." He brushed her tears aside with his thumbs. "There are many people depending on you, including me. Too many for you to take an unnecessary risk."

Her eyes glittered with unshed tears, and she took a deep, shuddering breath. "Make love to me, Sander. Please? I need you."

"I'll always need you, my love." He pulled her gently into his arms, the thought they might never love again after this night tugging fearfully at the corner of his mind. She offered herself willingly, opening her heart, her soul, her deepest thoughts to him without shield or subterfuge.

Sander sensed the separate levels of perception as Mara forged her own private mindlink with him. He hesitated but a moment, then opened his heart, his soul, his every thought to her.

They had shared before, but never with this intensity, not with this complete and total subjugation of self, this melding of identity, each to the other.

The subtle border between their thoughts shifted, blurred, then flowed together as one. Each stroke of Sander's sandpapery tongue across Mara's tender breast was a sensation shared by both. He knew the silken pleasure Mara felt when she raked her fingers through the thick pelt on his chest, shared the simple regret of abandonment when he stilled his tongue and shifted position.

As he dipped lower, tasting the subtle flavors in that honeyed spot between her thighs, Sander became Mara, became the woman he loved. His tongue filled her and she shared the lushness of his mouth, the overwhelming fullness of that unbelievable tongue tormenting, teasing, driving Mara to the brink.

Taking Sander with her.

Her small hand circled his engorged flesh, stroking the length and breadth of him and he felt the hot slick surface as Mara sensed it, a firebrand of molten steel filling her hand, his hand, the hand of each as one.

She shifted in his arms, turning and taking him into her mouth so that Sander tasted himself through Mara's senses, felt her warm lips surrounding him, tasted his own unsheathed penis, each sensation overlapping, one upon the other until Sander no longer knew the he or the she of the two of them.

Linked, forever forged in mind and soul, Sander balanced unsuccessfully on the brink of control. Gasping for air, grasping for one last particle of sanity, he turned Mara in his arms, clenched her hips from behind and without hesitation entered her with a bestial roar of pain and pleasure.

She was ready, hot and willing and so slick, so wet for him. She wanted more, all of him and more and Sander thrust deeper, mindless, mindful, aware on so many levels, knowing exactly what Mara wanted, what she needed, what she felt.

The link held. He was Mara, he was the young woman mounted by a raging, frenzied beast. He was the Beast, savage, untamed, filled with lust and passion and anger...tormented by love.

Linked. They were forever linked. Sander's roar shook the room, Mara's harsh cry of release stunned them both. Panting, drained, Sander's arms trembled as he grasped Mara's hips, eased her slowly to the tousled bedding, then curled up beside her, still tightly clasped within her quivering flesh.

They pulsed together as one, drained and exhausted.

Complete.

For this moment, complete.

* * * * *

Later, long sweet hours later, Mara arched her back, stretched her aching muscles, then once again relaxed against Sander. "Do you have any idea who the traitor is? Do you think it's Malachi?"

He considered the young doctor a moment before he spoke. "I don't know. He refused to join the mindlink and no one's seen him since he stormed out of the meeting at the Rec Center. I've maintained an open search for any telepathic messages to the WF and haven't picked up anything from anyone at all. I suspected your old friend

Haydon, but even though he hasn't linked, he's been helping Dr. Antoon with the telekinetics. Everyone else at the Institute has joined the effort, other than the few families who left this morning."

"I was sorry to see them go." Mara snuggled more tightly against him. His body responded to her heat and he shifted her in his arms.

"They had young children. There's no future here, not anymore, at least for those unwilling to make the journey to Mirat."

He let her think about that for a long moment. "For those who choose to stay, there's no assurance rescue is forthcoming. The risk is too great. They had no choice but to put their children's safety first. I'm very sorry, my love." He kissed the top of her head, inhaling the clean, fresh scent of her hair. Her fingers tangled in the thick mane falling across his shoulders and she arched her hips closer to his.

"Will I ever have your child, Sander? Is it possible?"

"I would have said no, before I met you. We are so different, but I've learned there's much in us that's alike."

He stroked her back, ran his hands along her sleek thighs, and gently slipped his fingers inside her.

So lush, so easily aroused. Hot and ready, waiting for him. He entered her slowly, reverently, and their lovemaking was quiet this time, a silent benediction to all they had gained, to the losses they faced.

When she cried out, when she tightened around him and shuddered in ecstatic release, he filled her with his seed, then wept great tears into her tousled hair.

* * * * *

Shouts, desperate, fearful. Pandemonium erupted just outside, spilled over into Mara's dreams until the banging on the door rattled the cottage. The clamor startled her awake, the pounding at the door and frantic shouts dragged both Mara and Sander into bewildered consciousness. Throwing her robe around her shoulders, Mara raced to the front door and flung it open.

"They're at the gates, Doctor." Tim Riley, his youthful face flushed and frightened, lunged into the room. "Armed forces, and they're demanding Captain Sander be turned over to them."

"Never." Mara dragged her fingers through her long hair, then turned frantically to look for Sander.

"How'd they get here so fast?" Jamming his arms into a clean skinsuit, Sander raced into the room.

"Whoever's informing on us must have given them specific directions through the passes. According to Major Tamura, they knew exactly which routes to take and where you'd be."

"Who's doing this to us?" Mara took a deep breath, fighting for control. Someone she knew, someone she cared about. The whole idea sickened her.

"I don't know, but we'd better get Antoon's Army linked and ready." Sander slipped his feet into his boots and grinned at Mara. "Forget the traitor, Mara. He's done his worst. Get dressed, my little general. We have a battle to fight."

"Men," she muttered, racing back to her room for clothing. "It's not a game, Sander," she called out.

All of them, little boys wanting to blow things to smithereens.

* * * * *

"I want to talk to them." Mara pushed her way through the gathered citizens of the Institute, then climbed the steps to the guard tower by the front gate.

"They're not inclined to listen." Shing Tamura stepped aside as Mara entered the protected platform.

She understood exactly what he meant when she looked down on the army massed before her. At least a thousand armed troops dressed in protective armor and a dozen large tanks capable of knocking down walls or firing explosive projectiles filled the broad plain in front of the Institute walls.

She glanced behind her. Sander stood head and shoulders above the others. Haydon was there, standing to the back of the crowd. She didn't see Malachi anywhere.

Barely a hundred Sensitives, some only minor talents, waited. She sensed their fear, their anxiety. But above all, she sensed determination.

Antoon's Army.

Supported by their strength, she turned and faced their attackers. "Captain Sander is our guest," she shouted, searching the helmeted faces below her for the one in charge. "We will not surrender him."

"Then you and all your people will die." A large, swarthy man of indeterminate age stepped up to the gate. "For harboring an alien and for the destruction of World Federation property. That was a very expensive satellite, Dr. Armand."

"But how?" Mara swiveled about to catch Sander's surprised glance. How do they know we did it? He shrugged and she turned back to face her enemy. The sense of evil flowing from their ranks made her tremble. The fear and loathing the invaders harbored against Sander and the members of the Institute formed a palpable wave of hatred. There would be no compromise.

Drawing a deep breath, she focused her attention on the commander. "I believe, sir, it would be in your best interest to remove your soldiers, now, before anyone gets hurt."

Channeling her energy, Mara projected a powerful emotional blast in the direction of the troops, fear, longing for home, desperation. A few of them shifted uncomfortably in the forward ranks, their leader among them.

Then he cursed loudly and raised and lowered his arm, a slashing motion that brought an immediate response.

Shells rained upon the Institute, great fiery explosives throwing cement and metal in all directions. Ducking, covering her head, Mara raced down the steps, directly into the linked arms of Antoon's Army.

Faces taut with concentration, the ragtag group of Sensitives joined their hands and their minds. Oblivious to the falling shells and blazing explosions, they formed a kinetic mindlink of more power than any one Sensitive alone could ever hope to achieve.

Mara heard the shouts at the gate, the thunder of heavy tanks moving against the solid stone walls of her beloved Institute. She felt the massed energy of the minds before her, power building upon power, then suddenly a shift, as if the atmosphere had bent and folded in upon itself.

The shells stopped their cascade of fire, movement ceased, then abruptly switched as the weapons of death and destruction reversed their direction to fall back upon the enemy.

Screams reverberated across the compound, the screams of men dying by their own weapons. Mara covered her ears, assailed by the agony of soldiers in the throes of death. Suddenly, Sander was by her side, holding her close, helping her shield the worst of the pain, his powerful mind forming a comforting protective cocoon around her beleaguered brain.

As a powerful empath, Mara sensed all, felt each individual horror as if it were her own. Now, surrounded by panic, fear and death, time lost all meaning, all relevance. Time was to be endured, an agony of dread and screams and torment.

Suddenly, all was silent. The small fires burning about the compound crackled and snapped, then sputtered and went out. A few birds ventured out of hiding and a collective sigh went up from the obviously exhausted, mentally depleted members of Antoon's Army.

Mara felt the slow withdrawal of Sander's protective mental shield, though his arms still held her tightly against his chest. She shuddered off the effects of the assault, then took a deep, calming breath and slipped out of Sander's embrace.

Fearing the worst, she tugged at his hand and led him to the top of the platform, unwilling to face the Stygian view alone. "My God, Sander...I never imagined."

Never imagined the horror their minds could create. Never dreamed the power inherent in the combined abilities of so many desperate Sensitives.

Tanks lay twisted and broken, their barrels bent, their treads separated and flung about. Relatively few bodies remained. Those men who hadn't escaped had burned beyond recognition when their weapons turned against them.

The leader's body remained where he had fallen, relatively untouched, a look of shock and surprise etched eternally on his dark face.

Mara shuddered. This horrible destruction could not be cause for celebration. She took a deep breath and clasped Sander's hands in both of hers. "They'll be back, won't they?"

He nodded slowly in weary acknowledgment. "Yes. They'll be back. I only hope we have the strength to hold out."

* * * * *

The enemy struck again before dawn and once again was repulsed. A third wave, fresher troops this time, hit the compound around noon and by evening, air strikes had begun, powerful helicopters sweeping in low over the walls.

Each aircraft made only one pass. Once within reach they were twisted from the sky, flung beyond the Institute's boundaries and dropped in pieces onto the men and machinery below.

Antoon's Army stood firm. The talented men, women and adolescents worked in shifts, repelling each attack before serious damage occurred.

Mara felt their exhaustion, knew this battle could not last much longer. There'd been no contact from a rescue ship, no assurance one was even on the way. Even Sander, as powerful a telepath as he was, looked haggard. She found him just before midnight of the fourth day, nodding in sleep, uncomfortably contorted into a small, straight-backed chair in Shing Tamura's office.

She set the basket of sandwiches she'd just made on an uncluttered patch of Shing's desk and knelt beside her lover.

"Sander, you must get some rest," she said, gently shaking his shoulder. "Come home with me, please, just for a few hours. We need you strong, not asleep on your feet."

He blinked awake, disoriented and spent, and for a moment merely stared at her. Then, finally understanding her plea but still obviously reluctant, he followed her back to the bungalow.

She helped him shower, but he fell asleep under the warm spray. The memories of their first shower together were bittersweet. So much had happened in such a short time!

She disengaged the hummer so they could be reached in case of another attack and helped Sander into bed. He collapsed across the burgundy spread, completely spent.

He slept restlessly beside her and she knew his dreams were troubled. Wrapping his huge, tawny body in her arms, Mara willed him into calm and peaceful slumber.

Chapter 9

The scream pierced her weary mind just before dawn, Malachi's call for help, a shattering cry of agonizing pain. Confused, disoriented, Mara wrenched herself from sleep and grabbed her clothing. Sander followed closely behind, stumbling in his exhausted, half-awakened state as he struggled into his skinsuit.

"Malachi? Where are you?" Her call was met with silence.

Sander shook his tousled mane out of his eyes. "The other side of the compound. Quick. We didn't actually hear his voice...he was projecting." He grabbed Mara's arm and pulled her along with him. They raced down the path behind her bungalow through the pre-dawn darkness, a shortcut to the hospital.

They found Haydon's body first, bloodied and crumpled in a broken heap beside the main entrance to the clinic, a laser pistol clenched tightly in his right hand, the powerpack spent.

Malachi lay in a spreading pool of blood just inside the door, white-faced, his shoulder nearly blown away. He clutched a small packet in one hand. Weakly he gestured to Mara.

"Not me," he whispered, dropping the packet into Mara's outstretched hand. "Haydon. It was Haydon."

"Don't talk, Malachi. Please, lie still. Sander? Can you help him?" She turned to Sander, hoping against hope, but Malachi struggled to raise himself to one elbow and reached out with his shattered hand, weakly clutching at the tight fabric of her skinsuit. "I killed Haydon. To save you, Mara."

"What? I don't understand."

Malachi glanced in Sander's direction, and something heated and powerful passed between the two. The physician's eyes closed and he slumped unconscious to the floor.

"Fred Haydon was our traitor." Sander gently stroked Mara's hair. "Malachi suspected him all along. That's why he's stayed out of the mindlinks. He didn't want anyone to know he was on to Haydon."

"But how? Haydon's telekinetic, not a telepath at all. He couldn't send a thought across the room."

"No," Sander said, taking the crumpled packet out of her hand. "But he could send written messages." He unwrapped the folded paper, then handed it to Mara. The coordinates of her bungalow were printed neatly across the page in Haydon's distinctive script, along with the fact she and Sander would be asleep for at least another couple of hours.

"They would have killed us. A single projectile wouldn't have been enough to alert anyone in time to protect us. Oh God, Sander. I've suspected Malachi all along and he's been trying to help me." She brushed a hand gently across the young doctor's brow. Even in his unconscious state she read the love he felt for her. "Can you help him? He's the Institute's only true healer..."

"And a healer cannot heal himself." Sander completed her thought aloud. "But if we can bring him back to consciousness long enough to complete a mindlink..."

Mara kissed Sander hard on the mouth, then ran for the kit of emergency supplies in the clinic office. Within seconds she was back, filling a syringe with a powerful stimulant, saying a brief but fervent prayer, then injecting it directly into Malachi's heart.

His eyes fluttered open; he groaned in pain. Mara immediately placed her hands on either side of his skull, drawing away his pain and projecting a sense of serenity to calm him. "Sander wants to link with you, Malachi. Can you manage?"

"Why?" His eyes darted suspiciously in Sander's direction, then back to Mara.

"A healer cannot heal himself, we know that," Sander said. "But if you link with me, I become the healer. I command your talent. It's worth a try."

"Why would you want to help me? You know what I think of you. You know that I would just as soon kill you as let you take Mara away."

"Please, Malachi. Quit being so damned stubborn." Mara swept useless tears out of her eyes and glared at her wounded friend. She wanted to project healing emotions to help him, but all she could sum up was a heavy dose of frustration.

"Your people have an old saying, Dr. Franklin. Physician, heal thyself. Please. If not for yourself, for Mara. She, at least, wants you to live." Sander held his hand out to Malachi and after a moment's hesitation the young doctor took it.

The transformation was miraculous. Mara had watched before when Malachi healed wounds, had seen the flesh close and the scars fade. Now, with the powerful boost from Sander's alien mind aiding Malachi's natural talent, shattered bone knit and reformed, torn vessels closed and throbbed with flowing blood and the terrible burns from the laser gun faded to healthy pink skin.

In a matter of moments, Malachi slumped to the ground, exhausted but no longer mortally wounded. Sander dropped to the floor beside him, his head lowered between his knees, his hands dangling loosely from trembling arms.

Mara watched the two men closely. She knew the power of the mindlink, knew the effect it had had on some of the Sensitives who had hoped to be part of Antoon's Army. Not everyone could handle the complete loss of self, the subjugation of ego that occurred during link.

Between men who hated one another, who saw each other as rivals...she glanced from one to the other, almost afraid to breathe. Neither Sander nor Malachi moved. The seconds stretched into minutes, until she could stand it no longer.

"Are you okay?" she finally asked, including both of them in her question. Sander raised his head and nodded. A moment later, Malachi struggled to sit up, a look of stunned disbelief on his face.

"I'm sorry, Captain," he said, obviously battling his emotions. "I owe you an apology, along with my life."

"No, Doctor, you owe me nothing." Sander's voice was barely audible, a hushed whisper. "You have given me a wonderful gift. I ask only that you follow your dream. The rebellion will need a good healer."

"What rebellion? What are you talking about?" Mara grabbed Sander's arm, surprised to find his shields locked firmly in place, his thoughts and emotions completely blocked.

"We tend to forget some of the extraordinary talents of the people around us," he said, smiling in a bemused sort of way. "Dr. Franklin is not only an excellent healer...he is precognitive, a seer of the future. During the link, we both saw much more than we expected. There will be a rebellion against the World Federation, and Antoon's Army will lead it."

"What else did you see?" Mara stood up and reached out to both men, helping them to their feet. "Will we...?"

"Yes, we will." Sander smiled enigmatically, then turned and held his hand out to Malachi. "Good luck, Dr. Franklin. I saw one more attack before my ship arrives. You need to be ready to make your escape the moment it lands. You'll have a better chance during all the confusion."

"Congratulations, Captain, and thank you." Malachi grasped Sander's hand in both of his and once again Mara knew something powerful passed between the two men. Malachi turned to Mara, and a sad smile flitted across his handsome features.

"I apologize for any pain I've brought you. Everything I did was out of love, Mara, but it was a very selfish love. I realize that, now. I'll think of you often, traveling the heavens. When I look at the stars, I'll remember what you did here, the path you followed. Take care." He leaned over and kissed her very gently on the forehead, then turned and left.

"I don't get any of that. What's he talking about?"

"Later," Sander said, compounding her confusion. "An attack is due any moment."

It happened as he said it would and the small army of talented Sensitives held the final assault off throughout that terrible day, long enough for the ship from Mirat to land, just as Sander and Malachi had foreseen.

It came in under cover of darkness, appearing suddenly as a shimmering opalescent disk just after sundown. Silent, powered by the minds of the crew within, it hovered inches from the ground over the large sports field to the rear of the compound.

Her final decision, after all, was not nearly so difficult as Mara had feared, not with World Federation troops massing for yet another violent attack, the beautiful ship hovering like a sacred beacon and Sander, his love for her like a coat of precious armor, standing strong and silent beside her.

Good-byes were brief and painful, then Dr. Antoon led his small army into the darkness, accompanied by Malachi Franklin and Shing Tamura. Tearfully, proudly, Mara watched them go.

The Rebellion had begun.

Close to a hundred Sensitives, including a number of families with children, boarded the alien craft, frightened, exhausted exiles on their way to another world. Sander's people welcomed them as brothers and sisters, as children of the same Mother, and the rescue ship spun silently into the heavens.

Hours later, when everyone had been settled for the journey, Mara curled up in Sander's warm embrace and watched the stars shimmer endlessly beyond the observation window in his private quarters. Had she done the right thing? Would her father have understood?

Sander had been oddly silent throughout their escape, his shields tightly drawn, his telepathic conversations with his crew brief and private.

Now he held her close against his heart and the steady *thump, thump, thump,* lulled her nearly into sleep.

"What did Malachi mean?" she asked, her voice a drowsy whisper. "About the path I followed and selfish love and pain he might have caused me? The only thing I understood was the part about the ship!"

Sander's voice rumbled in his chest, the deep grumbling noise she loved. "He blames himself for Haydon's defection. Malachi tried to turn the others against me, but not because he feared for the safety of you or the Institute. His motives were purely selfish. Once he suspected we were intimate, his jealousy made him say things that inflamed Haydon. He never expected the old man's extreme reaction. When he realized Haydon was the traitor, Malachi tried to stop him. He'd been following Haydon for days without discovering anything concrete. Praise the Mother he was following Haydon this morning. Otherwise he might not have caught him trying to transport that last message."

"Then he killed him, before Fred could have us killed." Mara thought about that a moment, about the years Fred Haydon had stood beside her, how he'd tried to fill Daniel Armand's role in her life. A love gone awry.

"What path am I following, Sander? What did Malachi mean by that?" She tilted against his chest to look into his eyes and saw happiness there, but no answers. "What?" she demanded, punching him lightly on the arm when he grinned down at her.

"The path between two worlds, Mara. The path between species." He brushed her cheek very gently with the side of one long, curved finger, then followed its path with a string of light, nuzzling kisses. "The impossible has happened. You carry our child, my love. A daughter. During the mindlink, both Malachi and I saw her and she will be beautiful." Tears sparkled in his amber eyes and he bent down and kissed her, a soft promise of a kiss that filled her with wonder.

Mara opened her mind to Sander's. He shared with her the vision of their daughter. A child of about twelve sparkled in sunlight, tall and slender, her coloring dark, like Mara's, a thick ebony mane curling about her beautiful face. She had eyes the color of emerald, a mouth much like her mother's and a slim, tufted tail that curved audaciously about her ankle.

Mara wiped the tears from her eyes with the back of her hand as the image faded, then stroked the sleek velvety line of Sander's jaw, aware of a connection beyond the physical, beyond the mind. A link of hearts and souls that could not be denied. A sense of the future, a knowledge of forever.

Very carefully Mara pulled the fastener of Sander's skinsuit aside, opening the fabric almost to his waist. She wrapped her arms around him, flesh against flesh, and buried her face in the thick pelt that covered his chest.

There. Right where it should be. His heart, beating strong and true. Beating for Mara. She sighed, remembering, and tightened her eyelids against the sting of tears. Her life would never be the same. With Sander by her side, she knew it would always be special.

"Remember, Sander, the first night we made love? You showed me stars. I knew then you could do anything. I love you, my great beast. I always will. With all my heart."

He didn't speak. He couldn't. Instead, he opened his mind completely, sharing once again the vision of their daughter, thrilling Mara with the brilliant future he and Malachi had foreseen.

He made love to her then, sweet, tender love filled with promise and passion.

Once again, he showed Mara the stars.

NIGHT OF THE CAT

Kate Douglas

Chapter 1

"Hey, Jenna. I'm making a trash run...got anything for me?"

Jenna Lang tossed a last handful of pens into her cardboard box, then grabbed a plastic garbage bag off the floor. "Thanks, Malcolm. This about does it." She looked around the empty cubicle and sighed. "Hard to believe it's over, isn't it?"

Malcolm Trent grabbed the bag out of Jenna's hand. "We're not the first dotcom to belly up. I doubt we'll be the last."

"Yeah...but it was a good gig while it lasted. I gotta admit, though...I'm ready for a change. Have been for a long time." Jenna leaned against her empty desk and folded her arms over her chest. "What are you gonna do now?"

"I've got some interviews lined up. There's always work for engineers. What about you?" Malcolm adjusted the bags of trash filling both arms. "Marketing jobs might not be as easy to find."

"Thanks for the vote of confidence." Jenna grinned. She'd always liked Malcolm, in spite of himself. He was funny and okay to look at. Tall and gangly, he resembled an overgrown teenager with a '70s Beatle haircut...cute in a geeky sort of way. It was hard to believe this overgrown boy was ten years older than she was.

She'd let her daytime fantasies run away with Malcolm on occasion, but in real life they'd never done more than have a cup of coffee together in the cafeteria.

Company policy forbade co-workers dating.

There's no more company. Hmmmmm...

Suddenly Jenna realized she was looking at Malcolm in an entirely new light.

She'd never noticed before, but he had the biggest hands and feet she'd ever seen on a man.

"Actually," she said, surreptitiously studying Malcolm's long, supple fingers, "I do have a job lined up. Similar work but not as frenetic a pace, thank goodness. I'm relocating to Sacramento...in fact, I'm moving in a couple days. Already have my stuff packed."

She smiled at Malcolm and he grinned back at her. His mouth wasn't bad, either. *Nice wide smile, full lips...but those hands...*

"Sounds good. From what I hear, just about everyone here has found work." He turned to leave. "Wanna go for a drink after we shut this sucker down?"

He must be reading my mind! "Sure. Works for me." Suddenly Jenna noticed something shiny through a tear in one of Malcolm's garbage bags. "What's that?" She reached through the hole and grabbed a brass statuette. "You're not really tossing Lucky Louie, are you?"

"Louie hasn't been all that lucky as far as I can tell. You keep him if you want. Maybe if you're the one rubbing his belly he'll grant *your* wish. If I'd gotten mine, I'd still have a job." He shifted the sacks once more. "I'll meet you in the lobby in ten minutes, okay?"

"Okay." Jenna barely heard Malcolm leave. She set Lucky Louie on the polished surface of her desk. The fat little statue glared at her out of brassy gargoyle eyes. It resembled a roaring lion with its tongue curling grotesquely from between sharp canines, but the body looked more like an overweight Buddha with a shiny, round belly and short, fat legs.

"Malcolm sure thought you granted his wishes when things were going well, didn't he, Louie?" The whole staff had teased the engineer about his habit of rubbing the statue's round tummy for luck. "I can't believe he'd just dump you in the trash!"

She rubbed the little statue's belly. "Maybe I'll get lucky with Malcolm tonight, eh, Louie? Can you fix it so there's something really hot under that dweeby exterior? You know what they say about men with big hands and feet..."

With any luck, maybe she'd underestimated Malcolm before now. The movers weren't due until day after tomorrow. A private little *bon voyage* party might be just the thing to send her on her way.

Grinning, Jenna stuck the little statue on top of her single carton of belongings, tucked the box under her arm and carefully locked the cubicle door behind her.

* * * * *

Jenna stared at the little brass statue on the bathroom counter. "Last time I rub your belly, you jerk."

Lucky Louie stared back with his gargoyle grin.

"If it weren't for you, I never would have invited Malcolm back here...remember, he was supposed to be hot."

She could have sworn Louie's little brass eyes twinkled.

"I was horny, okay? Besides, he lives with his mother. We couldn't very well go there."

Did Louie just wink?

"Well, he *sounded* like he knew what he was doing!" She glared at the grinning statue. "Talk about false advertising! With hands and feet like his, he should have been hung like a horse...I had no idea condoms came in *petite*!"

Louie appeared to hold judgment on that comment.

"Well, he knows his wine, he talked a good game...how was I to know?"

Obviously, Louie needed more details.

"Okay...so maybe I shouldn't have invited him home. What a fiasco. He said he was into 'light bondage,' then he totally freaked when I pulled out some silk stockings. He said he wanted to 'taste' me. Biting my neck is not the kind of tasting I'm interested in, dammit."

When she'd suggested he "taste a little lower," he'd practically turned green.

Then he'd asked *her* to go down on *him*.

"What a jerk!"

Louie's little brass shoulders seemed to droop with shame.

Muttering, Jenna stepped under the shower spray, then pulled the nozzle down and washed between her legs. Even though Malcolm had used a condom, she still felt yucky.

What a disappointment...even guys who weren't all that well-endowed could be decent lovers.

Malcolm, however, was not one of them.

He's not even remotely acceptable!

She adjusted the spray, turned the temperature up a little warmer and ran the pulsating jets over her breasts and belly with an occasional teasing shot at her clit.

Nothing. Not even a tingle.

Not a good sign when you can't even give yourself an orgasm, Lang!

If only she could get the blasted image of Malcolm out of her mind! Hell, she had more muscle definition than he did! Malcolm, naked in her bedroom, white skinned and pasty, a few scraggly little hairs on his chest and zits on his back, humping her leg like a damned teenager.

After all that talk over wine, the whispered things he'd like to do...*shit!* Obviously, the word *foreplay* was not in his dictionary. He hadn't even *touched* her...at least not where it counted! *What a waste of those wonderfully long fingers...*

No wonder he still lives with Mama!

Grumbling, Jenna turned off the water, toweled dry and grabbed Lucky Louie. She caught a quick glimpse of herself in the full-length mirror on the way out of the room. Tall, dark blonde and still slim and muscular from miles of jogging and hours of workouts...she worked damned hard to look good and what did it get her?

Bad sex or no sex. Take your pick.

Life definitely was not fair.

"Ya know, Louie, I'm not in bad shape for thirty." Jenna dropped the statue on her bed and looked in the closet for her bathrobe. "So, why can't I catch a decent man...and where's my damned robe?"

A soft thunk caught her attention. She whipped around, then realized the statue had rolled off the bed and landed on her packed suitcase.

Suitcase! She'd already packed the bathrobe. No wonder she couldn't find it.

"Thanks, Louie. I guess you're forgiven." Jenna picked up the statue and dragged her old quilt off the bed. Wrapping the worn blanket around herself, she wandered into the kitchen and dug an open bottle of Chardonnay out of the 'fridge. Juggling Louie, the quilt and the bottle in one hand, she grabbed her only crystal goblet in the other...everything else was already packed.

Jenna set Louie on the coffee table, lit a couple of candles, turned off the lights in the front room then, wrapped in the quilt, curled up in her favorite old rocker, surrounded by boxes and crates of her belongings.

Sipping at her chilled wine, Jenna stared at the brassy little statuette. Candlelight flickering off the shiny metal made him look like he was breathing.

"It's like this, Louie. I need to find a man. I thought you'd be able to help, but so far you're battin' zero...no, Malcolm doesn't count. Yeah, I know. Obviously, *he* had a wonderful evening." She snorted, then laughed out loud. "Ya know, Louie, that's got to be the first time I ever heard a guy whimper when he came! What a sad excuse for a man."

She shook her finger at the statue. "I am very disappointed in you, Louie. I asked for hot and you gave me Malcolm. He is not hot. He's pathetic."

The candlelight flickered brighter, then subsided. "Okay. I get your drift. I'm the one who's pathetic. Thanks loads. You are *so* good for my self esteem."

Jenna downed her wine then refilled her glass. "Where am I going to find a real man, Louie? Think there might be one waiting for me in Sacramento? Maybe I need to go on a cruise...you know, one of those singles fantasy find-your-man-on-board-ship cruises...nah...just a bunch of losers go on trips like that."

One of the candles flickered out. Jenna leaned over and tipped the lit candle to re-light the other, then sat back in the chair and wrapped the blanket tighter around her breasts. "You know what I want, Louie. Are you willing to give it another try? How about we skip the cruise and try for a cowboy this time? A big, tall, sexy, rugged cowboy."

Louie remained as inscrutable as ever. Jenna leaned over and picked him up. The brass felt warmed by candlelight. Absentmindedly, Jenna stroked her finger over the smooth belly.

"I have such great fantasies, Louie. Let me refresh your little brass brain. I want a lover like the one I dream about at night, one who's strong and tall and still has the element of the beast in him. I'm so damned tired of computer geeks with their wimpy muscles and wimpier personalities."

Jenna poked Louie in the belly. "Want to know what I dreamed last night?" She giggled. "All I will tell you is that it included me tied to a bed and a guy who was hung like a bull elephant."

She added the rest of the wine to her empty glass. "I didn't see him, in my dream, but my perfect lover has got to have hair on his chest, real hair, not that wimpy little scraggle like Malcolm's got...and muscles. Really big muscles."

She giggled, rubbing Louie's belly even faster. "C'mon, Louie...think you can do it? Can you find him for me? I want a man who likes the way I taste and smell and feel, a man willing to experiment a little with his darker side...and with mine."

The room spun a bit as Jenna finished the glass of wine. She probably should have eaten dinner tonight. *Damn Malcolm.* Talk about your cheap date. Now she was probably too woozy to even consider cooking anything.

There'd be time in the morning. She'd packed just about all her belongings, the new job didn't start until next week and there was absolutely no reason at all for her not to sleep in as late as she wanted. Yawning, Jenna snuggled further into the quilt, still rubbing Louie's brass belly.

Suddenly, the oddest thing happened.

She swept her fingers across Louie.

Something stroked between her legs.

She rubbed a little faster.

The sensation increased.

She slipped one finger between Louie's fat little legs, across the brass nub representing his cock and balls.

Something directly stimulated her throbbing clit.

She rolled her fingers in a circular motion over the fat little brass belly.

Something twirled deep inside her, filling her.

She rubbed the brass statue a little harder, a little faster. An orgasm bubbled near her surface.

This is weird...this is really, really weird. Louie, are you actually grinning at me?

Her strokes grew longer, smooth and slow, back and forth across the statue's brass belly, down between its fat little legs where she spent long moments circling his little brass nub.

Not once had she touched herself, yet each sweep of her fingers across the warm brass brought her closer to climax. Eyes half closed, breath coming in short, sharp bursts, Jenna felt the familiar tightening, the hot, needy undulations coiling deep inside.

Fingers flying, faster now, unbelieving, not caring this was entirely impossible, Jenna tottered at the edge, suspended over the abyss, gasping, each breath catching in a soft moan...suddenly she shuddered, cried aloud and sailed into darkness, passing through the most intense orgasm she'd ever known.

Her hands went limp. The little brass statue rolled to the floor where it lay on its back, grinning at the ceiling.

The candles sputtered and went out. The worn quilt settled to the empty chair, still damp from the spot where Jenna had once sat.

Chapter 2

Floating. So, so far away…

Jenna hovered halfway between sleep and wakefulness. She knew she ought to get up, but then she'd lose those glorious erotic dreams still simmering in her soul.

Nights were good. Last night was fantastic…*after* Malcolm left, of course.

Daytime sucked. Hopefully the new job would get her out of this funk.

Change is good. How many times had she repeated that phrase?

Maybe one of these days she'd actually believe it. Not that she'd liked her old job all that much, but losing it hadn't been part of her plans. Just a year ago, computer marketing specialists could call their own shots in Silicon Valley. Now they were practically sitting on street corners with cardboard signs, begging for jobs.

Somehow, Jenna couldn't quite picture herself sitting on a sidewalk. She definitely preferred her little Mercedes over a shopping cart, which was the main reason the offer in Sacramento had looked so good, even though it paid barely half the salary she'd been getting.

She'd joked with her co-workers about getting laid off; never dreaming the whole damned company would fold, taking her down with it. Not Jenna Lang, wonder-girl of the dotcom era, successful advertising ace and marketing guru. So what if the work had bored her to tears? Frustrated by long hours, repetitive projects and absolutely no time for a social life, she'd at least had a steady–and sizable–income. Thank goodness she'd invested that income wisely, or she'd really be in a panic.

Well, the big bucks were officially a thing of the past. At least it should be a lot cheaper to live in Sacramento…not that the state's capital was known for its night life.

*Cowboys…*that's what her assistant had told her. *It's hot in the summer, foggy in the winter, and when you go out at night, be prepared for cowboys.*

Jenna smiled. Cowboys were really not her style...*of course, who needs a night life with a fantasy life like mine?* No matter how bad the days, she'd always have her nights...but *cowboys?*

She felt her lips twitch in a slight smile. Once she'd gotten rid of Malcolm...damn, she'd had the most fantastic dreams! After she'd fallen asleep...*Wow*...there'd been shackles, restraints of some kind holding her face down on the bed. Pillows, something soft wedged under her belly, images of a large, almost bestial male looming behind her, mounting her, bringing her to one stupendous orgasm after another.

Had he actually roared?

Now where the hell did that guy come from?

Not a clue...but she certainly hoped he'd come back! Just thinking of the dream made her wet.

If only she weren't so cold. She must have set the thermostat too low. She tried to remember her last lucid thoughts from the night before.

Oh! Lucky Louie. Talk about weird! No way in hell could she possibly have had an orgasm rubbing that stupid little brass statue's belly! Must have been the wine. She'd finished an almost full bottle by herself.

Which explained the wilder than usual dreams...and the headache.

Damn but her head hurt. She needed to get moving. Had to finish packing, check with the movers, make sure the new digs were ready, utilities turned on.

Another couple days and she'd be settled in her new townhouse in Sacramento. *So what will you find there, eh Jenna?*

Definitely a bit more rural environment than she was used to. *Cowboys? Maybe*...that could be interesting...or not. She knew for a fact cowboys weren't all they were cracked up to be. Then again, she might enjoy finding out she was wrong.

Maybe you should just take Lucky Louie.

She felt a low throbbing between her legs, just thinking about that amazing orgasm.

Damn. Had to have been the wine.

Cowboys sounded better all the time.

A clattering sound intruded into her drowsy meanderings. *Good Lord!* Her teeth were chattering!

Struggling into wakefulness, Jenna shrugged off the last vestiges of sleep, yawned and raised her hands up over her head to stretch.

Chains clanked and rattled. Her hands jerked to a halt at ear level, elbows bent, wrists struggling against some sort of restraint.

"What tha...?"

"She's awake, Lieutenant."

"Thank you. That will be all."

"I'll be just outside your door."

Jenna's eyes flew open. She blinked, then blinked again and squinted against a blinding light that suddenly flashed on, blotting out all behind it.

"Where...?"

"Be quiet. You will speak only when addressed."

"Who the hell are...?"

Oomph!

Something warm and leathery cuffed the side of her head. Not hard enough to harm her, but it definitely got her attention.

Jenna bit down on her retort.

"I will ask the questions. You will merely provide answers."

The voice was deep, a bit raspy and raw, as if from lack of use. Jenna shuddered, shivering as much from cold as fear.

Other emotions warred...*anger...confusion...*

Anticipation?

A threat lingered in the potent silence.

Terror clawed at her belly, but remnants of the erotic dream flickered through her mind. How could she possibly think of sex right now?

You've been so damned horny for so long, you can't think of anything else! Jenna clamped her jaws together to keep from screaming. She'd damned well better think of something else...naked and shackled to a bed by an unknown captor might be one of her favorite fantasies, but the reality left a bit to be desired.

The image almost made her laugh. *Naked? Chained to a bed?* If only she wasn't scared shitless right now, this could be most entertaining.

Where the hell was she? Jenna blinked against the glaring light, trembling even harder from fear and cold. She wished she were back in her apartment. She had stuff to pack, movers coming, a new job waiting for her.

A future to live, dreams to dream...

The dream's over, sweetheart.

She took a deep breath. She'd learned control in the corporate world. She could deal with this guy, whoever he was.

"What WF unit do you call master?"

WF? What the hell is WF? She squinted her eyes against a sudden pain to her head. The question seemed to reverberate around inside her skull. Jenna concentrated on easing the pain, on controlling the tension mounting behind her eyes.

On not thinking about her state of undress.

The pressure eased.

"I asked you a question. You will answer me."

Jenna opened her eyes wide at the demand. She stared into the blinding intensity of the light and concentrated on the raspy but oddly melodious voice hidden in the shadows beyond. The accent was completely unique, unfamiliar to her.

"I haven't got a fucking clue what the WF is," she said. "Is that answer enough?"

A low, familiar growl reverberated from behind the light.

The fine hairs on the back of Jenna's neck stood up, and she blinked rapidly against the glare. Why the hell would a *growl* sound familiar?

"The World Federation. The ruling body on Earth. The bastards who are doing their best to wipe out all Sensitives, all extra-terrestrials, anyone who hails from a different world, a different way of thinking. *That* World Federation."

Jenna struggled to sit upright, tugging at the chains holding her against the bed. At least she thought it was a bed. The surface was hard and flat, not uncomfortable but certainly not the chair she recalled falling asleep in last night.

She sensed movement behind her and suddenly the tension on the chains released enough to allow her to scoot back against a cold, wooden backboard. She sat up. There was something about an upright position that left her feeling less vulnerable.

Pants and a shirt would have helped even more.

"I don't know who you are. I don't know what you're talking about and I haven't got a clue how I got here." She kept her voice level, forced her teeth not to chatter. It was so damned cold! She glanced at her chest and realized her nipples were puckered into half-frozen beads, the areola a pale pink instead of her usual deep rose.

Self-consciously, she drew her knees close together, almost completely hiding the bush of dark blond hair at the apex of her thighs. What did she care if her wax job was a month overdue? It wasn't like she was trying to attract this jerk, for crying out loud!

Not like she'd *attracted* Malcolm last night.

She felt a hot, angry flush spread over her body. *What a waste!*

A shame she'd been so successful. The damned statue had satisfied her better than Malcolm. Too bad Lucky Louie was just another fantasy...along with that unbelievable dream she'd had later!

Jenna shook her head, ridding herself of the final vestiges of dreams and fantasy.

This wasn't a fantasy. This was kidnapping, pure and simple. Kidnappers killed people. They did really bad things to their victims and then they got rid of the evidence. They...

"You were found sleeping in a chair in my residence at 0300. Naked, I might add. There was no evidence of a break in and I have never seen you in my life. Your presence cannot be explained by conventional methods. My orderly injected you with a light sedative before bringing you here, but I was unable to scan your thoughts. I see that you still have the block in place.

"If you are here in an attempt to seduce me for information about the Rebellion, you're wasting your time. Unlike other Explorers of Mirat, I do not find humans the least bit appealing. Other than as a first course, I imagine."

What the hell is he talking about?

Jenna stared at the glaring light, willing her captor to show himself. Nothing he said made any sense at all! If she could see his face, get some idea of what he was like...

Her head ached with the struggle to control her thoughts, the sense that somehow, if she wished hard enough, he would step beyond the light.

I want to see you. Why won't you let me see you? Something about that odd growl of his had sounded terribly familiar. *Is that why you're hiding? Are you someone I know?*

She focused all of her energy, her fear and anger on her captor. Concentrated with the entire force of will at her command.

A low growl filled the room. The light flickered, then swung aside.

Jenna pressed back against the solid wall behind her, an intense awareness of her own mortality suddenly flooding her body.

Tall and athletic, she'd always figured she could take care of herself in any situation. None of the situations she'd imagined, however, included anything remotely like this.

Shadows shifted, the light dimmed as a large shape passed before it, and suddenly a huge figure towered over Jenna.

Her grandmother's favorite little embroidered pillow suddenly came to mind, the phrase stitched across the front loomed in Jenna's thoughts...*Be careful...you might get what you wish for.*

She opened her mouth to scream, but the image in front of her was beyond screaming, beyond description, beyond any fantasy she'd ever imagined.

"I do not understand why I have shown myself."

Jenna clamped her jaws shut. She barely noticed the hollow, questioning tone in his softly spoken words.

He. She knew he was male. She just wasn't sure what kind of male.

The beast towered over her, his body encased in a skinsuit of palest silver. His physique rivaled any athlete's, his muscles rippled beneath the sheer fabric as though the material had been painted over them.

He stood just inches from her eyes, his huge thighs so close that, even though her wrists were tightly shackled, she could have reached out and stroked him if she'd wanted. The bulge of testicles and penis was unmistakable, though lightly disguised beneath the fabric. Muscles rippled across his abdomen, spread out to cover a broad chest.

Blinking, willing her rushing heart to settle back to a semblance of normal cadence, Jenna raised her chin so she could see his face.

She bit back a scream of pure terror. He was not human. Not remotely human. His muzzle was elongated like that of a large cat, his ears placed high and forward against his skull. A thick mane of dark hair parted in the middle, flowed down his back and over his shoulders. His amber eyes glared at her, half in anger, half in consternation.

It was that human expression, that questioning look combined with such obvious intelligence that stopped Jenna's scream. Her mouth fell open again.

Speechless.

She almost laughed. Jenna Lang had never been speechless in her life.

A sudden movement caught her attention.

A dark tuft of fur twitched and skittered near the beast's ankles. Jenna blinked, mesmerized by the flick and jerk of fur.

She clamped her jaws tight. It was all too much.

She giggled.

"Shit! You've got a tail!"

A deep growl emanated from the beast's chest.

"You're a fucking lion! A fucking TALKING African lion. This doesn't make sense. No sense at all." *Shit!* There must have been something in that wine...Louie? That dumb statue couldn't...? Jenna flopped back against the bed.

No, this couldn't be real. No one fell asleep in their own apartment and woke up chained to a bed by a larger than life, standing-on-two-feet African lion!

"I am not an African lion. I am an Explorer. A Lion of Mirat."

"You're for real, aren't you? You're not some sick fantasy, not something I've dreamed up?"

The growl was louder this time. Anger and frustration obvious. "You want real? I'll show you real."

A large furred paw skimmed the front of the skinsuit. The shimmering fabric parted at his touch. Jenna focused on the sharp, ebony-colored nails protruding from thick, powerful fingers. Focused so intently, she was almost slapped in the face by the huge penis that suddenly extended from the opening in the fabric.

That part definitely wasn't human, but Jenna had no doubt what it was. Long and thick, pulsing a deep burgundy red, it glistened and twitched as if reaching for her. A single drop of clear fluid shimmered on the broad tip, drawing her gaze.

The beast held himself lightly in one furred paw, his thick fingers barely encircling the immense organ quivering mere inches from Jenna's lips.

Jenna blinked, then blinked again and pressed herself back against the headboard. The beast made no attempt to force himself on her. He merely brushed her tightly closed mouth with the glistening tip of his penis.

Jenna clamped her lips together even tighter and stared, mesmerized by the contact.

She realized her teeth had stopped chattering, her skin no longer felt chilled. Instead, heat coiled through her gut, warmed her from the inside out...but why?

Why wasn't she terrified?

Because he is absolutely beautiful. He is every fantasy come to life. He is...intoxicating.

His essence coated her lips, tempting her to taste him.

She felt the heat of him clear through her jaws. Fought the urge to slip her tongue between her lips and lick away the tantalizing elixir, to open her mouth and take him in. She wanted to suckle the hot red length of him, knowing full well there was no way she'd ever get that much of anything in her mouth.

Another thought intruded, a reminder she was fully aware this wanting, this need she had for an unknown beast, was outside her understanding, beyond comprehension.

An intriguing odor filled her senses...cinnamon and something else, something totally unique and seductive. Like a drug to her conscious mind, it lulled and relaxed her, eliminated the last vestiges of fear.

Jenna felt her hands go limp in the shackles, finally licking his taste from her lips, savoring the salty-sweet flavors. Like his scent, his essence was an aphrodisiac, a pheromone-laden element of need and desire.

A moan slid from her throat. She tried unsuccessfully to call it back. She heard a deep chuckle, a most human sound, and her captor leaned forward, brushing that thick, hot member once more across her lips. Jenna closed her eyes against the powerful combination of heat and friction, taste and scent, then slitted them open barely enough to see him.

His hand stroked rhythmically along his own length and for a brief moment Jenna wanted those thick fingers stroking her, touching her intimately. She looked up to see his face. His eyes were closed, his lips curled back over razor-sharp canines in a rapturous, silent snarl.

Alien, but so very intriguing. A lion he might be, but his movements, speech and actions were totally familiar, completely human. Mentally bypassing all fear, she saw his beauty, the raw, unrestrained majesty of the beast.

She ached to touch him, to run her fingers through the tawny pelt covering his chest, to curl her fingers around that immense length of live, pulsing flesh. She swallowed, imagining the feel of him, the clichéd image of silk and steel filling her mind, tempting her.

Teasing her.

Damn the chains!

His testicles were pulled up tight against his body, the huge balls visibly throbbing with the same urgency Jenna felt. She arched her back, rejoicing in the sudden warmth from her body's response as much as the sensual touch from the beast. The last vestiges of fear faded into distant corners, held at bay by the beguiling scent, the tantalizing sweep of hot, slick flesh across her lips.

Reality retreated into some dark corner of her mind. Jenna gave herself over to the fantasy. Her taut nipples ached and throbbed and practically begged for attention.

Suddenly a dark nail flickered over each sensitive tip. Not just a nail…a claw. Catching, not piercing…just hooking lightly against the puckered flesh.

Jenna's moan caught in her throat.

The throbbing deepened between her legs, a rhythmic response reverberating throughout her body, timed to the hot sweep of smooth flesh against her lips, the almost painful torment of her nipples.

Once. Once again. A flickering touch, then exquisite pain as the nail caught the sensitive tip, hung there without piercing, a pinpoint of sensation that burned its way the length of her torso before settling in the wet heat between her legs. The rhythmic friction against her mouth continued until her lips grew slick with the taste of him. Jenna arched her back, parted her lips, licked them lightly with her tongue, offered a blatant invitation.

She closed her eyes, waiting.

Relaxed the tension in her jaws in anticipation.

The light friction against her mouth ceased. Jenna breathed lightly through her parted lips, a soft pant of need.

She moaned as each nipple was roughly pinched. Cried out as a sharp claw dragged the length of her belly, circled her clit with enough force to bring her pain along with intense pleasure.

The repetitious stroking continued around her over-sensitized clit. Her nipples peaked even tighter, begging for attention, but that sharp, ebony claw, slowly circling her bud was the only contact. Jenna strained at the shackles, arched her back, moaned aloud as he drew her higher and higher into a web of torment and longing.

Suddenly the swollen nub was crushed between the leathery pads of thumb and forefinger. Jenna screamed...peaked...and instantly climaxed.

Deep and painful, it left her panting, wanting more.

Sobbing out each gasping breath, Jenna finally opened her eyes. The bright light was back, the beast nowhere in sight. The air chilled her flesh. Now, her nipples puckered with need, not cold. The clenching, throbbing remnants of her climax underscored the pounding of her heart.

She lay quietly, waiting. She thought, but wasn't certain, the beast stood nearby, possibly just behind her. No sound gave him away, merely a "feeling" for him. She listened for the sound of his breathing but heard nothing.

A door opened. The subtle change in air pressure told Jenna someone else had entered the room.

"Take her to my quarters."

She'd pinpointed his location exactly. Odd, to be so attuned to this...*creature.*

"Put her in the spare room. Tell no one she is here. It could be too unsettling to the members of the Rebellion to know we've been infiltrated. She has a powerful block. I cannot read her thoughts though she appears to have the ability to compel my actions. I'm afraid it's going to take time we can't afford to break her before we can learn her mission."

"Yes sir. Do you want her chained?"

"Allow her use of the facilities first. Then I want her shackled hand and foot. A blindfold as well. Warm the room enough to keep her comfortable. Tell the troops I'm...away. As far as anyone knows, I'll be off world. "

Jenna swallowed, barely breathing during the long pause that followed.

"I'll need two, maybe three weeks. Her mind is very unusual, the shields she has unlike any I've seen." There was a pause. Jenna heard the sound of papers shuffling. A chair scratching across the floor.

"Contact General Antoon. Make sure he's aware of my absence but let him know you can reach me if there's an emergency. Other than the general, no one is to know I'm still on-site. Is that clear?"

"Yes sir. Your orders, sir. All honor to the Rebellion."

Jenna felt as much as heard the door shut. When she opened her eyes, the lamp had been turned to one side. Her captor stood in front of her, his ivory canines bared, his entire stance one of aggression and anger.

She stared at him, unblinking. Why didn't she feel more fear? Instead, a strange calm had settled over her, a sense of anticipation, as if somehow she knew more than she actually understood–would understand if only she concentrated. Jenna centered her thoughts on his eyes...those intense, amber cat's eyes studying her just as intently.

"You will tell me of your mission before the three weeks has ended," he growled. "If I am not satisfied with your answers, you will die. It's as simple as that."

As simple as that? Jenna threw her head back against the solid headboard and almost laughed at the absurdity of her position. She'd obviously tumbled down a rabbit hole of gargantuan proportions...right into her own little Twilight Zone. To think she'd been upset over an absolutely horrible one-night stand with Malcolm!

Malcolm was the least of her troubles. Jenna bowed her head, feigning submission. She had to get away, but first she had to figure out where she was or she'd never find her way home. Then she had to get moved, start her new job....

She could just imagine her new employer accepting her excuse for not showing up at work on time...*sorry, sir, but I was captured by aliens...it won't happen again.*

Why was she even concerned with such mundane thoughts as her job! Right now she needed to concentrate on survival.

This amazing beast wanted answers she couldn't give, not in a million years. Maybe this *was* an alien abduction. She wished she'd seen the other creature, the one who took orders from the beast. What did he look like?

Jenna thought of the latest martial arts class she'd completed. The instructor had done a whole week of intensive rape prevention maneuvers, but not one word about fending off the sexual advances of a six and a half foot tall lion.

A trickle of moisture pooled beneath her butt. Her breath caught in her throat as an errant thought fluttered through her mid.

Do I really want to fend him off? She'd never been so turned on in her life.

Nor been left wanting quite so badly.

It was all just a bit too much.

Suddenly a blindfold was slipped over her head and someone tugged at the shackles on her arms, releasing the restraints but holding her right arm above the elbow in a firm grip. Jenna followed blindly, managing a self-confident step in spite of her nudity.

She'd get out of this.

Whatever *this* was.

Chapter 3

Garan watched silently as his human orderly untied the female and led her away. The captive carried herself proudly, head erect, the thick, tawny mane lying heavy against her broad shoulders, her step defiant in spite of her nudity.

These humans! Would he ever understand them? Sander, a much decorated Explorer and Garan's mother's oldest littermate, had actually formed a life-bond with a human, the first Lion of Mirat to do so. He and the woman Mara had even created a child together. Now they traveled the stars, searching out other sentient species. Traveled and fulfilled the life goal of every young lion while he, Garan of Pride Imar was stuck here on this war-torn planet helping to direct a rebellion against the governing body of Earth.

His involvement went against every directive he'd been taught, every rule of contact he'd ever learned.

The Explorer's law: Study only. Interfere never.

Garan sat heavily behind his desk and sighed.

So much had changed since his world's first contact with Earth. Mirat was a peaceful planet, its people pledged to travel the stars in search of intelligent life. Then, when Sander the Explorer first contacted the Sensitive, Mara, when he realized there were others on Earth who communicated with thoughts and had learned to harness the powers of the mind...then everything had changed.

The simmering hatred between the xenophobic ruling body of Earth, the World Federation, and the Sensitives Mara's father had originally organized into a cohesive body had broken out into a full scale rebellion. Many Sensitives had escaped to Mirat, settling in among the various prides and clans, making a new home on Garan's world.

In the seven Earth years since the Sensitive human General Thomas Antoon first led his army into battle, many latent Sensitives who had originally supported the World Federation had come over to the side of the Rebellion. As more and more humans recognized their previously quiescent abilities, understood the power inherent in most human minds, the forces of the Rebellion grew.

Actual battles were few and far between. The members of the Rebellion preferred a war of words and education, steadily weakening the political power of the World Federation. They had learned to meld their mental powers, though, which gave the rebel armies a powerful weapon against the traditional guns and tanks the WF forces occasionally employed.

The Lions of Mirat did not join the actual battle. The ruling body of Mirat, the Council of Nine, had met and decided the formal limits of the Explorers' role. Theirs was a position of chronicling the war, of occasional intelligence gathering and a large part of the "behind the scenes" organization. Their exceptional mental abilities allowed them to safely question captives, to ferret out the occasional spy.

There had been many spies for the World Federation. Latent Sensitives, afraid of their own misunderstood powers, unaware of their abilities, loyal to the world masters intent on ridding the planet of anyone possessing paranormal talents.

They could be a powerful weapon against the Rebellion–capable of infiltrating and understanding the motives and intentions, if not the outright plans, of the ragtag group of rebels that had been dubbed Antoon's Army, after their charismatic leader.

However, the ones who had been captured by the rebels, who had finally learned to understand their powers, had also become powerful allies of the Rebellion.

Was this woman such a latent? She had blocked Garan more effectively than any trained soldier. Her mental shields were strong; her ability to project her needs and wants as finely honed as any member of his pride.

He felt the low growl rumbling in his chest...she had surely projected her needs. He'd never been even remotely attracted to a human before. There was something almost frightening when he recalled the furious need she had aroused in him. His cock still ached, tucked tightly away in his skin suit.

He wasn't sure what had compelled him to treat her as he had. Bondage and sadism were not interests he shared with others of his kind, but he somehow recognized the gentle touch would not work with this woman. If she were a latent Sensitive, however, she might have been directing his actions.

*Provocative idea, that…*Garan's lips curled back in a semblance of a snarl. He sent his thoughts to the young orderly currently chaining the human in Garan's room.

Take care, Haros. I believe our guest is a latent, most likely unaware of her mental powers. She might unwittingly control you. Keep your shields in place.

Haros's mental reply rang strong and true in Garan's mind.

I'm sure you're right, Lieutenant. I almost walked her out the front door and released her before I realized what I was doing! Take care with this one. She gives nothing, takes everything. Her powers are very strong. Her body might be chained to your bed, but her mind is free to work its mischief.

Garan laughed aloud at the orderly's candid assessment. He'd dreaded this post, found the boredom almost unbearable, the lure of the stars a hopeless dream. Breaking the woman's shields might prove to be an interesting challenge.

If she truly were a spy, it would be all the more satisfying.

If she proved to be as powerful a Sensitive as Garan suspected, if she could be brought over to the Rebellion, willingly choose to offer her loyalty to the cause, his satisfaction would be complete…and his rewards great. The Council would have to grant his wish to join the next starship on its journey into space.

Garan chuckled at the thought, considering his next move. Penetrating a strong shield could be difficult, but he had no doubt his powers were ultimately superior to the human's. There were ways to bypass strong blocks–if the mind were totally engaged in another activity, the concentration which held a mental shield intact could be sufficiently weakened.

Few creatures had the ability to maintain that concentration in the throes of sexual release.

He curled his lip back in anticipation, staring thoughtfully at the door.

Let the human wait a bit longer. Let her anticipate his next move. Let her wonder.

Then he would break her. Bit by bit, like peeling the layers from an onion, he would strip away the barriers and find the Talented woman beneath. The Sensitive he was certain existed behind those powerful shields. It might take many orgasms before her mind would open to him, but Garan could be patient when patience was required.

It might even be pleasurable. He'd gone much too long without a partner.

For a brief moment, Garan allowed himself to reconstruct the sensation of his hard cock against her soft mouth. The timid brush of her hot little tongue as it tasted him on her lips. The needy cries she'd been unable to muffle.

He rubbed himself through the thin fabric of the skinsuit, then stopped just before spilling his seed. No. There was no need to waste this feeling. Not when his goal was so clear.

Not only would he break her, he would bring her over to the Rebellion. While he was at it, he'd teach her exactly how to pleasure a Lion of Mirat.

Growling with anticipation, Garan locked the office door behind him and headed for his quarters.

* * * * *

"Lieutenant Garan said you could use the facilities. Be out in five minutes."

Jenna nodded, thankful for the chance to empty her painfully full bladder. They'd traveled for only a few minutes in some sort of silent, enclosed vehicle, then walked a few paces further on a paved surface before climbing a number of stairs and going through a doorway. The air had been quite cool against her naked flesh, adding to her discomfort and disorientation. She wasn't about to argue over time limits, especially since she didn't know if the person holding on to her arm was human or beast.

Somehow, after her little interlude with the lieutenant, she didn't feel up to tangling with another one of his kind, especially after getting a look at those canines.

Jenna closed the bathroom door behind her. *Dammit…no lock.* She ripped her blindfold off and glanced around the room, surprised to see familiar furnishings and typical porcelain fixtures. She'd almost convinced herself she'd become a victim of an alien abduction.

Somehow she didn't picture an alien sitting on a Standard brand toilet…at least, not an alien with a tail. She could, however, picture herself sitting on it.

I finally find something familiar and it's a toilet. Somehow, it seemed terribly apropos.

Relief gave her an entirely fresh frame of mind. She washed her hands and splashed cold water on her face and across her bare breasts. Her headache had receded somewhat and the water felt wonderful. She grabbed a towel off the rack to dry herself.

A subtle cinnamon odor clung to the soft fabric. She stared at the towel for a moment, thinking of the beast who had used it. A beast who obviously believed in cleanliness.

She made a quick search of the small room.

No windows. The mirror was large and stretched the length of the tiled counter. Jenna's reflection certainly wasn't awe-inspiring. Her hair hung in tangled waves past her shoulders; the circles under her brown eyes were dark and bruised looking and her complete nudity left her feeling powerless and vulnerable. Averting her gaze from the image in the mirror, she quickly looked through drawers and in the medicine cabinet over the sink.

Clues! She needed something to tell her where she was.

Nothing. No prescriptions in the medicine cabinet, no magazines or newspapers by the toilet.

Doesn't everyone read in the bathroom?

She might as well have been in a hotel room.

Towels were neatly folded, the soap in the dish looked unused. There was a hairbrush in one drawer. She picked it up, intending to run it through her tangled mop.

A few coarse strands of dark, tawny hair were caught in the natural bristles.

The image of that huge beast running the brush through his thick mane was oddly unsettling.

"Hey. You've been in there long enough. C'mon out."

Startled out of her snooping, she dropped the hairbrush.

Defiantly not replacing the blindfold, Jenna turned and opened the door. She got a quick impression of a neatly furnished bedroom without windows, but the young man standing impatiently in front of the door shocked Jenna all the way to her toes.

"You're human? But..."

"Of course I'm human. Now put the blindfold on. Lt. Garan specifically asked...."

"Wait a minute. He's not human. Why do you work for him?" Jenna clenched the blindfold tightly in both hands. "I don't get it. I thought you'd be like him. Who are you?"

"Paul Haros, Sensitive. I'm a corporal in the Rebellion. *Now*. Put the blindfold on or I'll do it for you."

Jenna stared at the young man for a moment. He was handsome enough. Brown hair, blue eyes, fairly well built. Intense. When he stepped toward her and reached for the blindfold, she quickly slipped it over her eyes. "That other guy," she said. "The lion...what the hell is he? He can't be from this world and I haven't read anything in the papers or heard on the news or..." She stumbled over the words. Where did she even start? There were so many questions! "He said something about a rebellion. We're not at war, at least not one where we're fighting battles on United States soil. What the hell is...?"

"Balls! What planet are you from?" Haros laughed as he grabbed her by the arm and walked her across the room. "There hasn't been a United States in almost thirty years. Not since the attack."

"What attack? What year is it?" *No United States? What the hell?*

Haros didn't answer. His movements were quick and efficient.

Neither did Jenna struggle when he pushed her gently down on a soft bed. He shackled her hands in smooth leather restraints and tied them above her head, then quickly bound each of her ankles.

He muttered as he worked. Jenna tried to move her right leg and realized it was already tied down. When Haros moved to tie her left leg, Jenna tried to pull her knees together.

"Look, I don't want to hurt you but the only things I've got to tie these to are the knobs on the footboard. Now relax and let me do my job."

"Why are you doing this?" Jenna bit back a sob. She hadn't cried, dammit, and she wasn't about to start now. If only she knew what the hell was going on!

Why would a human being tie up another human for an alien's pleasure?

"I'm doing this because I have a lot of respect for Lt. Garan. He's helped the members of the Rebellion even though he'd love nothing better than to be on his Quest. He's an Explorer stuck with Earth duty, but he does his job well. He wants me to tie you up...I'll tie you up. Believe me, lady, if he'd asked me to take you out in the woods and shoot you I'd have done it without question. I will do whatever it takes to aid the Rebellion."

Jenna stared at the blackness inside the blindfold. *Stuck with Earth duty. Rebellion. An alien working with rebels on Earth?* She tugged at her restraints and realized escape was not an option. At least not now. She needed answers. Desperately.

"What year is this? You never answered my question."

"I'm not supposed to tell you anything. My orders are to bring you to Lt. Garan's quarters, shackle you to the bed in the guest room and leave you blindfolded."

"What year is this? Please. I don't know who you think I am or what terrible thing I'm supposed to have done, but I have to know. What is the date?"

She felt his sigh as much as she heard it. Waited, pleading with her heart for this one bit of information.

Please!

"It's May 6, 2102. Year seven of the Rebellion. Year three since my enlistment and a year and a half since Lt. Garan took over the post."

Jenna barely felt the slight tugging at her ankles and wrists as he tested her restraints. She was only peripherally aware of the door opening and closing, though she sensed the moment Corporal Haros left the room.

Spinning thoughts erupted in a maelstrom of confusion.

May 6, 2102. Two thousand, one hundred and two. Twenty-ONE oh two.

Jenna laughed. Absurd! What kind of game were they playing? She'd fallen asleep in 2002 and awakened a hundred years later?

"I don't think so." She tugged at the soft leather shackles binding her hands. Tried once more to pull her widely spread legs closer together. She struggled a moment longer, then lay still. Her mind continued to swirl with unanswered questions.

Jenna heard the door swing open. The pressure in the room changed once more. She felt a cool brush of air between her legs and her nipples hardened in the sudden draft.

The spicy scent of cinnamon told her exactly who had entered the room.

"I see my orderly has followed my instructions to the letter."

Jenna didn't speak.

"It's not easy to find good help. So often they disappoint you."

She trembled, sensed him near the bed.

Something cool and sharp traced a trail from her left ankle to a spot just before her labia, a long, agonizing hint of what was to come.

"Corporal Haros made an interesting observation. Would you like to know what it was?"

Jenna clamped her lips tightly together.

"He agrees with me that you have powers. He thinks you're Sensitive and don't know it. He also told me you asked a very unusual question…" An uncomfortable quiet followed his words. Jenna kept her mouth shut. Finally she heard a "tsk, tsk," sound and an exaggerated sigh. "Doesn't the World Federation give calendars to its operatives?"

Silence followed his dry laughter.

Jenna tensed, waiting. Wondering. He hadn't really hurt her…not yet. Maybe…? She closed her eyes against the darkness behind the blindfold.

None of this is real…this is all a horrible nightmare. A bad dream.

A sexual fantasy gone awry.

Why couldn't she just wake up!

People don't fall asleep in their own living rooms and end up in another century!

She was a professional, dammit! A marketing analyst who'd lost her job and couldn't get laid.

Tied to a bed in a fucking nightmare.

Garan's laughter interrupted her thoughts.

"You're right, you know. From your viewpoint, I imagine it will be a fucking nightmare. I'm merely thinking about the fucking."

Eyes wide open against the black mask, Jenna stifled a scream. He was huge. He was a larger than life African lion with a penis the size of a baseball bat. He had her naked, tied to his bed in a time and place not of her own.

And he was reading her mind.

Chapter 4

"We're going to try an experiment."

Garan must have moved. She'd been almost certain he was on the other side of the bed. He'd made no sound at all for at least an hour, though Jenna couldn't be sure of the time.

She had quickly discovered time stood still when you were blindfolded and shackled.

Jenna turned her head to the left, in the direction of his voice. She hated to admit how much the sound intrigued her. The odd inflection...not really an accent...raspy, deep...*Good Lord!* She had to keep reminding herself...*this isn't a game.*

She swallowed. "What kind of experiment?"

She wasn't certain she really wanted to know.

"You're going to tell me your story. The truth. I want to know how you got here, what your orders are and who gives those orders."

"That's not an experiment."

"Actually, my dear, it is. I will know if you're telling the truth. I can read your mind, you know. Some of the time. Unfortunately, you have very powerful mental shields. Powerful enough to hide much of what you think. If I sense you are blocking, we're going to find a way to open your thoughts."

He'd moved again. Jenna turned to her right. "I don't know what you're talking about. I don't have any 'mental shields'. I don't know what the hell a mental shield is, for crying out loud."

"So you say. I'm waiting. I want to hear your story."

What is my story? She had no reason to hide what had happened. Hell, she didn't know what had happened!

"I don't really know where to start."

"The beginning works for me. Let's try your name first. Your age." The sound of a creaking chair told Jenna he'd at least settled in one spot. She almost felt thankful for the blindfold.

"Jenna Lang. I'm 30, a marketing analyst. I'm currently..." As of two days...two days and a hundred years ago, she reminded herself,

"...between jobs. I went out with a friend from work the day our company closed down. That was in San Jose, California. We went to a little wine bar, then back to my apartment. He......left. I took a shower and had a glass of wine. I must have fallen asleep in my chair. I woke up here."

She was not going to tell him about Lucky Louie...nor did she want to go into detail about Malcolm.

"Where is this San Jose? What is a 'wine bar'?"

"San Jose's in California. A wine bar is like a restaurant where they serve lots of different kinds of wine and beer."

"Where is California?"

Jenna huffed an exasperated breath...this could get difficult. "In the United States," she said. "On the west coast of the country, just south of a big city called San Francisco." When he didn't reply, she continued with her tale. "That's all I can tell you. I don't know any more. I was drinking wine in my apartment, getting ready to move to my new job, wondering if I ought to go on a cruise..."

"What kind of cruise? Planetary?"

"Excuse me?" Jenna suddenly broke out in a cold sweat. He didn't know where San Jose was, or California. He'd never heard of a wine bar. He thought a cruise was...could that young orderly be telling her the truth? Was it really a different century, a whole different world?

"An ocean cruise." She hated the squeak in her voice, the nervous stutter that would tell him just how frightened she was. "You pay for a room on a large boat that takes you to different places..." Frustration, anger, emotions she barely recognized slammed into Jenna. She yanked her hands, tugging against the shackles. "What the hell is going on?"

"You tell me. Open your mind to me, Jenna Lang. Let me see if your words are true. If they are..."

"I don't know how to open my mind," she screamed. "Let me go. Let me out of here. I want to go home!"

Panting, frightened by her own panicky outburst, Jenna slumped back against the bed.

"You leave me no choice."

Garan's voice simmered in her ear. He'd moved close, so close his heated breath brushed Jenna's cheek. She turned her head away.

"No choice at all."

No choice. What the hell does he mean by 'no choice'?

* * * * *

The human fascinated him. That in itself was unusual. Not nearly as unusual as her story, though. She told it so convincingly. He detected no deception, no subterfuge in her words. Her mind remained closed to him, but he would sense if she lied.

She spoke of things he'd read of, governments and countries no longer in existence, not since the alien invasion that had devastated Earth in the early years of the last century.

Explorers had monitored this planet for many years before actual contact was made. Garan knew Earth's history, recalled the superpowers known as the United States, China and Russia. They'd been brought nearly to their knees before the alien invasion by a series of wars and terrorist acts. Small countries with nuclear weapons had undone centuries of growth and civilization in a matter of a few short years.

The alien attack might have destroyed what was left of humanity on Earth, but the humans had shown amazing tenacity and an ability to unite against a common foe. The birth of the World Federation had spelled death to the invaders.

Unfortunately for the Explorers, the xenophobic backlash from the alien attack meant no extra-terrestrial was welcome. Even worse, Sensitives, those humans with paranormal powers, were treated as aliens among their own kind.

An Explorer marooned on Earth, protected by Sensitives, had brought the conflict to a head. When the small group of Sensitives discovered their ability to meld their kinetic powers into a single thrust, they developed a weapon more powerful than anything the World Federation had at its disposal...the combined kinetic talent of human minds.

The Rebellion was now in its seventh year. It showed no sign of ending, though the rebels appeared to be gaining the upper hand.

Garan sighed. He felt like he'd been stuck on this boring, warring planet for eons.

The human, Jenna, stirred. She turned her face toward his, unaware of his proximity. Garan exhaled, knowing full well she would feel the heat of his breath.

She jerked, turned her head away.

Her mental shields remained strong.

She was the most fascinating creature he had ever beheld. If she were indeed here from the past, Garan knew he held a treasure beyond price.

First, he must break through her shields, learn what was truly in her mind.

This human woman would not come to him easily. Garan smiled. He welcomed the challenge. He'd always brought females to completion. What could be so hard about achieving orgasm with this creature? For once he looked at his post here on Earth, his sworn duty, with a sense of anticipation.

So what if she was human? He could get past his prejudices.

* * * * *

It must be her imagination, but Jenna was certain she sensed an element of emotion, of anticipation, that was most definitely not hers. She listened to the silence, subliminally aware of the nearness of the beast, the sound of her heart beating in her chest, the sharp, choppy gasp of each breath she took, the occasional warm wisp of air as he exhaled near her cheek.

Another sound? Fabric? It wasn't tearing…it was…

Oh God, he's taking off his uniform! The same sound she'd heard when he'd bared his penis, slipping that huge organ out of his fitted skinsuit. This time the shuffle of fabric, the soft "thunk" as his boots hit the floor, the deep inhalation as he must have stretched those huge arms…all the sounds came together as a whole.

She didn't want to imagine him naked, his huge, muscular body stripped to the elemental beast. That long tail with the dark tuft, twitching erratically around his ankles.

She blinked against the soft folds of black fabric covering her eyes, thankful she couldn't see him. The blindfold was a blessing.

Jenna's mind whirled with tales she'd read of rape, of how some women endured by going away in their minds, by separating themselves from the reality of the violation.

The beast…Garan…she would think of him as Garan, pretend he was human, not a huge, hulking animal…not the beast of her fantasies?

The dream…was it only last night? Had she foreseen her own future?

She thought of his penis, that massive piece of solid, living flesh. If he tried to penetrate her, the size of him alone would kill her. No way in hell would that thing fit.

In the dream she'd experienced one orgasm after another.

There'd be no pleasure when Garan took her. Jenna shuddered, wondering how she would bear the pain, how long it would take her to die. Tears dampened her blindfold. So much she'd never experienced, so many things she wanted to do.

A bit melodramatic, don't you think, Lang? Hysterical laughter bubbled in her throat. She'd always been tough. She wouldn't wimp out now. She clamped her jaws tightly shut. He wouldn't make her scream. She would not beg for mercy. She would show this beast how tough a woman could be.

She stiffened, preparing for Garan's violent assault.

Something rough and damp caressed her ankle.

Jenna gasped. Jerked at her restraints. Felt the sandpapery texture of what could only be Garan's tongue as he slowly forged a trail up the inside of her left leg. There was no other sensation, no other touch. Merely that hot, wet tongue, rough and abrasive almost to the point of pain, lapping and licking its tedious path across her flesh.

He moved at a snail's pace, prolonging each touch and taste, defying Jenna to respond.

Fantasy! Pure, unadulterated fantasy.

Jenna clenched her teeth against the inherent pleasure.

She knew she should fight the sensation, not give herself over to the pure eroticism of his touch.

Knowing and doing were two entirely different matters.

Liquid heat pooled between her legs. She bucked her hips off the bed, fighting him, inviting him, all fear lost in the overwhelming arousal following that amazing tongue. Soundless sensation, an erotic caress like nothing she'd ever experienced, each slow stroke leaving her flesh quivering in its wake.

So slow! Hours! It had to be hours later when he finally reached the apex of her thighs. Jenna sighed in expectation, panting with need, praying that he find the sensitized, pulsating bud and give her release.

Damn! She bit off a tortured moan as Garan lapped at her pubic hair and the raised flesh of her mons, bypassed her aching clit altogether and began to work his way across her belly. He tasted her navel, the deep swirling sweep of his tongue making her stomach muscles ripple in response. Jenna bit her lips to muffle her frustrated cries. Garan took forever to circle each of her breasts without touching the nipples, licking steadily, nipping gently with those ivory teeth then soothing the flesh with his tongue. Her dampened flesh quivered with each abrasive sweep.

Suddenly he pulled away. She felt the restraints on her feet loosen along with the shackles at her wrists. Before she realized what he planned, Garan had picked her up as if she weighed nothing, flipped her neatly onto her belly and retied her to the bed.

Arms and legs spread wide, tied so tightly she practically hung suspended face down, Jenna couldn't even struggle against her bonds.

Garan's erotic torture began again, this time with the soles of her feet. He circled her toes with his tongue, suckled each one then licked from heel to toe, first one foot then the other.

"Stop! Please, please stop!" Bucking against the restraints, outraged, Jenna shrieked. Suddenly, her left ankle was caught up in his mouth, the sharp canines as powerful as the jaws of a steel trap.

Panting, terrified by this reminder of his dominion over her, Jenna stopped struggling.

He released her ankle, soothed it with his tongue, then once more made his leisurely way along the backs of her legs.

Jenna sobbed in frustration, all her promises to endure in silence shattered. Unable to see, incapable of any response other than her moans and curses, she cried and begged and bucked her hips against his touch. He never spoke, never changed the agonizingly slow, moist pace of his assault.

She felt only his tongue, that hot, wet, abrasive, mobile entity that had suddenly become the font of all sensation, giving the promise of pleasure but denying her fulfillment.

Not once had Garan touched her with his hands, other than to flip her over and retie her. Only his teeth and their tiny, teasing nips and his tongue, slowly laving its way up the inside of her thigh, reaching just to the apex and then moving beyond. Now he licked at the crease joining buttock and leg, first one side, then the other. He teased at her cheeks, firm and hard from miles of jogging, lapping with great swaths across her flesh.

Then he stopped. Jenna shuddered as the air chilled her damp and sensitized flesh. Where was he?

His hand slipped under her belly, raising her up against her bonds. Something soft and plump slid between Jenna's hips and the bed.

The pillows? Oh God. Just like the dream! Tied to a bed. Naked. Hips raised on a mound of soft pillows.

A beast mounting her from behind. Spearing her with his huge penis...and she'd had one orgasm after another.

Suddenly, she remembered the sound of him growling.

Recalled that low, bestial growl and broke out in a cold sweat. She might have been right about the growl, but Jenna knew for a fact his penis would never fit.

Suddenly, without warning, he grabbed her buttocks in his strong hands. She felt his claws, imagined them dark and sharp, digging into her flesh. She gasped, fearing the size of him, knowing she would rip apart when he entered her, no matter how wet and slick he'd made her passage.

She waited, teeth clenched, all the muscles in her crotch tightened in fear.

Garan clasped her tightly without piercing the skin, separated the tightly clenched muscles of her butt, baring her completely.

Jenna felt the bed dip from his massive weight as he knelt between her knees. His fingers tightened on her buttocks, opening her even more.

It would never be enough.

Her muscles froze in fear. She bit her lip, tasting the salt of fresh blood in her mouth as she waited for his invasion. A soft moan escaped her lips. She bit it back, tasting more blood.

Suddenly, without ever touching her clit, Garan slowly inserted his hot tongue between her wet folds.

Jenna cried out as the first orgasm slammed into her.

Ohmygod!

Pure sensation. Unbelievable pleasure!

Garan's tongue delved deeper than any lover had ever gone. Hot muscled steel stroked in and out of her flooded passage, the abrasive texture a sweet contrast to the miserable experience she'd had with Malcolm last night.

His furred jaws rubbed rhythmically against her inner thighs, his teeth ground gently against her anus and that tongue...that impossible tongue. Jenna's breath caught with each sweep as it stroked slowly, in and out, now reaching down, finally, to lap at her swollen clit, then tracing the crack in her cheeks, swirling about her tightly puckered anus, all the way to her waist before entering her once again.

Orgasm followed orgasm, each climax taking Jenna higher, farther than anything she could imagine. She couldn't come again, she knew she couldn't...and then she did.

She felt his laughter in her mind. Soundless, awe-inspiring to know he was there, sharing her thoughts, her feelings, her sexual release.

But how? Jenna tried to reach him, tried to reply with her mind, but Garan's mental touch slipped away. He released his hold on her buttocks, still delving deep inside her with his tongue, and grasped her breasts. He pinched at her nipples, tugging and pulling them until she cried aloud with the arousing combination of pain and pleasure.

Still his tongue lapped and soothed, alternately bringing her to climax, then bringing her down with almost tender ministrations. She no longer felt his presence in her thoughts, but the experience was one she would not soon forget.

Hours passed. Time lost meaning. Fear dissipated, swept aside with each successive climax. Any trepidation toward this huge beast had long fled. If he was going to kill her, Jenna could think of worse ways to die.

Now Garan lightly massaged her breasts, soothing the tortured nipples with his smooth, leathery palms. Jenna relaxed against the mound of pillows, uncaring if her hands and feet were tied, her butt still sticking up in the air with Garan resting behind her, his tongue softly lapping between her legs. She'd lost count of her orgasms. If there was any kind of limit as to how many a woman could have in one lifetime, she figured she'd just used up all of hers.

She must have dozed off, if only for a moment. Sated, relaxed, Jenna was only peripherally aware of Garan shifting his position behind her. The pad of his finger lightly stroked her clit. Jenna blinked in surprise when the greedy little bud immediately returned to life. It should have been worn away by now! Her inner muscles clenched and throbbed in reaction to his touch and she swiveled her hips slightly against the pillows.

The fabric was wet, soaked through from one orgasm after another. The moisture certainly hadn't come from Garan. He'd shared her mental reaction but she knew he hadn't had any physical satisfaction from his lovemaking.

Lovemaking? Definitely not rape; not what Jenna had feared. No, this thoughtfulness, this gentle attention Garan paid her could never be called rape. That concept was still bouncing around inside Jenna's head when she felt the gentle probe of something other than Garan's tongue, pressing between her legs.

The blindfold had slipped at some point. She rubbed her face against the bed to move it even further down her face, then craned her neck to look behind her. Garan knelt between her thighs, a huge maned and muscled animal towering behind her. The look on his face was one of pain, of fierce, bestial concentration. His eyes were shut, his fangs bared. He held his swollen penis in one huge paw, his long, thick fingers stroking the huge member.

He is not human. How can it be lovemaking if he's not human? Why do I find him so unbelievably erotic?

Suddenly Garan arched his hips, driving his huge cock up against her.

Jenna didn't even have time to consider the consequences of Garan inserting his part B into her slot A. She bucked her hips, an instinctive move to throw him off.

All she did was force him in.

Grunting with the pressure and Garan's weight, Jenna was shoved as far forward as the restraints would allow.

She prepared herself for pain.

She felt only pleasure.

Huge, hot and hard, Garan slowly eased his way inside her.

Gently, deliberately, with perfect control as far as Jenna could tell, he filled her with heat and sensation. His short, harsh bark of laughter brought an answering smile from her.

The damned thing fits! She wasn't certain if the thought was hers or Garan's, but the words echoed in her skull.

She tried an experimental wiggle of her hips.

Garan moaned his pleasure.

She wished with all her might that her hands weren't restrained, wondering how Garan would react if she could only reach back and touch him.

Besides, her shoulders were really beginning to ache.

As if he moved in slow motion, Garan reached up over her head and released the shackles on Jenna's wrists.

Without hesitation, she flexed her shoulders then snaked her right arm back, squeezed her hand between her belly and the wet pillows and gently wrapped her fingers around the soft fur covering his huge testicles.

Garan roared and bucked against her. Jenna stroked his balls, squeezing them gently and raking the underside with her fingernails.

She almost laughed when his roar choked off in a startled gasp. He grasped her hips and pumped his seed into her until the hot liquid ran down her inner thighs, until he gasped for air and finally collapsed against her.

Jenna didn't come with him. Reveling in the power of the huge beast's massive orgasm, she lay beneath his huge body, feeling as stunned as Garan by what had just transpired between them.

His chest heaved against her back, each breath he took compressing her lungs. His thick pelt warmed her, a living, breathing blanket. His gasps for air slowed, finally his breathing returned to its usual slow cadence. Jenna's breathing slowed as well. She drifted, still impaled on his now-flaccid penis.

Jenna thought of past lovers, other experiences, and sighed. No human had ever wrung so much response from her before.

Or made such a mess, either.

She'd heard jokes about the wet spot on the bed, but this was ridiculous.

As if he'd heard her, Garan slowly lifted himself off of Jenna. His organ slipped away from her, leaving Jenna empty and throbbing.

Then, slowly and gently, as if she were something very precious, Garan proceeded to lick her clean.

When he had bathed her thoroughly with his tongue, he found her clit. It was with a sense of reverence that Jenna reached her climax.

Whoever this guy was, whatever he was, she was not going to let him get away.

Chapter 5

Garan lay beside Jenna as she slept. He'd removed the rest of her restraints along with the remnants of her blindfold. He wondered when it had slipped from her eyes, how much of their intercourse she had seen.

Jenna hadn't awakened, even when he slipped the extra pillows from beneath her and changed the soaked bedding. He doubted she was aware of his actions.

Stunned, Garan could barely allow himself to consider all he had learned.

Though she blocked him now, even in her sleep, eventually she had opened completely to him through each successive orgasm.

The woman did not lie. She was an innocent bystander, somehow catapulted from her own time and space into the world as Garan knew it. She was also a powerful Sensitive, woefully untrained and unaware of her psychic abilities.

Garan sighed. What would he do with her? Neither he nor she had any idea how she'd arrived in his time, so there was no way to send her back.

Besides, he didn't really want to send her...anywhere. Idly, Garan reached down and rubbed his aching balls. To go for a year and a half without a sexual partner other than his own paw, then to find one as responsive, as overwhelming, as this human, was enough to kill a beast!

She'd been so afraid. He'd read that, her fear clearly defined in that beautiful mind of hers. She'd picked up his thoughts as well, though Garan wasn't certain she realized what she'd done. His people communicated telepathically. On Mirat, speech was reserved for ceremony and politics. In fact, speaking aloud was one of the things Garan had disliked about his post on Earth.

Thank goodness most of the Sensitives he worked with were powerful telepaths in their own right.

Knowing Jenna's thoughts had been an amazing experience. He'd picked her mind as thoroughly as he'd been able during the brief period when he'd still had his own wits about him.

He hadn't kept his wits for long.

This human woman had literally brought him to his knees.

Suddenly Garan felt great sympathy for the Explorer Sander, the first Lion of Mirat to mate with a human. All Garan's innate prejudices against humans had taken a huge shift after bedding Jenna Lang.

She stirred beside him. Garan shifted, bringing her even closer into the curve of his body.

Eyes still closed, she reached out and draped one graceful arm across his waist. Her long, slim fingers ruffled the thick fur on his hip and she nuzzled her face against the thicker pelt on his chest.

Sighing, smiling, she drifted back into sleep. Garan's lip curled in a brief but jubilant snarl in the darkness. Sleep had sounded quite appealing, until that brief movement of Jenna's had brought at least part of him fully awake.

He slipped his engorged penis between her thighs but did not enter her. The gentle clasp of her legs around him would be enough to keep him until morning.

Jenna rubbed one leg against the moist heat. Garan reacted without thinking, slipping farther between her legs. Sighing, Jenna draped one leg over his hip, opening herself to him.

The invitation was more than any young Lion of Mirat could hope to deny. Groaning, his usual sense of rightful arrogance in shreds, Garan slipped between her welcoming folds, praying to the Mother he might survive 'til dawning.

* * * * *

Jenna nuzzled against Garan's furred chest, inhaling the spicy cinnamon scent of him. For a brief moment she wondered if this was fantasy, another chapter of her dream, but the tenderness between her legs was proof all was as it seemed.

Her restraints were gone. The leather shackles had been removed as she slept. So, too the blindfold, though she was thankful that piece of fabric had slipped from her eyes during her bedding the night before.

Bedding. Not a word she would normally use to describe the most extraordinary fuck she'd ever experienced in her life. Jenna rolled the word around in her mind. She knew, somehow, she and Garan had communicated during sex, had communicated on a level totally unfamiliar to her. Without speech, without conscious thought she had spoken to him and he had replied.

Now, though, his mind was closed to her and the only thoughts she sensed were her own. At least she finally understood what Garan had meant by blocking her thoughts, but she wasn't quite certain how she did it.

Pragmatic by nature, the idea of communicating telepathically was not something Jenna had ever though about, especially in terms of herself. Garan had called her a latent Sensitive. She'd have to ask him more about such skills. He stirred beside her. She heard a low rumble, thought at first it was Garan, then giggled when she realized her stomach was growling. She couldn't recall the last time she'd eaten.

Over a hundred years ago.

She'd have to consider that later.

She raised her chin to look at Garan's eyes. He stared back at her, the deep amber shade of his irises narrowed to dark, slitted pupils. His truly were cat's eyes, but filled with intelligence and understanding. Alien he might be, a huge beast by comparison, but Jenna saw humanity and a trace of sadness in those glowing eyes.

"What is it, Garan? Why do you look at me this way?"

She spoke aloud. As she said the words, Jenna wished she could speak to him with her mind, communicate the way she'd sensed them doing during her most intense climaxes. There was so much she wanted to know, *wanted him to know,* mere words seemed incomplete.

Garan didn't speak. His intense stare shifted from her eyes to her lips, to the curve of her throat. Pressure filled Jenna's head and she clenched her teeth at the sudden pain behind her eyes.

Garan stroked her cheek with leathery fingertips. His voice was raspy when he spoke, as if he regretted the use of spoken words. "I want you to understand me here," he said, lightly tapping her brow, "and here." He ran one fingertip across her left breast, circling in the vicinity of her heart.

"But you block my thoughts too well."

"I don't know how not to." Jenna reached out and touched the soft fur along his jaw.

Garan smiled. "Maybe if you try speaking to me..." He sat up, pulling Jenna with him, folding his muscular legs Indian fashion on the bed. His long tail circled his hip and wrapped over his left thigh. The dark, brushy tuft lay still atop his crossed ankles.

Jenna mimicked his position, laughing at the incongruity of the situation, sitting on a huge, king-sized bed, knee to knee with a larger-than-life lion, one hundred years in her own future.

"Malcolm would never believe this, not in a million years."

"Who is Malcolm?" Garan curled his lips back over sharp canines.

Jenna assumed it was a smile. At least she hoped it was a smile. "Malcolm is a guy I knew from work. He, well, he was not a particularly good experience, but we've been friends for a couple of years. He's the last guy I saw before I…um…disappeared."

She glanced down at the tufted tail, the strong furred calves and the beautifully formed but fur-covered feet in front of her and sighed. "I wish I knew what happened. I was sitting in my front room, drinking a glass of wine. I had this dumb little Lucky Louie statue that I'd brought home from work." She laughed at herself.

"Damn. It is so embarrassing…. Malcolm and I had gone out for a glass of wine and he ended up coming back to my apartment. Somehow, we ended up in bed together. It was not a good experience, for me. Anyway, Malcolm seemed perfectly happy.

Anyway, after he left, I took a shower and went out in the front room. I lit a bunch of candles, poured myself some wine and ended up talking to the statue. Sounds dumb, doesn't it? Me sitting there in the dark with the candles burning and this stupid brass statue staring at me."

Only he wasn't just staring. He was doing so much more…

"Anyway, I was sitting there, holding the statue and rubbing its belly. That's all I remember. I must have dozed off. The next thing I knew I was tied to a bed in your office."

"All you remember? I sense you hiding something."

Jenna ducked her head. "It is so embarrassing. Weird, too. I rubbed the statue's belly. It was a joke at work, how Malcolm would rub Lucky Louie's belly and ask him to grant a wish. Well, I was rubbing his brass belly only…"

"Only what?"

"I had an orgasm. I rubbed my fingers across the belly of a dumb brass statue and I felt it all the way inside me. It was weird, but it felt so damned good."

Garan lifted her chin with the tip of one finger. His glowing amber eyes searched her face. "I see a large, shadowed room, candles flickering, boxes and cartons are stacked all around. A small brass statue is in your lap. It has a lion's head with a forked tongue, the body is fat and round, the legs short and square.

"You rub these fingers..." He grabbed Jenna's index and middle fingers of her right hand..."across the shiny brass belly of the statue. When you reach your climax, the statue falls to the ground."

Jenna reached out and grabbed his wrist. *He's seeing into my mind! I'm not blocking his thoughts...but how?*

Is your headache gone? Garan curled that lip again, a lion's version of a smile, she guessed.

Yes! But how?

Somehow, when you let your thoughts wander back to the last night, you dropped your mental shields. Your head hurt from blocking my thoughts. Try again to keep me out. See if you can block me. You'll need to know how to do it or everyone will know your mind.

"Sometimes even I don't know my mind!" Jenna released Garan's wrist and concentrated on keeping her mind closed to him. Suddenly it came clear, the steps she needed to take...steps Garan had somehow shared with her. She felt the familiar pressure, knew exactly when he tried to enter her thoughts, then felt the pressure ease as Garan backed away.

He stared at her, eyes filled with warmth and intelligence. There was little to read in his expression, but Jenna sensed sadness and resolution. His mental shields were tightly raised.

Jenna's stomach growled again. Garan grinned at her and tapped her lightly against the temple. "You learn very quickly, I think. Jenna Lang, you have more powers than many soldiers of the Rebellion. You will be a great asset to them, should you choose to stay and join the Cause."

What Cause? Jenna still felt as if she moved within her dreams. "Garan...I..." She reached out, touching his thick, heavily muscled arm. Warmth and life pulsed beneath the soft pelt. All of it alien, unreal. She stared silently at him a moment, studying the amber depths of his eyes.

"I've explained myself to you. Will you do the same for me? What's happened? Who are you and why am I here? None of this makes any sense at all to me. Will I ever be able to go home?"

Suddenly breaking her gaze, Garan unfolded his powerful legs and stood up. His long tail drooped behind him. Jenna was beginning to think of it as a tufted barometer of his moods.

"Later. I will tell you whatever you need to know. As far as returning to your own home, your own time...I don't think there is a way. You are here, now, and this is where I imagine you will stay. I've not heard of time travel among your kind, but there are people we can ask." He stroked the side of her face with the back of his hand. "First, though, we must bathe and then I suggest we feed you. Your fierce growling frightens me."

As if on cue, Jenna's stomach growled yet again. Before she could question Garan further, he had grasped her by the wrist and was tugging her along behind him to the bathroom.

He gave her privacy to shower and use the facilities. Jenna had hoped he might at least share the shower with her, but Garan returned to his own room to bathe himself. Something had changed in him when they'd talked, when he'd helped her discover some of the latent abilities she appeared to have.

She wasn't certain, but Jenna was almost convinced her Talent saddened Garan. She'd have to ask him about it later.

Later...damn, but she had so many questions she didn't know where to begin. She might still be on Earth but this was not the world she knew or remembered. Not only were her friends long gone, her country no longer existed. Jenna expected to feel grief, even despair...right now all she really felt was a deep emptiness when she thought of what she'd left behind.

You were ready for a change, kid...just not quite this much of a change...

She wondered if anyone had even realized she had disappeared. Had anyone looked for her? The movers would have come and gone without her goods. The new boss would have waited for her to show up on her first day of work, then arbitrarily fired her for flaking out on him. The rent was paid for the first and last month on the townhouse in Sacramento...had anyone noticed the new tenant hadn't arrived?

Her parents had been dead for years; she had no siblings, no cousins, not even a close friend to worry about her. Work had been so all-consuming there'd been little time for relationships.

Malcolm doesn't count. No, the more space and time Jenna could put between herself and that sad chapter, the better off she'd be.

Sighing, Jenna washed her hair and carefully scrubbed her well-loved body. She felt more of a connection to the huge beast after one night than she'd felt with any human at any time in her life...Garan's loving ministrations certainly went a long way toward easing her into this new world!

Her muscles might be rebelling at the workout they'd had the night before, but Jenna didn't regret a single ache. She'd always been a woman who prided herself on keeping in shape, but some of those muscles hadn't been exercised in years–never to the extent she'd had them worked last night!

She used the soft cloth to carefully clean between her legs, surprised she had any skin left at all after the thorough ministrations of Garan's talented but abrasive tongue.

"Maybe I'll develop calluses." She laughed aloud, turning her face to the warm spray from the shower. It would take a lot of sex to get those calluses.

Definitely something to anticipate in this strange, new world.

* * * * *

After his shower, Garan prepared a light meal of bread and cheeses. His orderly had left a bowl of fresh fruit outside the door, so Garan sliced an apple and a couple of oranges. Fruit wasn't one of his favorite foods, but he knew humans needed it.

He wanted Jenna strong and healthy. Praise the Mother, he wanted Jenna.

How could this be? Garan stopped in mid slice, recalling high points of the past night he'd shared with the human. His member twitched and he willed it back to sleep. This was not something he welcomed, this immediate reaction whenever he thought of what he and Jenna had done.

What they had shared.

She weakened him, practically unmanned him with her ripe body and needy soul. She had drawn an unexpected response from him, exhausted his loins, given him strength and brought him to completion. He had done things to Jenna Lang he'd never even imagined with another mate.

Garan was well aware he'd given pleasure to the females of his own species, but that was the way of his kind. Sex was a casual expression between male and female unless the two joined in a life-bond. Garan had heard bonding changed things, but he'd never chosen to pair with a female for more than a single night.

With Jenna, though, everything last night had been different. She had become, for want of a better word, a drug he must have. Even now, after spilling his seed but once within her heat, he fought a powerful need to take her again, to taste her sweet essence, the flavors at once so foreign and yet seductive.

Garan suspected Jenna had initiated some of his more innovative moves herself. The powers of her mind were strong, though untried. Much of what Garan had done to excite Jenna had been new to him, not acts he would have imagined on his own.

Was she, a mere human, strong enough to control a Lion of Mirat? To control him without even understanding her own powers? Garan shook his head, shamed to admit he would do almost anything Jenna Lang asked of him, subliminally or otherwise.

He'd shown himself to her yesterday during the early part of her interrogation. That had not been his intention, but it had been hers. Her unspoken order that he reveal himself had compelled him against his own wishes.

Again, last night, when he'd untied her, flipped her over to her belly and taken her with his tongue.

He grew hard again, recalling her sweet taste, the tight clench of her vaginal walls against his tongue as she climaxed against him. Absentmindedly rubbing his aching groin through the soft fabric of his skinsuit, Garan shook his head, bemused.

That hadn't been in the plan, either. His original intention had been to remove her blindfold and mount her from the front, forcing entrance without preparing her for his large size, baring his teeth, maybe even nipping her breast and hurting her in order to gain her fear and compliance.

Garan, post commander and Lion of Mirat, was not known for gentleness. In fact, he'd taken pride in being referred to as an arrogant bastard on occasion.

Oh, how the mighty have fallen.

He certainly hadn't expected the night they'd shared. He had intended, eventually, to bring her to orgasm, to open the secrets of her mind.

He'd done more than that. He'd definitely gained her compliance. In fact, he feared he'd even gained her love.

He'd been fighting the fact all morning that she had his.

Garan wanted Jenna. Again. Now until forever if she were willing, his lifemate if she would choose him.

Impossible. His commitment would end in six months. He'd been counting the days until his post ended, begrudging each minute of this boring duty until he could finally take his rightful place among the Explorers. His life's goal wouldn't be met until he traveled the heavens in search of other planets, other species.

Jenna was of the Earth. There was no reason for her to risk the unknown frontiers of space. Once the leaders of the Rebellion discovered her powers, unschooled and untried though they might be, she would become a powerful asset in their fight against the World Federation.

Garan would go on to travel the stars. Jenna would remain on her home world, most likely as a recognized leader among her people.

She'd been brought to this time for a purpose. Garan was certain of that. He was also just as certain he would set her free when it was time for him to leave.

"I heard you tell that orderly it would take at least two or three weeks to break me."

Startled by Jenna's nearness, Garan almost sliced himself with the knife. "I didn't know you were out of the shower yet." He turned around and glared at her.

He did not want to desire her. Not like this!

By the Mother...I don't merely desire her...I need her. He curled his lip back in a silent snarl of denial. She was human, not of his kind. He could use her, he could manipulate her...he could not *need* her.

Her scent surrounded him. He took a deep breath, held her essence deep within. His hands practically shook with the need to take her.

Need.

His shoulders slumped in defeat.

Obviously unaware of the turmoil seething within Garan, she rubbed against him like a cat in heat. "I just wanted to know if I was broken yet." She flashed him a cheeky grin. Garan's composure broke. He almost felt like crying. Instead, he laughed aloud.

She'd wrapped herself in a cotton robe, an old one of his. The sleeves were folded back against her wrists and the hem dragged the floor, but the pale blue fabric emphasized the olive tones of her skin and the deep brown in her eyes. Her hair was damp and darker than usual, almost the color of his mane but a thousand times softer than the coarse hair flowing over his own shoulders.

Jenna's had felt like silk, brushing against his shoulder, tickling his nose as she slept. He reached out now to touch it, thought better, and dropped his hand to his side. There was no point in hiding it…before long she would read his thoughts as clearly as a printed page. "I don't imagine you will ever be broken, Jenna Lang. However, I do believe you've broken me."

"Oh. My…I hope not!" Without warning, she reached out and touched his aching groin, her long fingers fondling his balls as if she inspected him for injury.

Garan moaned. This time the small knife clattered to the floor.

Jenna's stomach growled. "Down, boy!"

"Are you ordering your stomach or my prick?" Garan gestured at the huge bulge now straining against the fabric of his skinsuit.

Jenna gave his taut balls one last lingering caress, brushed his erect penis with the backs of her fingers, then rubbed her own belly and sighed. "My stomach. After last night, I'll never give that part of you an order. It does quite nicely on its own."

I wonder.

Jenna's eyes flashed wide open and Garan knew she'd caught his wayward thought. He sighed, tendered no further explanation and offered her a seat at the table before retrieving the fallen knife.

You've created a monster, I think. A truly insatiable monster. She grinned at him as the thought filled his mind. Grunting in answer, Garan passed the tray of fruit to Jenna and wondered if she might be right.

* * * * *

They talked of the Rebellion as they ate. Garan tried to explain Earth's recent history so Jenna might know and understand what the last hundred years had wrought. Much had changed in her world. Wars, a violent alien invasion, a new world government. Earth's new association with his world, Mirat, through the Sensitives and Talents fighting in the Rebellion.

Garan opened his thoughts to Jenna, showing her his birthplace, the twin moons shining over the savanna, the jagged cliffs near the sea. Then he switched to views of Earth cities he'd visited, many of them nearly abandoned over the past hundred years of attack, invasion and Rebellion.

Nothing was the same as the world she'd left. Everyone she'd known was long dead.

Garan reached across the small table and lifted a tear from Jenna's dark lashes with the tip of one ebony claw. "I cannot explain how you came to be here, but I believe there is a reason. It won't be easy for you to accept all you've lost, but please think of what you stand to gain. What Earth stands to gain. I believe the Rebellion needs you. I truly believe that's why you're here, but I want you to know that I grieve for all you left behind."

She nodded in silent agreement, closed her eyes a moment as if in prayer, then swiped her napkin across her damp face, removing all vestiges of her tears.

"I left no one behind. No family, no brothers or sisters, not even a close friend. I didn't even have a pet, Garan. I guess I never realized how empty my life was until you started talking about how all of what I knew was gone. The world I knew was, for me anyway, a very lonely place. I lived for my work. My relationships, if you could call them that, were nothing more than brief encounters. I don't grieve for the empty life I left behind, Garan."

She bowed her head for a brief moment, then smiled sadly at Garan. Her eyes sparkled with unshed tears. "Any grief I feel is for the horrible lives my contemporaries found in their future, the destruction of so much potential. In my time, we truly believed we were on the way to peace. Obviously, we were wrong."

Jenna stood up and adjusted the robe around her waist. She reminded Garan of a soldier girding herself for battle. This time when she looked at him, her eyes were clear. She projected a sense of strength and purpose. "I need to put my past behind me. I guess, if I'm really here to stay, I need to learn more about this world as it is now...the world and the Rebellion you keep talking about!"

Her emotional strength was truly as amazing as her mental powers. As Garan led Jenna into his room in search of extra clothing he wondered how he would have dealt with the loss of all that was familiar.

Not nearly so well as Jenna.

She didn't respond to his projected observation, nor did she speak while he dug around in the back of his closet. She did smile when he managed to find a child-sized skinsuit that had been left by a visiting council member's son.

Smiled and pointed out the neatly stitched opening in the back.

After sewing closed the hole for the tail she didn't possess, Jenna slipped into the shimmering suit. It literally fit like a second skin, molding her body and making her thankful for the long hours she'd spent in the gym.

She paused a moment, brought up short thinking of the many acquaintances she'd exercised with at her local club, the ones with whom she'd teased and shared stories of work and dates and politics and gossip.

They'd been the closest thing to real friends she'd had...and she couldn't recall the last name of a single one of them. None of them had known her any better. Had she lived her life in such a shallow, uninvolved manner that no one had even missed her? Had anyone wondered where she'd gone when she didn't show up at the new job, didn't return to the gym?

She hadn't told anyone she was leaving. Hadn't even returned to the gym once she learned her company was closing. No, she'd been so tied up with final projects and finding a new job and apartment; she hadn't cared enough to let anyone know.

Of course, that worked both ways–probably none of them had cared enough to worry.

It wasn't easy accepting the fact they all were long gone. It was even more difficult realizing what little imprint she'd left on her world. She would accept, though. Accept and move on. She really had no other choice...besides, hadn't she wanted changes in her life?

Jenna blinked at the sudden insight. Was that her problem?

Maybe she needed to think about *making* changes…making enough difference somewhere that she'd at least be missed if she disappeared.

Right now, she merely felt empty, unable to consider anything beyond the immediate future.

Sighing, Jenna smoothed the fabric down over her hips and glanced up at Garan.

He watched her like the predator he was. The intense expression in his amber eyes was an aphrodisiac all on its own, wiping all vestiges of sorrow from her heart. She would grieve later, when the reality of her losses finally hit her. She was pragmatic enough to accept that inevitability.

Now, though, under Garan's intense gaze, Jenna's breasts tingled and her nipples hardened to stiff peaks clearly visible beneath the sheer fabric. A low pulsing began in her belly, a throbbing sensation only Garan could soothe.

"We have two weeks," she whispered, taking a step closer to him. "Two weeks for you to break me."

"Three, if it takes that long." Garan closed the small gap between them.

There were no restraints this time, neither shackles nor blindfold. Free to run away or mold herself against Garan's hard body, Jenna made the only reasonable choice.

Slipping her fingers along the seam of her skinsuit, she carefully removed the garment she'd just fastened.

Garan matched her actions, removing his own clothing as well. Something brushed against Jenna's ankle and she jumped, then realized it was the dark tuft of Garan's thick tail.

Garan's laughter filled her soul. *Yes,* he said, projecting his thoughts, his need. *It does tell my secrets, that damned tail of mine. Right now it's telling me I want you very, very badly.*

Oh…I want you badly, as well. Jenna traced the dark fur around one male nipple with her tongue. Her left hand caressed his tight balls until Garan moaned aloud. She licked his nipple once more, then dropped to her knees in front of him, still fondling the solid sac between his legs.

Let's see just how bad I can be.

Chapter 6

Jenna's lips touched the glistening tip of Garan's penis and his knees buckled. *Praise the Mother,* the bed was close behind him or he would have landed ingloriously on his backside on the floor.

To think my intention was to break you! He lay back on the bed, both legs hanging over the edge, his tail twitching wildly about his ankles, and groaned with the pleasure of her gentle ministrations.

Jenna licked the hot length of him, encircled the crown with her lips and suckled with an amazing strength. Her small white teeth nibbled at the very tip, then she drew him farther into her mouth than he'd thought possible.

Garan swept his hands through her thick hair, unsure what to do while she milked him with her soft lips. This was something he'd never experienced, a sensation he'd never even considered.

It was also one he imagined he could easily grow to crave.

He'd long prided himself on control. At this moment, this time, he had none. Snarling, clenching his buttocks tight against the mounting pressure and incomparable pleasure, he grabbed at the blanket covering the bed, shredding it.

She had to stop. She must release him now or be forced to take his hot seed in her mouth.

Suddenly she stopped, glanced up at his face with heavy-lidded eyes.

Forced?

The look she gave him was almost coy. Before Garan had time to consider the meaning of that one word of hers floating in his mind, she grasped the base of his member in one hand, his sac with the other, and gently squeezed.

His world went black. A huge roar escaped his lips; his seed flooded her mouth, running down her chin, along her throat. Jenna's fingers continued their rhythmic pressure; her lips sucked him dry and Garan's ferocious roar ended on a kitten's cry.

As if you have any say in the matter. Jenna crawled across his chest, resting her mons against his semi-erect penis. She wiped her face against his furry chest, then kissed him full on the mouth. He tasted his seed on her lips and felt himself stirring again.

She rolled her hips against him, sliding his cock between her wet folds without actually mounting him, bringing him back to life. After the orgasm he'd just experienced, this erection was almost painful.

I think not, my lovely Jenna. You have worn me out.

She slipped back down the length of him, once more covering the span of his newly restored penis with kisses. She licked the underside, suckling the furred testicles that stirred at her touch.

Turn about is fair play, she said, her mental touch strong and true. *Your, ahem,* interrogation, *took me beyond limits, beyond anything my body has ever known…I was ready to beg you for sleep…then your tongue would find me and suddenly sleep was the farthest thing from my mind. Don't you think you should share the experience?*

With a devious, throaty chuckle, she wrapped one hand around his cock, the other around the thick base of his tail. She'd yet to play with that particular part of his anatomy, though its jerking, twitching movement appeared to fascinate her.

She squeezed each body part in unison.

Garan almost whimpered at the multiple layers of sensation.

Wondering if her plan was to kill him, Garan suddenly flipped Jenna around and stabbed his tongue deep into her passage. Her grasp on his manhood and the sensitive base of his tail tightened, she clamped her lips around his balls, drawing one round, solid testicle into her mouth.

Garan cried out, taking Jenna over the precipice with him in a tangle of mouths and hands, lips and tongues.

Garan's seed soaked the bed covering and Jenna's liquid release filled his mouth with her taste. Gasping, laughing, moaning, Garan dragged Jenna into his arms to lie with him, completely satiated.

A few moments later, Garan rose up on one elbow to plant a soft kiss on Jenna's breast, laving the nipple with his tongue. He stared at her for a long moment, slowly shaking his head from side to side. "You win," he said, chuckling. "I formally surrender to you, Jenna Lang. It didn't take two weeks, it certainly won't take three. You've broken me, my love. Praise the Mother, I raise the white flag to your superior strength."

* * * * *

This time they showered together, washing one another, exploring without shame the differences and similarities of their bodies. They shared their thoughts, as well. Jenna saw more of Garan's world of Mirat through his memories, then took him to the California she loved from 2002.

She was certain, someday, Garan would show her his world in person.

Jenna's world, as she remembered it, no longer existed. Her memories were bittersweet, though not as painful as she had expected. Not with Garan's arms around her. The closeness she felt to him helped soothe the loss of friends she'd barely known. It was also a reminder, once again, of how little impact she'd made on her world in her time.

That, Jenna realized, was the real tragedy. To have lived a life so devoid of meaning that you could completely disappear and leave nothing of yourself behind.

Except for the cute little, paid-for Mercedes in the garage...

Exactly. A car. That, Jenna, is the epitome of shallow.

She had no doubt she was capable of change. There was nothing shallow about the depth of passion, the unbelievable emotion she felt for Garan.

She would never be able to explain how quickly she'd grown to love Garan, though having someone crawling intimately through your mind certainly allowed two people to become acquainted much faster than the old-fashioned methods.

Jenna had no doubts about Garan's methods.

She was sorry when their shower ended. Feeling almost shy with the huge, dripping feline, she dried him carefully, rubbing his thick coat with the towel and mussing ridges in his damp fur. His use of the towel was more inventive. Giggling, she tugged it out of his hands.

He licked her damp shoulder, purring like the big cat he was. Jenna stepped back and grabbed her skinsuit off the hook by the door. Sighing dramatically, Garan stepped into his suit and carefully slipped his long tail through the opening. He twitched the end of his tail so that it encircled Jenna's ankle.

She stepped back again, bumped into the counter, but managed to get herself dressed before Garan could distract her any further.

"Garan! Open up. Lt. Garan...hurry!" Loud pounding followed the shouted order. Garan held his finger to his lips in the universal sign for silence, then raced into the front room and peered through a tiny spy hole in the door. He quickly stepped aside and opened the door, allowing a tall, lanky human to enter the room.

"Garan, thank goodness! It's good to see ya. I was afraid you might really be away from the compound and we've got an emergency. Your orderly said I could catch ya'll here."

"General Antoon. Come in." Garan closed the door behind the general, then led the man into the kitchen where Jenna waited. "I'm glad you're here, Thom. I've got someone I want you to meet."

Jenna stepped forward and, after a moment's hesitation, held out her hand to the general. He took hers in a firm grasp. "Jenna Lang," she said, practicing her newfound skills by lowering her natural mental shields as she shook his large hand.

"Mah Gawd." Antoon hung on to her hand, his mouth hanging open in shock. Jenna felt a subtle searching of her mind, not intrusive but definitely inquisitive. She waited patiently while the general satisfied his curiosity. After a few silent moments, he shook his head and grinned. "Where tha hell did you come from?"

Garan chuckled, slapped him on the back and offered him a cold drink. "Now, that's a bit of a difficult question to answer."

Antoon stared at Jenna.

"Your question might be better phrased as *when*. Somehow, it appears I've come from another time." Jenna fiddled with the chilled fruit juice Garan had placed in front of her.

"That would explain the images. Ah see things in your mind I've only seen in history books...memories of places and things that haven't existed for decades."

"Or a hundred years." Garan's soft comment brought a quiet expletive from Antoon.

"You're really here from...?"

"Night before last, I fell asleep on May 6, 2002."

"Where?"

"Not far from San Francisco, California. In a rocking chair in my apartment in San Jose, to be exact. And no, I haven't got a clue how I got here." Suddenly Jenna frowned at Garan. "In fact, I'm not even sure where 'here' is."

"We're not far from the original compound where the Rebellion began, in your American Southwest. We're in a mountainous area called the Sangre de Cristo Range. There was a large city nearby during your time...Santa Fe? Is that correct, Thom? I'm not real good with the names."

"That's right. Santa Fe, New Mexico. The city was completely destroyed during the alien invasion of 2074. Hell, most of the major cities around the world, including many in the United States, had already been destroyed by terrorist attacks and war." He turned to Jenna.

"The World Federation started out as a good thing, Jenna. Don't get us wrong. If the surviving armies of the world hadn't finally managed to stop blowing each other up and work together, we'd all have ended up as blue-plate specials on another planet. Unfortunately, the WF has grown very powerful and very corrupt in a relatively short time. Common folk disagree with their rule and want to return to a democratic government, but most of 'em are just so danged busy trying to survive, they've not been able to organize."

Jenna shook her head in dismay. "So many changes. It's hard for me to take it all in. I can't believe I'm in New Mexico! I've never even been to New Mexico..."

"The New Mexico you recall no longer exists," Garan said. "Most of civilization's infrastructure around the world was destroyed. Enough people survived to keep the race and the memories alive. That's part of the reason I've been stationed here...to aid the leaders of the Rebellion as they try to re-establish a democratic government while the WF stays busy rebuilding the bridges and roads and such."

"They have engineers working on power grids and communication...in fact, the WF even got a communications satellite launched a few years ago..." Thom chuckled.

"That's the one your kinetics managed to blow out of orbit with their first successful mind meld, if my history serves me correctly." Garan added.

"Then are they the good guys or the bad guys?" Jenna was growing more confused by the moment. "If they're rebuilding everything, why are you fighting them?"

Thom sighed. Jenna had the feeling he'd given the explanation many times before. "It's like this, Jenna. As they rebuild, they also educate. They're teaching the people to fear and disavow psychic abilities.

"Unfortunately, since the invasion almost thirty years ago, the human race has undergone a dramatic evolution...most of the children born in today's world exhibit various telekinetic or telepathic powers, powers that have most likely always existed in a latent form but are now very much a part of the conscious mind.

"Many adults are finding capabilities within their minds they never suspected before...it's most likely a genetic response to the near-annihilation of the human race. Unfortunately, the adults are jailed or sent to mental institutions–the ones who don't find their way to us–and the children are taught from the beginning to bury and ignore their abilities.

"Eventually, without training or the proper stimulation, the talents appear to subside and, in many cases, completely disappear."

"They're being cheated of their birthright," Garan added. "Having lived in a world where the mind's abilities are accepted as a part of normal development, I can only compare it to being purposefully blinded as a child. It's wrong. The goal of the Rebellion is to fight through education and reform...and the occasional battle when the WF gets too aggressive. "

"Our Rebellion is a war of words, not bullets–most of the time," Thom added.

It was all too much. Jenna blew out a puff of air that ruffled her bangs. "Whew! This is a lot to take in, but I can tell you one thing, I'm a lot farther from California than I thought!"

Antoon just shook his head. He took one of her hands in his again, turning it palm up and studying her fingers. "California. That's where my great grandparents hailed from. Tell me, were you a practicing Sensitive in your own time?"

"She's a latent," Garan said, answering for her. "Just coming into her powers which, I believe, are quite extraordinary."

"I have to agree." Antoon focused his attention once more on Jenna. "I actually feel your power, here, in your hand...and here it's even more obvious." He released her hand and rested his fingers on her temple. His touch was not at all intrusive, merely professional. With his thick Southern drawl, he reminded Jenna of a country doctor, not a general in charge of an organized Rebellion.

"You have no idea what you're capable of, do you, m'dear?" He turned his attention back to Garan. "This changes everything, you know. Malachi was right. We may just have a chance."

"Your emergency?" Garan downed the chilled glass of water he'd poured for himself.

"Our emergency. We've got word of a new weapon. Last week, operatives intercepted intelligence of a prototype mechanism the WF has been testing. It's designed to disrupt the powers of our kinetics. Uses some kind of radio wave to interfere with the kinetic link. Rumor is, it can turn the power back on the Sensitives...like a mirror, it reflects the power back at them, literally burns out their brains.

"We found out today they tested it on four captives. Let them think they were going to be able to escape by forming a mind meld, then hit 'em with the signal."

He shook his head sadly. "They are nothing more than walking dead, Garan. They were left at the front gate this mornin', shackled to a post...staring off inta space...just Zombies, like in the old tales. Mindless creatures."

"Can they be healed? Is there any..."

"I had Malachi try a healing. There's nothing left ta fix, Garan. Nothing ta heal."

"That's horrible." Jenna shifted her gaze from Garan to the general, then back to Garan. "Who's Malachi?"

Garan answered. "Malachi Franklin. He's a very powerful healer. He's also a precog...he can often foresee bits of the future. Thom, what did Malachi see? You said something about Malachi being right?"

"The boy's good, that's for sure." Antoon's laugh was nothing more than a dry, humorless bark. He turned his gaze on Jenna. She heard his words in her mind even as he spoke them aloud.

"Malachi said a powerful woman with a tawny mane would meet the World Federation and match them. He seemed very confused by what he saw, but your story, unbelievable as it is, offers an explanation...one I might have had difficulty believing if not for our young healer. He said, and I quote, 'I sense a very old Talent, but the woman is young. I see ancient skills in her mind. It makes no sense.'"

Malachi had foreseen her arrival? Jenna's arms suddenly prickled as a shiver ran along her spine. Maybe this was the reason she'd been brought forward in time. She hadn't managed to leave a mark on her own world...was she being offered a second chance? Jenna swallowed deeply, knowing the decision she was about to make would once again change her life.

She really had no other choice. "General, whatever I can do to help, you know I..."

Garan's harsh words interrupted Jenna. "What are the risks? I won't have her ending up a mindless shell of..."

"I agree." Antoon shook his head. "Thank you, Jenna. I think you are much too important to us to risk. You will need to be trained and trained well, but I believe the Rebellion will find success with you among the ranks. We have some time. Not much, though. You really don't understand your abilities at all, do you?"

She shook her head, ashamed.

Why would you feel shame? Garan's words entered her mind. She knew he directed them to her alone. The general appeared to recognize they carried on a private conversation. He turned his head away as Garan pressed his point. *You have only just discovered you even possess Talent. You can't be expected to understand powers if you don't even know they exist. A true Sensitive spends a lifetime learning to master his Talents.*

Thank you, Garan. But how will I learn in time? How can I help if I don't understand?

"That's where the good general comes in. Thom? Can we do it? Can she master her talents before they're needed? Do we even have time to figure out exactly what they are?"

"That she can, Lieutenant. Indeed she can. We'll start her out with the kinetics this afternoon." He turned to Jenna. "Telekinetics. They lift and move objects with the force of their minds. I have some ability but this team has really expanded on their original gifts. As far as what she can do..."

The general shook his head and laughed. "Malachi looked like he'd seen a ghost when he got the precog on his mystery woman. When I asked him what her Talent was, he just shook his head and said, 'Everything. She can do it all'."

Antoon stood up and held his hand out to Jenna. He gave a courtly bow over her hand, then straightened up and winked. "Jenna Lang, you are going to put the rest of us to shame...and I believe you will put the World Federation troops on the run."

* * * * *

The huge block of granite held steady, approximately eighteen inches off the ground. One by one, each of the other telekinetics removed his mind from the meld. Fourteen men and women eventually stepped back from the circle.

Jenna stood alone, arms at her sides, a calm, determined look on her face. There was no sense of effort–she merely stared at the three tons of stone, holding it aloft with the power of her mind.

Garan watched. He stood behind her, off to the left. He did not want to interfere with her concentration. He knew the pride he felt in her achievement, after mere hours of training, must be evident.

Tim Riley, a tall, darkly handsome young man and leader of the group of kinetic Talents, stepped close to Jenna. He'd surprised Garan when he'd gone out of his way to welcome Jenna into his close-knit group of talented men and women. Generally the young human was quite territorial about his team.

Now he leaned over and spoke softly to Jenna. "Can you rotate it without losing the lift?"

Jenna didn't answer, but the huge rock slowly began to rotate to the left. "Or did you prefer clockwise?" she asked, smiling for the first time since this exercise had begun. The boulder slowly spun in the opposite direction.

"You tell me." Tim shook his head, obviously awestruck. "You do whatever you like with that little thing."

"I think I'd like to put it there, by the back of that shed." She pointed to a spot on the far side of the compound.

The subtle gasp from the small crowd gathered behind Jenna was the only sound as, almost faster than the eye could follow, the huge stone shifted across the open space then gently came to rest in exactly the spot Jenna had indicated.

Stunned silence erupted into spontaneous applause. Jenna turned with a wide grin on her face and took a deep bow. Garan grabbed her up in his arms for a resounding kiss. "How? No one here could show you how to…"

"I just knew. Garan, it is the most amazing thing. It's like my mind has just opened up. There's so much I can do." Sudden tears filled her deep brown eyes. "Once the mindlink occurred, I could see how the process worked. When we linked arms and minds, it's like I suddenly managed to absorb the collected knowledge of the entire group! Once I knew how to move an object, I realized there are no limits. None. Garan...I don't know how to explain, but I really believe I can do almost anything. All I need is someone to show me the way."

Suddenly she burst into tears. Covered her face with both hands and sobbed. Garan held her in his arms, felt her shoulders trembling beneath his touch. He stroked her arms and back, willing her to relax, to accept. Her distress pained him, made his heart ache for her.

It had all been too much. Too much too soon.

Their sexual discovery of one another last night, her self-discovery today.

Praise the Mother but he loved her more than life.

"C'mon, team. This calls for a beer."

Tim gathered the rest of the kinetics together and herded them away, allowing Garan and Jenna some privacy. Garan held Jenna a moment longer, smoothing her hair and rubbing her shoulders with his huge hand.

It's a paw, Garan. A big, sexy, paw. She'd teased him about his hands this morning, studying the thick, blunt fingers and razor-sharp claws. Without meaning to, she'd reminded him they were two totally separate species. Then she'd pushed the situation even further, flicking the tuft on his tail in play, batting at it as a kitten might, running her fingers through his thick mane, even going so far as to trace her slim fingertip along the soft points of his upright ears.

Pointing out their differences.

He could have felt shame. He might have felt anger and resentment. Instead, her teasing had led to more touching and loving until Garan realized they were truly reveling in both their similarities and their differences.

Would the thrill of their discovery be enough? After watching her this afternoon, would any man, lion or human, ever be enough? She had discovered powers they could only estimate, hidden abilities yet to be understood. Jenna had absolutely no idea how her life would change. She was going to command more power, more esteem and respect than any woman since the Mother.

Who was he, a mere lieutenant, not even a tried Explorer, to think he could hold her heart? Garan rested his chin atop Jenna's head and sighed. Time would tell. In the meantime, he would protect and honor her. Hopefully, she would not forget the one who loved her most of all.

Chapter 7

"It's a pleasure to meet you, Malachi."

Jenna shook the young doctor's hand while Garan and Thom Antoon stood aside. Garan found no pleasure in the meeting. Malachi Franklin was about Jenna's age. Brilliant, an important leader of the Rebellion. He was the group's foremost healer and their only active precog.

From gossip Garan had overheard, Malachi was considered quite an attractive male by the women in the camp.

He was also human.

Would Jenna prefer his company to Garan's? Garan stifled a low growl deep in his throat. No, he definitely was not happy with this meeting.

"I've heard a lot about you, Ms. Lang." Malachi led them toward a small sitting area in his office.

"Please, just Jenna. I've heard a lot about you, as well." She smiled, flashing those perfect white teeth Garan found so appealing. He'd always thought human teeth were useless, practically bovine. Now he knew what kind of pleasurable pain Jenna could achieve with those blunt-looking canines. They'd proved quite effective when she applied them to his...more *sensitive* parts.

He'd experienced those perfect little teeth this morning, in fact— the little nips and bites that had left him a shivering wreck in Jenna's arms. He stirred with the memory, still half angry with himself over his weakness, his *need*, for the human, then quickly took a seat to hide his burgeoning discomfort.

Malachi sat directly across from Jenna. She took a seat next to Garan. He reached out and covered her small paw with his much larger one, establishing ownership as subtly as he was able.

"From what Thom tells me, you entered the compound—and our time—as an unschooled latent, but you have the ability to absorb and learn the talent of any Sensitive with whom you link. That's amazing! You had no idea...?"

"No." Jenna shook her head. Her tawny mane swept her shoulders with the motion. The scent from her shampoo filled Garan's nostrils. "I mean, I always felt I had good instincts, but in my era people didn't really believe in the paranormal. People who said they could read minds or move objects without touching them were looked on as crackpots."

"The high number of active Sensitives on Earth is really a fairly recent development," Thom said, expanding on his earlier explanation. "Somehow it relates back to the alien attack, almost thirty years ago.

"It was shortly afterwards when science began to recognize more and more people with extrasensory abilities. Dr. Daniel Armand, founder of the Armand Institute, believed the very real thought of genocide, of the destruction of the entire human race, forced a species-wide acceleration of mental abilities. We know for a fact that children born since the attack almost all posses extrasensory powers, something the World Federation continues to deny.

"Thank goodness Dr. Armand was able to bring a large group of those people with their various talents together to better study the newfound powers of the mind, or the Rebellion might never have been able to organize." He grinned knowingly at Garan and Jenna. "Dr. Armand's daughter, Mara, was the first human to make contact with Explorers–the Lions of Mirat. She has since formed a pair-bond with Captain Sander, the Explorer from Lt. Garan's home world."

Suddenly Antoon was all business. "Of course, this here is not just a social visit, Jenna. I have something to ask of you and Malachi that I wouldn't even think of requesting under normal circumstances."

Garan felt the hair along his spine raise. He was no precog but he knew what was coming, wanted to fight it with every fiber of his being. Unfortunately, General Antoon was right. These were not normal circumstances.

"I'm waiting, General." Malachi glanced at Jenna, then turned his attention back to Antoon. Jenna squeezed Garan's hand. He tried to reassure her with a slight return of pressure.

"I want you and Jenna to do a comprehensive link. I want to see if she can absorb the Talent of a healer, possibly even become a precog like yourself. So far, every time she's linked with the kinetics, she's not only learned the skills of each person, but mastered them more powerfully than the teacher. Those links have all been functional only, without the depth of a comprehensive link. I know it's asking a lot, Malachi…"

"I think it's up to Jenna." Malachi turned to Jenna and smiled. Garan thought about punching him. Instead he kept his shields strongly in place and held tightly to Jenna's hand.

"I haven't got a clue what you're talking about." She shrugged her shoulders and looked up at Garan. He felt her questions but kept his shields intact. Frowning, Jenna turned her attention back to the other two men.

"A comprehensive link, or mind meld, means you have no secrets," Malachi said. "To put it bluntly, you and I will know each other better than we know ourselves. Anything you have ever done, ever thought, ever felt, will be open to me. " He paused a moment, then flicked a quick glance at Garan.

He knows, Garan thought. *He knows I don't want to share that part of her, of us.* His respect for the young doctor grew, along with his jealousy.

"I don't mean to embarrass you, Jenna, but what Malachi is trying to tell you is that everything in your memory and knowledge will become part of his." Antoon glanced from Jenna to Garan. "For instance, whatever you and Garan have between you, whatever you have said or done, will be open knowledge to Malachi. As will his life open to you."

"I live like a monk," Malachi said, laughing ruefully. "I doubt my thoughts will be all that entertaining."

Jenna smiled nervously. "Garan? You should be a part of this discussion, don't you think?"

"It is your choice." Garan took a deep breath and willed his furious libido to calm. "Thom says your mind has abilities you've barely discovered. Adding Malachi's talents and then going him one better by improving on them could help tip the scales for the Rebellion." He took both Jenna's hands in his and looked deeply into her soft, brown eyes.

This time his thoughts were private, personal… directed only to Jenna. *I do not want to share you. I want no man, no person, to intrude on what I have found with you. I leave this decision to you, though, with the knowledge that I want the Rebellion to succeed and I have never in any way doubted Malachi's dedication in reaching that goal, nor his honor in how he goes about achieving victory. I believe him to be a man of the utmost integrity, or I would never, ever condone such a personal invasion.*

Jenna bowed her head and sighed, then looked away from Garan to face the other two. "I can't answer you right away. Is later this afternoon okay?"

Thom Antoon and Malachi both stood. "Of course," Malachi said. "This isn't a decision to make lightly." He touched Jenna's shoulder and then Garan's, almost in benediction. "Whatever you choose will be acceptable. If you decide against the link, the subject will not be raised again."

✳ ✳ ✳ ✳ ✳

"Why does the thought of linking with another man besides you terrify me so much?" Jenna pulled the drapes closed and paced back and forth through the near darkness of the great room in Garan's quarters. "I've linked with the other kinetics and it was all business. What's so different about…"

"Even when we have linked, my love, it has not been complete." Garan's uncharacteristic soft words ended on a rumbled sigh.

"What do you mean?" Jenna stopped her pacing directly in front of Garan. "You're hiding something from me? Aren't you being honest when we…?"

"I'm hiding things that might be, well, awkward." Garan dipped his head.

"Like what?" She thought of stomping her foot, then decided that was a bit childish.

Garan stared at her for a long moment, an almost sheepish expression on his face. He shrugged his shoulders in resignation. "Like females that came before you. Times when I have been less than honorable, times in my youth where I was foolish…things I'd just as soon not share with the woman I love!"

"Oh…what? You really love me?" Jenna dropped her shields but not her anger.

"Of course I love you." He snarled, his rancor obvious. "Do you think I would even consider this if I didn't?"

"I don't know." Jenna sighed as her indignation left her. *You're willing to let me share all my secrets with a complete stranger but not with you?*

I'm certainly not happy about it, but I think it needs to be done. Once again Garan dipped his head and shrugged his powerful shoulders.

Jenna studied the bowed head in front of her. So unlike Garan, this submissive, accepting creature. There was still so much about him she didn't know. So much she wanted to learn.

Okay, I'll do it. But only if you show me how. You and I do a comprehensive link, a complete and total mind meld. We hold nothing back. NOTHING! If you're willing to open yourself to me, only then will I do it for the Rebellion.

Garan's chin snapped up. He straightened his shoulders and glared at her, his amber eyes narrowed to fiery points. The tuft on his tail twitched and jerked. Jenna thought of a cat stalking prey.

She wanted to stomp on the damned thing, will it to be still.

"You may regret this." Before Jenna could put thought to action, Garan pulled her into his lap. "You may find out things about me you don't really want to know."

"Works both ways, buddy. How do we do it?" She punched him lightly in the shoulder, breaking the tension.

"Naked works for me."

"I am not getting naked with Malachi Franklin!"

"You're damned right you're not. You are, however, getting naked with me."

Her arrogant Lion of Mirat had returned!

That I can do.

Jenna parted the seam down the front of Garan's skinsuit and peeled the soft fabric over his broad shoulders. He copied her every move, pausing long enough to run his tongue across the sensitive tips of her nipples.

Shivering from his touch, Jenna stood and faced Garan. He sat on the edge of the bed, his knees spread wide enough to allow her to stand between them. His erect cock was proof he was no more immune to Jenna than she to him. "What do we do now?" She glanced knowingly at his erection.

"We ignore that...for the moment, anyway." Garan placed his hands on either side of her temples, then leaned forward and pressed his broad forehead against hers. "Put your hands on my head…yes, just like that."

The position felt oddly erotic, to be connected physically, forehead to forehead, palms to temples. Jenna had sudden misgivings about touching another man this intimately, even though they would both be fully clothed.

"Now, I want you to completely lower your shields. You'll be aware of me searching through your memories, but don't go with me. Once you see how it's done, I want you to do the same thing to me. You'll feel as if you're walking through miles and miles of dark passages. You'll see flashes of light, sparks of activity, but as you move through my mind you'll be absorbing my memories, the essence of everything that makes me who I am."

"You've done this before?"

"With my father, once, when he was very ill and we feared he might not survive. So that our family heritage and history–essentially the archives–of Pride Imar would not be lost. You will know as much about my family as I do when we are finished."

"Oh." Jenna swallowed, then closed her eyes. She felt the subtle probing of Garan's thoughts, understood the process he used to find her memories. For a brief second she fought the urge to block, to stop this intrusion into the essence of what made her the woman she was. He would see old lovers, her childhood, all the humiliating and stupid things she'd done with her life…her weird little interlude with Lucky Louie, her disastrous, humiliating night with Malcolm…

As I will also see your strengths, your honor, your bravery and loyalty. Jenna, you are a remarkable and complex woman. Now leave your memories and follow mine.

Chagrined, she noted the process Garan used then allowed herself to enter his mind. This was nothing like the mindlink with the kinetics! Then, the meld had been used to accomplish an action, to move an object with the strength of their combined Talent.

Here, the link opened a door into Garan's life. She saw his childhood through his memories, absorbed his love for his parents, his siblings, the other members of his family, of Pride Imar.

She knew the first young female with whom he had mated.

Jenna expected to feel jealousy but instead experienced only tenderness at the awkward, almost humorous first mating of this huge beast she loved.

She loved him even more.

Suddenly and unexpectedly, Jenna discovered an area of his mind filled with hatred and anger, a black, roiling pit of darkness out of place with the rest of Garan's thoughts. After cautiously searching its source, she realized she had come across the memories of Garan's father from the earlier link, memories Garan carefully guarded and contained so they might not pollute his own beliefs and personal integrity.

Unwilling to linger amid such animosity and bigotry, Jenna moved on into the brighter areas of Garan's mind.

She followed his career, knew his disappointment at duty to Earth instead of the stars. She finally understood his arrogance and the self-doubt that lay beneath it. So many of Garan's personal battles appeared to link to his father's hostility. Jenna sympathized with the child/man inside Garan, fully understanding the familial baggage he dealt with on a subconscious level. Garan's father hated humans...hated them with a depth of passion beyond description. No wonder Garan struggled with his love for Jenna!

He did love her, though. Traveling the long corridors of his memories, she found herself. There, filling his thoughts, sparkling with a thousand lights, Garan held his love for Jenna almost enshrined within his mind. She knew how he felt when she touched him, understood the deep, sensual pleasure he experienced at their coupling. Moving deeper, she felt his dismay at what he considered his ultimate weakness—loving a human.

She lingered there, understanding more of Garan, more of the nature of the beast who was his father's son. He didn't love less...he loved more, even though loving her went against his very nature, against all his father had attempted to teach him.

Jenna realized, for the first time, how Garan honored her with his love. She wanted to weep with the beauty of his passion.

Time stood still. She might have spent a lifetime, Garan's lifetime, learning his memories. Regretfully, she knew when she had absorbed everything he had to give. It was with a great sense of loss she withdrew, aware of a subtle withdrawal of Garan from her mind as well.

Before she could mourn the loss of contact, Garan suddenly lifted her, easing her slowly down on his erect cock. Impaled on his shaft, she wrapped her legs around his waist as the swirling aftereffects of the mindlink coalesced into one great surge of need.

He gripped her buttocks, driving her body against his until she felt the hot surge of his climax, rocked with the full-throated roar of a Lion of Mirat. She shuddered with her own release, clinging to him, crying out with the full pleasure of their mating, the complete knowledge and understanding of the man inside the beast.

"My God." Jenna slumped against Garan's chest, clinging to him like a kitten. Her labored breathing caught on a whimper and he felt her trembling in his arms.

"I probably should not have done that." He chuckled and nuzzled the damp mane at the side of her throat. "I don't want you to think every mindlink ends with a mating."

"Only you, my love." She punctuated her whisper with a soft nip of his lower jaw. Garan growled in pleasure. She would know, now, how much her nips and bites excited him.

There were no secrets between them.

Just as there would be none between Jenna and Malachi. Did he really want her to do this thing? Link with another male? Pair-bonds went entire lifetimes without such a link. It was almost unheard of between mere acquaintances.

Jenna stirred in his arms, wiggling her bottom against him, bringing life back to his flaccid penis. He felt himself stirring, filling her once again. She sighed and nuzzled his chest. "Don't worry, my love. I can do the link with Malachi and walk away with nothing more than knowledge. Trust me?"

"I will trust you," he growled. "I do not, however, have to trust Malachi. Nor do I have to like the idea of sharing any part of you, especially your thoughts, with another man." He bucked his hips so that she rode his huge cock. He wanted each stroke to emphasize his words.

"Good." Jenna rubbed her breasts against his chest, then quickly dropped her feet to the floor so that he slipped out of her. She stood away from Garan. "Then I want to do it now, while your seed is in me and your scent on my body. Malachi will be very aware of where my heart lies."

During a minimal clean up, Garan couldn't quite contain his joy. He had wanted just such a thing before the mindlink. Now Jenna shared his wishes as well as his heart.

* * * * *

"Well?"

General Antoon's soft drawl seemed to come from far away. Jenna realized she no longer touched or linked with Malachi Franklin. He lay back in his chair, his eyes closed as if in sleep.

Jenna blinked herself awake and grinned at Malachi. He opened one eye and winked back, then laughed aloud. "That was fucking incredible," he said, sitting up and leaning forward. "Thank you, Jenna. Unbelievable. I see how you do what you do, but I can tell you right now, I don't have the mental strength or ability to achieve the same level of power as you. In fact, just linking with you has left me a bit scrambled."

"I think I understand healing, but try as I might, your precognitive Talent escapes me." She had tried to understand the tangle of neurons Malachi summoned when he searched the future, but their patterns eluded her.

"Damn." Thom Antoon pushed himself to his feet. "I was really hoping for a stronger precog."

"Well, at least I think you'll have another healer." Malachi stood up, stumbled, grabbed the arm of the chair and steadied himself. He laughed. "In fact, if I don't get my legs back soon, I may have use of her." He turned to Garan and nodded his head in a quick bow. "I envy you, my friend. Thank you for sharing this woman with me. I promise you your faith and trust will not be mistreated in any way."

With a brief wave, Malachi left the room, leaning heavily on General Antoon's arm. Jenna dipped her head, unwilling to look Garan in the eye quite so soon after her link with another man. It had truly been an intimate experience, though nothing like her link with Garan. She had feared a sense of violation from Malachi's passage through her memories, but felt only a sense of having shared something meaningful with a dear friend.

Could Garan understand that? Or would her intimate knowledge of Malachi somehow come between them?

Garan watched her without speaking. His arms were folded across his chest, his amber eyes expressionless. His tail, however, was another matter. Jenna grinned when she realized it twitched this way and that, the dark tuft jerking about like an agitated mouse.

Now was as good a time as any to soothe the angry beast. She stood up and approached him, sauntering across the room with much more bravado than she actually felt. Stopping directly in front of Garan, Jenna suddenly reached down and stroked between his legs.

He snarled as if angry but pressed himself against her hand.

"I've got something for you," she said, rubbing a little harder, just a bit faster against the growing bulge inside his skinsuit. "Just so you'll never have to wonder what I shared with Malachi, I thought we'd go back to your place and try another link."

"Another?"

"Malachi linked with Captain Sander during the early days of the Rebellion. It was done to save Malachi's life. Something he learned about Captain Sander and the woman Mara fascinated me."

"Go on...I find this conversation...stimulating." His breathing had grown labored now. Jenna raked the area behind his balls with her fingernails, then drew her hand away and linked her fingers behind her back.

"I feel like a voyeur because it's as if I watched this from Sander's point of view, since that's how Malachi saw it, but Sander and Mara would do a complete mindlink during sex. She experienced his sensations as well as her own. The same for him."

Jenna lowered her voice so that she practically growled. "He felt her orgasm when she climaxed as if it were his own, tasted himself on her lips when he came in her mouth, experienced the fullness of penetration as if *his* vagina were stretching for his cock. We need to try this, Garan. I've had just a taste of the feelings you've shared with me...I never dreamed we could have it all..." She gave him a saucy grin and flipped an imaginary tail. "...but only if you think you can put up with another full link."

She barely had time to prepare before Garan had grabbed her up, thrown her over his shoulder and started across the compound at a near run. Laughing, Jenna clutched at his mane and arm to keep from falling as he hauled her off to his private quarters.

Chapter 8

"So. Do we link first?" Naked, though with his soft pelt he would never appear as naked as a human, Garan stretched full length on the oversized bed. His erection speared the air like a flagpole.

Feeling oddly nervous, almost virginal, Jenna scooted to the foot of the bed where she could study the man/beast she loved beyond all others. "I think Mara and Sander just did it without thinking...it's not like it was something they planned."

"Ahhhh...then you think we should just begin and let things happen?" Garan walked his fingers close to Jenna's bare toes. "Go into this experiment, um, open-minded?"

"Quit teasing me." Damn, she hadn't felt this embarrassed with him from the beginning, even when he held her prisoner.

Of course, then she'd just been pissed.

"I'm sorry."

Jenna didn't think he looked the least bit contrite. She studied him a moment, realizing how easy it now was to read his moods, his very human expressions. At first, when she'd looked at Garan she'd seen a frightening beast, a huge, man-like lion with ivory canines and a flowing mane, brilliant amber eyes and a flat, triangular, leonine nose.

Now she saw warmth and humor, a fierce determination to do the right thing, to protect those weaker than himself, to fight anyone trying to oppress freedom. He could be brash and arrogant, or tender and loving. She'd never seen him fully angered but imagined he would be a fearful beast, more primitive than not.

He was everything she'd ever dreamed of and more. Her ultimate fantasy come to life. Watching him through narrowed eyes she opened her thoughts and invited him inside.

* * * * *

Garan linked and melded with Jenna, expecting much the same experience they'd shared this morning. Now though, with the ease of experience, she invited him into her mind without the typical connection of foreheads touching, fingers at temples…she merely opened the door to her memories and he crossed over the threshold.

He felt her humor first of all, then the overwhelming love she had for him blended with his feelings for her.

Stunned, breathless, surrounded by the flashing synapses of emotion, passion and need, Garan paused to savor the depth of feeling wrapped within their linked minds.

He was vaguely aware of Jenna inside his head, her mental touch gentle and true as she slipped through his memories once again.

Suddenly, warm lips surrounded his erection, a growing suction he sensed in the muscles of his own cheeks. His tongue was Jenna's, laving the hard shaft, tasting the salty-sweet flavors. Awareness flooded his senses.

So this is what she means!

Inspired, he positioned Jenna beneath him, still nursing at his growing cock with lips and tongue and teeth. She nipped and suckled, sharing her pleasure, his textures and tastes. Struggling for control against this overwhelming flood of sensation, Garan lapped at her mons, then dipped his tongue deep inside her. The pressure on his cock increased–the dual experience of suckling at Garan's rigid shaft as he lapped the tight folds surrounding her clit, knowing from their shared experience he was slowly driving her insane.

He gave her taste and texture, sharing the flavors, the musky scent of excitement and need. Caught up in a frenzy of linked experience, he nipped at the soft flesh of her bottom, laved the tender bites with his tongue, all the while growling and snarling his pleasure.

She raked his balls with her fingernails, nipped at the glistening crown of his cock, then licked him from base to tip as if he were nothing more than a huge lollipop.

Growling, clenching his buttocks against the rush of sensation, Garan delved inside her with his tongue, swirling and lapping at her moist heat, biting at the tender folds then finally latching onto her pulsing clit with lips and tongue.

He suckled harder, tasting Jenna, tasting himself. He felt Jenna rise up, a long keening wail disappearing as she drew him deep into her mouth. When her fingers wrapped around his tight balls and squeezed, Garan's world disappeared.

Sensation! Pure, uninhibited release!

Orgasm robbed him of conscious thought. His seed spurted deep into Jenna's throat. He felt the pressure of his own release melded with the clenching spasms around his tongue as Jenna reached her peak.

Panting, frenzied with the overload of dual sensation, Garan spun around in the bed, grabbed Jenna by the waist, flipped her over and plunged into her from behind. She arched her back, crying out and he felt the pressure as he filled her, knew the stretching pain/pleasure of taking him deep within.

She grabbed the bars on the headboard as if to steady herself. Garan slammed into her, over and over, reveling in the power of his thrusts, knowing exactly what Jenna experienced, each spasm within her vaginal walls, each level of excitement breached as climax followed climax.

He spurted into her once again and her cries echoed his. Still hard, he steadied himself to pull out and give her rest, but his mind filled again with her need and he thrust again, then again in shared pleasure.

Garan reached around her flat belly and spread his fingers over her mons, stroking her clit. He might have been stroking himself so intense was the sensation. Jenna bucked against him as he filled her, cried out as he stroked her to yet another peak.

He knew her climax was upon her, knew the moment when she would break.

He knew!

Gasping, trembling like a newborn kitten, he carefully wrapped Jenna in his arms and tumbled to his side. Still pulsing within her, he experienced the last tremors of her orgasm with a deep, clenching release of his own.

Panting, gasping, he was barely aware of Jenna's voice in his mind.

Remember what Malachi said?

Malachi? *I don't want to think of Malachi right now. I don't even want to think right now.*

He felt her laughter deep within his soul.

He said the mindlink was fucking incredible. He doesn't know the half of it. Now this *is what I call fucking incredible.*

This time Garan laughed aloud. *No, Jenna. I call this incredible fucking. Now go to sleep.*

Practically purring, she curled up in his arms and, for once, did exactly as he'd asked.

* * * * *

"Sheesh, Garan…what's that horrible noise?" The screeching siren sounded both from without the bedroom and within her head. Jenna's shields had absolutely no effect on the decibel level.

"Alarm! Quick…get up. It means we're being attacked!"

Jenna shook her head to clear her thoughts. Last night's loving had been an incredible experience, but this morning she felt like she had the world's worst hangover. *Must be all that mental exercise,* she thought, crawling out of bed. *Not to mention the physical.*

The damned siren didn't help any, either.

Garan had already thrown on a clean skinsuit and raced to the door. He flipped a switch and the ear-splitting blast immediately silenced. He threw the door open as Jenna stumbled into the great room, fastening her own suit at the neckline.

One of General Antoon's officers waited impatiently on the porch. "It's here, sir. The WF's new weapon. General Antoon said it was stationed just outside the gates some time during the night."

"None of our sentries heard it?"

"They're all dead, sir. Or as good as…their minds are gone."

Garan's body appeared to go rigid at the news. His chest swelled with the deep breath he took as he turned to Jenna. "Jenna…please wait here and…"

"No, Garan! All this training wasn't designed for me to hide in your quarters. I'm coming with you." She glared at him, daring him to make her stay behind.

His amber eyes studied her with more sadness than anger. Finally, without a word, he stepped back and allowed her to lead him out the door.

The short ride to compound headquarters was totally silent. Jenna couldn't avoid the contrast: a night of totality, two minds and bodies melded together as one. Today, each of them cocooned in their own silent shells, unreachable, alone.

"Lieutenant Garan, over here!" General Antoon gestured toward them as the transport eased into a space by Antoon's headquarters. "Jenna, it's good to see you." Thom Antoon shook his head, his frustration obvious. "I wish we had more time. Somehow they got this damned aberration parked just outside the gates. No one's manning it so it must be remote-controlled. We brought in three sentries...they're with Malachi now."

Garan studied a video cam of the strange machine just outside the gates. It reminded him of an ancient mobile weapon, a tank, but without the metal tracks. The turret was obviously designed to spin, the long barrel to deliver whatever mind-destroying ray it used, but the bulk of the machine was crudely attached to a simple trailer. It must have been moved in by foot soldiers. Men very much like the three young sentries now with Malachi Franklin. Garan sighed and looked away from the screen. "Any hope? The sentries..."

"None that we can tell. Jenna, can you go to Malachi's quarters and take a look at them? Maybe you picked up something in the mindlink yesterday that can help Malachi."

"Of course. Garan? Will you be okay?" She rested her fingers on his arm. He ignored her touch...blocked her completely. Finally, after an uncomfortable moment, Garan turned to her and nodded. *Help Malachi if you can. I'll be fine here.*

Jenna turned and headed for the doctor's quarters. If Garan didn't want her help, far be it from her to force herself on him! Brushing angry tears from her eyes, she raced across the plaza area where she'd once moved three tons of stone. So few days ago! Yet it felt like a lifetime. Had last night meant so little to him?

Malachi worked over three comatose young men in the clinic attached to his private quarters. When Jenna arrived he looked up. The relief on his face was obvious. "Jenna! Lord, woman, am I glad to see you. Take a look at this guy...see if you can read anything at all."

Jenna reached out and touched the temples of the young man lying on the table. He appeared to be sleeping. His face held a peaceful, restful appearance. Only after trying to link with him did she realize it was merely the look of one without a functioning mind. The brain stem appeared to be the only working part, that area of the brain keeping the most basic functions alive.

She tried pressing her forehead directly against his. The boy's face was damp with perspiration but the active clamor of a healthy brain was silent. She reached deeper, searching for any remnant of his former self.

Nothing.

"He's alive. He's apparently healthy but...Malachi? What horrible thing can do this?"

Malachi ran his fingers through his dark hair. Jenna couldn't help but think he was attractive, but after knowing Garan...

"I wish I knew how it worked. Somehow, it takes the power of the Sensitive mind and flings it back with such force that, well...the only way I can describe it, it's like reformatting the drive of a computer. Whatever makes the person an individual, whatever gives him his humanity, is destroyed. The brain itself isn't harmed at all, merely the memories it contains, the essence of the person inside."

He shook his head. "The sentries were warned against directing their thoughts at the damned thing...it must be able to grab the energy from any direction and return it to the sender...God, I wish I knew more." Malachi turned to her, his hands outstretched in agony. "This kid is just twenty years old, Jenna. What am I going to tell his folks?"

"Do you know him?" She grabbed his hands, hoping a sharing of strength would help.

"Yeah. I set a broken arm for him a couple of years ago. He fell out of a tree trying to rescue his sister's cat. Dammit, Jenna. It's like he's not even there."

Jenna, Malachi, quick!

"That's Thom." Malachi glanced at the young man lying still as death on the table. "There's nothing we can do for him, at least not now. Not for the others, either. Let's go."

They raced across the compound in time to see the front gate splinter. Sensitives raced from all corners of the compound, weapons in hand, minds ready. Tim Riley quickly organized a group of kinetics in an attempt to physically lift and remove the awesome machine.

"No!" Jenna screamed, interrupting their link. "That's what they want. You don't have to be directing the energy at it...Malachi thinks it's set up to take whatever you send in any direction and return it to you in deadly force. We can't link and we can't send it any energy. It will only destroy us."

Suddenly the barrel of the strange looking machine turned toward Jenna. The scent of ozone filled the air. A vibration emanated from the machine and a blue glow appeared along the barrel. Before she could react, a narrow yellow beam caught Jenna in its trajectory.

She fought it. Calling forth all her newfound knowledge, Jenna narrowed her entire being into one single thread of hatred, a lazar sharp line of white heat, directed right down the barrel.

The heat increased, a pressure that built inside her skull in a nanosecond and threatened to overwhelm her, when suddenly, barely visible in her peripheral vision, a tawny streak launched itself directly at the machine.

Garan!

Before Jenna could react, Garan had thrown himself at the turret. Roaring loud enough to shatter stone, he ripped the offensive barrel from the machine and redirected the beam of energy. It released Jenna and struck the reflective glass of the uppermost guard tower, then bounced back to its source, a flash of white-hot energy that detonated the fuel tank and caught Garan in the forehead, throwing him a full twenty feet from the weapon.

He lay, unmoving amid the rubble of twisted metal and smoking plastic. Jenna raced to him, her head still throbbing with the aftereffects of the beam. Garan's eyes were open, their amber light darkened in shadow. She pressed her hands to his temples and felt only warm flesh beneath his soft pelt.

The life, the man she loved, was gone.

* * * * *

"God, Jenna, I wish I had better news for you." Malachi turned away from the still form of Garan. "I can't find him. I keep thinking he's in there, that a guy as brilliant and alive as he was just moments ago can't be gone, but there's nothing. No sign of any brain activity other than basic life maintenance. I wish I had some idea how to help."

Jenna didn't cry. She'd felt numb since the moment Garan saved her life. Had felt nothing since he collapsed in the compound, the life gone from his beautiful amber eyes.

"I want to take him home."

"I'll have a couple of the orderlies help you. I think that might be best. I really can't care for him..."

"No, Malachi. *Home.* Mirat. I want to take him back to his people. You know, for all his arrogance and strutting, Garan loves his home and he loves his family. I think he needs them now."

Malachi bowed his head. "You're right, you know. I'll talk to Tim Riley. He and the kinetics have set up a regular communication with Garan's home world. We'll get a ship here in a few days. Are you sure you want to go, though?" Malachi shook his head with a tired smile. "It's not Kansas, Dorothy."

Jenna wiped a tear from her cheek. "You still say that? Even now, so many years later?"

"Yeah. Would you believe that's one of the favorite old movies that survived."

"Somehow, yes. I do believe it." Jenna brushed the thick mane back from Garan's eyes. The lids were partially open, the amber depths barely visible. "I'm taking you back to Oz, my love. Kansas has not been very good to you."

* * * * *

Jenna met later that night with Thom Antoon, Malachi, Tim Riley and a group of engineers. They sat facing each other at one of the long tables used for classes during the day. Malachi was next to her, much as he'd been all day. His presence was a welcome comfort after all that had happened.

The machine that had stolen Garan from her lay in a heap on the auditorium floor, completely dismantled. It made her ill to even look at it, so she stared at her folded hands instead.

The voices of the men floated in and out of her consciousness. It was all she could do to concentrate on their words. Garan needed her. She should be with him in the quiet darkness of Malachi's clinic, not here with the metal carcass of the perversion that had stolen his mind.

"I can't believe the solution is as simple as polarized lenses." Thom Antoon held up a small jumble of computer chips and circuitry and shook his head. "You're sure that will intercept the beam?"

One of the engineers nodded. "We ran all the tests we could, rebuilt the guts of the machine to get it to run and tested it again. Polarized lenses completely diffuse the effect of the ray, essentially rendering it harmless."

"So you're telling me we can fight this aberration with a set of cheap sunglasses?" Malachi shook his head. "Hard to believe it could cause so much damage to such strong minds…Tim, can you get glasses issued to everyone by tomorrow?"

"We have plenty in the storeroom. I'll take care of it."

Thom interrupted. "What about the sentries? Any luck bringing them back? Jenna?"

Startled into full awareness, Jenna raised her head. Malachi handed her a clean handkerchief before she even realized she'd been crying. "Thanks," she mumbled, wiping the tears away from her eyes and cheeks. She blew her nose.

"I'm sorry. What did you ask?"

Thom patted her gently on the shoulder. "It's okay. Take your time. Malachi told us earlier you were going to try and reach the sentries. Did ya find anything?"

"No, Thom. Nothing. But I sense they're still in there, somewhere. I just don't know how to find them."

"And Garan?"

Jenna sighed. "Nothing. I tried going into his mind like we did during a link and it's like walking into a dark and empty room. There's just…" Her voice broke and she covered her eyes with both hands, unable to speak. She took a couple of shuddering breaths, fighting for control, then finally just projected what she'd seen. *He's not there, Thom. There's absolutely no sense Garan ever existed, none of the miles of sparkling lights, the synapses of energy and memories I found before. He's gone. Completely gone. I can't find him at all.*"

Sobbing quietly, struggling for control of her overwrought emotions, Jenna buried her face in her folded arms. She absorbed the heartfelt sympathy from the small gathering seated about her, all friends of Garan's, with a deep sense of gratitude and a terrible sorrow. Garan had known these men for barely a year and a half and yet they loved him like a brother, ached for him and for Jenna's loss.

They cared for her, as well. The genuine love pouring into her from this group shattered the last remnants of her control. She let the tears come.

"I am so sorry, Jenna." Tim Riley's soft apology filtered through her misery. She sensed something else behind his words…a confession?

She raised her head and looked at him.

Tim's tear-filled eyes stared sadly back at her. He raised his hands, as if in supplication, then let them drop to the table. "I don't know how to explain this," he said. "You've all wondered how Jenna got here...I think it's my fault."

Shocked silence followed his words. Jenna fought an insane urge to giggle. Lucky Louie's little brass image came immediately to mind.

Thom Antoon broke the silence. "What tha hell are you talkin' about, Tim?"

"It started with Malachi's pre-cog, about a powerful woman with an ancient talent." Tim nodded to Malachi. "I'm sorry, Malachi. I guess I was experimenting with stuff I really know nothing about. I'm a kinetic," he added, and Jenna knew the explanation was intended for her. "I can move things with my mind, find things far away and bring them here..."

"And you found me, in the past, and brought me here?" Jenna knew her mouth hung open in shock. She made a conscious effort to shut it. "But how? How could you find me if you didn't know who I was?"

"Malachi let me 'see' his image of you. I don't think he realized how detailed a sense of you he had, but as a kinetic I saw the qualities and coordinates I'd need to move you from one point to another. I've just never tried doing it through time before. I really didn't think it would work," he mumbled.

Thom exhaled a huge gust of air. "Will we ever truly understand the powers of the human mind." It was a statement, not a question. "This is something we'll have to study with great care, Tim. Something that could have great implications on all of us. Jenna, I..."

Jenna shook her head. "No. Please. None of you owes me an apology. Don't you understand? If Malachi saw me here, Tim must have been fated to bring me." She stretched her hand out and grasped Tim's. "If you hadn't managed to defy logic, time and space, I would never have met Garan. I wouldn't feel as if my life finally had purpose and meaning. You've given me more than you can possibly imagine, Tim. I..." Her voice broke. She choked back another sob. "I need to be with Garan. Please...I..." She looked frantically for Malachi, knowing this time she'd not be able to control the tears.

Malachi pushed his chair back and stood up. He helped Jenna to her feet, his strong arms practically carrying her along. "I'll take her back to the clinic. I'm keeping Garan there until the ship from Mirat arrives. I have him on an IV to keep him hydrated. Jenna, you'll stay there as well."

There was no reason to argue. Wherever Garan lay, Jenna would be close by. She let Malachi take her arm and guide her from the room, grateful for his understanding and support.

* * * * *

The ship from Mirat arrived three days later. Silent, ethereal in its moonlit shell, drawn by the wishes of the human kinetics, powered by the minds of the flight crew within, it hovered just above the playing field to the back of the compound.

Malachi had talked of sending the brain-damaged sentries along with Garan in the hope of a cure, but since a couple of them were showing some minor signs of improvement he decided to keep them in familiar surroundings. In the end it was only Jenna and her unconscious beast boarding the starship for Mirat.

Chapter 9

She wondered, later, about the trip. At the time, Jenna barely noticed the stars, the colors of the universe, the swirling shades of blue and green that marked her home planet as they sped away from Earth, literally at the speed of thought.

There was no wrenching sense of loss, no feeling whatsoever for the third planet from the sun. Her home, no matter where she went, would always be by Garan's side.

Her friends and companions had seen her off. Tim Riley had apologized once again, then had begged her to come back when Garan was healed. Jenna had cried when she hugged him, then had to explain she was grateful for what he had done and just as grateful to know all of them believed she would find a way to restore Garan to himself.

The Rebellion needed her. Right now, Garan needed her more.

She fed, bathed and cared for him during the journey. It might have been a burden, but she had the support of the crew, a half dozen young male and female lions of Mirat. None of them singled her out for her humanity. Instead they honored her for the love she showed one of their own.

Jenna knew only Garan. She held his limp paw, willing him awake. She bathed his body and kept him warm. At one time she attempted another mindlink, only to retreat once more from the empty shell she found.

That night she cried for long hours. Members of the crew stopped by to offer comfort. She awoke, hours later and nearing Mirat, wrapped in the comforting arms of a young lioness. "I'm sorry." Embarrassed, Jenna disentangled herself from the woman. "I don't even remember falling..."

Please. You don't realize...I am Sheyna of Pride Imar. Garan is my brother. We are not of the same mother but we share a sire. You honor our pride by the care you give our brother. You honor us.

Jenna looked closely at Garan's sister, searching for a resemblance. It was there, in the intelligent amber eyes, the quirk of her lip when she spoke. She closed her eyes against the quick sting of tears, then took a deep breath.

Garan loves all of you so much. Please know that...we did a link, a complete mind meld, and I felt the love he has for you and the rest of your family. I'm sorry I didn't recognize you. It's just been so...

You did a meld? Comprehensive? Everything? The lioness grabbed Jenna's hands in hers. *There's hope! We can save him...I know we can!*

I don't understand? How...?

When you did the link, when you shared your thoughts with each other, you essentially recorded everything that Garan is! I don't know how to make the transfer, but the elders will certainly know the way. Somehow, we need to plant those memories back into Garan. You have him in your mind, don't you realize? You are Garan!

* * * * *

Three days later, dressed in a new, more formal skinsuit shimmering in shades of silver and pearl, Jenna stood nervously before the Council of Nine, the ruling leaders of Mirat.

It had not been easy to arrange the audience, but Sheyna had persisted. She cared deeply for her brother. Somehow the young lioness had managed an audience for Jenna in spite of the typically long waiting list. Still, there was a definite sense of irritation emanating from the venerable group seated on the raised dais.

Humans had lived on Mirat since Sander the Explorer brought the first small wave of refugees here from Earth. Some had returned to join the Rebellion, but others had made the long journey and taken their places, anxious to escape the constant upheaval on Earth. They'd established residences in the smaller villages where they were more likely to find acceptance.

Still, Jenna had learned many of the older generation Lions resented the small human settlements now scattered about the planet. There was also growing resentment against the increasing number of inter-species pair-bonds.

Well aware she would not be readily accepted by everyone on the council, Jenna had spent the past two days studying as Sheyna coached her in proper protocol and behavior. Now she stood here with more confidence than she might have otherwise felt.

She knew the council members studied her surreptitiously, though she'd not felt any of them trying to enter her thoughts. In their flowing dark robes, the mixed group of male and female elders reminded her of the American Supreme Court of old. They sat in a half circle upon a slightly raised platform, bathed in a rainbow of colors reflected through the domed ceiling of the council chambers.

She counted three male and six female members, the longer, fuller manes of the males the only thing to differentiate their sex. All had the grizzled, time-worn look of the old, but there was no questioning the obvious intelligence and awareness of each member.

The air in front of them shimmered with tiny dust motes. Sheyna had described the protective shield guarding the council members, a shield that would allow them to read Jenna's unblocked thoughts without divulging their own.

Looking from face to face, Jenna realized she was getting better at telling the citizens of Mirat apart. At first, all the people on this planet had looked alike. Now she saw their individual characteristics, the subtle differences that made each one special.

Garan had once said something similar, how when he first arrived on Earth all humans looked alike. Jenna smiled to herself, noting the gray strands in the hair of one older female, the heavy jowls and scarred visage of one of the males. Another male reminded her much of Garan. He stared at her with the same arrogance, the same sense of superiority. Jenna squeezed her eyes tightly shut.

Somehow, she must find a way to bring Garan back.

Suddenly, the lights in the chamber dimmed, then brightened again, a signal, she knew, for the proceedings to begin.

Thank you, Sheyna. She had no idea what she would have done without her friend's help. Suddenly Jenna felt the subtle, individual searching scans as the council members intimately studied her. In response, she dropped her personal shields completely, allowing each member of the council full access to her every thought.

She nodded to acknowledge the joint sense of approval at her openness and was rewarded by more than one smile. She relaxed a bit, adopting a military "at ease" posture with feet slightly spread apart and her hands clasped behind her back.

Jenna had only a brief moment to reflect on the astounding circumstances of this meeting, that she, Jenna Lang, late of San Jose,

California, Earth year 2002, should find herself addressing the ruling body of another planet as a supplicant for her alien lover.

As amazing as it was, to be here in this time and place, there was also a sense of desperation, the knowledge she might be all that stood between Garan leading a normal life, or spending the rest of his days suspended within a living death.

She'd not left his side since arriving on Mirat. Sheyna had joined her, sitting by Garan's still form, coaching Jenna in the manners and bearing necessary to face the renowned Council of Nine. Touching Garan, laying her face against his chest to hear the beating of his heart, had kept Jenna going when she was ready to abandon her quest.

She'd never imagined a love such as she had found with her great beast. She was not willing to let it go.

When she'd made her wish on Lucky Louie's little brass belly, Jenna'd certainly had no idea of the future awaiting her.

"We welcome you to Mirat, Jenna Lang." The speaker, a handsome female seated at the center of the Nine, nodded her head, snapping Jenna to attention. "We have learned of the sad circumstances of your journey from Sheyna, of Pride Imar. We are not so certain, however, that her solution has any merit."

"Garan is an honored Explorer." This speaker was a darkly maned male, seated to the far right. He coughed, took a sip of something from a large cup, then continued. "He has served Earth well and we are dismayed by his current condition. However, we have never done a complete restoration such as he would require…"

"Nor have we ever used a human as a source." Another male interrupted the first. His belligerent manner almost made Jenna smile.

Almost. He reminded her very much of Garan.

He continued, leaning forward aggressively and speaking directly to Jenna. His anger was almost palpable. "Human minds are not as powerful as ours. Your bodies are weak and your abilities, though better than some of the sentient species we have encountered in our Quest, are no match for the Lions of Mirat."

"I disagree, sir." Jenna faced him, quaking inside. She had to convince the council or Garan was lost to her! "I have been told my mind is as powerful, if not more so, than what is normally found in most sentient species. I would prevail upon the esteemed council for permission to aid Garan of Pride Imar through a full link."

"You risk bringing him back as half a man. I will not allow that to happen to my son!"

Garan's father!

No wonder he looked so familiar!

"Sir, I beg to disagree." If she could stand up to the younger version, she could certainly face the elder. Jenna turned so that she faced Garan's sire full on. "Garan and I have done comprehensive melds twice. I have him here…" she pointed to her head, "and here." Jenna pressed her hand over her heart. "My mind is strong enough to hold his true self. I only need to know how to…"

"Ha!" Garan's father lunged to his feet. "My son would never love a human. Your minor telepathic abilities are *nothing*! I hold you responsible for his injuries. If not for you, he would be himself, he would not be this damaged shell of a…"

Jenna glared at the raging beast and blasted him with her telepathic words…*You're right! He was protecting me. Garan loves me as I love him. You have no right….*

"I have every right. I am his sire! He is my son!"

The other council members pulled back, as if giving Garan's father the opportunity to battle wills with Jenna. Suddenly and without warning, with a ferocious growl, teeth bared and claws extended, he leapt from the dais.

Jenna caught him kinetically, caught and held him in mid-air, mere inches from her throat. A collective gasp escaped the remaining council members.

"Gard of Pride Imar will be removed from Council chambers." The elder female, obviously the leader, waved her arm in the direction of an armed sentry. "Take him to his chambers. We will discuss his punishment later." To Jenna she bowed her head. "Please accept our apologies. His behavior is reprehensible…totally inexcusable."

"I disagree." Jenna continued holding Garan's sire immobile. His frustration radiated in psychic waves of impotent anger as he floated, still poised to kill, in mid-air. "This man is Garan's sire. He rightly holds me responsible for his son's condition. I will not, however, allow him to keep me from helping Garan."

Looking directly at the infuriated beast hovering in front of her, Jenna narrowly directed her thoughts at him. *I can and will help your son. You obviously can't break free of me right now, so let's just assume I am mentally strong enough to restore Garan. If you truly love him, you'll stop this ridiculous posturing and let me set you down without fear of getting my throat ripped out. I am his only hope. Think on that a bit, okay?*

His struggling ended. Shamefaced, Garan's father bowed his head, reminding Jenna even more of the man she loved. Carefully, she released her hold on him and eased him gently to the ground. The sentry reached for his arm, but the elder raised his hand. "I would like to apologize to this human and request the Council's forbearance. I was wrong to doubt..." He sighed, curled his lip in what could only be called a "rueful" smile, and held his hand out to Jenna.

"Peace, my daughter?"

"Peace." Jenna grasped his hand in hers, recalling something Garan had told her. "Your son did a comprehensive meld with you..."

"That was many years ago. He has grown since then, become a man any father could be proud of."

"But if we work together to restore him, aren't the odds better that we'll get it right?"

"You would do that? You would share this with me?"

"I know how much Garan loves you. I felt that love when we linked. I would be honored to work with you."

She watched the emotions cross his face, doing her best to ignore that black pit of hatred she'd found during her link with Garan.

* * * * *

"Sheyna. Thank you for coming. " Jenna grasped the young woman's hand in greeting just outside the small clinic where Garan rested.

I could not stay away and leave you to Gard. My sire can be a bit overwhelming at times.

At least I know where Garan gets his attitude. Jenna grinned, shrugged off the events of the morning and followed Sheyna's silent laughter inside.

Garan lay immobile on a clean pallet, covered only by a light blanket across his hips. The intravenous line Malachi had placed in his arm on Earth had been changed to one of Miratan design that fed directly into the large vein in his groin.

His smooth coat had lost its shine, the thick, dark hair of his mane tumbled about his head and shoulders in disarray. Jenna knelt beside him, overcome by the silent figure so unlike the proud beast she loved.

She touched his temples, her fingertips softly grazing the proud structure of his brow. *Nothing.* Garan's spark had, for all intents and purposes, been extinguished. At least now she had instructions from the Council, advice on how best to restore Garan to himself. The process was not so difficult, merely different from a typical link.

Anxiously, Jenna leaned forward, prepared for the complete loss of self she knew would come with the first contact.

A loss that would, with any luck, bring Garan back to her.

"I would ask that you allow me to be first to link with my son."

Jenna spun about, startled by Gard's soft request.

"My earlier meld with him does not reach the present but should allow a stronger foundation of his past self. I have spoken with the Council and they agree. I will bring Garan to the point where we last linked to better establish his early years. You will give him his present and what details I may have lost. Is that acceptable?"

His mind was shuttered, blocked tightly against her subtle probe. She knew she had the power to force herself within Gard's thoughts, but common courtesy held her back. Jenna glanced at Sheyna, who merely shrugged.

Sighing, Jenna deferred to Garan's sire. "I agree. My link with Garan will follow yours."

Struggling with her need to touch him, Jenna backed silently away from Garan. Gard knelt beside his son, placed both broad hands at his temples and rested his forehead against Garan's brow.

Jenna clasped Sheyna's arm, fighting an overwhelming need to join in Garan and Gard's link. The gasping breaths of both males filled the room, the harsh intake as Garan struggled against the re-emergence of his memories, the steady pant from Gard as he replaced the thoughts so recently destroyed.

Finally, long minutes later, Gard broke contact and, breathing hard from exertion, sat back on his heels. Garan settled into a quiet slumber. Jenna anxiously stepped forward, prepared to complete Garan's knowledge of the last five years.

"No." Gard held his hand out. His eyes narrowed, as if daring Jenna to come closer. "Give him time to assimilate what I've transmitted to him. The thoughts will be chaotic, their placement almost random. I am hoping his brain still has the ability to sort and group his memories correctly. Let him rest."

Oddly uneasy with Gard's demand, Jenna sent a subtle probe toward the older version of Garan.

Still blocked! Why are his shields so firmly in place? What is he hiding? She couldn't forget that dark pit of Gard's memories in Garan's mind, the bigotry and hatred of humans. On the surface he seemed fine with her, but what if…?

Sheyna grabbed Jenna's wrist when she would have ignored Gard's request. "Come. We will rest. After the evening meal there will be time enough to link with my brother."

Gard's intense stare eased. Jenna backed off, reluctant to leave Garan alone with his father. As if aware of her discomfort, Gard stood up, brushed his hands along his thighs in a most human-like gesture and silently passed by Jenna and Sheyna on his way out of the small room.

Sensing Gard's sudden hostility, Jenna flashed one last uneasy look at Garan before following his father and sister.

"I will be in my quarters." Gard bowed briefly to Jenna and Sheyna, then turned away quickly and left them just outside Garan's door.

"Is he always that gruff?" Jenna shook her head, well aware, now, where Garan had inherited his arrogance.

"Actually, I think he's behaving quite well…for Gard." Sheyna grabbed Jenna's arm. "C'mon. My rooms are just across the square. We can rest there."

"No." Jenna glanced over her shoulder, toward Garan. "I'll just sit with him. I promise not to link until you both return."

"You're sure you'll be okay?"

"Yeah." She sighed. "It's hard, seeing him like this, wondering…"

"The Mother will watch over him."

"I certainly hope so. But just in case, I'll be here, too."

* * * * *

Jenna sat, legs folded, on the floor next to Garan's pallet. She rubbed his limp hand, tracing the strong tendons and bones beneath the soft pelt. It was hell, holding her searching thoughts at bay...she wanted to link, *needed* to link, but she'd promised Gard. Still, shouldn't she feel something of Garan in his hands?

Nothing. No sense of life, no awareness. Did Gard's meld work at all?

Time passed slowly. Shadows shifted across the room. Jenna's mind drifted, filled with memories of Garan as she knew him. "Garan? I know you're there." She reached out her hand and touched his brow, swept the unruly mane back from his eyes.

His eyes! Had his eyelids flickered? Once more, Jenna ran her fingers through his mane, leaning close, so close she felt the soft *puff* of each breath. His chest rose and fell, his fingers clasped, fist-like, then relaxed.

She spread her hand across his chest, feeling the steady thump of his heart, the proof he lived.

Garan's eyes blinked, the lids opened, then shuttered closed once more.

Jenna held her breath, willing him to consciousness, willing him to *be*!

Once more he blinked, held the lids open, stared at her with narrowed pupils of endless black within their amber irises.

He frowned, his lip curled in a snarl, a warning.

He studied Jenna, his look of confusion giving way to comprehension, then distaste and loathing.

Confused, Jenna rocked back on her heels, her hand still splayed across his broad chest.

The snarl intensified into a low growl, an angry rumble vibrating beneath her fingers. Jenna snatched her hand away.

Garan's huge paw grabbed her by the wrist, pulling her off balance. She tumbled across his chest. He lurched upright, holding her tightly against him.

She struggled, terrified, screaming. "Garan! Garan, it's me, Jenna!"

She twisted in his frightening embrace, looked fully into the furious jaws of the enraged beast.

A door slammed open. Sheyna and Gard rushed into the room.

"No! Garan! Let her go!" Gard grabbed Jenna around her waist and pulled her out of Garan's grasp. Sheyna quickly drew her to one side.

"It's okay, my son. It's okay."

"Who is she?" Garan waved his hand, dismissing Jenna. "Why does this human attend me? What has happened to me?" Suddenly he pressed both hands to his temples and bowed his head, as if suffering excruciating pain.

Jenna stepped forward, her hand outstretched.

Sheyna gently tugged her back, out of Garan's line of sight.

Gard tenderly swept the tumbled mane back from his son's face. He turned and stared somberly at Jenna with a contemplative expression. "My son does not know you. I have returned him to a time before he posted to Earth, before he consorted with a human. It is better this way. You should go now."

"Sire! How...?" Sheyna drew up quickly as Gard aggressively slashed his hand across the space between them.

"I have spoken. You and..." The disparaging look he gave Jenna chilled her to the bone. "...this human will leave now. My son has no further need of you. Go. Now! I demand it!"

Shocked, betrayed, her mind a jumble of chaotic dreams dashed, Jenna stumbled from the room.

Sheyna followed, the anger emanating from her in deep waves. *He has no right. No right at all. I know my brother must have loved you. This is wrong...we must go to the Council...we...*

No, Sheyna. Calm stole over Jenna, an idea simmered just beyond reach. *No the Council will not help me, not now. I can't completely blame Gard...he loves his son and I am an interloper, someone he blames for bringing harm to Garan. Somehow...*she turned, smiled at Sheyna, mentally soothed her new friend's distress. *There are better ways.*

You're not giving up? Sheyna stopped, grabbed Jenna's arm.

"No, I have no intention of giving up. Come with me. I have an idea but I'll need your help."

* * * * *

Jenna paced the floor, anxiously considering the folly of her next move. Where was Sheyna? Would their plan succeed? Two long days had passed since Garan's reawakening. Sheyna said he recovered slowly, that his mind had not completely assimilated all of Gard's transferred memories. He remained confused, unsure of himself.

The physicians were uncertain why he struggled so. Sheyna had spent much time with Garan and though he seemed to know her, he also appeared bewildered by her appearance.

She said he had no memory at all of his work on Earth. No memories of loving a human named Jenna. Instead, Garan had absorbed his father's bigotry and hatred of humans, a loathing beyond reason.

Why didn't I see it? Her gut feeling had been to scan Gard's thoughts before the meld, to link surreptitiously, something she could easily have done if only she'd listened to her soul. Instead, she'd let manners overrule common sense.

Now she impatiently paced the dimensions of a luxurious hideaway hollowed out of solid rock in the side of a mountain near Heáz, the capital city of Mirat. Surrounded by private parklands belonging to friends of Sheyna's, it boasted a single sleeping/living area, small kitchen for food preparation and a fascinating sunken grotto heated by one of Mirat's many hot springs.

It more than met Jenna's requirements.

Thick carpets covered the floor and elegantly embroidered tapestries hid the rock walls from view. A sleeping pallet filled a small alcove, the thick mattress piled high with blankets and soft pillows.

Jenna had been assured of complete privacy for as long as she required. She sent a mental search for Sheyna, knowing full well not to expect anyone until after dark.

She checked the food supply, adjusted the blankets on the sleeping pallet, checked the sturdy restraints bolted to the walls at each end of the alcove.

Thick leather straps reinforced by heavy chains should be more than enough to restrain an angered beast.

Jenna knew Garan would be very, very angry once he awoke.

Sweet-smelling lamps burned, fueled by the oily fruit of the nara tree. They cast a golden glow about the room, giving it more the look of a sultan's small palace than a prison.

Garan's prison. Would he ever forgive her? Jenna stopped pacing near the sleeping alcove and sighed. What if it didn't work the same with Garan as it had with her? She knew he'd never voluntarily link with her, never let her beyond the powerful shields he'd erected against her mental touch.

She *had* to meld with him, must form a complete and all-inclusive mindlink. Only then could she return to Garan those memories they shared, memories of love and laughter, of joining body and soul in a manner unlike anything either had experienced before.

Only in the deepest throes of orgasm, when the mind is completely involved, only then would the strongest shields give way.

Garan had explained it all to her...and then he'd taken her to places within herself she'd never suspected could exist.

That's how you found me, my love. That's how you penetrated my blocked mind. Jenna smiled sadly with the memory, fingering the soft leather restraints near the foot of the bed. *It has to work.*

She could leave Mirat. Return to the Rebellion and the people who desperately needed her Talent.

Not yet. Not until I've tried everything.

Suddenly Jenna sensed a presence. *Sheyna!* Where was Garan?

She raced to the heavy plank door and slid it open along the metal track holding it in place. Sheyna stood just outside the door. Behind her, two soldiers, Lions of Mirat as large as Garan, carried a stretcher between them.

He is unconscious. That's why you can't feel his presence, but the drug will wear off quickly.

"Thank you, Sheyna. I was afraid..." She glanced at the soldiers standing silently behind the young Lioness. *Gard..?*

These are two of Garan's brothers. Not all of Pride Imar dislike humans. Sheyna smiled at Jenna and stepped aside. The soldiers nodded to Jenna with respect, then carefully brought the stretcher into the room and set it on the floor near the pallet. Without a word, they lifted the blanket-shrouded figure of their brother and placed him on top of the bedding, then turned and left as quietly as they had entered.

"We must hurry. The drug will be wearing off soon...and I intend to be far away when he awakens." Sheyna smiled as she bent over Garan's sleeping form. Without hesitation she removed his soft boots while Jenna slipped the skinsuit off his upper body. Together, the women tugged the tight fitting garment down over his thighs.

Jenna took one last pull to slip it off him, but it suddenly stuck.

Sheyna rolled her eyes at Jenna and carefully slipped the garment over Garan's tail. Jenna covered her mouth with her hands to stifle the giggles. *It's gonna work, Sheyna. I know it is.*

I certainly hope so! She finished tugging Garan's skinsuit over his long, muscular legs. Within seconds they had him completely naked, chained hand and foot to each end of the alcove. Sheyna checked the restraints then gave Jenna a quick hug.

If you need me for anything, call me. I will hear you.

Garan groaned and shifted on the soft pallet.

I'm going. He's all yours.

Jenna looked at the slowly awakening beast chained to her bed. *I know. Thank you.* Garan rolled his head back and forth on the pillow, then gave a slight, experimental tug at the restraints.

Hurry. Jenna hugged Sheyna once more, then slid the heavy door open. Her friend disappeared into the night.

"I will kill you, you know."

The raspy voice sent shivers along Jenna's spine. Lord, how she'd missed the sound!

"It won't be easy." Jenna sauntered across the room and stood over the pallet, smiling down at Garan. "Your father tried and failed."

"My father is an old man." Garan jerked at the restraints, rattling the chains until the muscles in his arms and shoulders visibly knotted. "Why? I don't know you and yet you torment me. Why?"

"But I do know you, Garan. I know you intimately. I will know you again, just as you will know me." Jenna slowly released the seam along the front of her skinsuit.

Garan frowned.

She slipped the snug-fitting sleeves down over her arms and pushed the stretchy fabric to her waist.

Garan's frown deepened. "I do not find humans the least bit appealing," he said.

"...other than as a first course. I know. I've heard that before." Jenna continued undressing. She slipped the skinsuit off her feet and tossed it to one side.

Garan stared belligerently at Jenna as if daring her to...

What? What if she couldn't arouse him?

She stood there a moment and studied her captive. He was Garan, yet he was not. His body was the same—strong and lean, the musculature evident even beneath the soft pelt that covered him. The only unusual thing about him was his completely sheathed and flaccid penis.

Jenna grinned, remembering. Garan was rarely so...*relaxed*.

Could she change that? Did she still have the power to excite and entice him as she'd done just days before? The man she loved had five more years of experience, his arrogance tempered by age and battle, his knowledge of humans, the distrust and dislike he felt now, overcome by months of working side by side with a species he had reluctantly come to admire.

There's only one way to find out.

Tentatively searching, Jenna projected a subtle search of Garan's thoughts. He blocked her, his shields tightly drawn against her touch.

Much as I once blocked you, eh Garan? I guess it's only fair.

His eyebrows raised. He *was* reading her!

She grinned in reply, then curled her legs beneath her and sat next to him on the pallet. He bucked his hips, tugged at the restraints, then sagged back against the pillows with a snarl curling his lips.

Jenna studied his face, remembering. Her thoughts flowed freely, recalling the night he'd restrained her, the slow, excruciating torture as he'd bathed and laved her with his tongue. Up one leg, down the other, teasing and licking, bringing her to the brink but not over, holding her there at the edge of ecstasy...

The snarl left Garan's lips as he absorbed her projected memories. He would see himself in her thoughts; know the excitement Jenna had felt at his sensual assault on her captive body.

"Why do you show me this ridiculous fantasy?"

His harsh exclamation snapped Jenna out of her reverie. "It's no fantasy, Garan. It really happened. Tell me something...did your father explain why he linked with you?"

"He said I was attacked and badly injured. It was the only way to restore my mind."

"Did he tell you where the attack occurred?" Jenna trailed her fingers along his thigh, tracing the line of muscle from groin to knee. "Did he tell you that, Garan?"

"Why do you touch me? I find it...unsettling."

"Where were you attacked, Garan?" She raked her fingers back against the grain, raising small tufts of tan fur, soft as mink, in their wake.

"I...I do not remember."

"Earth, Garan. You were attacked on Earth by a squadron of the World Federation using a new weapon adapted to destroy the minds of Sensitives."

"You make no sense. I've not been to Earth. I am an Explorer. My work will be to search out new peoples, new worlds. I'm not a peacekeeper to maintain a ragged horde of rebels."

"Is that what you think of us, Garan? Or is that what your father thinks, what he wants you to believe?" Jenna swept her fingers closer to the bulge beneath Garan's sheathed penis. Her fingers touched his balls and he jerked in response. She continued her gentle fondling, smiling to herself as his huge cock began to strain against its sheath.

"Link with me, Garan. Let me into your mind. I have five years of your life, Garan. Don't you want it back?"

He curled his lip in a disdainful snarl. "I would never link with a human. Never! You lie. You tell fantasies about something I have not done. Your minds are as weak as your bodies. I do not find humans the least bit attractive. "

"Part of you does." Still smiling, Jenna swept her fingers lightly over his straining cock. The soft sheath slipped away. Suddenly, his rampant erection strained against her hand. She gently stroked him as she spoke. "Haven't you wondered about the last five years of your life? Think about it, Garan...you awaken from the link with your father, and little Sheyna is all grown up...you are larger, older, a man grown. Haven't you wondered why?"

Ignoring his furious growl, the rattle and slap of the restraints as Garan once again struggled against his manacles, Jenna crawled up higher on the bed and knelt between Garan's legs...she leaned over and slowly drew him into her mouth.

His strangled gasp inspired her further. Licking the hot shaft with the tip of her tongue, she sighed against the familiar flavors and scents. Nibbling, sucking, drawing him deep into her mouth, Jenna lost herself in loving Garan.

His struggling ceased. He held himself still and she sensed the struggle within. Finally he arched his hips, offering himself to her as she suckled him. She licked along the length of him, withdrew, then encircled his cock with her fingers as she suckled first one, then the other testicle into her mouth.

He groaned, tightened his muscles. Jenna felt him stiffen, knew orgasm was eminent.

Releasing him before he could climax, she sat back on her heels and wiped her lips with the back of her hand. "Okay, now are we willing to talk link?"

His growl reverberated back off the stone walls.

"No? Well, maybe you just need some time to think." She scooted back and leaned against the wall between his manacled feet. Garan snarled, raised his head to glare at her, then lay back down.

Jenna draped her legs over Garan's. He grunted but did not respond.

She cupped her breasts in her hands, playing with her turgid nipples until they peaked and hardened even more. Though Garan pretended to ignore her, she knew he watched her through slitted eyes.

Playing to an audience of one, Jenna carefully suckled the fingers of her right hand then slowly reached between her legs. She stroked herself, imagining Garan's tongue filling her. Fingers were a poor substitute but Garan didn't appear to mind.

He studied her, his eyes open now, his hands clenched tightly about the chains holding him to the bed. His cock strained skyward, pulsing a deep red, and his testicles were drawn up tight and close to his body.

Knowing he watched her was a powerful aphrodisiac. Jenna surprised herself with her immediate response, the deep coiling heat in her belly, the swelling, pulsing need centered in her labia and clit.

She opened her thoughts, allowing her excitement to pass freely to Garan's mind, should he choose to receive.

From the unsteady sound of his breathing, he was definitely receiving.

She stroked long and slow between her legs, dipping into her hot vaginal opening, gathering up the moisture on her fingers and sliding once more across her sensitive nub, a motion that reminded her briefly of her interlude with Lucky Louie. Now that had been an orgasm!

Her inner muscles clenched at the memory.

Jenna bit back a gasp.

Garan's tension transmitted itself where their flesh connected, right at the point where Jenna's thighs rested on his calves. The muscles between them shivered and trembled.

She thought of stopping just before her release, but the touching, the teasing was much too pleasurable. As Garan watched, Jenna took herself over the top, peaking with a groan and a shudder that racked her body.

Fully aware of his rapt attention, she continued stroking her quivering flesh, reveling in Garan's obvious excitement, before collapsing in the pillows piled up against the wall.

After a moment, she withdrew her fingers from her pulsing vagina and held them up for Garan's perusal. They glistened with her fluids. She leaned forward and wrapped her wet hand around Garan's pulsing cock. He groaned and thrust his hips, driving the hot flesh between her slick fingers.

Jenna allowed him just three short, sharp stabs before releasing him.

He didn't even attempt to quell his frustrated growl.

She touched him again, dragged her fingers the length of his shaft, trailed them against his balls, then leaned back against the pillows.

His cock futilely stabbed at the air, painfully engorged, rampant with his anger and unfulfilled lust.

Jenna shook her head in mock dismay. "Ah, Garan. You still don't appear very receptive. In fact I'm concerned you might be just a bit...overheated. I think maybe we need to cool you down." Eagerly anticipating the next step in what she was beginning to think of as *Garan's education,* Jenna crawled over his legs and off the sleeping pallet. In the kitchen area she found the waterproof bag she'd prepared earlier, partially frozen and filled with small ice cubes and water.

As Garan watched her through half-lidded eyes, Jenna crawled back over his legs to straddle his right thigh. The moment her sensitive crotch connected with Garan's powerful muscles and soft pelt, her nipples peaked in response. She raised herself up on her knees, just enough to begin a rhythmic slide back and forth along his hard thigh.

Garan snarled at the sensual contact. "Why don't you just take what you want, human? Why do you insist on this pointless exercise in futility?"

"You know I can't force a link, Garan. It would be totally counterproductive for me to even try. You must welcome the meld for it to work. Until you invite me in..." She let the thought dangle, along with the ice-cold bag she held in her hand. A few drops of condensation dripped from the bag, hitting the very tip of his cock.

He twitched at the freezing contact. Jenna gifted him with her sweetest smile.

"It would be rape, Garan. I don't believe in rape...though I'm certainly not above a little persuasive coercion."

She leaned over and, without touching him with her hands, carefully took his rampant cock between her lips and licked the cold droplets from his hot flesh. He shuddered beneath her. She knew he was close to orgasm...and he was fighting her every step of the way.

She nibbled and licked the length of him. The thick scent of cinnamon filled her senses, Garan's scent, almost overwhelming with his arousal. Jenna rode his hard thigh, nearing her own climax, clutching the icy bag in both hands.

She knew the moment Garan's muscles clenched, sensed the huge orgasm ripping through his body. Gently, almost as if in benediction, Jenna released his straining cock from her mouth and pressed the frozen bag against his balls, completely enveloping his straining testicles in a blanket of ice.

Thank you, Sheyna, for finding a soundproof cave! Garan's roar would have shattered glass if there'd been windows. He climaxed long and hard, his thick seed covered Jenna's throat and breasts and still it spurted forth. He bucked against the ice-filled bag, his cock still rigid and upright, his growls filled with anger and frustration.

He'd come, but Jenna knew there'd been very little satisfaction for him. She projected a quick thought, a memory of the first orgasm he'd given her, that brutal twisting pinch of her clitoris after bringing her slowly to the edge of ecstasy.

This time, Garan's mind didn't close against the image. He glared at her, hate-filled eyes narrowed to amber slits. Jenna was thankful for the strong shackles holding him down so firmly.

She lifted the ice-cold bag away from his balls. They'd drawn up tight and hard against his body, doing their best to escape the bitter cold. Jenna leaned over and blew a hot breath of air against them, smiled at Garan, then carefully wrapped his upright cock with the cold bag.

This time he didn't move, as if daring Jenna to do her worst.

She knew the bitter cold encircling his penis must be agonizing, even though it wouldn't injure him in any way.

Other than your pride, you great, hardheaded beast.

She held it there for long moments. Her fingers grew numb with the cold and Garan's breathing was choppy and fast. She glanced at his hands and saw that his fingers were wrapped tightly around the chains as he fought what must be overwhelming cold on a part that had been so hot.

Finally, when her hands were stiff from the ice, Jenna took the bag away and set it on the floor.

Garan's erection had disappeared completely.

It was time for the next lesson.

Chapter 10

Garan endured her careful bathing of his belly, groin and legs in stony silence. Jenna took great delight in washing him with a soft cloth dampened with the aromatic waters from the pool in the bathing area. She found the thick steam filling the small, dark room slightly intoxicating, filled with the scent of unfamiliar minerals leaching from the rock.

Garan was obviously appalled by the surging erection he developed the moment she touched him.

"Your mind may not remember me, my love, but this part of your anatomy certainly appears to." Jenna lifted his heavy testicles and swirled the warm cloth around them, cupping each ball in her hand to carefully inspect and cleanse the furred pouch.

She stroked his huge cock with the damp cloth then draped it over the crown like a tent.

"Maybe I'll just leave it there." She sat back and grinned at the image–furious beast, angry erection, cloth tent–and knew she'd just about reached Garan's boiling point.

She left him that way and sauntered into the small bathroom. Thick, aromatic steam almost obscured the pool, a natural hollow in solid stone fed by a hot spring that bubbled and trickled over rocks through a cleft in the wall. Overflow from the pool spilled out the opposite end and disappeared into a crevice in the floor.

Sighing, Jenna slipped into the hot water. The mineral-laden pool immediately soothed and relaxed away some of the tension coiling in her soul. What if her plan failed? Garan was furious with her, but she was banking on his powerful emotions of hate being closely linked to love. If she could get him to *feel* enough, she might have a chance.

He had to welcome her link, had to open himself to the truth.

He has to!

Tilting her head back to wet her thick hair, Jenna let the tears flow. She hated what she was doing to Garan...it was not her nature to be cruel and barbaric. Since linking with Malachi, her need to nurture and heal was even stronger than it had been in the past, but this was the only solution she could think of.

She scrubbed her face and cleansed her body thoroughly before toweling off and returning to the main room.

Garan's erection had not faded and his glare was as angry as ever. For an arrogant male such as he to suffer humiliation and ridicule had to be the ultimate punishment. Taking pity on the beast, Jenna quietly removed the wet cloth, then leaned over and soothed him with her lips and tongue while her fingers softly stroked his warm balls.

"How long do you intend to continue this charade?"

Jenna stopped her ministrations and smiled at Garan. His question lacked his typical arrogance. He almost sounded curious.

"As long as it takes, my love." She pulled his thick penis back between her lips and glanced up, catching Garan's intense stare. Maintaining eye contact, she worked her lips around the broad crown and traced its contours with the tip of her tongue.

Blood surged into his cock, stretching the skin taut.

"Why do you think this violation of my manhood will make me change my mind?"

Jenna sat back and bit her lips. The arrogance was definitely gone. Now she heard mere resignation in his voice.

"I'm only following your lead. What you taught me when we were on Earth."

"I don't believe you. I was not and have never been on Earth. You may resume what you were doing, however. I'm actually beginning to appreciate what little talent you have in this area."

He nodded his head in her direction, as if giving her leave to continue.

*Why of all the arrogant, egotistical...*Jenna caught her self up short. He *was* arrogant and egotistical. Wasn't that what she loved about the beast?

She glanced at his erection and sat back on her heels. "Well, I'm not a one trick pony, you know." Jenna pulled herself forward into a sitting position, trapping his fully engorged penis between her legs.

Still hot and full, it throbbed against her needy clit, teasing her as much as she hoped to torment Garan. She raised up on her knees, hovering just over the tip of his erection. Garan strained upward, attempting to force entry. Jenna allowed him just close enough to feel her heat.

God, but she was wet and ready again!

Jenna lowered herself on his huge cock, slipping carefully down until he filled her. She felt as much as heard Garan's sigh of pleasure.

Without breaking her slow rhythm, Jenna studied Garan through half-closed lids. He'd shut his eyes completely, given himself over to the sensation, the heat and friction of their mating. She tested his mental barriers and realized they were slowly falling, slipping lower with each gentle motion of her hips. His hands clasped the manacles as if they were all that held his sanity.

He's opening to me!

Suddenly, he looked directly at her.

Unbind me, he pleaded. *Let me touch you.*

Only if you let me into your mind, Garan. Link with me, find yourself and the years you've lost. Please?

He snarled his answer.

Jenna lifted herself up and away from his straining body. She leaned down and blew a cool breath of air over his slick cock, then ran her fingers down the length of him for good measure.

Anger radiated from Garan in palpable waves. If her mind had not been so strong, Jenna knew she would have bowed to the mental demands he made.

No, my love. I will not free you. Not yet.

Jenna sat close beside him, observing the enraged and shackled male before her as clinically as she was able. Garan focused on his restraints, jerking and pulling against them in a futile effort for freedom.

She knew exactly how he felt. Jenna reached over and stroked his rampant erection, enraging him even further. Then she slowly stood up and walked away.

Suddenly she remembered the blindfold, how vulnerable it had made her feel. How protected.

Rummaging through a closet in the bathing area, Jenna came across a soft shawl. She almost giggled out loud when she returned to the main room. If anything, Garan's erection had grown even larger. He glared at her with absolute fury in his eyes.

He swung his head to meet her hands, his teeth bared. Jenna concentrated on holding him immobile with her thoughts.

His eyes widened in surprise. Obviously, he had no idea of the mental abilities he'd helped her develop. Unable to move, he glared at her until the soft folds of the shawl hid his angry amber eyes from view.

Jenna released him and sat back on her heels. "So, Garan. How does it feel to be totally helpless? To know I can do whatever I want to you. You can't see me...you have no idea what I'm thinking...and I am thinking, Garan."

He snarled, then clamped his jaws shut. Smiling to herself, Jenna decided to let him wait a little longer.

✷ ✷ ✷ ✷ ✷

Surrounded in darkness, Garan tested the restraints. They weren't painfully tight but he certainly wasn't going anywhere soon. The only pain he felt was the pounding ache in his groin. His balls must be as hard as rocks right now...he knew his cock was. Damned thing, standing straight up in spite of his attempts at control. He'd done his best to ignore the ministrations of the blasted human, but...

His breath escaped in a loud *whoosh*. *By the Mother!* He'd never felt anything like he'd experienced with her. Frustrated, he jerked impotently against the restraints, wondering what she planned next.

Anticipation made him ache even worse.

If only he knew what had brought him to this state! So dreamlike since he'd first awakened...as if he moved in a body not his own, reasoned with thoughts and memories glimpsed through smoked glass.

The blindfold merely intensified the sensation.

Since awakening in the clinic, he'd felt oddly unsettled, incomplete. His sire had explained his illness, but that didn't account for the added years he'd seen on Gard's visage. Nor did it explain the lovely development of his sibling, Sheyna. She'd been barely a kit when he last saw her...in his mind, only days before.

How much of what this human said was true? Gard had always been a manipulative, bigoted bastard, sire or not. He was not necessarily the one to turn to for truth.

Trust a human? This human?

"What are you doing?" Jerked out of his thoughts by something cold as ice against his balls. "What is that?"

"What does it feel like?"

He knew exactly what it felt like, still ached from the unfulfilling orgasm she'd wrung from him earlier with that damned ice pack. His balls throbbed with the memory–and his damned staff swelled in anticipation.

He felt her breath against his ear…hadn't realized she'd moved so close to him. *What is she doing?* Garan bucked his hips, vainly trying to escape the icy hot sensation burning its way across his balls, now sliding up and over his cock.

"Take away the blindfold! Now!"

"I'm not going to hurt you, Garan. I love you. I would never hurt you…not really. "

Hot fingers followed the cold, stroking him, squeezing just enough. He moaned, bit back the sound and gasped when the cold suddenly reappeared.

If only he could see! *If only*…sensation blossomed. Lost in darkness, securely bound, Garan could no more ignore the magic she practiced on him than choose not to breathe.

The shackles! He'd fight the shackles, dismiss the overwhelming awareness of her magic, he'd…*lost.* Lost in sensation…*lost in hot fingers circling cock, cold, burning ice cold sweeping over balls, behind them to base of tail then back, hot, cold, intense, almost painful pleasure, small, strong fingers squeezing, ice melting, pooling between legs, under butt, so cold, so…ahhhhhhh…hot lips, her lips sucking away the cold, licking drops, drawing icy balls into mouth, hot cavern of a mouth, tongue sweeping around one, then the other…so close…coiling tighter, mouth covering cock, suckling, teeth nibbling, coming, so close to….nothing.*

He tried to bite back the low moan escaping his lips.

So close. By the Mother, so damned close.

His chest heaved as if he'd run a marathon. His damned cock waved hungrily, searching blindly for that hot, wet mouth.

He would not beg.

Nor would he link.

Yes, Garan. You will. I've had enough of this fooling around. You're the one who taught me, remember? Garan, please! I want you to remember.

Garan bit back a retort. He would regain control. Somehow, he would escape her bondage and take her, show her the wrath of a Lion of Mirat was not something to toy with. He would...

...*die with the succulence of her body.* She straddled him, her strong, smooth legs clamped against his hips, the hot, wet passage she'd denied him suddenly swallowing him, taking him deep in long, lush strokes timed to his breathing, clenching muscles holding him, taking him...where?

Suddenly he felt soft palms against his temples, the pressure of her smooth forehead against his broad skull, her throat close, so close he could tear the life from her, end her foolish existence as if she'd never...

The hot sweep of flesh over flesh, instantly thoughts pooling, blood surging, hot, clenching need...he needed...needed...*By the Mother! Her! He needed this human, this woman giving him climax strong and hot, sweeping him over and into darkness*...and she was there, sweet and hopeful, filling his mind with light and love, sharing his climax, sharing her own, giving him back his memories and dreams, hopes and frustrations of the last five years of his life...giving him his future as she returned his past.

Long, long moments later, Jenna reached up and released the shackles holding Garan's wrists, then collapsed across his chest.

He thought she was gasping for breath, much as he'd been doing, until he realized his chest was wet with tears. He swept his hands up and down her spine, soothing her shuddering body and whispering softly to her, loving her as he had from the beginning.

She trembled, her sobs tearing at his heart when he thought of all she'd risked to bring him home. During the link he'd experienced the trip from Earth to Mirat, seen his still form lying death-like aboard the ship. He'd felt the all-consuming love Jenna had for him, the fear he might not recover, her joy when she realized there might be hope.

Garan brushed the tears from her cheeks with the pads of his thumbs. She blinked, hiccuped, then giggled. Garan moved to sit up, realized his feet were still shackled.

Jenna turned and released the restraints and Garan pulled her into his lap. There were no words. What could he say to the woman who had risked all to give him back his life?

"I love you, Garan of Mirat. I have missed you so terribly and I am so thankful you've come back to me."

He looked into her tear-filled eyes and tipped her chin up with his forefinger. "I love you, Jenna of Earth. I will never, ever be able to repay you for all you have done for me." He tapped her on the nose with the pad of his finger. "Hard to believe you had all that is me..." he tapped her forehead, "...in there."

"Do you remember?"

His mind felt clear, purified after linking with Jenna. Her powerful mental touch had obliterated every last vestige of his father's intrusive, clumsy meld.

Now his past, his memories and thoughts, were all in their proper order and place. His last coherent thought as Garan ended with their final link when they'd last made love, but he picked up Jenna's point beyond.

He recalled his last day through her mind, recalled the battle, Jenna's horrifying fear as she was trapped in the beam from that terrible weapon, his own desperate lunge at the turret in a final, successful attempt to deflect the beam from Jenna.

Saw her rush toward him, his still body on the ground, the sadness of the rebel fighters he'd actually grown fond of during his time on Earth.

The concept stunned him. "They cared for me, your humans. I always thought..."

"What, Garan? That they looked at you and saw nothing more than an arrogant bastard?" Jenna pressed her palm against his jaw. He felt the warmth and strength in her fingers, the love filling her heart. "You are, you know. But you're also someone they respect, someone they care about. They're going to miss you."

"My duty on Earth is not over. I have six more months left to serve." He thought about the feelings of those he left behind, realized his job on Earth was far from over. "I feel a great duty toward the Rebellion. Their battle has...*meaning* for me."

She snuggled closer, her look one of charming innocence. "During the link, my love, I think you absorbed a bit of me."

"What do you mean?"

"I am human. I will always feel a loyalty to my kind, to my world, just as you do to yours. When I was bringing you home to Mirat I didn't care if I ever returned to Earth. All I wanted was you, healthy and whole again. Now that I have you back, I can think once again about my duty to the Rebellion. When we linked, just now, I imagine you picked up some of my sense of loyalty to my own kind."

Garan brushed her thick mane back from her eyes. The texture felt softer than the finest silk. He kissed her forehead, nuzzled the sensitive point behind her ear. "The Rebellion won't last forever. Even Malachi has seen an end to it, though he doesn't know when. No matter...all that is important is that, by the grace of the Mother, I have found you."

"The Mother didn't have anything to do with it. Tim Riley brought me here."

Garan pulled back and looked into her eyes. *Surely you jest...?*

"I don't think he really planned it. In fact, he was very apologetic for ripping me out of my own time, but Malachi had shared his vision of a young woman with an old talent. He let Tim see the vision during a link. Tim understood nuances of the message that Malachi, who lacks kinetic ability, missed. Somehow he managed to coordinate everything in such a manner he was able to bring me forward, to this time."

"Amazing...and obviously something we'll need to study...but what about the brass statue?"

Jenna giggled. "I have absolutely no idea. I didn't mention Lucky Louie to Tim and he didn't bring it up, either. I have to believe in fate — Malachi saw me in this time before Tim brought me forward. It was destined I come here."

"Fate or not, you are mine, Jenna Lang. You are not going back to your own time."

"Of course not. The Rebellion needs me." She ran her fingers along the side of his jaw. Garan leaned into her gentle touch.

"Ah, Jenna," he whispered. "The Rebellion doesn't need you nearly so much as I do. As my life mate. Jenna, I love you and ask a lifebond of you, a commitment unbroken till death."

"I have already given you my bond, Garan of Imar. You have my heart and all that is mine." She kissed his jaw, then knelt between his legs, her hands grasping his thighs. He wanted her again, this slim, naked, almost hairless human.

Would he ever get enough of her? He wrapped his arms around her, breathing in her scent, inhaling the sweetness he would always associate with Jenna Lang.

He experienced a fleeting but bittersweet sense of loss, that in gaining her love he most certainly must turn his back on the stars. Earth, however, had a new allure for him with Jenna by his side.

Not forever, my love.

Hmmm? He tilted her chin up to look deep into her eyes.

She smiled at him and snuggled closer, wrapping her slim arms about his waist. *You said yourself Malachi foresaw the end of the Rebellion. I believe it will end sooner than later. Once I've fulfilled my duty to my world, I want to experience yours. I want to see the stars with you, my love. You have your StarQuest to fulfill. Will you take me with you?*

"You would do this? Give up your world to risk the heavens?"

"What would I be giving up? If I'm with you, I have everything."

A sudden commotion sounded just outside. The huge door slid open on its track. Before either Garan or Jenna could react, Gard stalked into the room, followed by Sheyna.

Garan tugged a blanket free to cover Jenna, then wrapped another around his hips and stood up.

"You wanted something, Sire?"

Gard halted. Sheyna almost collided with him. Instead, she stepped around the older man and raced to Jenna. "He's okay? It worked? Garan, it's so good to have you back."

"Thank you, SheShe." He leaned over and gave her a quick hug, the familiar nickname falling from his lips. "I asked you, Sire, what you wanted."

Gard practically vibrated with rage. Garan studied him for a moment; deeply aware the man he had always feared and often hated was worthy only of his scorn. "I think you need to leave, Sire. You are not welcome here." He turned to the young woman hugging Jenna's arm. "SheShe, you have risked a lot to help me. For that you have my lifelong gratitude. Is there anything…?"

"Will you and Jenna take me to Earth? I need to go there, Garan. He…" She glanced at Gard, then dismissed him with a look, "…has forbidden me to leave Mirat. Garan, I've read about the Rebellion and have talked to many of the humans who've settled on Mirat. I've also talked to the physicians about your recovery and they have some ideas that may help restore the minds of those young men targeted by that terrible machine. I want to help."

"I think we can do that." He turned and smiled gently at the woman he loved. "Jenna?"

She laughed. "Yeah, we can definitely do that. I know Malachi will welcome whatever assistance you can offer."

"We'll leave within the week. Can you be ready? It means you'll not see Mirat for a long time, my little sister."

"I can be packed in an hour! Thank you." Sheyna hugged Jenna and kissed her brother's cheek. Giving her father a look of unrestrained loathing, she quickly left the room.

Garan stared at his father in disgust, tired of the lies, the anger, and most of all sickened by the fanatic hatemonger the man had become.

"Why, Gard. What were you trying to prove?" Garan pulled Jenna close against his side. He needed her there, safe beside him.

"You will address me with respect!"

Garan shook his head, finally accepting the fact his father would never change. "No, old man. You are not worthy of my respect. You did your best to raise us as bigots and worse. Thankfully, it appears all of your offspring have minds of their own. Those few days I spent filled with your narrow-minded, intolerant thoughts taught me much, none of it good. Now go."

Gard's eyes narrowed with hatred. His muscles tightened as if he prepared to attack, then obviously thought better of it. He glared first at Jenna then at Garan before turning quickly and leaving. The air crackled with his passing. When the door shut firmly behind him, both Garan and Jenna released pent-up breaths.

Garan wrapped his arms tightly around Jenna, nuzzling the sweet fall of her hair. He had come much too close to losing her...even closer to losing himself. The exchange with his father left him feeling soiled and unclean.

Jenna purified his soul.

*There is a large pool of very warm water in the next room, my love. Spring fed, thermal heated to a most perfect temperature...*Her smile intrigued him, the subtle undulation of her hips against his a blatant, sensual invitation for a more thorough cleansing.

Big enough for two?

Of course.

Garan the Explorer needed no further invitation.

PRIDE OF IMAR

Kate Douglas

Prologue

You look pensive, little one. Do you regret your decision to leave Mirat?

Sheyna of Pride Imar turned away from the view port at her brother's soft mental touch. His concern was obvious and very touching, but Garan had always known her better than anyone else.

Of course, there'd been very few on Mirat who had cared to know her at all.

No more of that! Sheyna pushed the self-pity aside. A new world awaited her. A new life. The past would remain where it belonged — on Mirat.

Still…

It's almost physical — the pull of our homeland. It calls to me now, as it never has before.

Garan growled deep in his throat and wrapped a powerful arm around her shoulders. He gave her a comforting squeeze. *Are you worried what you'll find when we finally reach Earth?*

She thought about that a moment before answering. It was not so simple a question.

I worry my promise of help might not be enough. What if my healer's instincts don't work on this new planet? What if Winn's instructions were incorrect and I harm the young rebels more than help them? Jenna said all of them were beyond her reach, that the damage to their minds appeared even greater than the injury to yours. What if their wounds are beyond my ability?

"Then you will know you tried, even if you fail," Garan replied aloud. "They can't ask for more, SheShe. You've made a grand and generous offer, to leave the world of your birth to help strangers. A very brave and courageous offer. My mate believes in you. I believe in you."

"You and I both realize what little holds me to Mirat." Sheyna leaned against Garan's strong shoulder. She practiced her smile even as she sighed. So much to learn about dealing with humans. To think a baring of teeth was a form of friendly greeting! "I guess it's up to me to believe in me, eh? I wish I had just half the courage you and Jenna seem to think I possess."

"You'll do well, my sister. I've always known you were much stronger than you ever admitted."

As an empath, Sheyna sensed better than most her brother's love for her, his pride that she should take such a risk for another species. It warmed her and reaffirmed her decision. Still, she wished for just an ounce of Garan's arrogance and courage. He believed himself stronger, better, braver—and so he was.

The door to the observation deck slid open. Sheyna turned quickly to see who intruded on this quiet moment with her littermate.

"There you are. I've been looking for the two of you." Jenna, Garan's human mate strolled onto the deck. "Can you see Earth yet? Is it visible?"

"Not yet, sister of mine." Sheyna held her hand out to the woman. Jenna was never an intrusion. She was, in fact, the truest friend Sheyna had known. "Are all humans as impatient as you?"

Garan laughed and wrapped his arms lightly around both females. "No, SheShe. They're worse."

Jenna took a teasing swing at him and Garan ducked.

"I know when I'm not wanted," he said, spinning nimbly out of the way when Jenna took another punch in his direction. "I'll leave you two ladies to discuss what's most important on this ship...me."

The door slid shut behind him on a gust of air. "Has he always been this insufferable?" Jenna smiled broadly, her expression giving away all the love she felt for Sheyna's brother.

Sheyna's claws remained carefully sheathed. It had not been easy, learning the difference between a snarl and a smile.

She carefully curled her lip in reply. "Worse. He's twelve years older than I. We have different mothers, but on Mirat, if a pair-bond is not involved, the offspring are claimed by the sire's family once they're mature enough to leave their mothers. I grew up with him as 'the older brother'."

At Jenna's snort, Sheyna flashed her a wry grin. "You've probably guessed, Gard is not big on pair-bonding."

Jenna rubbed Sheyna's shoulder sympathetically. "I'm amazed your sire could even find a female to mate with him!"

"Oh, I imagine he can be quite charming when he wants to be...much like his son."

Jenna's knowing grin brought an answering smile from Sheyna. It was growing easier all the time, this human expression. Some day she'd have to tell Jenna how difficult it had been for her to learn to read the human face.

"Garan had seventeen summers when I came to Pride Imar as a five year old kit. I was horribly shy and frightened of all the new faces. He was upset at being charged with my care and even more upset I wasn't male. He teased me unmercifully."

"But you love him now? It's obvious you two are very close. What changed?"

"Gard."

"Ah…our favorite non-pair-bonding un-father figure." Jenna grimaced, as if merely saying the man's name was painful.

"Exactly. Gard returned from his StarQuest when I was about ten and discovered I had been added to the pride. Not only was I female, I was the wrong race and genetically deformed, a throwback."

"You mean you're not the same species as Garan?" Jenna shook her head in confusion.

"Look at me." Sheyna spread her slender arms wide. Lithe and petite in comparison to other lionesses of Mirat, she knew her resemblance to Garan was based on her feline appearance as compared to human. To Jenna, she most likely appeared similar to her littermate, though she was nothing like him at all.

"Not species — races. I'm no taller than you…smaller than a full-blood lioness, my coat is pale and short, and my features more like pictures I've seen of your house cats! My mother neglected to tell Gard her complete genetic background. He knew she was of the panther group, a bit lower than the ruling class of Mirat, but still acceptable as a mate.

"Unfortunately, her genetic background has a number of ancestors of an even lower caste. I understand I take after my grandmother. Gard just automatically made his legal paternalistic claim to me without realizing what I really was."

Sheyna tried to disguise the bitterness in her voice. Her genetic history was certainly not Jenna's problem.

She practiced her smile once more on her human sister of the heart. It would have been so much easier to just *show* Jenna what she was struggling to explain. Garan insisted she use human talk when she communicated with humans, even though most Sensitives, like Jenna, heard Miratan mindspeak just fine.

"Once claimed for Pride Imar, I could not be returned to my mother's pride as a member of a much lower caste," she said, still searching for the correct words. "Along with my obvious deformity, I could never expect full rights as a member of Pride Imar. I was, and am to this day, an embarrassment to my sire."

Jenna lifted one dark eyebrow. Sheyna paused, struggling to recall the meaning of the raised brow. Finally she remembered—Jenna's expression meant question or confusion.

"You're not just being polite?" Now Sheyna was the one who felt confused.

This made no sense.

"Obviously not. Why are you considered deformed? You look perfectly normal to me. In fact, you look absolutely gorgeous, if you want the truth."

"Think of what I lack that my kinfolk flaunt so proudly." Sheyna turned her back to Jenna and bowed her head.

"I don't...oh my! You don't have a tail!" Jenna laughed as she circled Sheyna.

Stunned, Sheyna grabbed the back of a chair for support. To think Jenna hadn't even noticed! "Would you believe you are the first person I have ever met..." She took a deep breath, for the first time wondering how it might be, existing among a race of people who didn't care about her abnormality. "No, you're the *only* person I've known who hasn't made some critical or disparaging remark about me?"

Jenna shook her head in disgust. "This must be where Garan comes in."

Sheyna took a moment to answer. Her heart pounded. Blood rushed in her ears. *Jenna didn't care...a tail, or lack of one, meant nothing to her.* Something so essential to the people of Mirat went totally unnoticed by a human.

Sheyna forced herself back into the conversation. There was much for her to think about—later, when she could be alone. "Ah...Garan. He was terrible. His teasing went on for years, though I have to admit he was never cruel. Not like our father. It wasn't until Gard returned and publicly ridiculed me that Garan had a change of heart."

"Your brother's a big softie, you know."

"I know that now. When I was a kit barely five summers old, away from my mother for the first time, I thought he was wicked and mean. He changed in a heartbeat, the moment he saw how badly Gard treated me. From that day on he was my protector and I loved him with all my heart."

"At least you won't be teased about not having a tail on Earth." Jenna gave Sheyna a quick hug. "I honestly didn't notice."

Amazing…no tails, no problem. Sheyna curled her lip and realized it actually felt like a smile. She waved her hand lightly, practicing a dismissive gesture.

"What do you know about Malachi Franklin? I understand I'll be working with him. He's the local healer caring for the young rebels."

Jenna laughed. "He doesn't have a tail, either."

"I must admit, now I think of it, the idea of an entire bipedal race of intelligent beings without tails has its draw."

Jenna giggled at Sheyna's dry comment. "You're the first lioness of Mirat to actually come to Earth to stay. Did you realize that? Only the men of your planet have actually set foot on earth."

"Our men are the warriors. That's why only the males have been assigned to duty on Earth. I volunteered as a healer because there is nothing on Mirat to hold me. My mother has been dead for many years; my other littermates tolerate but do not love me. Garan has been my only champion. When he chose you as his mate, he chose your home world as well. This mission is…" Sheyna struggled for the right words. "It is important to me."

How could she explain her desire to aid the wounded, the innate knowledge that only she could accomplish such a feat, without sounding even more arrogant than her brother?

When in doubt, the truth usually worked. "I know the ones who are the living dead need me," she said. "It's something I've sensed from the beginning, from the moment you told me Garan wasn't the only one affected by that terrible machine."

"Then you've made the right choice to come." Jenna smiled and glanced over Sheyna's shoulder at the view port.

"Look!" Jenna pointed at the shimmering blue-green orb floating ahead of them in space. "It's beautiful. I didn't even see it when we left. All I saw was Garan and my own misery."

Sheyna studied the jewel-like planet hanging in the ebony depths of space and experienced a sense of homecoming. "I understand. The last time I saw Earth, I hated all it represented. Your world had wounded my brother, mortally, I believed. I came here to take him home, not understanding that *home*, for Garan, now existed wherever his mate resided."

Jenna grabbed her hand, circling her long fingers around Sheyna's broad paw. Sheyna glanced down at their linked hands, the smooth olive skin of Jenna's, the soft ivory colored fur of her own.

She kept her razor-sharp nails carefully sheathed.

Garan had cautioned her to believe in herself, to trust in her own strength. Holding that thought to her heart, she gazed once more at the shining world ahead.

It was indeed beautiful. It filled her with anticipation, with hope. More than beauty, she knew it held answers to questions she'd not known to ask, to a future she hadn't even dared imagine.

Taking a deep breath, Sheyna let her soul fly free.

My destiny. I know this world is my destiny.

Chapter 1

"How's it hangin', Doc."

Malachi Franklin tucked a blanket around the silent young man in the hospital bed and turned gratefully at the softly drawled question from his closest friend. As usual, he bit back a grin. Thom Antoon was just the guy he needed right now—Malachi's polar opposite in personality, Thom always knew how to bring him out of whatever despair held him captive.

"Hangin' long but lonely, Thom. Gotta find me a woman." Standard answer. Same answer he always gave. It might be funny if it weren't so damned true.

Thom chuckled and shook his head. "Unfortunately, I'm all too sympathetic."

Tall, lanky, deceptively average, Thom did not look like the leader of a powerful rebellion. Even Lieutenant Garan, arrogant and egotistical as he was, openly admitted his admiration for the man's brilliant mind and logistical skills while managing to poke fun at his Southern drawl and country manners.

Garan. There'd been no word on his condition for the past month. Mal wondered if he'd ever see the big cat again. He hated to admit how much he'd missed him.

Thom paused by the nearest bed. "Any change?"

"There's no improvement, if that's what you mean. They're no better, no worse." Malachi checked the IVs on the seven young men in the ward, then quietly led the way out of the room. "It's so damned frustrating, Thom. I sense they're in there, that their minds are still intact *somewhere*. I just don't have a clue how to reach them."

"You might have help on the way."

Malachi swung around to face his friend, noticing his broad grin for the first time. "What kind of help?"

"Jenna and Garan are returning. He's been restored, Mal. It's hard to believe after the shape he was in, but the bastard's okay. Tim Riley just picked up a message from their ship. They should be here in a few hours."

"How? My God…" The sharp sting of tears surprised him. He was not a man who wept easily. "I never dreamed Jenna'd be successful, that she'd figure out how…" Malachi grabbed his handkerchief and wiped his face. His hands shook. "Damn, it's been a long month…not being able to help even one of these kids."

"It's probably been harder on you than anyone," Thom said, awkwardly patting Malachi on the shoulder. "The kids and Garan…I know how you feel about Garan, Mal." He laughed. "Never thought I'd see the day you'd be so shook up about *him* gettin' hurt."

Malachi grimaced. "Don't ever link with someone you enjoy baiting. Takes all the fun out of it."

"You didn't link with Garan, did you? I thought your meld was with Jenna."

"It was—about twenty minutes after she'd done a really comprehensive meld with Garan. His thoughts were so fresh in her mind it was like a damned party of three. Everywhere I went, *essence of Garan.*"

He laughed, unwilling to admit aloud just how heavily Garan's mental destruction had weighed on him. Looking at the big cat through Jenna's adoring mind had shown Malachi a human side to Garan he'd never suspected.

"Well, it sounds like he's back to his old self. You know what that means." Thom slapped Malachi's shoulder and laughed. "The Lord of Arrogance has returned."

"He is insufferable. Thom, it also means…" Malachi glanced at the ward where seven young men survived a partial existence. Once more he grabbed his handkerchief out of his pocket. "I'd give anything to help these kids."

"We don't know how she did it, or if she's even the one who healed him. All Tim got is the message they're returning, Garan is healthy and irritating as ever and he's bringing a healer with him—a woman, Tim said."

"One of the exiles? Do you think she's the one who healed him?"

Thom shook his head. "I don't know. The message was brief. Tim was so excited to hear the lieutenant was okay he didn't get a lot of details. " Once again Thom squeezed Malachi's shoulder. "You okay?"

"Yeah. Sorry…it's just been a bit much, ya know?" Malachi straightened, struggling to regain his composure. "I know these boys,

Thom. I've grown up with some of them, even baby-sat a couple when they were children, if that's not enough to make a guy feel old. It hurts like hell to see them this way."

"It won't happen to any more of our soldiers, if that's any consolation."

"I know." Malachi shoved his handkerchief back in his pocket. "Thank God for that...but who's going to help these poor souls?" He gestured toward the darkened room.

"Maybe Garan's healer?"

"Let's hope so."

* * * * *

Malachi didn't realize he was holding his breath until the large bay door of the Miratan ship *whooshed* open on a gust of air. "It's that silent arrival—gets me every time," he said, not really expecting Thom to answer. "You see that huge ship suddenly appear out of nowhere, absolutely soundless..."

"And you know it's just the minds of the crew controlling it, taking it through deep space with kinetic power alone," Thom added. "It is utterly amazin'."

The small group of Sensitives waiting to greet the ship cheered as Garan and Jenna appeared at the open bay door.

"Look—there's Garan. Quite a change from the limp carcass they hauled out of here." Malachi laughed. "I had no idea I'd miss the cocky bastard so much. It's good to see him healthy again and back where he belongs." He took a closer look. "He's lost weight."

Thom laughed. "Hey, Doc...don't necessarily blame the World Federation's new toy for that. From the smile on Jenna's face, I imagine he's been getting some pretty heavy aerobic workouts since his recovery."

"You're probably right. Lucky reprobate!" Grinning ruefully, Malachi raised his hand in greeting. "Hey Jenna! Garan!"

"Oh Mal, it's so good to see you!"

Jenna practically flew into his arms for a welcoming hug. Thom and Garan embraced as well, then Garan turned to shake hands with Malachi.

"It's good to have you back...I mean it." Malachi clapped him on the shoulder. Garan grunted in reply. He hid his jealousy well. Mal figured the big cat might never get over the healer's relationship with Jenna, but at least Garan appeared to have gotten used to it.

Mal fondly recalled the link he'd shared with Jenna. Because of that one, brief connection, he would carry a special bond with her to his grave. She had become an integral part of him during their very comprehensive meld...as had Garan.

Of course, Malachi had no intention of easing the jealous feline's mind. It was much too entertaining to let the big cat think Malachi felt something special for Jenna, something beyond the normal sense of family such a link created.

Poor Garan. Malachi grinned. Hard to believe a guy with Garan's attitude could feel insecure over a woman, especially one like Jenna. Her devotion to Garan was an open testimonial. It uplifted all who knew her.

A love that strong could never be breached.

No, Malachi realized if there was any jealousy, it was all his. Would he ever experience love such as theirs?

Suddenly Garan turned away and pulled a third person into the group.

As if all the air had been sucked from his world, Malachi forgot how to breathe.

Blindsided.

How else to describe the feelings sweeping over him, the coil deep in his gut, the sudden racing of his heart?

Vaguely aware his mouth hung open, he made a conscious effort to shut it. He blinked, then blinked again to better focus on the newcomer.

To prove to himself she was real, not his wildest fantasy come to life.

The creature standing timidly between Jenna and Garan was something out of a wet dream, obviously feline but so breathtakingly beautiful, so overwhelmingly feminine compared to Garan's strong masculinity as to appear a separate species.

Tall and slender, fine-boned and fragile in comparison to the huge male, she was the color of old ivory. Her body was encased in a soft yellow skinsuit that molded every contour of her frame, from her slim hips and well-shaped legs to the slender column of her throat, down her long and willowy arms to end at tight cuffs around slim wrists.

Like Garan, her hands were a cross between a human hand and a cat's paw, the fingers blunt, the partially retracted claws dark as ebony. She clenched her fingers, a nervous gesture not lost on Malachi.

His own palms had begun to sweat the moment he saw her.

Well aware he'd been staring, Malachi raised his head and smiled at the newcomer. Definitely feline, every inch a woman. More catlike than lion-like, her small, pointed ears showing through the dark mane that swept back from her broad forehead. It flowed to her shoulders, a sleek chestnut counterpoint to the soft pelt covering her face and hands…and most likely the rest of her body.

He wasn't quite prepared to let his imagination wander that far afield.

She watched him every bit as closely. Her beautiful amber eyes held him with the strength of her unblinking appraisal.

Jenna's soft laughter penetrated Malachi's mind. Slowly, he turned away from the newcomer to focus on her introduction.

"…is Sheyna of Pride Imar, Garan's sister and a healer from Mirat who has trained under some of the best doctors their world has to offer. Malachi Franklin, our own healer, who I'm sure will be more than happy to show you around the clinic once we get you settled in."

Garan's sister. Shit.

Jenna grinned at him, her brown eyes twinkling. She knew. She must know, as powerful as her Talent was. Malachi glanced back at Sheyna, wishing his precognitive abilities hadn't chosen this moment to desert him entirely.

"Nice to meet you," he said, mentally kicking himself at his inane greeting.

Jenna bit her lips in an obvious attempt to control her laughter. "We need to take Sheyna, Mal. You can have her later."

*I'd rather…*suddenly he realized he was broadcasting. Clamping down on his thoughts, Malachi glared at Jenna. Sheyna slanted one more curious glance in his direction, nodded, then quietly followed her brother and Jenna across the compound.

Chapter 2

"This will be your room." Jenna opened the door to a brightly furnished room in Garan's residence and led Sheyna inside. Her luggage had already been delivered from the ship, a small mountain of bags with Sheyna's distinctive healer's emblem embossed on each one.

"It's beautiful...this is a sleeping room?" She ran her hand over the smooth surface of a chest of drawers. "You build much with wood. On Mirat we use more stone." Sheyna crossed to the window and pulled the curtains aside, allowing a bright flash of sunlight into the room.

So far, Earth looked very much like Mirat. Dry, rocky hills, dark green trees, burned grasses blowing in the wind. A brilliant blue sky above.

Sheyna had a direct view from her room of a small group of buildings just across a wide, open area.

Garan, Malachi and a third man stood out in front. From the movement of his hands, the physician was obviously speaking to the tall general she'd been introduced to. For the life of her she couldn't recall his name, though he had a nice smile and gentle eyes.

The healer, however, was a different matter. Sheyna felt as if his image had been permanently seared into her brain. "What's he like?" she asked. From the grin on Jenna's face, if was obvious she knew exactly which *he* Sheyna referred to.

"Malachi's very special. Remember when I told you about doing the comprehensive mindlink in order to learn healing skills? That was with Mal. Garan was *not* happy about our link, but I've never regretted taking that step."

"You did a comprehensive link with a male of your own species? I'd forgotten about that." Sheyna tried to imagine the loss of self Jenna must have endured, to link with a male she was not bonded to. "Was it...awkward?"

"It should have been...could have been, actually, with Garan sitting right next to me radiating so much jealousy you could practically feel the sizzle in the air! Malachi had linked years before with Captain

Sander, so he knew what to expect. I had just linked with Garan less than an hour earlier to learn what a comprehensive link was like...I didn't want to do it with another man before Garan."

"I imagine it's very intimate." As if she even understood intimacy! Sheyna curled up on the bed and leaned against the wooden headboard. Tired from the long journey, she relaxed and let Jenna take over the conversation.

Jenna plopped down in a rocking chair, prepared for some quality *girl talk*. With any luck, Garan would be busy with Malachi and Thom for a while.

"It is. More intimate than I ever imagined. I hadn't been here very long and had barely discovered my own Talent. Thom was hoping I'd be able to learn how Malachi's healing and precog talents worked and develop them even further. I'd been able to do that with other skills. That's why I agreed, though I didn't have a clue what I was agreeing to!"

"But you'd just linked with Garan. You must have..."

"I was already in love with Garan. It's different, to link with someone you love. The only reason I did it with Garan first is because I wanted my first time to be with someone I loved and trusted completely. There's no fear of losing your *self* because you've already given it.

"I barely knew Malachi. I was essentially linking with a stranger, but once we linked it was like I'd known him all my life...or at least all *his* life."

"Can you tell me about him?" Sheyna's eyes practically glowed. Jenna shook her head.

"Only what I know from observation. I would never breach the sanctity of a link. I can tell you he's honorable, intelligent, has a wicked sense of humor and a marvelous healing Talent. He's precognitive, though he hasn't got much control over what he learns of the future. He's not telepathic unless he's physically touching someone. Even then he's not always clear."

Jenna grinned and leaned closer to Sheyna. "He's also really handsome and he doesn't have a mate. In fact it's a running joke he lives like a monk, but not by choice."

"A *monk*?" Sheyna shook her head. "I don't know the word."

"A religious person...a celibate. Someone who doesn't have sex."

"Ah." Sheyna glanced away and sighed.

"What's the matter?" Jenna scooted the chair closer to the bed and patted Sheyna's knee. "What'd I say?"

"I have a few things in common with your healer." She curled her lip in parody of a human smile, but the similarity didn't reach her eyes. "I have lived my entire life like one of your monks. It's not by choice, either."

Jenna frowned. Was Sheyna telling her what she thought she'd heard? "Are you saying you've never…?"

"That's exactly what I'm saying." She plucked at the bedspread, a nervous gesture Jenna hadn't noticed before.

"But…you're beautiful. You're not a child, your society certainly doesn't frown on open sexuality among adults…I don't understand?"

"You think I'm beautiful, but you're applying human standards. On Mirat, because of my genetic heritage, my body is too fragile, my color too pale, my features too narrow, my fur too short…and then of course there's that missing tail." This time her grin, a reaction Jenna knew Sheyna worked to perfect, reached her eyes.

"The men of my world were not at all interested. My body did not excite them. I sensed Malachi's interest. He didn't try to hide it." She giggled, a very human sound. "I think I'm going to like Earth."

Jenna laughed aloud. "I think you're going to like working with a certain healer…just as he's going to like working with you. Believe me, the pheromones were thick out there! Let's refresh ourselves and check out the clinic."

✱ ✱ ✱ ✱ ✱

Sheyna rested her fingers on the brow of the last of the seven young men Malachi kept hooked up to IVs and feeding tubes in his clinic. Just as the others, this one appeared to retain only the basic brain functions needed to keep his body running.

She struggled to focus her concentration on the young man, certain she detected his essence hiding deep within the damaged mind. It was so easy to falter; so aware was she of Malachi standing close beside her.

She must focus…if what Winn had believed was true…

"Anything? Do you feel them at all?" Malachi was completely professional here in his hospital. The admiring gaze he'd given her earlier had been replaced by one of respect for her abilities as healer. For the first time in her life, Sheyna realized she would have preferred another healer's admiration of her as a female.

"I think so." She turned away from the comatose young man and quietly led Malachi out of the ward, then followed him through a series of doors into his private quarters, which were attached to the clinic.

He walked with almost catlike ease, his long legs as strong and powerful as any lion's, his broad shoulders and trim waist barely disguised beneath the shapeless white lab coat.

Focus.

Easier said than done. "I sense a block so powerful it actually prevents the mind from recognizing itself," she said.

Malachi turned and studied her intently, his blue eyes clear and unblinking. His mouth curved slightly downward and she wished she understood human facial expressions better.

Focus.

She spread her hands wide, gesturing for emphasis. "It's as if the mind, in the immediate moment of trauma, threw up a protective barrier so complete, so impervious, it essentially cut itself off from the functional part of the brain."

"You're saying they're blocking their thoughts from their own minds?"

Did he have to sound so skeptical?

"Exactly. And from us as well. I know you originally felt the beam from that machine had essentially reformatted their minds, wiped them blank of all memory. That's what we thought happened to Garan, why we used the mindlink to restore his thoughts, the very essence of himself."

"Which we can't do with these kids because none of them, as far as we know, had linked with anyone before the attack." Malachi shook his head in frustration. He pulled a chair out for Sheyna. She sat across from him at a round wooden table in the kitchen. "So, what is your theory, Lioness of Mirat?"

Sheyna blinked at the sudden formality of his address. Had she somehow offended him with her ideas? Haltingly, she attempted to explain. "I was lucky enough to study with a powerful and well-respected Miratan healer, Winn of Pride Reale. I went to him shortly before coming to Earth. I shared with him my observations of Garan's trauma. I wanted to see if he had any ideas how we could help your soldiers."

Malachi continued to study her without comment. Was he mocking her suggestions? His face told her nothing. If he'd been a lion she would know by the twitch of his tail, the flattening of his ears. How did humans *read* one another?

Lowering her voice so as not to offend, she continued. "Winn thinks your premise is incorrect. He said both leonine and human minds are similar, at least among the Talented. He believes the comprehensive link saved Garan, not because we replaced his memories so much as allowed his memories their freedom. That brief time frame during the link where another mind relieved the weight of the trauma was enough to free the trapped thoughts."

Malachi merely nodded. At least he wasn't telling her to shut up!

"I understand Garan's told you the story of what happened, how Gard inserted his own block when he first linked with Garan, essentially blotting out the five years since they had last had contact. Once Jenna was allowed to link, she removed Gard's block and Garan's memories returned, at least to the time of injury."

Malachi rubbed his eyes and rested his head in his hands. "I don't know, Sheyna...sounds pretty far fetched to me."

"Will you allow me to attempt a link with one of your patients?"

The slow shake of his head was entirely negative. "We've tried. Both Jenna and I tried to link, but you've got to have something to link with! There's nothing there. Trust me. It won't help."

Praise the Mother; she'd come too far now to quit. Gathering courage, Sheyna leaned forward to make her point. "I disagree. You've asked for my help. I've offered it. Why do you turn it down?" Suddenly, she grabbed his hands in both of hers. His long fingers immediately curled around her shorter ones.

She closed her eyes against the need, the hot coil of desire that flooded her body with his touch. Malachi's? Her own? An empath should be able to discern one from the other.

She'd not realized how dangerous it would be to touch this man. She had to touch him, had to make him feel hope for his patients. Sheyna accepted the inevitable, that she had no choice, no matter the risk.

Somehow, she must convince him to try.

Malachi stared silently at their clasped hands, at the ebony nails curling sharply against his palms and the soft, fur covered fingers wrapped tightly around his, and knew he was lost.

Need twisted his gut, shortened his breath, left him rock hard and wanting—and feeling terribly unprofessional. What was it about this creature? He'd been fighting for control since the moment she'd stepped into the clinic. Had struggled to remain aloof and professional when all he'd wanted to do was touch and taste all over her wonderfully exotic body.

He'd never reacted to any woman this strongly in his life…not even Mara Armand in the bloom of what he considered his most ill fated romance.

With thoughts of Mara and the mental bonding she and Sander had shared, Malachi immediately strengthened his mental shields. He certainly didn't want this innocent woman to sense the lust that engulfed him!

Had Mara responded to Sander this way? Was this how Jenna felt when she first awoke to Garan's touch? Almost afraid to look into Sheyna's eyes, Malachi raised his head.

He saw the same shocked need mirrored there, the same surprised desire.

Too much, too soon. He squeezed her hands, then with a strength of will he wasn't certain he possessed, released them. This was neither the time nor the place.

"I find it impossible to argue with your points." He smiled sheepishly and pulled Sheyna's chair back so she could stand. "I'm probably just a bit territorial and protective with these kids…totally unprofessional. Are you up to giving it a try right now?"

Sheyna nodded without meeting his eyes.

Had she sensed his lust, his desire for her? Somehow, had he offended this marvelous creature? Unsure how to proceed, Malachi took the safest course of action. He led Sheyna back to the clinic to give her theory at least one good try.

Chapter 3

"Garan, as much as I hate to admit it, it's damned good to have you back." General Antoon sprawled in a well-worn old couch in the lieutenant's residence. Jenna had gone into the kitchen in search of a glass of wine. The men each held a cold beer. "It's especially good to have you back with all your marbles intact...or at least as intact as they're gonna get."

Garan grunted his reply and took a long swallow of beer, refusing to rise to the bait. It felt much too good to be home to sling verbal arrows at his friend.

Home? He'd never thought of Earth as home before. Not until Jenna. So much had changed. "How are things going? Any more attacks?" He rubbed his fingertip along the chilled side of the can, reveling in the cool drops of moisture condensing against the smooth metal. *Simple pleasures.* He'd never appreciated what he had until he'd almost lost it.

"They tried hitting us with another one of those machines, figured it didn't work anymore and backed off. We all look a little silly running around in designer sunglasses, but so long as the polarizing filter defuses the beam, I'll wear mine." Thom leaned forward in his chair, glanced toward the kitchen as if checking for Jenna and lowered his voice.

"Our biggest concern is, they've got a new battalion commander for this area, a guy named Merrick White. He's supposedly the inventor of that damned machine, sort of a mad scientist type. Some of his troops have recently deserted, come to us even though they're not Sensitives. They're more afraid of White than they are of us. They think he's crazy...dangerous crazy."

Garan was suddenly assaulted with the images Thom privately showed him...images the general had culled from the minds of the deserters.

Perversions inflicted upon captives...rape, torture, even deviant behavior against his own troops, all of it directed by a corrupt mind, totally mad, completely devoid of morality.

Garan shuddered and backed away from Thom before he realized what he was doing. "Praise the Mother...how'd he get to a position of power?"

"The WF, at least their military, is truly beginning to crumble. The rebellion has spread worldwide. Earth's citizens have watched the battles on the nightly news for seven years now. They've heard our side of it, seen that the rebellion is made up of decent men and women who want to use their very special abilities to help make this a better world.

"Another thing in our favor is the citizens are giving birth to a higher percentage of children with Talent. They love their babies even when they fear what they don't understand. They see us as a better way for humanity, the answers to a lot of questions.

"As the WF weakens, as their better officers begin to question the war against us and politicians realize their constituents no longer support the oppression of the Talented, a void has opened up at the top. It's allowed men like White into command positions without the checks and balances that would normally control his deviant behavior.

"This man is truly a danger. Garan, keep an eye on Jenna. Word is out White's trying to kidnap some of our people. He'll naturally go for the leaders. He wants power and he'll do anything to get it."

A low snarl emanated from deep in Garan's chest. "She needs to be told." Garan glanced toward the kitchen as Jenna walked out with a bottle of wine in one hand, an empty glass in the other. *I could not bear it, should she be hurt...could not survive should I lose her.*

"I was hoping you'd feel that way. I didn't want to frighten her unnecessarily, but..." Thom scooted to one side on the long, low couch where he sat and patted the spot next to him for Jenna to sit. "Darlin'," he said in his slow drawl, "'we've got to talk."

* * * * *

He was so unlike the men of her world. Tall, lean but broad shouldered, his skin smooth, almost olive toned. The dark dusting of fine hairs on the backs of his hands, the black slash of eyebrows, the waving black hair on his head...so different from the sleek pelt that covered her own body, the dark mane that flowed from her high forehead, down to curve about her shoulders.

The hair on his head was shorter than hers...Jenna explained it would grow quite long if left alone, but Malachi's was trimmed neatly around his ears, curling just against his collar in the back. Sheyna liked it. Wished she had the freedom to run her fingers through the thick waves, to see if they felt as silky as they looked.

His eyes were blue. Sheyna had never seen blue eyes quite like his before. Their brilliant color fascinated her; the intelligence in their depths intrigued her. His features were finely drawn, almost pretty, she thought, but there was a strength of character in the line of his jaw, the broad, full-lipped mouth.

His mouth was definitely interesting. It was difficult not to stare at his lips. He had a fascinating smile...she was definitely getting used to smiles. Did he growl when he was angry?

What sounds would he make during sex? She'd heard the males of her species snarled, growled, even screamed. Did he purr when he was content?

Sheyna knew he was attracted to her, felt his passion as clearly as her own. She'd told him she was a healer. She hadn't mentioned she was also an empath. From their first meeting she'd sensed his desire for her. It had left her shaken, an unfamiliar heat coiling in her womb.

The idea of joining with him held much fascination. She wished she knew more about males of *any* species, much less this one! Hopefully, time and familiarity would teach her.

Smiling at her own naiveté, praying to the Mother for patience and wisdom, she followed him into the ward.

Malachi lowered the lights and directed Sheyna to the first bed by the door. She turned and smiled at him, unsure of herself. "Malachi," she finally said. "You must promise me. No matter how long this takes, no matter what sounds I make or how distressed I might appear to be, you will not interfere. Winn has warned me this will be neither painless nor quick. Nor is it without risk, but it's my risk and you must promise me you will not intervene."

After a long moment of silence, Malachi nodded his head in agreement. Sheyna sat on the edge of the firm mattress and lifted the blanket, exposing the lean length of her patient, gasping in sympathy at his thin, flaccid body.

Gently she touched her forehead to the young man lying so still.

Her fingers covered his temples, her hip pressed against his, completing the contact. Still, she had to force Malachi's image from her mind in order to search for the injured sentry's thoughts.

She entered his mind, slipping silently into the dark recesses of his wounded brain. Malachi had told her his name was William and he was 20 years old. His parents and sister wanted him whole and healthy again. William's fate rested heavily with her.

She carried his name in her heart as she searched for the familiar synapses and current of an active brain, knowing she would not find them here. Darkness filled his thoughts—a black shroud covering his intelligence like a thick blanket of mucous, just as Winn had told her to expect.

Sheyna would have to part the cover without damaging the mind beneath...if that mind actually existed. She focused her thoughts, searching for a glimmer of intelligence, anything that would help lead her to the memories buried beneath their protective covering.

There! Something flickered, some minor spark of life, barely visible but enough to guide her. She followed it, her searching thoughts a hound on the trail, fighting the clinging blackness, aware of the slick, viscous texture of the protective sheath.

It disappeared. Only blackness remained.

Hours she searched—it must have been hours. Maybe Malachi was right. Maybe there wasn't anything here to heal. Maybe that spark had only been her own longing.

Sheyna's body trembled with the effort, her head ached and the pressure of the shroud threatened to envelop her mind as well as the young sentry's.

Nothing.

Sobbing with frustration, she slowly backed away from the darkness.

Malachi was waiting for her when she emerged from the meld. She tumbled into his embrace, the guilty pleasure of touching him, being held by him, an even greater transgression because of her failure.

"Did you find anything?"

"No. Nothing. I thought, once, I felt a flicker of life. I couldn't find it again." Her voice was muffled against the soft white lab coat covering his chest. His scent filled her nostrils; the smooth fabric tantalized her with the contours of his muscles hidden beneath. "I'm so sorry, Malachi."

His arms wrapped tightly around her shoulders and he held her even closer. His chin rested on top of her head. "I think you should try again."

She pulled away, looked him directly in the eye. "But you thought I was wasting my time. You said…"

"I was wrong. Sheyna, when you linked to William, his eyes fluttered. His lips twitched…not a lot, but enough. I saw movement in his toes and fingers, movement that wasn't there an hour ago. Something happened. I believe you're on the right track. Do you have the strength to try once more?"

She nodded, gathering energy from Malachi's encouragement. He handed her a cup of something hot and dark. The scent tickled her nose. *Coffee.* Garan had given her some of the restorative during their flight. She sipped quietly at the bitter brew, eyes half closed in silent meditation.

A few minutes later, balance restored and mind alert, she knelt once more beside William. Again she touched him, entered his mind, fought through the darkness.

This time, however, she searched the darkness knowing that Malachi believed. His faith gave her strength—a newfound strength that guided her, gave her the tenacity to struggle through the enveloping shroud.

Finally she sensed it yield, felt the fabric part, heard a ripping, tearing shriek of unimaginable pain and then…

Lights! Thousands and thousands of tiny, sparkling surges of energy…all here, right where they belonged. Here, protected beneath the darkness, hidden from even the brain that held them, the memories, the intelligence that gave humanity to this boy!

Instinctively, following her healer's tenants, Sheyna repaired what little damage existed, removed the heavy shroud and disposed of the last of the protective covering so William's body could re-absorb it. As a last act, she lulled his mind into a deep, healing sleep. A sleep from which he would awaken, whole, healed, himself once again.

Slowly, so slowly, she withdrew from the peacefully sleeping mind. Once again Malachi caught her as she fell away, held her trembling body tightly in his arms as her own mind returned to its normal state.

Sheyna opened her eyes, aware on so many levels of the man embracing her. She sensed his concern, his worry she had stayed too long in her trance-like state. Most of all, she felt his need, his deep desire for her as woman.

It was a new feeling, one she would have to consider. She smiled, not attempting speech, not yet. Malachi brushed her thick mane back from her forehead, his crystalline blue eyes filled with worry. For her. He worried for Sheyna.

That, too, was a new feeling.

"Are you all right?" His voice was troubled, deep, melodious. She shivered, exhaustion robbing her of will.

"I am very tired. There are six more to heal."

"Six who will wait until morning. William sleeps. You should, too. If you try to do too much tonight, you could easily cause more harm than good."

"But, I came here to…"

"You've done the impossible. You've shown me you can heal my boys. I am sorry I ever doubted you. Trust me. The others will be fine until tomorrow."

"If you're sure?" Sheyna glanced at the young men, all peacefully sleeping. Only William snored.

Malachi merely smiled at her protests. He shook his head and stepped away from Sheyna, covered William with a light blanket and quickly checked on the other patients.

Before she realized his intentions, he'd swept her up in his arms, carrying her as if she were just a small kit.

His arms were strong and warm across her back, beneath her knees. His face was mere inches from hers, his lips barely parted, an unreadable expression on his most beautiful face.

She could grow quite used to that face, Sheyna decided.

If only she could sense what he was thinking. His thoughts were unreadable, but his intentions quite clear.

Just as she realized the consequences of his very human lips so close to hers, they were touching her forehead, her cheeks. He was kissing her mouth, his kisses growing bolder and more passionate as she tentatively answered him with kisses of her own.

So new! She'd never been kissed, not by her own kind, certainly not by a human! His arms tightened around her, his lips parted so that she tasted his tongue, tasted the unique flavors that made him human.

She wrapped her arms around him, kneaded the muscles of his back and shoulders, parted her lips and invited his tongue deeper, sparring with it, surprising herself with her own uninhibited response.

He carefully shifted Sheyna's weight in his arms and carried her through the clinic door, shutting out the light and heading straight for his residence.

Sheyna took one last look at the young soldiers. William pursed his lips as he quietly snored. The others were silent. She would heal them come dawning. For now, she anticipated...*what?*

Desire coursed through her body. Need. A hunger long denied. She pressed her mouth to the warm column of Malachi's throat.

Malachi had never felt so terribly unprofessional, nor so expectant in his life. He told himself Sheyna needed the rest, the long trip had tired her, healing William had obviously exhausted her.

So why was he carrying her back to his quarters and not to the small room she had at Garan and Jenna's?

Sheyna's arms tightened around his neck and she nuzzled his collarbone. He sensed more than heard a deep, rumbling purr.

No way was he taking her back to her room!

The couch was long and wide. He wished he could just carry her into his sleeping quarters, but what if he'd read her incorrectly? As beautiful and appealing as he found her exotic feline features, Malachi wasn't quite certain how to read her expressions.

At least with Garan, you could watch his tail twitch! It suddenly dawned on him what Sheyna lacked.

Malachi sat heavily back in the overstuffed cushions with Sheyna across his lap. He stroked her smooth bottom through the sleek skinsuit; privately pleased she didn't have a tail.

Her fingers caressed his shoulder, then lingered at the buttons on his lab coat. She looked up at him, her amber eyes glowing in the gloomy light from one small lamp burning in the next room.

Uncertainty ebbed from her in waves. Malachi covered her hand with his, taking strength from her confusion, then helped her unbutton his coat. The day had been warm and he wore no shirt underneath. When her partially sheathed nails found his flesh, fire slashed across his bare chest. She stretched her fingers out and the smooth palm of her hand branded him.

Practically trembling with need, he slid the fastening open on her skinsuit and slipped his hand inside. She felt like warm mink, her heart beating rapidly against his palm, her small, firm breast filling his hand, the taut nipple calling to his lips.

Malachi looked into her eyes and read the invitation there. He leaned over, suckling her nipple, circling it with his tongue and drawing it into his mouth. She arched her back and a low growl deep in her throat sent shivers along his spine.

Growing bolder, Malachi tugged her skinsuit over her shoulders. When she slipped her arms free then tightened them around his shoulders and raised her hips, he obeyed her invitation.

Her skinsuit and soft boots dropped softly to the carpet.

Her naked beauty made him gasp. Long and lithe, covered completely in a soft pelt of ivory mink, she rippled like molten silver in the pale light. She turned in his arms, sliding off his lap to one side and kneeling next to him on the couch so that he could remove his own clothing.

Malachi slipped the unbuttoned lab coat off and unsnapped his pants. He struggled to pull them down over his straining erection. He'd barely gotten them past his hips before Sheyna had her fingers wrapped around his cock.

He snapped around to look at her, surprised by her aggression, then laughed aloud at the eager look of curiosity on her face.

"It's so hot," she said, frowning at him. "I had no idea it would feel this hot. Or be this hard...or this big."

"Because I'm human?"

"No. Because you're male."

"Are you telling me you've..."

"Never done this before? Jenna didn't believe me either." Still holding on to his penis, Sheyna studied him a bit longer. "I've always been curious, but I've never felt so...well..." She looked at him very seriously. "I'm feeling things. My chest is tight; there is a sensation of heat, of yearning in my womb. I *feel* my clitoris...that's not a body part I'm usually all that aware of."

She stared at him, then carefully curled her lip in a smile. Unselfconsciously, she began to touch herself, rubbing her finger between the folds of flesh between her legs. Malachi shifted his hips and prayed for endurance as she changed tactics and stroked him slowly with both hands, her smooth palms driving him beyond lust.

"It's getting bigger. How much bigger is it supposed to be?"

Malachi groaned. "I take it this question is for medical purposes only?"

There was a twinkle in her eyes when she answered. "As a healer, I've seen many pictures of Miratan males and their parts. They're still a mystery to me. Humans are a *complete* mystery."

She squeezed him, then swept one ebony nail across the head, catching a drop of liquid and popping it into her mouth. "Salty. Sweet, too. How unusual."

Before he could respond, she'd leaned over and taken him into her mouth. Her lips encircled him; her long, abrasive tongue wrapped itself around his length. He felt the hard ridges of her sharp canines against the sides of his cock.

His testicles tightened against his body and he fought the urge to thrust harder into her mouth. Who know what those teeth might do, should he surprise her! Warily, Malachi reached between her legs and gently stroked the hot, wet folds. He found her clitoris, a fleshy protrusion larger than a human female's.

When he rubbed it between his fingers, she moaned, the sound vibrating the length of his cock. He opened her wider with his fingers and she raised her hips to accommodate his touch. He stroked her now with his entire palm, inserting his fingers into her heat with each forward thrust. She moved against him, increasing the rhythm, tightening her mouth around his cock until he knew he couldn't last much longer.

So close. He felt her tremble, knew she hovered on the edge of orgasm, sensed her surprise at the sensations, the lush promise of…

A loud knock sounded at the clinic door.

Sheyna jerked back. Malachi's cock waved forlornly in the cool air.

"Shit." He shook his head in disgust and grabbed for his pants. "Someone's at the clinic. I've got to see who it is."

He stood up and shoved his withering erection into his pants and fastened the zipper. Sheyna lay on the couch, staring up at him with glazed, lust-filled eyes. "Hold that thought," he whispered, leaning over to kiss her. "I'll be right back."

* * * * *

Jenna peered through the window on the kitchen door at Malachi's residence. Garan grumbled angrily at her side. She knocked. When there was no answer, Jenna quietly opened the door. Garan lunged ahead of her.

"Wait a minute, big boy. Sheyna's a grown woman. If she decided to stay the night with Mal, that's her choice."

Garan snarled at her. "She's untouched. She doesn't understand what..."

"She's tired of being untouched, Garan. Let her have a life, okay?" Jenna pushed her way ahead of him and headed for the clinic.

William, looking pale and unsteady but gloriously awake and alert, met her in the hallway. "Jenna! What are you and Garan doing here? Have you seen Malachi?"

"My God!" Jenna rushed forward, grabbed his arm and looked him over completely. "She did it, Garan! She found them! William, how are the others? There were seven of you...what about...?"

"They're asleep, Jenna. I can't wake them up. I tried. What the hell are we all doing in the clinic? Last thing I remember, I was in a Federation holding cell. What happened?"

"Later. I'll explain what I can later. Where's Malachi? What about Sheyna?"

"I haven't seen Malachi. I was looking for him. Who's Sheyna?"

"Jenna. Quickly. In here!"

Garan had gone down the hallway to search Malachi's residence. He called to her from the front room. Jenna and William reached the doorway at the same time.

"What happened?"

"Nothing good." Garan stood amidst chaos, his fear and anger a palpable entity within the room. Chairs tipped over, a table broken and splintered, muddy footprints and shattered glass.

He picked up a piece of bloodied cloth and showed it to Jenna. It looked suspiciously like the lab coat Malachi usually wore. Sheyna's yellow skinsuit and boots were piled in a corner, Malachi's boots shoved under the couch. "Can you get a read on the room? Now, before the essence is badly disturbed?"

Jenna closed her eyes, concentrating on the air, the very molecules within the room. She turned right, then left. Garan and William backed away, leaving Jenna to her psychic search. She leaned over and touched Sheyna's skinsuit. The smooth yellow fabric slipped between her fingers, carrying with it a sense of curiosity, the heat of passion, the lush warmth of discovery.

Jenna held the garment close to her, absorbing Sheyna's last moments in the room. She swayed with the emotions emerging from the very molecules in the air about her, shuddered as her questing mind went deeper.

When she had absorbed all she could from Sheyna's garment, she took the lab coat Garan handed to her. The blood was still fresh. She pressed her fingers against it, feeling the cold, sticky substance with her mind as much as her sense of touch.

Malachi's blood.

Pain assailed her. Pain and fear and a sense of outrage beyond anything she'd ever experienced. Shocked, she stared out the front window and attempted to organize her turbulent thoughts.

"I sense darkness and evil." She turned to Garan with tears flowing freely down her cheeks. "Evil and fear. I think Sheyna was unconscious...drugged, maybe...but Malachi was hurting. Hurting and very, very afraid."

Chapter 4

She regained consciousness very slowly, almost as if her mind struggled to protect her body from the circumstances. Sheyna sensed she was not alone, knew she was naked, felt the residual touch of having been examined and explored by something or someone strange—and *wrong*.

She was not chained or shackled, but movement was impossible. She cast her thoughts about, sensing confinement by some auxiliary means, whether by an electrical field or some other mechanical device. There was no blindfold covering her eyes, but she saw nothing, had no awareness of her position, what she might be lying upon, where she was.

Feeling nothing, seeing nothing. Touching nothing. Panic welled deep in her chest. She struggled to breathe, to draw air into her straining lungs. Her arms and legs twitched against unseen shackles. Whatever passive restraint held her, grew more powerful the more she fought.

Sensory deprivation. She'd studied it, experienced it just once during training. Likened it to being lost in space, floating for eternity, knowing death.

She gasped for air. There was no sound of indrawn breath.

Calm. Calm down.

She had to remain calm.

She searched for Malachi, then realized her thoughts were contained, somehow, within a narrow field. Still, Sheyna knew she was not alone.

Suddenly a narrow beam of light spotlighted her.

Sheyna blinked against the brilliance, realized she was laying spread out on a lightly padded surface as sense and feeling slowly returned to her body. She curled her fingers against her palms but could not raise her. She pointed her toes to experiment, but could not move her feet.

"You are absolutely fascinating."

The voice echoed mechanically. Sheyna willed herself not to react.

"Intelligence said there was another alien among the rebels. I expected a male, not a female of whatever species you are. We know the last one was destroyed, his mind perfectly erased by my beautiful machine."

He's talking about Garan! They think I've been sent here as his replacement. Malachi, where are you? I need you, Malachi!

"You cannot escape. I am going to free you from your restraints. By the way, I do hope you're impressed by the immobilizing features of my table." A dry laugh crackled through the speaker. "Remember what I said. I would hate for you to die before we get to know one another."

Sheyna heard a soft *click*. Absolute silence replaced a low-level mechanical *hum* she hadn't even noticed until it ended. The entire room was suddenly bathed in light.

Something in the table must have been the source of sound. She wondered if the table itself had immobilized her, encased her within some sort of powerful force.

Sheyna raised her chin to see where the voice had come from. A speaker with a small camera attached was mounted on the wall just above her. The lens stared back at her, a malevolent, unblinking eye.

She studied it a moment, wondered who watched her.

She must disregard the lens. She would also ignore the man behind the voice. She must disregard everything except escape. She cast her thoughts about, experimenting with the amount of sensation and freedom slowly returning to her, searching for Malachi.

She sensed him. *Nearby?*

Slowly she turned her head, realized her arms and legs were free to move as well, though she felt as if she were reawakening from some sort of powerful drug. She sat up and turned to study her prison more completely.

Plain walls, an unshielded commode in one corner and…She gasped aloud.

Malachi lay in a naked, bloody heap against the far wall.

Stumbling, her feet unwilling to obey, balance practically nonexistent, Sheyna scrambled across the room to him. "Malachi? Oh, Malachi…"

She knelt beside him, felt his steady heartbeat beneath his chest, the thrum of blood rushing through the large artery at his neck. "Praise the Mother, you're alive!"

Her first instinct was to heal, to place her hands at his temples and will his battered body to repair itself.

She touched him, opened her mind to her healing ways.

No! Do not heal me. Sheyna...do you understand? We can't let him know.

His body remained still, his eyes closed. His mental speech was weak, as Jenna had told her it would be.

I understand your words but not your reason. Malachi, you are badly injured. You might die without healing.

I'll live. I look worse than I feel. Quickly...hear me. You must know I can only speak telepathically if we are in actual physical contact. If we don't touch, I can't hear you. I'm not powerful enough to transmit my thoughts, not like you and Garan...or Jenna. Just help me to the table as you would any injured person...examine me, but do not heal me! *Healing my injuries would tell him more than we want him to know.*

Sheyna restrained from nodding and helped Malachi slowly and carefully to his feet. "What happened to you?" she asked aloud.

"It appears the WF battalion commander enjoys watching someone get the crap beat out of them. In this case, I was the star of the show." Malachi leaned heavily on Sheyna's arm as she steadied him before beginning their slow trek across the room.

"Is this behavior common among humans? It's very rare among our people, though I have studied some aberrations." Sheyna babbled on, slowly helping Malachi to cross the few steps from the wall to the table.

"I find it disgusting...how anyone..." She propped him against the table, all the while surreptitiously checking his body for further injury.

"Ahhhh...careful. Ribs..."

"I know they hurt. I'm sorry. I'll be more careful." *I sense no broken bones, but there's hardly a place on you that isn't bruised or bleeding. I'm going to request water and towels to bathe your injuries. Is that okay?*

Yeah. I think that's okay. Just don't do anything to let on you have any Talent at all. That's all we've got going for us. If he learns we can communicate silently, I can guarantee we won't be allowed any contact at all.

Who is our captor?

I'm afraid it's the new WF battalion commander. I've heard a lot about him...none of it good.

Oh Malachi..."Okay. Do you want to sit, or...?" Sheyna helped him lie back on the lightly padded table. Malachi moaned as if in extreme pain. She hoped most of it was an act for the overhead camera.

Looking at the glass eye focused directly on her face, Sheyna fought the compulsion to snarl. "I need warm water and towels. Some bandages. This man is badly injured and needs treatment."

Immediately, a previously hidden door slipped open. The requested items sat within a small wire cage. Sheyna could see them but not touch them. She frowned.

"Touch yourself."

"What?" She stared at the speaker, at the strange command she'd just received.

"Touch yourself and you can have what you asked for."

"I don't understand. Touch myself where?"

"You're a female. Your species must find sexual gratification like any other species. I want to see you touch yourself. If I am satisfied, you can have what you requested."

Horrified, Sheyna glanced at Malachi. She touched his knee as if for balance.

Don't do it, Sheyna. I'll be fine. This guy is sick.

I need to see how badly you're hurt. I can't tell with all the blood. Malachi, I have to do what he says.

No!

Defiantly, Sheyna broke physical contact with Malachi so she could no longer hear him. She glared angrily at the camera and ran her palm slowly across her left breast.

It hurt when she rubbed the nipple. *Why?* She dropped her hand to her side and continued glaring at the camera.

"Not there." The mechanical sounding voice might have been a robot for all the inflection she heard. "Your breasts are hardly large enough to count as an erogenous zone. You will part the folds between your legs. Touch yourself as if you search for pleasure. I know what you look like. I want to know if you react at all like a human woman."

Swallowing back her anger and shame, Sheyna stepped far enough away from Malachi to be certain he couldn't sense her feelings. She was aware when he turned his head away. Was he ashamed of her or giving her privacy?

She used her fingers to part her labia. Vaguely aware of the mechanical sound of the camera moving, swiveling on its mount to follow her action, she slowly dipped one finger into her cunt. She was dry and unusually tender, but she rubbed the edge of her finger against her clitoris once, twice, then again before stopping.

She glared at the camera. Her heart thudded in her ears and shame rippled across her body.

Remembered shame? Something flickered, just beyond consciousness, a sense of filth, of evil…something beyond the evil surrounding her now? She shuddered and the memory faded.

Rigid, angry and embarrassed, she waited for a response, any response. Mere hours ago, she'd touched herself just like this for Malachi. Remembered passion made her shiver.

Fear left her cold and wanting.

A loud, clanking sound startled her. Sheyna spun around. The cage door opened slowly, making the water and towels available. Without a word she grabbed up the items and returned to Malachi.

He lay on the table, his back to her. Sheyna dipped the towel in the warm water and slowly washed the blood from his battered flesh. There were cuts and bruises wherever she touched, as if he'd been both whipped and beaten. She rested one hand on his naked hip to communicate. *I want you to know I would do whatever he asked if it meant I could help you.*

You don't deserve to be treated this way.

Neither of us does. I think, however, if we wish to survive, we must be prepared for more of the same. Personally, I intend to survive. Now, do not acknowledge what I am about to do.

Before Malachi could reply, Sheyna carefully *healed* his internal bruises and the deepest cuts. He would not appear healed, but there would be less pain. She worked quickly, disguising her restorative work under the slow sweep of the damp cloth.

Praise the Mother, Malachi was right. His injuries were not life threatening, but she knew they must be horribly painful. Whoever had beaten him had taken great pleasure with the whip about his groin and thighs. Bloody ribbons crossed the damaged flesh; his testicles were swollen and bruised.

She washed him as she might a child, careful to control her healing power to the injuries beneath the skin.

His back bled freely by the time she finished cleansing the blood and dirt away from his wounds. At least she'd repaired the bruises to his bones and deep muscle tissue.

I've done all I can. I'm sorry, but any more and the healing will be visible. If you can turn around, I'll help you off the table.

Malachi grunted, hesitated.

What's wrong? Are you still in much pain?

It's not what you think. Slowly, he rolled over as she'd instructed. His cock jutted out, erect and hard. *I'm sorry...I don't want you to misunderstand...it's not because of what that bastard made you do to yourself, it's...*

She stared at the swollen flesh, transfixed. In spite of the contusions marking him, the sight of Malachi's rampant erection sent a coil of heat through her gut. Just as suddenly, reality intruded. Sheyna blinked away the desire building within. This was neither the time nor the place. She brushed her hand lightly along Malachi's welted thigh, steering well clear of what she really wanted to stroke.

It's from the healing. Sometimes my touch has that effect on my patients.

The corner of his mouth twitched into a smile. *I imagine your skill makes you the most popular healer on Mirat.*

"Hold still," she said, studiously ignoring his erection and wiping at the blood on his chest a bit more vigorously. "This might hurt a bit."

"Ouch!" Malachi glared at her but his blue eyes were twinkling.

The speaker overhead clicked on. "You are obviously not hurt as badly as I imagined. Fascinating. I never expected a human male would react sexually to something as alien and bestial as this creature."

Another click left Malachi and Sheyna in frozen silence, alone except for the watchful eye of the camera.

Chapter 5

"What have you got?" Garan glared at his group of officers. They'd spent the past hour searching for Malachi and Sheyna. He'd searched mentally, as well, counting on the strong link with his sibling to help him find her.

There'd been nothing. Sheyna was either unconscious…or dead.

"We put our best empaths on it right after we discovered they'd gone missing." Shing Tamura, in charge of security, spoke first. "They started in the front room at the residence and picked up mindprints of four men, all World Federation troops."

Shing paused a moment as he studied Garan. "It appears they were sent to capture your *replacement*. They think Sheyna is the new Miratan lieutenant. Obviously, they don't realize you've returned mentally intact. We might be able to use that misinformation to our advantage."

"Damn." Thom Antoon slammed his fist on the table. "How the hell did they get past our guards? The clinic and Mal's residence are a good two hundred yards from the nearest gate."

Jenna walked into the room and shut the door behind her. "They managed to get in through the service entry at the back of the compound. Both sentries are dead. Security just recovered their bodies. Blunt trauma, blows to the head. They probably never knew what hit them."

"What?" Antoon leapt to his feet. "I checked that gate myself, first thing. Locks were up and the sentries were on duty."

"Unfortunately, I imagine the *sentries* you saw were WF lookouts wearing our kids' uniforms. They probably stayed at their posts well after the abduction to confuse any searchers." Jenna threw herself down on the low couch. "We must have been just minutes behind them."

Thom buried his head in his hands.

Shing continued as if he'd never been interrupted. "That fits. The empaths followed their trail through the service gate to that canyon just past the north ridge. It disappears there, which leads me to the conclusion they had aircraft, most likely a helicopter."

"Yet none of us heard a thing." Garan bowed his head, absorbing the pain of those around him. Malachi was both loved and respected by everyone in the room, yet he sensed the same depth of concern for Sheyna, a Miratan lioness many of these people had never met. "Do you know where this commander, Merrick White, has his headquarters?"

"I believe he's taken over an old armory near the ruins of Santa Fe. It's well fortified but not impenetrable." Thom Antoon walked across the room to a large map on the wall. It was quite old and many of the cities no longer existed. Still, he found the area just north of Santa Fe and pointed it out.

"Here. I've been inside the place, though not for years. According to our intelligence reports, Battalion Commander White has renovated much of the building without government approval."

"If he's willing to work without approval, that would explain kidnapping." Garan looked at his officers, weighing the abilities of each one. "Even the WF doesn't condone abduction of civilians."

"True. Which might mean we can go after what's ours without fear of interference." Shing Tamura folded his hands in front of him as if contemplating the possibilities. "We have a unit of Sensitives based near Santa Fe."

"Good." Garan turned to Antoon. "Thom, I'd like to command this raid, if you don't mind. Sheyna is…"

"I understand, Lieutenant." Thom nodded his approval to Garan.

Garan took a deep breath and said a short prayer to the Mother. "Okay, then. We'll work with the Santa Fe unit. Shing, why don't you contact them and set up a meeting point. We'll need telekinetics, empaths, telepaths for communication…" Ticking each Talent off on his fingers, Garan ran through the list of skills a rescue mission would require. Jenna moved to stand beside him. "…And of course, Jenna."

"With your permission, I can have a party assembled in about an hour." Antoon stood, obviously relieved to take action.

"I'd suggest we keep our group small. No more than a dozen. The Santa Fe unit has over a hundred members." Shing appeared satisfied when no one disagreed.

"We leave in an hour. It'll take Tim that long to get the ship ready, provisions loaded. We'll assemble here in forty-five minutes." Garan stood, effectively dismissing the meeting. Jenna's hand rested on his arm, transmitting the raging anger she obviously worked so desperately to control.

We will find them, my love, Garan said. *This commander has no idea the dangerous beast he has unleashed.*

Jenna looked up at him. Her eyes sparkled with tears but she smiled at his broad statement. *Are you referring to yourself, my love, to me, or to the rebels as a whole?*

I think any of us will be more than a match for Commander White.

* * * * *

"How long have we been here? My last memory is of two men rushing me in your quarters." Huddled together against the wall, Sheyna kept her voice low but chose to speak aloud. Malachi had grown weary from his wounds and it was harder for him to understand mindspeak.

"I think we've only been here a few hours. The guy who knocked on the door flattened me with some kind of gas...I think I saw at least three others. After they grabbed me I imagine they shot you up with some kind of drug or used the gas."

"That would explain my disorientation. The table itself immobilized me. I was aware of a hum coming from it, something mechanical."

"I saw it," Malachi said. "There was some kind of beam surrounding your body. It was barely visible in the dark, sort of a green glow. You didn't start moving until it shut off."

"Oh." Sheyna closed her eyes and leaned against him, hoping she would appear to be falling back asleep. She wasn't certain whether or not their captor observed them. She wrapped her hands around Mal's arm and projected her thoughts as clinically as she was able, hoping Malachi would understand.

I did not want to tell you, but you need to know...I believe I was intimately examined while unconscious. My breasts are smaller than those of human women but our nipples are still erogenous zones and quite sensitive. Mine are badly bruised, as if they've been pinched and twisted. I am sore inside, though I don't believe I've been raped. I have, however, been penetrated by something...his fingers, I think. There is no ejaculate on me, no sense of full penetration.

Malachi tensed and almost jerked away, but her grip on his arm tightened. *Control yourself,* she demanded. *I considered not telling you what I suspected because I did not want this reaction from you.*

I will kill the bastard. If he so much as touches you again, I will kill him.

The pure malevolence in the threat left little doubt he would follow through on his promise. Sheyna considered her words very carefully.

That is the reason I am telling you this. I don't believe he intends to touch us again. I think he intends for you to touch me.

Why do you say that? What makes you think...? Malachi turned to face her. Sheyna read the fierce struggle going on inside him.

I am a strong empath. I sense him, sense his sexual excitement, when he is watching through the camera or speaking to us. He must not be far away, possibly just on the other side of the wall. He is a voyeur, but a dangerous voyeur, one who enjoys inflicting pain, who derives his only sexual satisfaction from the pain of others. I believe he is sexually impotent, yet to him, sex is power. He will want to exercise that power through us.

He can't force me to rape you. I have that much control over my own body.

Sheyna held Malachi's face between her hands and saw herself reflected in his brilliant blue eyes. *In my studies of healing I learned of mental aberrations, including some about his type. There are many different ways to force actions from the innocent. I have told you my suspicions to prepare you for what might come, as well as to let you know that, whatever the consequences, whatever may come, I do not hold you either accountable or responsible.*

Malachi narrowed his dark brows and stared intently into her eyes. *You already sound like a victim,* he said. *Don't give up so easily.*

She thought about that a minute. There was no anger in his silent comment, merely frustration. Sheyna suddenly realized how different she and Malachi were. *The circumstances of our lives mold us. I have been a victim my entire life. As an outcast on my home world, I learned that, to survive, one must often take the route of least resistance.*

She prayed Malachi would fully understand her acceptance of what was to come, as well as her warning. Watching his brilliant blue eyes, she knew the moment he'd worked his way through the denial, the disgust and the frustration.

She felt him channel all of it. Direct it into an anger so powerful it became a living, breathing entity between them.

He touched her face, the thick mane cascading over her shoulders, closed his eyes a minute, then opened them, control intact. He moved away from her, his chest heaving with exertion. Suddenly, she heard his voice, a powerful voice in her mind without benefit of physical contact, Malachi's voice, powered by passion and anger.

I will always be responsible for my actions. I promise I will not hurt you. I also promise, on whatever honor I have, we will get out of here alive and make him pay.

Chapter 6

"You have rested enough. There is food. Eat. You will need your energy."

Malachi startled awake, surprised he could have slept in such an uncomfortable place. He detected an odd scent in the air and a strange, coppery chemical taste in his mouth. *We've been gassed. It appears to be venting now. Are you okay?*

Sheyna lifted her head from his shoulder and wrinkled her nose in disgust. *I have a terrible headache. Must be from the fumes.* Aloud, she said, "'There's a horrible stench in the air. What is it?" She glared at the camera when she spoke.

"Just something to help you sleep. Eat now. You will do as I say."

Glancing at Malachi, Sheyna stood up and stretched, as if putting on a show for their voyeur. "We've had visitors," she said, nodding at the new furnishings in the room. The long table she'd first awakened on was gone. In its place was a small dining table with two chairs, silverware and covered trays.

There was also a large metal-framed bed against the wall, directly beneath the roving camera. Leather shackles hung from both the headboard and footboard.

Malachi followed Sheyna across the room.

He pulled the chair out for Sheyna as if they dined in a fine restaurant, as if both of them were fully clothed, then sat across from her. *Is the food safe, do you think?*

I have no idea, she answered. *But I'm hungry enough to risk it. My last meal was on the ship.* She looked up at him and twitched her lip into a smile. *You've channeled your anger quite well. I hear you loud and clear.*

It had to go somewhere productive. I must admit, I can't believe I can communicate this well. Malachi gestured at the chicken dinner in front of them. "Can you eat this?"

You're doing great. "I'm okay with fowl and other meats, so this should be fine. Vegetables, too, but not starches like potatoes or your pasta. That's definitely human food. I can eat some fruits, but I don't really like them."

Do you think he'll question our inane conversation? Malachi took a bite, wondering aloud if the food had been drugged or poisoned.

I don't think so, but we need to keep talking as if all we have is verbal communication. "This tastes okay. I don't detect any chemicals."

They completed their meal in silence.

The waiting bed loomed like the proverbial white elephant in the parlor.

Sheyna grew more and more agitated as the meal progressed. She'd wondered about sex since she'd first discovered her clit when she was still a child.

She'd learned to ease the pressure of her needs through self-stimulation, but it had never been enough.

Suddenly, unexpectedly, the unwelcome vision of her sire flitted through her mind. Sheyna shuddered, equating Gard, somehow, with the invisible monster watching through his camera lens. Why would she suddenly see them as one and the same?

With long practice, she pushed thoughts of Gard from her mind.

If only she could dislodge her awareness of Malachi, the unexpected yearning she felt for him.

She fought her growing arousal. It was wrong to anticipate anything that would satisfy the perversion of their captor, but it was so easy to picture herself with Malachi, his smooth skin against her soft pelt, his hard cock finding entrance into her virgin passage. Her clit throbbed and the small nipples barely hidden beneath her fur ached as blood engorged the bruised flesh. Troubled, she glanced at Malachi.

He watched her, his expression serious, searching. *What are you thinking?*

That I am as perverted as our captor. My body tingles, my breasts ache. I hardly know you. I am the captive of a madman and yet I am very much aware of the bed across the room, of your strong body across the table.

She glanced down at the almost empty plate in front of her, struggling to control her sense of shame, of humiliation. *I am ashamed I think of you, of us, when there are still six young men in need of me. Ashamed that much of my anger over our capture is because our lovemaking was interrupted. My only concern should be the fact I've not healed your young patients.*

Malachi reached across the small table and covered her blunt fingers with his long, slender hand. She felt the connection, a shock that took her breath and jolted her heart into overdrive.

Malachi's self-deprecating words filled her mind. *The young rebels will be fine. They will be cared for until our return...and mark my words. We will return. As far as your shame...you would see, if I were to stand right now, that my mind travels the same roads as yours. I think our biggest problem should be that we can't let him know we might actually anticipate what he has planned for us.*

Troubled, Sheyna turned her hand in his and squeezed. She stared at their linked fingers for a moment, then raised her head to study the man across from her.

Assuming, she projected, *that* is *what he has planned...*Sheyna shivered as her thought dangled between them.

Chapter 7

"Garan? What is it? What do you sense?" Jenna rested her hand on Garan's arm, hoping his faraway look meant contact with his sister.

After a moment he sighed and lowered his head. "I had her. Just a brief sense of Sheyna, then it was gone, but...she's alive." He glanced at the clock over his desk. "We'll save them both. I have no doubt. The team's due here in a few minutes. Tim should have the ship ready by now."

"Tim said he's never powered it this far before." Jenna stuffed her remaining gear into a bag and threw it on the floor next to Garan's. "Think we can make it all the way to Santa Fe?"

"And back." The confident turn of Garan's head filled Jenna with love — and relief. She had been so certain she'd lost her great beast. Her hatred for Merrick White was without bounds...hatred of the madman who invented the device that almost took Garan away.

Jenna knew if she'd been born with claws like her mate's, they would be extended, much as his were. It hadn't taken her long to learn to read Garan's emotions. From the deep slant of his ears against his broad skull to the rapid twitch and flick of his long tail, she knew Garan, just as she, looked forward to the coming battle.

* * * * *

"Do you think the food was drugged?" Sheyna gestured toward their empty plates. "I don't sense anything *wrong*..."

"I don't think so. I do wonder, however, what our host has planned for us." Malachi glanced at the ever-watchful eye of the camera.

"You will secure the female to the bed. There are shackles." The disembodied, mechanical voice echoed out of the speaker.

Malachi glared at the camera. "What if I choose not to do as you say?"

"Then the same methods that restrained you will subdue the female. I have a number of willing soldiers ready to do their duty for

God and country. Of course, since she is female, their tactics may prove a bit more…intrusive."

Malachi shoved his chair back and stood. "No one will lay a hand on this woman."

"That remains to be seen, now, doesn't it?"

Sheyna placed her hand on Malachi's arm. "Don't fight him. Not now." *I sense madness…he will kill us both without remorse. Do as he says, for now.* Something else floated in the back of her thoughts. Another's madness? Puzzled, she stood up and walked across the room to the waiting bed.

She was regal, her step proud, her back straight, head high. Malachi swallowed his anger, giving into the moment to admire her strength and bravery, the lithe curve of her spine and the rounded sweep of hip. She was no victim, not this woman.

Her beauty, alien and unfamiliar, drew him like filings to a magnet. He shook his head, physically clearing his need for Sheyna from his mind. Then he quietly followed her and attached the restraints around her wrists and ankles as she lay back on the mattress.

The shackles were adjusted in such a manner that her arms were pulled directly behind her head, thrusting her small breasts forward. Her legs were spread wide, leaving her helpless and vulnerable.

Her thoughts were closed, as were her eyes. Malachi realized she did not want him to look into her eyes as he restrained her.

Deadening his emotions didn't work. He had little control over the passionate storm that left him shaking with rage. He took a few deep breaths, struggling to find an inner peace he'd long ago lost. The trembling in his hands eased.

Then he realized his movements had gone mechanical when Sheyna needed his strength more than ever. As an empath, she would feel his anger as well as his withdrawal.

I'm sorry, so very, very sorry…

She took deep, even breaths, as if struggling to contain her panic. *We will survive this. It is not your fault. Please, I do not blame you, Malachi. Do you see anything? Jenna said you were precog…*

I can't see my own future…yours, either. It's as if I feel so tightly linked to you; your life is hidden within mine.

Sheyna opened her eyes and stared solemnly at him. *I like that. It's good; to think we are linked so strongly.*

"Step away from the bed."

Malachi jerked in surprise. He'd managed to put their observer out of his mind for a brief moment. He turned and glared at the camera, then backed away a few paces.

Suddenly a door flew open. Sheyna cried out and tugged frantically at her shackles, her amber eyes wide with terror.

Four men rushed into the room and grabbed Malachi, hauling him farther away from Sheyna.

Malachi struggled, a madman out of control. "No, dammit! No!" Biting, clawing, twisting beneath their blows, he fought them even as they bound him with straps against the wall opposite her bed.

Chest heaving, he hung against the cement surface like a trophy, made helpless by a series of restraints over his thighs, waist and chest. He jerked his hands, grunting with the effort, but his wrists were manacled tightly to the rough wall, his ankles restrained the same way.

Cursing, threatening, he raged impotently against his bonds.

The four soldiers stood at attention, as if awaiting orders. Malachi stopped his cursing and directed his thoughts at Sheyna. He'd not tried it from this distance before.

Are you okay?

She nodded her head, but her attention was fixed solely on the four men. *I am attempting to control their movements. I've never tried it, except when I'm healing and need to restrain my patient. Do you have any kinetic ability?*

Very little. A bit of residual ability I retained after the link with Jenna. I've only used it with her, in gestalt.

If we get a chance alone together, we need to do a comprehensive link. It's the only way we'll be able to achieve a total meld of powers.

"You have your orders, gentlemen." The mechanical voice interrupted their silent conversation. The men eyed Sheyna with apprehension, curiosity and lust.

Malachi's blood ran cold.

"Sergeant...I understand you won the draw? You have fifteen minutes with the female." A dry chuckle echoed over the intercom. "We know she's female, don't we?"

Bloody rage stole Malachi's breath. Were these the animals that had already *inspected* her, who bruised and hurt her?

"There will be no penetration—not at this time, but you are allowed to be as...*creative*...as you wish. Make the creature orgasm. I'm curious to see if their responses are at all similar to humans. You will be rewarded for your success. Of course, there will be punishment for failure."

The men glanced apprehensively at one another. Malachi had heard tales of this deviant's idea of punishment.

The camera swiveled until it pointed at Sheyna. She looked directly into its glass eye and growled low in her throat, then turned to glare menacingly at the approaching soldier.

Malachi had not seen this side of her, the feral gleam in her eye, ears flat against her skull, her lips curled back to expose the sharp canines as she snarled like the cat she was. It was so easy to forget her feline ancestry, so enamored was he of the woman he was beginning to know.

The sergeant circled the bed warily, then ran his hand across her breast, keeping well away from her sharp teeth. He plucked at one tightly budded nipple, then grinned at his companions. "Small tits, that's for sure. 'Course, I never screwed a cat before."

"Yeah...I guessed that much, Sarge," one of the privates said. "Figured you stuck with sheep."

"Well, there's a first time for everything." The sergeant laughed nervously. He continued pinching her nipples, then leaned over and sucked one into his mouth. Sheyna bucked against him, but her moves only seemed to increase his interest. She snarled, tilting her head forward so that her snapping mouth was mere inches from the man's ear.

Anger is good, Malachi told her, feeling the red-hot tide of hatred rising in his veins. He'd been afraid she wouldn't fight. "Leave her alone," he shouted. "I'll kill any bastard who touches her."

"Shut the fuck up." The oldest of the four, the corporal Malachi remembered for his painful blows during the beating, raised his arm in a threatening gesture. "Go ahead, Sarge. Go for her clit. You've got time."

The sergeant grinned as he nibbled at first one puckered nipple and then the other. "Hell, I haven't tasted titty this nice in a long time. Hard to believe it's an animal...course if I close my eyes I can pretend she's a real woman."

He slurped noisily at her nipples.

"Only way you're ever gonna get any titty, Sarge, so's you might as well enjoy it. No real woman's gonna let you touch." The corporal laughed crudely at his idea of a joke.

"Yeah, well...they're little but real sweet." The sergeant stroked himself through his fatigues.

"Sergeant. I would suggest you use your time wisely." The disembodied voice brought the man to attention. He released Sheyna's nipple and circled her bed, studying her intimately. He finally settled himself between her legs and released his erect penis from his loose fatigue pants. Long and narrow but fully engorged, the organ bobbed proudly through the open zipper. It was obvious he enjoyed showing himself off to his companions.

The other three men openly fondled themselves, obviously fascinated by the bound creature on the bed as well as their sergeant's abuse of the captive.

The sergeant settled himself between Sheyna's legs, pressed his penis against her clit and began to rub against her with long, slow strokes. He kept up his rhythmic motion for almost five minutes without any reaction from Sheyna other than a low growling.

"You're running out of time, Sarge." The corporal tapped his wristwatch and giggled nervously. The two privates watched their sergeant through eyes glazed with lust as they continued stroking themselves through their army fatigues.

"Shit. That always works. She's as frigid as a damned iceberg. Maybe cat people don't come like real women." The sergeant climbed awkwardly off the bed and used his fingers on Sheyna. She snarled and bared her teeth, her fury a palpable force in the room.

Sarge backed away, breathing heavily. His erect cock still poked through his open pants. The biggest man there in girth and height, he dwarfed the young lioness. Malachi held his breath. Sheyna had kept her thoughts buried throughout the ordeal. He felt her anger and disgust but she didn't appear to feel shame. Thank God...there was no shame in her behavior.

"You have five minutes."

The sergeant glanced nervously at the speaker over the bed then once more stuck his thick fingers between Sheyna's legs. He rubbed vigorously at her clit while he tugged at his own swollen cock. Sheyna twitched her hips to avoid his touch.

It hurts, she said to Malachi. *He's hurting me.*

"You're hurting her, damn you. Stop it!"

The sergeant grinned maliciously at Malachi. "Nah, she likes it. See, she's movin' her hips." Suddenly he stopped rubbing and grimaced as his hand rapidly pumped his stiff cock. Groaning, he ejaculated on Sheyna's belly.

The three soldiers watching him laughed. Playing the showman, the sergeant carefully wiped his semi-erect penis on Sheyna's thigh before grasping it once more in his fist. He carefully stroked himself back to an erection, then, using his spilled semen as a lubricant, began rubbing vigorously at her clitoris once again.

I will kill them…every damned one of them. Malachi hung there, strapped against the wall, frustration and hate tearing at his gut. These men would die. He would see to it personally, even if they took him with them.

Sheyna snarled. Malachi felt her physical pain as she bucked her hips and twisted her body. The sergeant eyed her snarling mouth dubiously.

"Stop." The mechanical voice crackled to life. "Obviously this is not going to work."

The sergeant swung his head around to stare at the camera. He continued steadily pumping his erection as if totally unaware of the action. "Uh, Commander, I'd sure like ta finish my shot at her. I mean…"

"I agree, Sergeant. I believe, however, limiting your time is not going to work. Take all the time you want. Bring her to completion. Yourself again, as well, if you can." The voice paused. "Impressive."

The sergeant grinned proudly, obviously missing the sarcasm emanating from the speaker.

"As an incentive, if you fail, I will kill you."

Malachi noticed the man's erection immediately disappeared within his meaty fist.

"But…"

"That's all, Sergeant. Remember, no penetration. Now begin."

Chapter 8

Malachi, I am a healer. I cannot let him die. No matter how much I want him dead, I have taken an oath not to kill. Help me!

The bastard deserves to die! They all do. Malachi lunged ineffectively against the restraints. Blood trickled from his wrists and ankles where the webbing bit into his flesh. The soldiers ignored him. Their attention was all on Sheyna and the bulky sergeant studying her.

Sheyna's empathic senses were on fire. She'd managed to block most of the others' emotions, but now she felt the panic building, coiling in the pit of her gut like a live thing consuming her from the inside out.

Not mine, she realized. *I feel anger. The fear comes from the sergeant.* This man was as much a victim as she was. She could not be instrumental in his death.

Lunging frantically against her restraints, bucking her hips across the surface of the bed, she sent another urgent plea to Malachi.

Malachi! I am a healer. I cannot kill…if I do, I can no longer heal. Please, help me!

His frustration boiled across the room, frightening Sheyna with its power. *They deserve to die.*

They are victims, just as we are. I cannot live with this man's death on my head. I can't heal if I kill him. Don't you understand? You must help me.

How, Sheyna? He jerked against the shackles. *How can I help you? What if you just pretend? Can you act like you're coming?*

The sergeant glared at her from the foot of the bed, then walked around to the side. He'd tucked his flaccid penis back inside his pants. He touched her leg and Sheyna shivered in disgust as all his horrifying emotions suddenly blossomed within her mind. Unable to block the man, she focused on Malachi, on the anger and frustration pouring out of him, enveloping her with his own passionate desperation.

Too much! The burgeoning emotions swirled about her, overwhelming her with anger, fear, lust and pain. Spiraling higher and higher, sucking her deeper into a whirling tornado of multi-faceted passions.

Desperation empowered her. Marshaling her mental powers, Sheyna managed to throw up a partial shield against the sergeant's fear. The maelstrom of emotion paused, flickered and finally eased.

She slumped against the restraints, breathing deeply as she regained control. Resigned, she answered Malachi. *No...faking an orgasm won't work. The bed has sensors. I am aware of them. They will read my body's functions and responses and our captor will know.*

I have an idea. Malachi's blue eyes, even at this distance, seemed to crystallize with his intensity. *You will have to concentrate on me. Only me. Not on the man touching you.*

I can do that. I have him partially blocked.

Fantasize making love to me. Tell me what you would do if we were together, alone in the privacy of your quarters. What would have happened between us if we'd not been interrupted. I will do the same for you. It won't be acting, not for me. I've wanted you since the first moment I saw you. With any luck, with our minds working together, we may actually be able to control a bit of what he does. The only problem is, I don't know if you've felt any attraction to me or not. Is there any chance...?

Sheyna closed her eyes, limp with relief. *A good chance, Malachi. An excellent chance.*

*You're an amazing woman, Sheyna. You...*Malachi jerked angrily at his restraints when the beefy sergeant suddenly knelt between her legs.

Sheyna shuddered as the man separated her labia with his thick fingers. In spite of the block, she clearly perceived his fear of failure, his growing disgust at what he considered "rutting with an animal," his frustration with her lack of physical response to his touch—all wound tightly together with an overwhelming hatred of his commanding officer.

She had known immediately that none of the men in this room respected their leader. All feared him. All were disgusted by him. She might have felt sorry for each of the soldiers if not for their treatment of Malachi. They had enjoyed beating him. They wanted to do it again.

They would rather beat *her* than participate in this intimate assault.

A beating, she thought, would be preferable.

Suddenly, a beefy finger ran from her anus to her clit. At least his touch, for all his size, was not as hurtful as it had been earlier. Still, she was dry and sore from his diligent rubbing. Even a good fantasy wouldn't help if he continued to treat her roughly.

The other three men shuffled about near the bed. The acrid scent of fear and sex permeated the air. Sheyna couldn't allow herself to be distracted. She focused on Malachi.

Malachi...please, now, Malachi!

Sheyna twisted against her restraints and looked frantically across the room. Desperation and outrage poured from Malachi.

Malachi! Make love to me. Please?

She sensed the struggle in him as he fought to control his anger, as he searched for the fantasy he'd promised. She fought every instinct that told her to buck her hips, to jerk away from the sergeant's crude fondling. Instead, she slowed her breathing and focused on Malachi.

When she concentrated on his face, on the angles of his jaw, the perfect shape of his lips, the finger rubbing back and forth between her legs was not nearly so invasive.

She focused on Malachi's hands, strapped securely in their restraints. Blood dripped steadily from his wrists and she thought of the religious icons of old earth, the crucified Christ humans had worshipped.

He had been a healer, too.

Malachi's hands were healer's hands; the fingers long and supple, the nails neatly trimmed. She imagined his fingers massaging her labia, dipping into her vagina and spreading the hot moisture about her genitals. She shared that image with Malachi, let him see what she was fantasizing, invited him to join with her, to take the image and run with it.

Suddenly, Malachi's thoughts filtered into her mind. He'd closed his eyes. She knew he couldn't bear to watch the man touching her in such an intimate assault. Malachi's words came to her, soft and controlled, filled with passion and lush promises.

I'm touching you now. Can you feel me? My fingers are so sensitive to your heat. You must feel my touch as I stroke your flesh. You're hot...hot and wet...I dip my fingers into your moist center. The passage is tight but I feel your flesh yield. It yields for me...only me.

A soft moan escaped Sheyna's lips. *Malachi*...Malachi was the one touching her. Suddenly a rush of slick moisture eased the passage for his fingers.

I find a rhythm, the rhythm of the ages as I stroke in, then out, then back again. Two fingers, now three. You buck your hips against me, drawing me in deeper.

I have calluses on the pad of my thumb. I use them, gently brushing the taut little nubbin at the apex of your thighs, stroking that point of nerve endings and synapses that bring you pleasure. I imagine the callus rough against your sweet flesh, slick with your desire…hot.

She sensed her growing heat even as Malachi took her there. Her legs trembled with his touch; her breathing grew choppy, erratic.

I want to know your secrets, what makes your body tense and shiver, what draws the heat from your womb. I want to feel the subtle quivers and clenchings of your vaginal muscles, the inescapable truth of your passion.

Silky liquid pools between your legs. It eases the passage for my fingers. Slick heat surrounds my fingers. I imagine my mouth on you, your muscles tightening about my tongue. I want to taste you, excite you with tiny bites and warm kisses. I want to know you with my mouth.

Sheyna responded as Malachi's thoughts slipped like quicksilver through her mind. *Breathing is difficult. I gasp for air, panting, my breath coming in short, sharp bursts. Your fingers control me; take me where I've not been before.*

I've never been touched like this, never felt the passion growing and coiling in my womb, engorging my clit. My breasts ache…oh how they ache…I feel them throb and swell, my nipples are puckered and tingling with desire. I wish your lips were on my breasts, biting and nipping at them as you stroke the hot folds of flesh between my legs.

As if he was being directed by both Sheyna's and Malachi's thoughts, the sergeant turned his attention to her nipples, gently rubbing them with his free hand while he continued his gentle strokes between her legs. With Malachi's fantasy filling her mind, Sheyna let her excitement grow, knew the first tremors of orgasm hovering just beyond the moment.

Your breasts will have to wait for my mouth — now I kiss your belly, the soft mound above your clit, then encircle that wonderfully sensitive little bud with my tongue. Your taste is foreign but sweet, unlike anything I've ever experienced. I dip my tongue into your soft folds and lap the dew like honey. The strokes of my tongue are deep and slow, but so long as I can use my mouth, both my hands are free to touch your breasts.

Though tightly wrapped in Malachi's silken words, Sheyna still watched the man who touched her body. Frowning, a look of denial and confusion on his swarthy face, the sergeant slowly crawled up on the bed and knelt between Sheyna's outspread legs.

He lowered his face between her thighs and began lapping at her labia, taking particular care with her swollen clit. His big hands reached up and gently fondled her nipples, tweaking and pinching them into stiff peaks, each action following Malachi's fantasy.

The man's tongue swept slowly between her legs, just as Malachi described it, teasing at the entrance to her vagina but steering clear of the forbidden penetration. Sheyna moaned, hovering on the edge of orgasm, Malachi's passionate words filling her mind.

He was the one who tasted her. His hands tugged at her sensitive nipples and massaged her small breasts until they tingled and throbbed. Malachi's tongue lapped at the moisture pooling between her legs, his lips encircled her clit and suckled, so gently she wanted to weep.

Come for me Sheyna. Come, my love. Let me taste everything you have to give me. Let go and love me.

She whimpered, a mewling, kitten's cry, grinding her hips against his face, wanting him inside her, wanting him to fill her with heat and life.

I need you inside me, Malachi. I need to feel you inside!

Suddenly his tongue speared into her, the penetration she'd so far been denied, and she cried out, a harsh scream like a panther's cry, a shuddering explosion of passion, of need and anger.

She bucked against his face, grinding her swollen tissues against his mouth as he frantically licked and suckled, covering him with the liquid heat of her climax. Then, with a final shudder, her body went limp.

The sergeant rolled away from her, his face shiny with her fluids, his look one of disgust and relief.

The other three soldiers cheered and jeered until he stood up and silenced them with a curse, violently wiping his face clean of Sheyna's release. "Not a word, do you hear me? Not a word to anyone."

He turned and glared at Sheyna, eyes filled with hatred. He knew. He knew she had directed him, forced him to service her.

She might be the prisoner, but he had done her bidding.

Malachi hung from his restraints, his cock out-thrust, engorged and erect. His eyes were closed, his mind shuttered to her searching thoughts.

Tears coursed down his cheeks, dropped silently to the floor below.

Thank you, she said, closing her eyes as well. *Thank you, Malachi.*

Chapter 9

"Well done, Sergeant. Tell me, did you enjoy yourself?"

The sergeant looked ready to vomit. "No sir, I did not."

"You don't find our guest attractive?"

"No sir. The tits were okay, but it's an animal. I just been licking an animal's cunt. It's disgusting."

"I didn't tell you to do that, Sergeant. I would assume that approach was your idea."

"No sir. It wasn't. I never did that with a real woman before. Why would I do it to that?" He jerked his head and nodded in Sheyna's direction.

"Interesting. Why indeed?"

"It's unnatural, I tell ya. Unnatural. Something musta made me do it."

There was a long pause. "You may release the female's arm restraints. She'll be able to take care of her other bonds. I would suggest you leave the room quickly and stay out of reach once her paws are free. Her teeth and claws appear quite...functional."

"Corporal, release her manacles." The sergeant growled his command as he headed for the door.

The corporal looked around as if searching for an escape, then grabbed the shackles over Sheyna's head. He released her wrists and jumped out of reach in one movement.

The four men were gone from the room before she was able to free her legs and reach Malachi. She untied him, then stepped away, out of his reach.

"I'm filthy. Don't touch me."

Malachi reached his hand out, but again she stepped beyond his reach. "Sheyna, you..."

"I need to bathe myself. It's disgusting, what he did to me. I want his stink off my body."

Malachi turned to the ever-present camera. "I want warm water and towels and I want them now!"

A door opened and the requested items appeared. Malachi led Sheyna to a corner of the room, far from the prying eye of the camera and the sensors on the bed, and sat her down. He placed his own body between her and the ever-present camera, grabbed the bucket of water and the towels and proceeded to bathe her as if she were a child.

He cleaned the semen from her belly, then had her lie back on the floor. At first she balked, knowing what he intended.

I need to do this, he said. *Please. Let me wash their touch from your body. I should have protected you. I failed. I must do this, for both of us.*

She nodded and lay back as he asked. She'd been defiled by the sergeant's touch. When Malachi used the warm cloth to clean her belly and the tender folds between her legs, Sheyna began to understand the depth of the healer's caring.

He had entered her mind, given her the fantasy she'd begged for, the orgasm she'd needed to save the life of his tormentor. He'd been beaten, drugged, restrained and forced to watch her assault, forced to participate, and still he treated her like a precious and fragile thing.

No matter what the future brought, Sheyna knew she owed him more than her life.

*   *   *   *   *

Garan quietly addressed the assembled Sensitives. "We've made contact with the unit near Santa Fe. They're expecting us. There's a warehouse where we can hide the ship and a number of folks familiar with the armory and the layout of the base. Are you ready?"

"Yes, sir." Tim Riley swung his gear aboard the small scouting ship, one of Miratan design used rarely and then only for emergency travel. Earth's population was growing more familiar with the possibility of friendly aliens living among them, but for many the memories of a disastrous attack years earlier were much too horrific. It was better for all concerned to keep alien airships out of the sky.

The members of the rebellion kept their ties to Mirat as low key as possible. At some point they would formally introduce Garan's people to earth—once the rebellion ended. For now, the alien presence remained as much rumor and conjecture as absolute fact.

"Thom, give everyone the coordinates. You're captain on this run so we'll follow your lead." Garan settled himself in the co-pilot's chair and fastened his safety belt.

Thom's soft drawl took over. "Jenna, would you please link with me and give my lift a boost? The rest of you, join once Jenna and I have the ship airborne. We'll let you know when we're ready."

As often as she'd practiced this form of travel with the other Talents, Jenna still thrilled every time she took part in powering a vehicle through the air with the kinetic abilities she'd so recently discovered within herself.

She settled comfortably in the seat directly behind Garan, fastened her safety belt and steadied her arms on the padded rests. Thom's mind touched hers with the destination coordinates and she grinned in anticipation, opening her mind to all its power so that he could draw on her Talent.

Within seconds they were airborne, eleven Talents working in gestalt to power the small ship through the afternoon haze. Garan remained apart from the group, a single powerful mind not linked with the others, available in case of emergency.

Travel this short distance was practically instantaneous. Within seconds they hovered over the landing site, a small parking lot in the ruined outskirts of Santa Fe. Immediately after Garan reported contact with the local commanding officer, wide doors on an apparently abandoned warehouse swung open and the ship slipped silently into the darkness.

Jenna gave a great sigh of relief the moment they touched the ground. Thom gave a "thumb's up" and Shing Tamura crossed himself.

"I will never get used to that," he said, releasing his safety belt and standing up. "It is absolutely unnatural."

"Sure beats walkin'." Thom Antoon gave Shing a friendly pat on the shoulder, gathered up his gear and followed the rest of the rebels out of the ship.

They gathered in the darkened interior, approximately two dozen members of the Santa Fe unit and the twelve-person team from Rebellion Headquarters. "Lieutenant Garan? I'm Steve Canon, captain of the units in this quadrant. Welcome. We've been looking for an excuse to take out Commander White for a long time."

"Good to meet you, Captain. I understood he was fairly new to the area?" Garan slung his gear over his shoulder and followed the men to a conference room at the back of the warehouse.

"He's the new battalion commander, but he's been around for about three years. Actually, he's probably done more good for the rebellion than he has for the WF...over half our units are made up of deserters from his command."

"I will admit, from what I've heard of him I am growing more concerned for my sister's and our healer's safety." Garan glanced at Jenna. She sensed the amazing control under his calm demeanor. Merrick White most definitely did not have a clue about the beast he'd unleashed.

"I heard you were caught in that machine of his. It's good to see you're okay. Too bad about the others." Canon nodded his sympathy.

"Garan's sister, Sheyna, healed one of them, Captain. We need to bring her back safely. There are six more young men who need her. We have to get her back." Jenna's voice broke. Garan's arm wrapped around her shoulders and she felt his strength pour into her.

"Supposedly, White's got a lot of toys he likes to play with. Let's hope he's not had time to use them on his captives. Luckily, we've been making plans to go after him for quite some time. Here's what we're going to do..."

Chapter 10

They lay in the darkened room on a makeshift pallet of towels and the bedding taken from the large bed where Sheyna had been tied. They had to believe there were no sensors in the floor.

Malachi kept his arm wrapped tightly around Sheyna's shoulders. She had burrowed into his side, hiding her face against his chest as if trying to hide her shame.

He stroked her sleek flank, offering what comfort he could. He'd never felt so helpless. Many women of the rebellion had been raped and assaulted over the past few years. He'd offered what help, as a healer, he was able to give.

He'd never witnessed their assault, had absolutely no idea of the true degradation they'd suffered. He knew he would never treat another woman as he had in the past. Not after what had happened today.

Malachi?

I hear you. Are you okay?

I have something more to ask of you, Malachi. Something important.

Anything. You know I will do anything for you. He tilted her chin and kissed her. The room was dark, so dark there was not form or substance for him to see, only the memory of her sleek beauty, of her powerful response to his words.

Love me. Now, while our captor sleeps and the room is dark. Show me what love feels like.

Are you sure? After what happened…

After what happened, I want to feel clean. I want to feel the weight of your body on mine, shiver at the touch of your hands…must I beg it of you, Malachi? Do you see me as an animal, a beast, as that man did?

She shuddered in his arms. Suddenly Malachi realized how difficult it had been for her to make such a request. His admiration for her grew — admiration and something more. Something that tugged at his heart, worried his mind…something he'd not felt for any woman before.

Could he make her understand?

I see you as someone precious to me beyond value, perfect in every way. I felt it the moment I first saw you, as if the one most important thing in my life, forever missing, had finally been found. He brushed the tangled mane back from her eyes and kissed her brow.

In the dark, he could easily have imagined her as a human woman in his arms. Instead, his mind lingered on her cat-like beauty, the panther's gleam in her amber eyes, the thick mane framing her lovely face. He stroked the soft fur covering her shoulders and shivered with the pure eroticism of the silky pelt against his palm.

I imagined this. Just yesterday when I held you in my arms in the early morning hours at the clinic. I had watched you heal William, a young man I'd given up for lost, had envied him your soft touch and warm concern. I wanted you then, all of you. Felt the need to bury myself in your heat so badly, but I was afraid.

Afraid? She reached up and brushed the side of his face with the backs of her fingers. He nuzzled the soft fur; the silky warmth of her hand, then kissed her palm.

Afraid you would be insulted by the direction of my lustful thoughts.

He felt her soft laughter as much as he heard it in his mind. *Then I probably shouldn't tell you where my thoughts were…are.*

I'd rather you show me…or maybe I'll show you. He wished for light, but darkness and a good imagination would have to do. Malachi raised himself up on one elbow. Leaning over Sheyna's quiet form, he stroked her inner thigh with the tips of his fingers, then followed with his lips.

She was sleek…sleek and warm like close-cropped mink, but when he reached the apex of her thighs the mink was hot and slick, already wet with her release.

Are you okay? I don't want to hurt you…

There is no pain when you touch me. Only pleasure.

He lapped at the soft folds and tasted flavors unlike anything he'd imagined. *Cinnamon…you taste of spice to me. Cinnamon and brown sugar.*

She arched her hips when his tongue found her, but her cries were soundless words in his mind. Malachi grasped her firm buttocks and held her, kneading at the flesh as his tongue discovered the creases and folds, the pulsing nubbin he knew would bring her pleasure.

He felt her struggle for silence, knew she bit her lips to keep from crying out as he explored her as intimately as he pleased.

His fingers found the crease between her buttocks, stroked the sensitive flesh and teased her until she trembled. He let his tongue wander, delving into her wet passage, lapping at the engorged folds, encircling her swollen clit until she grasped at his hair with fluttering, lifeless fingers.

Suddenly she pushed him away. *No...I do not want this alone. I want you inside. I want to feel you swelling against me, thrusting inside me and know you are as aroused, as frenzied with need as I am.*

Malachi gasped for breath and prayed for control. He turned Sheyna over on her stomach and raised her hips. He knew from his link with Sander, so many years ago, exactly how to please a female of Mirat.

She was slick and hot and oh, so tight. He held his cock in one hand and opened her virgin passage with the other. One finger, then two until she bucked against him, begging with her body for more.

She was wet and hot, ready for him. He entered her slowly, engulfed in her heat, struggling against an overwhelming sensation — the rhythmic clenching of her vaginal walls against his hard cock.

He grasped her hips in both his hands, holding her steady, supporting her body

The rhythm drew him deeper, past the slight obstruction of her virginity. He paused, afraid he might have hurt her, but she pressed her hips back against him, the sweep of her taut buttocks a universal invitation for more.

Finally, after what seemed an eternity, Malachi was buried completely inside, control hanging by a thread. *If you move, I am lost.*

If you don't move, I may have to kill you.

He almost laughed aloud. Instead, he slowly withdrew, then thrust into her with a bit more force. His hands slipped along her sides to cup her breasts. She tilted her hips back against him. Taking her lead, Malachi drove into her hot passage once more, then again, gaining speed and force with each penetration.

He trailed his fingers along her belly and found her clit, swollen and waiting for his touch.

She groaned, a long, low moan of pleasure as he gently encircled the little organ in his fingers, rubbing and stroking with the gentlest of pressure.

*I can't...I can't...oh, Praise the Mother, Malachi...I...*her incoherent mental babbling was lost in a silent scream, her shoulders curved forward and her back arched against him, driving him to even deeper penetration.

Her muscles tightened around him, a series of pulsing contractions that rippled the length of his sensitive cock. Gritting his teeth to avoid crying out, Malachi felt his balls tighten and retract, drawing up tightly between his legs. He shuddered with the hot coil of pain and pleasure rippling from his belly to his cock.

Thrusting, driving deeper, harder, her slick heat enfolding him, surrounding him in pure liquid sensation, he rode her climax into his own. Gasping for air, he caught her strong thighs in both hands, pulling her tight against him.

One thrust, another, and Malachi spiraled into the abyss with her. Sheyna fell forward, obviously spent. Malachi lowered himself with her, still deeply imbedded within her wet heat. Her muscles continued to spasm around him, his cock continued to twitch with each tiny movement, and he was certain the thundering beat of his heart must echo against the walls of their prison.

When the speaker in the wall remained silent, when nothing appeared to disturb their rest, Malachi finally allowed himself to relax against Sheyna's warm body. He pulled a blanket up to cover them and rolled to one side. Still buried within her welcome folds, he finally allowed himself to drift off to sleep.

Sheyna's soft *thank you* lingered well into his dreams.

Chapter 11

Garan sensed Tim's return long before the lanky young man emerged from the tree-shrouded hillside. "Is everyone in place?"

"Yes." Tim's low-pitched reply didn't hide his excitement. "We've got the entire compound covered and the outermost sentries have been neutralized. Members of the Santa Fe group have taken up the positions."

"Jenna? Do you sense anything unusual?" Garan knew his pride in her was obvious to anyone within hearing. He also knew there wasn't a more powerful Sensitive in existence than his beautiful life-mate.

Jenna shook her head, frowning. "I sense something but I'm not sure what it is. Some type of force, very faint, almost as if it's a part of the earth around us. I haven't been able to determine its origin."

"Is it mechanical or natural? This area has long been thought holy by the native people. Do you sense its nature? Can you tell what it does?"

She flashed Garan a wry grin. "I'm good, Garan, but not that good."

"I wouldn't say that." He wrapped his arm around her shoulders and gazed westward. The sun had long since set. Now a slender turquoise ribbon against the mountain peaks hinted at the last light of day. "Continue to monitor. Most likely it's a natural emanation from the rock formations."

Steve Canon slipped quietly into the clearing. "I think everything is as ready as it's going to get. White'll have them in a room he calls his dungeon. From what a few of the deserters have told us, it's set up with all kinds of equipment for observing and torturing his prisoners. The guy is sick and if we want to save your people, we need to move quickly."

Garan closed his mind to thoughts of SheShe. He could not, would not, let his fears for her interrupt his concentration. She'd been captive of this madman for close to twenty hours now. "I want specifics. I need to know everything about him."

"He's into rape and forced sex, but from what his men say, he's impotent. They've been ordered to rape prisoners, do lots of degrading things. He likes torture, usually of a sexual nature. He's never in the room. Watches it all on camera from a private booth. He stays in there, sometimes for days at a time."

"How has he managed to retain control of his troops?" Thom Antoon shook his head in disgust. "Why haven't all of them deserted?"

"A lot of them have, but the rest? They're scared to death. If they're caught, they're sodomized by other soldiers. It appears White has collected enough degenerates who enjoy his brand of *recreation*. Afterward, if the deserters are still alive, they're put to death by their fellow soldiers, but it's never done quickly. The depravity goes pretty deep—it's all filmed and the rest of the troops have to watch. I imagine it's a pretty forceful lesson."

"This is something I will never understand." Garan's lip curled back in disgust. He took a deep breath, searching for control. His anger seethed like a separate entity, deep in his chest.

"We know he is, at some level, a genius," Canon added. "He invented the machine that got you, Lieutenant, and we've heard of other projects he's been working on. All of them work with forces just outside current science, as if he's a step ahead of everything else the WF has got, or the Sensitives, for that matter. That weapon was not approved by the World Federation. Even they won't stoop so low."

A low growl rumbled through Garan. "Jenna, it will be up to you to scan for this bastard, once we get close enough for you to feel him. If he has harmed Sheyna in any way…"

The soft threat, unspoken, hovered in the cool evening air. Following Garan's lead, the Sensitives moved as one toward the compound in the valley below.

* * * * *

A coppery, chemical taste was the first thing Malachi noticed as he returned to consciousness. That, and the fact he was once again shackled to the wall. His shoulders ached and his head pounded in time with the beat of his heart. *Dammit Sheyna, the bastard's gassed us again. Are you awake?*

Sheyna?

He opened his eyes to the glaring brightness of the overhead lights. The door hung open.

No one else was there.

"Sheyna!" He jerked against the restraints, twisting his body in a futile effort to free himself. The stiff leather abraded his wrists and ankles, tearing the already wounded flesh.

Sheyna! Where are you?

Silence met his cries. Where once he'd felt her soft mental touch, *nothing.*

"Sheyna!"

His scream ended on a sob. Beaten, hopeless, Malachi sagged against the restraints. Blood from his torn wrists trickled along his forearms. More blood dripped from his chafed ankles to the cold floor.

Silence. Overwhelming silence. Even the omnipresent buzz from the overhead speaker was gone.

There was absolutely nothing he could do.

* * * * *

The Sensitives slipped quietly through a back gate to the compound. Jenna felt the hair on the back of her neck rise, sensed the ever-present *something* grow stronger, more defined. Blending into the shadows with the other troops, including Shing, Tim Riley and Garan, she reached out with her mind, searching for the source of whatever power existed here.

I don't like this, Garan. We're being watched...studied in some way. Do you feel it?

No, but I don't doubt your feelings. Silently, Garan passed Jenna's warning on to the other combatants. *Something watches us. Take great care. Alert the sentries.*

Have you searched for Sheyna? Jenna touched Garan's arm in the darkness. *Is there any sign of her?*

Suddenly, Jenna halted. *Malachi? But he can't project any distance...*

A primal scream shattered her thoughts.

Sheyna!

This way! Hurry! I hear Malachi! Jenna leapt over a small retaining wall and raced down a dark corridor. Garan and half a dozen soldiers followed close behind her.

Suddenly, Jenna halted, stopped midway by something invisible but compelling. She felt the force of some sort of shield, knew it attempted to hold her, but her superior mental strength broke her free of its binding.

"Careful." She traced the contours of the field with her mind while the others waited impatiently behind her. *There.* She pointed to a small crevice in the ceiling. *Together!*

Working together like the well-trained team they were, Jenna, Garan, Shing and Tim focused their kinetic ability on the mechanism controlling the force field.

The ceiling split and a small circuit board dropped to the floor, shattering into a dozen pieces. Jenna didn't hesitate. Without a backward glance she raced through the corridor for another fifty paces, then halted at an open doorway.

"Ohmygod. Garan! It's Malachi."

Bruised and bloodied, he hung lifelessly from the wall. Jenna reached him at the same time as Garan and Shing. Garan grabbed his body, supporting him as they quickly unlatched the shackles holding him upright. When he was free, Garan lifted Malachi away from his bonds and laid him carefully on the floor.

Calling on the healing ability she'd gained from Malachi during their link, Jenna used his own powers to bring him back to consciousness.

He blinked, obviously disoriented, then struggled to sit up. "Sheyna? Have you got Sheyna?"

"No." Garan eyes narrowed and darkened. "Do you have any idea where she is?"

"Bastard!" Malachi spat the word, then lowered his head to his hands. "We have to get her back. There's no telling what that madman will do to her."

"Lieutenant! Hurry!" Steve Canon appeared in the doorway. "There's a chopper leaving from the recreation yard. Looks like the woman might be on board."

"Don't worry about me. Go!" Malachi shoved Jenna toward the door even as he pulled himself to his feet. Cursing his injuries, his weakness, he stumbled after them.

Garan, Jenna and Tim were already outside when Malachi reached the door. They stood together, hands linked, staring intently at the helicopter disappearing in the night sky. Suddenly Jenna broke the link.

"We can't. It's too dangerous to try and turn it kinetically. I've got a good link on White, though. Sheyna must be unconscious. I don't feel her at all. I'll know where he goes, though. Thom, can you and Tim get the ship? Just the two of you? Garan and I can round up the rest of our group."

Garan turned to Steve Canon. "Have your men secure the area. Don't touch any of Commander White's toys. We may need to know how they work if we're going to rescue Sheyna."

"Will do." Canon nodded to Malachi. "You gonna be okay? We've got a good medic."

"Thanks. I'm okay. What I really need is a pair of pants." He turned to Garan. "I'm going with you."

Garan curled his lip in what Malachi assumed was a humorless smile. "I assumed as much." He paused, then looked intently at Malachi, as if really seeing him for the first time, as if sensing a connection to this man who was so closely linked to both the women in his life. "How is my sister? As a healer, what is your opinion? Has she been harmed in any way?"

Malachi sighed. "Physically, she will recover. She's been badly abused and I know she feels degraded by that abuse. Merrick White is a madman. I won't sugarcoat it. We have to get her back, Garan. Soon."

Steve Canon handed Malachi a pair of camouflage pants and a tee shirt. Another soldier appeared with canvas boots and a couple pair of socks. The Miratan ship hovered over the field as Malachi finished tying up the laces.

He boarded the ship with the twelve members from his home base. Twelve strong Sensitives and a battered healer going up against one madman.

Malachi only hoped it would be enough.

Chapter 12

A hood covered Sheyna's eyes and her hands were tightly bound. Her feet had been left free so that her captors could drag her onto the helicopter without having to carry her. She went without a struggle, her mind tightly shielded.

For now.

She knew anything she did to fight the madman who held her would jeopardize Malachi. Though she'd been immobilized by the gas when the soldiers dragged Malachi away from her, Sheyna had sensed his absence with every beat of her heart.

She slumped against the leather seat; concentrating on the heavy *thump, thump, thump* of the blades as the pilot prepared for escape. Suddenly, the tiny craft lifted off, tilting wildly to one side in a scatter of wind and noise. Her body lurched against the seat belt holding her securely in place.

She carefully lowered her shields and reached out, wondering how many were aboard, how many she would have to kill in order to be free.

Three. There were three others aboard, all male. Two were terrified, uncertain, their minds a disturbing tangle of fear and subservience.

The third...*blocked?* A Sensitive mind, here, among Federation troops?

Sheyna tested the edges of the powerful shield, then withdrew before discovery.

The madman has Talent. But does he know? Or, is he latent, unaware of the power he might unleash?

Treading on safe ground, Sheyna cast her scattered thoughts about for Malachi.

Nothing.

Was he dead? Had this monster killed the healer while they slept, unconscious from the gasses pumped into the room? While they slept, Malachi's flaccid cock still resting within her sated flesh? His arms wrapped tightly around her waist, his face buried in her thick mane?

Sheyna moaned quietly. To have finally found the satisfaction, the pleasure she'd only heard of, the man she'd never expected, and then to have it all snatched away.

Suddenly she had a greater awareness of the pain Jenna must have felt when Garan was first injured.

Jenna had her lover back.

Where are you, Malachi?

A subtle but familiar touch warmed Sheyna's fear.

Jenna?

Thank goodness you're alive! I couldn't find you…I thought you were dead. Malachi's with us. With Garan and me. He's safe.

Praise the Mother! I feared him dead!

He's okay. I swear it. Do you have any idea where your captor is taking you?

No. We just left the compound a few moments ago. I don't know my directions on this world. None of the points feel familiar to me. I'm sorry.

We'll find you, Sheyna. Hang on. Keep your mind open to my thoughts. I'm here.

I know. Please, tell Malachi I'm sorry.

Sorry? For what?

This monster wanted me. Malachi got in the way. He tried to protect me. He…

Sheyna? Sheyna…where are you?

"I don't understand, Garan. We were in direct communication and suddenly her mental touch disappeared." Jenna shook her head in frustration.

"He knows." Malachi's soft voice radiated a hatred none had felt from the healer before. "He knows when she communicates. We thought we were keeping it secret, but the bastard has Talent. I'm sure of it."

"That would explain a lot." Garan's soft reply contained his anger well. "Here's the ship. We know they were headed almost due west. Let's assume they're on the same course, at least for now."

With silent nods the company quickly boarded the Miratan ship. Thirteen, now, with Malachi added. Jenna joined the link and the ship lifted silently into space. Once they were airborne, she withdrew her power from the gestalt and searched the heavens for Sheyna.

It was a slow process, but chafing at the speed of their search would not help Sheyna. Jenna let her mind float free; her senses open to Sheyna's fear. Malachi moved closer and grasped her hand. *Feel my love for her. Feel my anger. I can't reach her, but let my passion give you power.*

Garan stepped up and grabbed Malachi's other hand. The strength of the link grew with Malachi at its center. Jenna felt the power of their combined mental prowess, the passion of the three who loved Sheyna most.

I feel her.

As do I. Malachi's hand trembled in Jenna's and she squeezed his fingers. Garan nodded in reply.

"She's afraid, but she is okay," he said.

"Actually, she feels really pissed off to me." Jenna gave Malachi's hand another squeeze.

Malachi sighed, a catch in his throat the only evidence of the barely controlled emotions tangling his thoughts. "I hate for her to be afraid. She's..." He looked down at Garan's huge paw still clasping his hand. He thought of Sheyna's, the way her hand felt stroking his face, the soft brush of the warm fur.

"Garan, I..." Malachi shoved both hands in his pant pockets. "Sheyna is...I..."

"I know, my brother." Garan's lip curled in a brief smile. "I feel your love for my sibling in everything you do and say. It's good. My lifemate has convinced me I am not to act the overbearing, older brother."

Malachi gave Jenna a sideward glance, then nodded at Garan. "We have to find her. We've got to get her away before that madman harms her any more than he already has."

"I've got 'em!"

Tim Riley's voice echoed over the speaker system.

"Coordinates, please?" All business, Garan quickly strapped himself into the co-pilot's seat.

Thom Antoon, Jenna, Shing Tamura and Malachi took up positions directly behind. The rest of the group readied themselves for action.

Tim relayed the information to everyone on board.

"I recognize that area," Thom said. He pulled a much-folded map out of his pocket. "It used to be a national monument. Bandolier, I think it was called. There's a really deep canyon, lots of old Native American cliff dwellings, places of ancient civilizations."

"Accessible by helicopter?" Garan turned around in his seat to glance at the map.

"Possibly. Once we're closer, let's try and pinpoint their exact location, then land on the rim above. It'll be easier to work our way down than to try and climb up."

Within seconds, the linked minds of the crew located Sheyna's familiar mindprint. Working together, they moved the silent ship to a hidden position on the canyon's rim, slipping it beneath a copse of fir trees.

The midnight darkness enveloped them in a silent shroud.

Malachi reached out with his thoughts, praying for the strength to find Sheyna on his own. A familiar touch, a brief whisper of love caressed his mind, a promise of hope. Smiling grimly, he joined the others outside the ship.

Chapter 13

"Be certain she is secure. Those claws look fully functional."

That voice!

"Yes, sir. Should I remove the hood, sir?"

"No. Leave it in place. Pull that leg tighter, Corporal. You're sure she can't get free?"

"Absolutely, sir. Prisoner is secured."

Sheyna felt a rough hand on her lower leg, as someone tested her bonds again. She forced herself to remain motionless, unmoving. To concentrate on the voice, the shackles holding her hands above her head, her legs stretched wide, the unseen surroundings.

The surface they'd secured her to was hard and rough, the texture of sandstone or granite. She couldn't be certain. She smelled the thick stink of burning kerosene, glimpsed a narrow ribbon of lantern light beneath her blindfold.

One thing she did know—this place was ancient, filled with the spirits of humans long gone. She felt their souls, sensed their essence in the very air she breathed, in the brush of wind against her cheek in an otherwise still room.

Suddenly, the rapid tattoo of automatic weapon fire shattered the silence.

Sheyna heard a groan, a cry...the soft *thud* of bodies hitting the ground.

"I apologize for startling you."

There was no doubt. Even without the metallic buzz of transmission, this was the voice she'd heard through the speaker when she and Malachi were first imprisoned.

Was it only yesterday?

"However, I no longer wanted them here. I've decided you're the only one I need...for now, anyway."

There was the sound of something heavy sliding across the floor, the clatter of rocks and debris as if it was pushed from an edge of…*what*…? Again, the same noise, a grunt, as if from exertion, the clatter and rattle of rocks…the sense of two fewer souls in the room.

"I know you speak English. I've heard you. Fascinating, to hear civilized speech coming from the lips of an animal. I am Merrick. The other man, the captive? He called you Sheyna. That's a lovely name…a lovely name for a fascinating creature."

Sheyna struggled to control her breathing, her fear and anger. It escalated, built upon itself and something *else*…something evil, something long hidden in the depths of her mind.

Why can't I remember?

A single finger traced the length of her thigh. It reached higher, paused in the soft, thick fur covering her pubis.

Again a memory tickled the corners of her thoughts before fading into fear.

His thick fingers cupped her mound.

She trembled.

"Amazing. Feels like mink." His hand rested between her legs.

She sensed the coiled desire in him, the need for control, the frantic search for physical satisfaction so often denied him. He broadcast his needs so explicitly, Sheyna knew exactly what he wanted of her, what he expected.

In graphic detail.

Malachi had been right. This man was Sensitive, possessed of a powerful latent talent he didn't recognize.

"You're not human, but what are you? I saw pictures of the other one, male, I assume. First proof there really were aliens in that damned compound. I took care of him, though." There was a dry chuckle, an indrawn breath.

He rubbed his fingers between her legs. Sheyna held herself rigid. His loathsome touch was a parody of the sensual strokes Malachi had given her mere hours ago.

"You know, first time I explored you, you were unconscious. I find it much more stimulating, knowing you are aware of my touch. Did you know that? Were you aware how closely I examined you?"

His voice deepened. "Did you find it exciting, my lovely alien? Did it make you hot, imagining what I might have done while you were sleeping? Do you have any idea how closely I touched?"

He giggled. The sound of madness. Sheyna clenched her jaw to keep from screaming. "I bit your nipples. Couldn't help myself. That was exciting. I couldn't get enough of them. Ah, but the sergeant...suckling your nipples, even licking you! Imagine, that idiot having the temerity to stick his tongue between your legs. It was...nice...to watch. Very nice."

Sheyna heard nothing but his quick, shallow breath, felt his hands convulsively grasping between her legs. Suddenly, he paused.

"Oh my! What have we here?" His fingers clenched tightly in her fur and she sensed his surprise. "For you, my lovely guest. In your honor. It looks like the General is making his appearance."

Sheyna barely controlled a shudder. She'd been so certain Merrick was impotent. Somehow he'd managed an erection. Now she sensed lust, his uncontrollable desire for sex. His fingers grabbed the thick fur covering her mound, squeezing her flesh in a painful grasp. She bit her lips to keep from crying out.

Something black, evil and horribly familiar boiled in her brain.

Frantic, Sheyna reached out with her mind, a mental scream of primal fear.

Malachi! Where are you Malachi? I need you!

* * * * *

"Do you hear her?" Malachi grabbed Jenna's arm. "Sheyna. She's calling for help!"

Jenna paused in mid stride and narrowed her eyes in concentration. "Below us. To the left. Garan? We have to hurry."

Silently, Malachi, Jenna and Shing Tamura scrambled over the edge of the rocky cliff. Garan, Tim Riley and Thom Antoon circled around from the opposite side, crawling like spiders across the steep slope above an ancient cliff dwelling.

Sheyna? Sheyna! We're coming. Hang on! Malachi felt the rage growing as his sense of danger grew. He followed Jenna's silent figure along the narrow trail she'd somehow discovered. Cut sharply into the face of the cliff, it offered no room for error.

Jenna glanced back at him; her moonlit eyes all that were visible in the darkness. *You didn't used to be able to project your thoughts. I hear you loud and clear.*

Once before, when Mara Armand and her mate, Sander were threatened. I called her to me. I haven't been able to since, not until Sheyna.

We'll save her, Malachi. Jenna paused behind a large outcropping of rock. A pale glow of lantern light spilled out from the opposite side. Shing and Malachi moved in silently behind her.

Malachi! Help me!

Let's move!

Sheyna's mental cry and Garan's silent command threw the six members of the team into coordinated action. Jenna went in over the top with Shing and Malachi circling in from the side. Garan, Thom and Tim Riley raced directly into the ancient room.

Malachi knew he would never forget the ugly scene that met them.

Sheyna's nude body tied to a stone altar stained with the blood of ancient sacrifices, the floor and walls spattered with the fresh blood of Merrick White's soldiers. White himself, his camouflage fatigues draped around his ankles, kneeling between Sheyna's outstretched legs.

Before Malachi could act, Garan grabbed White, one hand around his throat, the other in a death grip between his legs. He held the man above him mere inches from his bared fangs and roared in unrestrained bestial fury. Malachi rushed to Sheyna's side as Garan hurled his screaming captive out and over the ledge.

Merrick White's strangled shriek ended abruptly in a clatter of stones.

"My Gawd, Garan. That's effective." Thom Antoon's soft southern drawl seemed horribly fitting in the charged silence that followed. He leaned over the edge and swept the beam from his flashlight across the rocky plain below.

"Very effective." He flicked the flashlight off. "Though I would like to have allowed him more time to consider his imminent death."

Malachi carefully untied Sheyna, touching the torn skin at her wrists and ankles, healing each abrasion as carefully and quickly as his power allowed.

She would not face him. Her body trembled but her eyes and her mind remained closed. He ached to hold her, but sensed her withdrawal from his touch, no matter how gentle.

Sheyna? Are you okay? Did he…?

Jenna suddenly appeared next to Malachi. "Let me," she said, touching him lightly on the arm. "Go with the men. I'll bring Sheyna up in a few minutes."

Malachi nodded. He slipped his cotton tee shirt off over his head and handed it to Jenna. "Here. It's big enough to cover her." Then he reached out and brushed Sheyna's shoulder with the backs of his fingers before he left.

She felt cold to his touch, even through the mink-like softness of her fur. Cold and frightened and very far away.

Chapter 14

"No, Jenna. I don't understand why she won't see me." Malachi leaned over the table in Jenna and Garan's dining room, his hands planted firmly on the polished oak surface. "It's been two weeks. I've been patient. I haven't bothered her...hell, I haven't even seen her, for crying out loud. It's not just me, dammit. I've got six young men who are only half alive...six young men she might be able to help. Why won't she talk to me?"

Jenna covered both of Malachi's hands with hers and smiled. At the moment of contact, he felt his anger fade.

"You're doing it to me again, aren't you? Pulling your little *calm the pissed off doctor down* routine?"

Jenna grinned at him. "Works, doesn't it?"

Malachi pulled his hands out from under Jenna's. "Yeah. Every time. That's what happens when you try and get mad at someone you've linked with. It's like shouting at yourself."

"Mal, be patient. That's all I can advise. This was a horrible, traumatic event for her. For you, too, for that matter. Are you doing okay?"

Jenna wished she could explain Sheyna's state of mind in terms Malachi would understand. Right now, the young lioness was brittle beyond imagining, her vibrant personality shattered into fragments, her world a tattered remnant of what had been before.

Jenna was beginning to suspect her trauma went even deeper than the recent kidnapping and assault. What it might be, however, she couldn't tell.

Malachi walked away from Jenna to stare out the window. "I'd do a lot better if I could talk to Sheyna. You're sure that bastard didn't rape her?"

Jenna sighed. "He didn't have time to penetrate, if that's what you mean. It doesn't matter. She was raped by him all the same. Not just by White, either. Sheyna told us about the assault by the other soldier. It was a horrible experience for a young woman, especially one who was still untouched."

Jenna stood up and walked across the room. Malachi shoved his hands in his pockets and sighed, but he didn't move away from her.

She knew how much Mal was hurting, knew he needed Sheyna's touch just as much as Jenna was convinced the young lioness needed the healer.

"Sheyna told me how you helped her through it, how you used your mind to build a fantasy for her. That fantasy helped her survive, Mal."

"It wasn't enough. I couldn't save her from them."

"You did what you could. Especially later, when you made love to her."

Malachi whirled around and stared at Jenna. "She told you about that?" He looked away, his jaw tightly clenched, hands shoved even deeper into his pockets. "Lord, Jenna. I'm such a bastard. I shouldn't have touched her. I don't think I've ever wanted a woman so much...but after what she'd been through...I'm no better than Merrick White."

"That's just so much bull crap, Mal, and you know it." Jenna grabbed his arm and felt his muscles tighten under the soft cotton shirt he wore. "Sheyna told me she begged you to make love to her even when you resisted. I think she actually feels guilty for forcing you. Give her time, okay? A little more time."

Malachi's shoulders slumped. Jenna felt the life go out of him, the spark of anger that had kept him charged and ready. Now she felt defeat — Malachi's defeat.

"Link with me, Jenna. I can't say the words, but I want you to know how I feel. Please? Link with me?"

Without hesitation, she grabbed both his hands and opened her mind. His was waiting, a sense of desperation coloring his thoughts, his love for Sheyna adding light and life...and urgency.

The sensations overwhelmed her. The love, the respect, the need. Trembling, Jenna pulled back, and then drew Malachi into a fierce hug.

"She has no idea how strongly you feel. How much you love. I don't think I did, either. Right now she feels defiled, worthless. She doesn't want you to see her like this."

"I need to. Please, Jenna. Will you talk to her?"

Jenna nodded. "I'll do what I can. She's with Garan now. She's...Mal, I don't know how to explain it, but Sheyna has been horribly affected by this. In some ways I think she's stronger, but in others...she's not herself. Not at all. Garan's worried about her. So am I."

Malachi turned away from Jenna and opened the door. His blue eyes sparkled with determination and Jenna realized, for the first time, how truly handsome the healer was. Tall and lean, his thick, dark hair in need of cutting, his olive-toned skin and the dark slash of his eyebrows highlighting his intense nature, he was a man not used to hearing the word *no*.

Currently, those eyebrows were drawn together in a scowl. "I will see her, Jenna, whether she wants me to or not. You might let Garan know I'd appreciate if he didn't interfere. He tends to get a little protective of his baby sister."

Jenna couldn't have stopped her smile if she'd wanted to. "That's an understatement. Tell you what—this may be a mistake, but I don't think so. Garan and I are meeting with Thom and Shing tonight. Sheyna will be here by herself around sunset. You might want to check in on her."

Malachi nodded his appreciation and turned to leave.

"Um, Mal?" Jenna touched his arm. "We won't be home until at least midnight. Just in case you need to know."

"Thanks, Jen. I owe you."

* * * * *

Malachi paused at the entrance to Garan and Jenna's quarters. Sheyna was here. He sensed pain, a deep-seated anguish so unlike his earlier perception of her. His healer's instincts immediately kicked into high gear. She needed him. She might not know it yet, but the young Lioness of Mirat needed Malachi as badly as he needed her.

He raised his hand to knock, thought better of it, and stepped inside. The rooms were gloomy, shades drawn and lights extinguished. He headed unerringly in the direction of Sheyna's room.

The door was closed. Malachi knocked quietly and waited, holding his thoughts to himself. After a moment, he opened the door and entered.

Wrapped in a faded afghan, Sheyna sat in a large, overstuffed rocking chair, her knees drawn up to her chest, arms wrapped tightly around a tattered stuffed kitten. She stared out the window, away from Malachi.

He paused in the doorway, waiting. After what seemed like forever, Sheyna finally acknowledged his presence. Her voice was low pitched, dull...lifeless.

"Hello, Malachi."

"Hello, Sheyna. How are you? I...I've been worried about you." He crossed the room and knelt in front of her. She was every bit as exotic, as beautiful, as he remembered, even with her dark mane tangled and her eyes awash with unshed tears.

It took her a long moment to respond. At first her voice crackled over a growling, mewling cadence Malachi had never heard from her before. She bowed her head, started anew. "You and everyone else. I think Garan's fed up with me. Jenna too. For that matter, I'm fed up with me."

"Not fed up. Only worried. Concerned. They love you, Sheyna. This isn't like you."

"How do you know it isn't like me?" She turned, then and looked directly at him, finally showing a spark of emotion. Her voice shook with repressed anger, her words escaped on a sibilant hiss. "You don't really know anything about me. All you know is the victim."

"Not true." Malachi stood up and grabbed her hands, pulling Sheyna to her feet. "You were a captive like me. Never a victim. A prisoner of war, certainly no martyr."

"I'm going home. I've decided to return to Mirat." She wouldn't look at him.

NO! Malachi took a deep breath, steadied himself and took another. "No," he said aloud. "We need you here, on Earth. The rebellion needs you. Those six young men waiting for your healing touch need you."

Sheyna turned her head. She addressed the carpeted floor, her feet...anything but Malachi. "The young soldiers will recover. I have nothing to give...not anymore. You know what they need. The madman is dead. Your rebellion is drawing to a close...it has no need of me."

"I have need of you." Malachi cupped her chin in his hand and forced her to look at him. "I want you to stay. I want..."

"What about what I want, Malachi? What about that?"

"You can't possibly want to go back to that half-existence you lived under Gard." He grabbed her upper arms, forced her to look at him. "You can have a life here, a wonderful life. You can do so much good on this world."

She tore herself from his grasp and stepped back. "Oh yes. I came to this world to do good. To heal. In less than twenty-four hours I'd been assaulted, defiled and terrified beyond anything I could ever imagine. Humans debased me in the most disgusting manner then had the temerity to call *me* a beast, an animal. Even animals aren't that cruel to one another. Maybe Gard was right. Maybe we should be wary of humans."

Malachi bowed his head. Her pain washed over him. "Is that how you felt when I made love to you? *Defiled?* Sheyna, I have relived that time my every waking moment. I should never have touched…"

"Oh, Malachi. No. You are the only decent thing that's happened to me since landing on this Mother-forsaken planet. Don't you see, though? What might have evolved between us, what might have become something deep and lasting, was tainted by everything else. You will always see me bound and helpless, at the mercy of a madman and his soldiers. You witnessed the most degrading acts…"

"I witnessed a woman, more beautiful than I could ever imagine, maintain her pride and dignity during the most degrading experience imaginable. I saw her defy her captors, show mercy to her tormentor and give strength to her fellow captive. There's no shame in what you did! Try and see yourself as I see you."

Shoulders drooping, Sheyna stared at the floor, her ears flattened against her skull. Slowly she shook her head in denial. Her hands opened and closed, sharp claws protruding with each extension of her fingers. "I can't. Logically, I know I wasn't at fault, but I can't wipe the images from my mind. Why is it when I remember you, so badly beaten and hurting, I remember only your bravery? When I think of myself, it's with fear and disgust. I think it would be best for all concerned if I just went home."

Talking wasn't getting him anywhere. Malachi slowly drew Sheyna into his arms and tucked her head under his chin. She fought him for a moment, claws extended, teeth bared, then with a soft mewling sigh, relaxed into his embrace.

It won't work, Malachi.

I will make it work. Look at me, Sheyna.

He tenderly lifted her chin with one finger. Her dark amber eyes gazed back at him so filled with pain and need it made him ache. Her beauty was not human but it called to him, made him shiver with desire.

"I want you to know I had not been with a woman for almost four years before you. Since loving you, even under those circumstances, I desire no one but you. You would be so selfish as to take yourself away forever?"

She smiled then, a bittersweet smile that broke his heart. "There's nothing left in me, Malachi. Nothing left to give. No desire, no urgency, no passion. They took that away from me. It's gone. I can't give you what you need."

"Oh, Sheyna… Please? Will you at least try?" He leaned closer to kiss her.

She shuddered and turned away. "No…please." Gently, Sheyna slipped from his embrace. "It's best this way. I've requested a ship for transport. I'll leave within the week."

She turned her back on him and picked up the stuffed kitten. Stroking its tattered coat, she stared out the window. Malachi watched her a moment and wished he knew the words to make her stay. "You're a healer, Sheyna. You can heal those young men, but you cannot heal yourself. I want to help you, but you have to let me. I can't force a healing on you. Nor can I force love. I wish I could make you understand."

Finally, when he realized she wasn't going to answer, Malachi turned and left the room.

He felt her pain as if it were his own.

She's leaving. I'll never see her again.

Something cracked open and bled, deep within his heart. Stopped him at the doorway. Made him pause for air.

Malachi realized the pain truly *was* his own.

Chapter 15

"I think your ankle will be just fine." Malachi rubbed his hands together to release the energy from his healing. The young soldier twisted his foot in every direction, grinned at the healer and hopped down off the examining table.

"Thanks, Doc. Doesn't hurt a bit." He bent over to pull his boot on.

"Next time you decide to impress the girls, I'd suggest you don't jump off a twelve foot retaining wall. Unless of course, you're into levitation."

"Who, me?" The youngster glanced up at Malachi. "I do languages. Levitation is a bit beyond me."

Languages. Malachi scrubbed down the table after his patient left, walking carefully on an ankle that had been cleanly broken just two hours earlier. *So many new talents. More and more all the time.* Nowadays, he didn't know half his patients, had never expected the wide range of psychic skills.

He knew the six young men in the clinic, though. Knew them intimately. How was he ever going to heal them? Sheyna said he could do it...Malachi knew she was the one with the ability.

All he could do was keep them alive. *Amend that,* he thought. *Half alive.*

He glanced at the clock. Almost three. Sheyna would be boarding the Miratan ship in just under an hour. He wondered if Garan had had any luck convincing her to see Malachi at least once before she left.

Suddenly, as if his questioning thoughts had willed him there, Garan's huge frame filled the doorway to the clinic. Malachi sighed. From the concerned look on the big guy's face, he hadn't had any luck.

"Change in plans, Mal. Big change."

Malachi carefully hung the towel over the edge of a chair. "Is she gone already?"

"No. She's not going."

"She...?" *Maybe...?*

It's not what you think." Garan stepped into the room and shut the door behind him. "We've been contacted by the head of the World Federation. A courier arrived just over an hour ago. Turns out the president's youngest son is showing signs of Talent. We've been asked to see him, secretly, and test the boy. He's about eight years old and showing strong kinetic ability."

"How does that affect Sheyna?" Malachi leaned against the examining table. "Why would she stay?"

Garan at least had the decency to look sheepish, if a Lion of Mirat even had that ability. "It was Jenna's idea. We convinced Sheyna we needed a powerful empath, someone who could sense subterfuge or danger. Jenna has the talent to do it, but..."

"Thanks, Garan. I owe you."

"We'll also need a healer along on the trip."

"Jenna's idea?" Hope bloomed in Malachi's heart. A chance to work with Sheyna, to break through the barriers she'd thrown up against him, against all men.

"Nope. That was mine." Garan turned to leave. "I thought you should know...we've contacted Mara Armand and Captain Sander. This could be the break we've been waiting for, the beginning of the end of this mess. We felt they should be involved in any treaty discussions that might occur. They may or may not be here in time. I know you once had something going with Mara, so I thought..."

"Thanks, Garan. What Mara and I had was over a long time ago. We've stayed friends over the years. It'll be good to see both of them...and their daughter. She must be about six or seven, now."

"Good. I wasn't sure. I'd forgotten about the child. Amazing, isn't it? Two totally separate species producing offspring?"

"Maybe we're not so separate after all." Malachi took a steadying breath. "You really think this could signal the end of the rebellion?" He tried to imagine a world without war, without the constant threat of attack; the chance to once again feel like a productive citizen of a stable society.

Had he ever known that feeling?

"This could be what we've hoped for. We've long believed there were many more Talented among the general human population than anyone suspected. When their president's own child shows abilities associated with the enemy, maybe the leaders of the World Federation will be ready to reconsider just who the enemy really is."

Garan paused just outside the door. "For what it's worth, I hope this will give you and Sheyna the opportunity you both need. I agree with Jenna. Both of you have a lot of healing to do. It would best be done together. We leave at dawn. Pack light. I doubt we'll be gone more than a few days. Riley, Tamura and Antoon will travel with us as well."

Malachi stared at the closed door for a long time after Garan left. His chest felt tight, his mouth dry. He felt a faint stirring of precognition, a sense of danger in this meeting with the World Federation leader, but hope, as well.

Would there finally be an end to the rebellion after seven long years of war?

He thought of Sheyna, of her sleek beauty marred by the fear in her amber eyes. Somehow, the Mother willing, he would replace that fear with love.

The Mother. Not one of his usual epithets. Malachi chuckled to himself as he closed up the room. *You've been too much among these Lions of Mirat, Doc.* He gazed in the direction he knew Sheyna's home world lay and realized he could never spend enough time with one lioness in particular.

I would pray to You without hesitation, Mother of All, if I thought you would heal her heart.

* * * * *

"Everything's packed." Jenna shoved her bag against the wall, alongside Garan's. "I'm exhausted, my love. I'm going to check on Sheyna and head for bed."

Garan grunted in reply. He was deep in his maps, checking out the route they would follow tomorrow. The distance was great, the need to bypass cities and heavily populated areas greater still. Jenna knew this meeting must remain totally secret.

Jenna knocked lightly on Sheyna's door, and then entered. Sheyna lay in the fetal position, curled tightly on the bed with covers pulled to her chin, the ever-present stuffed kitten beside her on the pillow. Sheyna's eyes were open but Jenna knew she was a million miles away.

It broke her heart to see her sister of the heart like this, so badly traumatized by her assault, so unwilling to accept anyone's help...unable to accept Malachi's love.

Almost as if you believe you deserve what happened?

Something more was going on here. Something...it came to her in a flash, the reason for Sheyna's withdrawal. *Gard.* Sheyna's father had spent a lifetime breaking her spirit...and more? Why did Jenna sense Gard, here in this room?

Jenna thought of the young woman she'd first met, the changes she'd watched as Sheyna had grown and built upon her newly won self-confidence. Always, though, there had been a shadow, something unseen, which impacted all that Sheyna was.

Merrick White's assault had destroyed the fragile hold on her newly won confidence.

Jenna kept her thoughts to herself. Instead, she lightly stroked Sheyna's shoulder, said a soft *good night,* and quietly left the room.

Garan waited for Jenna in their bedroom. He sat on the edge of the bed, looking tired and rumpled and very dear. His skinsuit was partially unfastened, his mane tangled from running his hands through the thick strands as he'd worked.

Jenna knew she could never have loved anyone, human or otherwise, as much as she loved her powerful Lion of Mirat. He glanced up and smiled at her.

She closed the door and walked across the room, coming to a halt directly in front of him, inserting herself between his powerful thighs.

I want Sheyna to know the kind of love we share. Jenna smoothed the rumpled hair back from Garan's broad forehead.

He leaned into her touch. *It will take patience and understanding.*

She needs to break through Gard's teachings, to find something in herself to love.

Gard? Garan appeared to ponder the thought a moment. "You're right. I never made the connection. He spent years crushing her spirit. She can't go back. It would destroy her."

"I'm not sure if all he did was crush her spirit. I worry there is more in her relationship with your father."

Garan's brow furrowed and his eyes darkened as Jenna's implications sunk in. He curled his lip back in a snarl. "If what you suspect is true, I will not allow her to return. Sadly, I can easily imagine

Gard capable of anything, no matter how heinous, though I can't believe Sheyna would protect him."

Jenna paused, wondering how to make her beloved understand the depths of guilt and fear that often accompanied abuse. "Sometimes, a child's mind protects them from what they can't accept. I don't think Sheyna even realizes what makes her so afraid...at least, if my suspicions are correct."

"I've never known you to be wrong, my love. She will not return to Mirat. Not while Gard is alive." Garan wrapped his arms about her waist. Jenna leaned against his broad chest, close to the steady rhythm of his beating heart.

Thank you. I'm glad she'll stay. Malachi needs her. The young soldiers need her.

So you've said. Right now, though, I need you even more.

Jenna leaned back to better see Garan's face. "I hoped you would say that."

Life these past weeks had been much too serious. Now she was certain Garan understood the need to keep Sheyna away from Gard, Jenna felt as if she could finally relax.

Garan was in charge. All would be well. Jenna slanted a sexy grin at her large beast. Tonight was a time to ease some of the worries from his soul, just as he so capably eased her own.

She dropped to her knees beside the bed and nuzzled the warmth between his legs. The slick material of his skinsuit stretched tightly over his erect cock. Jenna nipped him playfully through the fabric.

He groaned and his eyes slipped shut. He buried his hands in Jenna's thick hair and thrust forward. Answering her mate's need, Jenna slowly peeled his uniform over his shoulders, past his hips, and then stripped it over his long legs and suddenly mobile tail.

How she loved that tail, an appendage rarely noticed until Garan's emotions overwhelmed his careful control. Anger, lust...just now it jerked and twitched as if it had a mind of its own.

She knew perfectly well he wasn't angry.

So much the beast, but even more the man. He was beautiful...a creature of wild, untamed majesty who brought Jenna to her knees.

She stroked his muscled thighs then shoved him back on the bed. His unsheathed claws raked the bedding as she teased him, touching everywhere about his belly and legs, rubbing her cheek lightly against his fully erect penis, kissing the tip, tickling the silky shaft with her fingers.

He groaned, a rumbling, purring sound emanating from deep within his broad chest. He reached for her but she caught his big paws in her hands and held them back against the bedcovers. He bucked his hips against her, pleading silently until she took his hot shaft in her mouth, suckling him deep and hard.

She felt his muscles bunch and quiver, knew he was seconds away from coming. With a teasing grin, she licked him once more then backed away. "We want this to last, don't we?"

He answered her with a long, low snarl.

She nibbled him, running her teeth just over the tip of his shaft while she lightly fondled his testicles. He thrust against her mouth but she teased him further, blowing a cool wisp of air along his swollen penis.

Jenna knew the moment when Garan reached his limit. He grabbed her about the waist and tossed her beside him on the bed, stripped her clothing off in a single, economical motion, then planted himself between her knees.

"Enough, my dear." He leaned over and blew hot breaths against her belly.

"But I like being in control." She spread her legs wide and slanted her eyes. "Pleasure me."

Before Jenna realized what he was up to, Garan grabbed a colorful scarf off the bedside table, looped it around her wrists and secured it to the headboard.

"You've had enough of control," he growled. "I've been waiting for just this opportunity." He knelt once more between her outspread legs.

Giggling, she tried to put her knees together. He grabbed her legs, forcing them apart and holding them down with his huge paws. His cock jutted forward, hot and ready, but he ignored it in favor of Jenna.

Struggle as much as she might, Jenna knew she was no match for a Miratan male in his prime, especially one as sexually aroused as her mate. Garan held her firmly in place. His rough tongue left a trail along her inner thigh; circled across her belly, around her breasts where he spent long minutes on each swollen nipple, then back to a point just above her aching clit. She raised her hips, begging silently for more of his touch.

He stroked her with his tongue, holding her immobile while he teased and licked, circled her clit then backed away, taking her almost to completion then changing direction until she cried out in frustration.

He brought her to the brink, then sat back on his haunches and grinned. "We want this to last, don't we?"

"You will pay for this, my love." Slipping her hands from the loosely knotted scarf, Jenna lunged forward and knocked Garan to his back. Laughing, he rolled exactly as she wanted, playing the kitten to her display of force.

This time she took her work seriously. With teeth and tongue and lips, she made love to his erect cock, his hard testicles. Projecting her pleasure, linking her thoughts with Garan's, she shared the tastes, the textures, the sensations that thrilled her, pulling her lifemate deep into the sensual ecstasy exactly as she experienced it.

She knew he neared the limits of his control, sensed the faint pulsing in his hard shaft, the beginning of his orgasm. When he would pull himself away from her so that he might give Jenna pleasure before his own climax, Jenna suckled him harder, then nipped him sharply with her teeth.

Still projecting her own pleasure at pleasuring him, Jenna tickled and massaged his balls with the fingers of one hand, stroked the base of his tail and the cleft between his buttocks with the other.

He shuddered with the increased sensation, his body trembling beneath her touch. She knew he fought release, struggled for control so that it became a game for her, to take him over the edge against his wishes.

She let him know she fully intended to win.

Once more she suckled his balls, now drawn tightly against his body as his arousal grew. She stroked his slick cock, squeezing the hard shaft in her fingers, long, smooth strokes guaranteed to drive him over the edge.

Still he fought release. She almost laughed at his competitive nature, his stubborn arrogance.

You haven't got a chance…I'm about to pull out the big guns.

Without giving Garan time to consider her threat, Jenna took his cock between her lips and grasped his buttocks in her hands.

Her fingers crept closer to the cleft beneath his tail; she suckled the slick cock between her lips and breached his tightly puckered anus with a quick thrust of her finger.

She sensed his shock, his gasp for breath and the overwhelming pleasure of release as his seed filled her mouth.

Gotcha! That will teach you, my stubborn love.

His laughter ended on a moan...and a promise. *You have merely given me new ideas, my dear Jenna. I hope you're prepared.*

She grinned, lapping the remainder of his seed from his semi-erect cock. The sweet spicy taste of cinnamon and brown sugar was an aphrodisiac all its own. Expectation hummed through her. Garan always carried through with his threats.

Jenna barely had time to consider the implications before he picked her up and reversed their positions on the bed.

He held her down, tickling her in the process until her skin shivered and she giggled uncontrollably. Batting ineffectually at his hands, she was helpless against his attack.

Laughing with her, Garan fell beside her on the bed. He took a deep breath, grinned at Jenna and flipped her over on her belly. She struggled, her laughter muffled against the mattress. Garan shoved a pillow beneath her hips, nipping at her buttocks when she fought him, then stretched her legs apart, managing to run his rough tongue across the soles of her feet in the process.

She loved this side of Garan, the playful, foolish side he rarely showed anyone, including Jenna. She wiggled her hips as his tongue teased her, then sighed as he licked and stroked the tender flesh between her legs.

He found her clit almost at once, touching it lightly with the rough tip of his tongue, encircling it, then licking her from front to back in long, lush strokes.

Once again, the abrasive texture of his tongue made her shiver—when he slipped it deep inside, she felt the muscles contract and expand against her vaginal walls.

After a moment of pure sensation, he withdrew his tongue and once again gently lapped at the crease between her buttocks, taking long, slow licks from her clit to her waist.

Suddenly he switched his technique and licked roughly across her butt, using the sandpapery texture of his tongue to his best advantage.

Within moments, Jenna's buttocks tingled as if she'd been soundly spanked.

She cried out at the pleasure and pain of his less than tender massage and felt his answering chuckle in her mind.

As I said, you've given me some new ideas, my love.

He licked at her muscled buttocks, pulling Jenna to her knees, massaging her clit with one hand as he squeezed her breast with the other. His tongue continued its abrasive, tortuous path over her butt, first one side, then the other. He matched the rhythm with his fingers between her legs, the other hand tugging at her taut nipple.

Jenna wriggled and squirmed at the overwhelming sensations. She bucked against him, against the climax building deep inside.

Suddenly he grabbed her thighs in both paws, lifting her off the bed. He blew a cool breath across her sensitive ass, then drove his long tongue deep inside her vagina.

She screamed. Screamed and bucked against his mouth. Writhing with the pleasure, the surprise, the sense of fulfillment she'd never found with another man.

Her muscles clenched violently around his tongue. Suddenly he slipped his tongue out of her, and then filled her again, this time with his huge cock. Thrusting fast and hard, he quickly hauled her once again into oblivion.

Garan shuddered, his massive body covering hers as he climaxed. The link was almost automatic now, the total mind meld they shared with each sexual release. Jenna felt Garan's pleasure even as he knew hers.

She gasped for breath as she slowly surfaced once more from their shared passionate spiral. Garan's broad chest heaved against her back; his arms held her immobile and she felt his hot seed spurting into her with each spasm of his orgasm.

Her legs hung limply in his grasp.

Long moments later, Garan gently settled her back to the bed and rolled to one side, a huge smile on his face. *Any more new ideas?*

Not that I want to discuss right now. Laughing quietly, she ran her fingers along the side of his powerful jaw, studying him through a haze of love. Beast he was, as well as lover, leader, soldier, mate.

She almost told him then, thought better and snuggled instead against his warm chest. There was time enough.

Before the year was over, there'd be a new title to the litany of descriptions befitting Garan, Lieutenant of the Rebellion and StarQuest candidate.

Jenna smiled, wrapping her thoughts around the sweet music of the word.

Father.

In the morning she would tell him, before they left on their journey.

It would do him good to know how his life was about to change.

* * * * *

Sheyna knew she shouldn't eavesdrop, shouldn't listen to the sounds of laughter and love coming from her brother and his mate's room. She tried to ignore them, blot them from her consciousness, but they shimmered about her, filled her empathic senses until she burned with a deep hunger all her own.

Huddled in her bed, wrapped in the protective blankets, she let herself remember the one time she'd known fulfillment.

She ached, reliving the passion, the wondrous touch of the only man who had ever made love to her.

Malachi.

Why was it, here, in her lonely room, she dreamed of him, yet when he came to her she rejected him?

Her self-disgust knotted into a hard kernel of pain just below her heart. So long as it held tightly to that spot, there would be no room for love.

Arms wrapped tightly around the ragged stuffed kitten, the only witness to her soft mewling cry of anguish, Sheyna wept alone in her quiet room.

Chapter 16

Malachi strapped himself into place between Shing Tamura and Thom Antoon. Sheyna huddled in the seat just ahead, protected by Jenna and Garan on either side.

Something was obviously going on between those two...Garan hadn't quit grinning all morning and Jenna was acting particularly odd, casting quick glances at her lifemate, touching his arm, his shoulder, any part of him that was close, whenever she thought no one was watching.

Malachi sighed as he tightened the belt. Would he ever know that intimacy, that eternal link, with Sheyna? They'd come so close.

Tim Riley piloted the craft, projecting coordinates for the series of kinetic hops that would bring them to the meeting place high in the Rocky Mountains, near what had once been the city of Denver.

"I wonder if we'll ever give our cities new names?" Shing Tamura's quiet comment brought understanding grunts from the rest of the crew. "Everywhere we go, it's *that used to be the city of...* I think it's time we build new cities, create a new civilization, not perch temporarily upon the bones of the dead."

"Which is exactly why I wanted you along on this trip. You've always been able to think beyond the battle." Thom Antoon's soft drawl was interrupted by the blinking light signaling *lift off.*

"That time will come, my friend. I just hope it happens while I'm still here to enjoy it." Thom settled back into his seat next to Malachi and closed his eyes.

Malachi's mind filled with the coordinates, a mental picture that allowed him to direct his energy with the rest of the group. Though not a kinetic, his mind working in gestalt with the others would help power the ship for lift off.

Sheyna's mind was obviously missing from the group.

Sheyna would block, Jenna 'pathed to Malachi. *This is not a good time for her to link.*

Of course. Malachi hadn't considered the fact Sheyna would shield her thoughts rather than link with any of the men on board, including himself. A sigh caught in his throat. He clenched his hands in his lap to keep from reaching forward to touch her.

She was so close, but a universe away. As Malachi studied the curve of her cheek, the smooth line of her neck, Sheyna hunched even lower in her seat. Jenna must be explaining the reason for her exclusion.

Malachi's heart went out to her. The ship lifted silently into the morning sky and Mal quietly withdrew from the link. Once airborne, Tim Riley and Thom Antoon had enough power to move the small craft where they needed to go.

Automatically, Malachi's thoughts leapt to Sheyna's. Instead of her welcoming mind he came up against a dark wall of pain.

He settled back in his seat and let his mind return to the link. At least that would keep him from thinking of Sheyna and what might have been.

* * * * *

The president's private security forces were already waiting at the compound's small airstrip when Tim quietly brought the ship in for landing. The rebels remained on high alert during the short drive to the president's private compound, but other than sensing curiosity and disbelief at the two Miratans' existence among the humans, there was no sign of danger.

Sheyna immediately felt herself relax and noticed that Jenna, the strongest empath among the seven, did the same.

At the front door of the residence, they were met by the president himself, a casually dressed man of average size and what appeared to be mostly American Indian heritage.

"You're not at all what I expected," Thom Antoon said, stepping forward as leader of the small band of rebels.

The president shook Antoon's hand, but his attention was on the imposing figure of Garan standing just to Antoon's left, as well as on Sheyna, who stood just behind her sibling. "Neither are you," the man said, breaking into a wide grin. "Neither are you."

Just then a small boy about eight years old came tearing around the corner, an older woman in hot pursuit. "Daddy, Daddy, didja see the…"

He skidded to a halt just in front of Sheyna. She immediately knelt down to his level and smiled, fighting the urge to laugh at his childish look of wonder and surprise.

The little boy stared at her a moment without speaking. Suddenly, Sheyna felt a stirring against the mental shield she'd unconsciously thrown up. She lowered the shield and projected a soft *hello, Tad.*

The little boy giggled in delight. "Daddy, the cat lady's talkin' in my head. She knows my name. She said 'hello'."

The president didn't say a word, just stood there with an odd grin on his face. After a moment, he shook his head in disbelief. "I know," he said. "I heard her as well."

* * * * *

"The sunset is beautiful here in the mountains, isn't it?"

Malachi stepped up behind Sheyna on the far end of a deck overlooking the vast range of snow-capped peaks. For once she didn't pull away from him, though she didn't look at him, either.

"I've never seen anything like it. The country around the compound is much like my home world. This is totally alien to me."

"You were wonderful with little Tad, and with his father as well. President Barton has finally stepped off his fence and decided to support our cause in any way he can. I didn't really feel I belonged at tonight's meeting, but I recognized a number of world leaders at the table. They're all a bit enthralled by your brother. He's quite the statesman when he wants to be. Still, it will be President Barton who swings their opinion."

"I'm glad I could help. I'm surprised he didn't suspect his own Talent. The man has strong empathic abilities, some precognition—and he's a natural telepath."

"Probably why he's been so successful in politics. You notice he was very quick to request we not discuss *his* abilities, only his son's." Malachi chuckled, projecting the image of Howard Barton's consternation when his many Talents were revealed by Jenna and Sheyna's brief study.

This time, her shields stayed down. She felt the gentle humor in Malachi's take on their afternoon, his relief that the long nightmare of the rebellion might finally come to an end. He didn't push her for anything more, made no attempt to reach beneath the surface of her thoughts.

It wasn't enough. After loving him, Sheyna knew this would never be enough. If only it wasn't too late. "I understand Mara Armand and Captain Sander are due to arrive some time tomorrow. Jenna said you and Mara…"

Malachi's gentle chuckle held more self-deprecation than humor. "I'll never live that down. No matter how many years pass. I thought we were in love. Turns out I was in lust and denial and she wasn't even on the same page. It was years ago. Once I linked with Sander and discovered what the two of them shared…well, I knew then what I felt certainly wasn't love. Nothing could compare with the passion between them, the commitment. It was an amazing experience, to feel that— *adoration*—between two people."

"She was your first, though. Your first love is always special." *And you are mine,* she wanted to scream. *You will always be my first love.* She blocked her deepest thoughts though, merely smiling with Malachi at his memories of Mara Armand.

"Link with me, Sheyna."

Malachi's unexpected request startled her. Link? A complete meld with this man? She'd wanted it once, before… *No, Malachi, no, I can't. I can't let you see…*

His fingers caressed her cheek, then turned her so that she couldn't help but face him. By the Mother, he was beautiful to look at. How could she have ever thought humans as alien and strange? Malachi's beauty lay in his strength of form and kindness of nature, the dark sweep of his hair, his crystal blue eyes, the obvious love he felt for her.

Sheyna swallowed another retort, another defensive plea, though she shivered from his touch. He caressed her arms with his hands, neither holding her close nor pushing her away.

His feelings engulfed her, overwhelmed her empathic nature. *Passion…fear?* Not disgust, not for Malachi. Only for herself. She tried to block the thoughts he shared with her. At the same time, she drew them into her soul and trembled with the emotion she could no longer check.

Don't you understand? Malachi's impassioned plea went straight to her heart. *You are my first love, not Mara. You are the one I burn for, the one who holds my heart. I want no secrets. I want to open my life to you, share my failings, my weaknesses, along with the strength of the love I feel for you. Please, Sheyna.*

"I'm afraid." She swallowed against the bile rising in her throat; the realization of how deep her fear lay within her soul. "I am afraid, once you see the darkness, the filth inside me, you'll hate me."

"No, my love. There is no darkness within you. You are my light."

She touched his cheek, remembering his gentle loving, the passion he'd shared with her under the worst possible circumstances. Could they actually achieve that once again, in a normal world?

She felt Malachi's fingers tremble against her cheek, then suddenly still. Garan's soft, rumbling voice carried through the open door, followed by Jenna's laughter. Sheyna stepped away from Malachi. She was not ready for anyone to view them as a pair. She sensed his hurt at her rejection, but he quickly buried it beneath a somber smile.

Later.

The single word drifted through her mind, echoed over and over. She wondered, as Malachi turned to greet his friends. Was it a threat, or a promise?

* * * * *

"How'd it go? You guys look like you're celebrating. Is a treaty possible?" Malachi purposefully turned his back on Sheyna. He couldn't bear to be so close, yet so aware of her distance.

"I think a treaty is a given." Garan hitched one hip up on the railing and draped his arm around Jenna. "Turns out every one of the leaders of the WF has some form of Talent, most of them latent, some very aware of their abilities and not above using them. It's why they're the leaders, why they're as powerful, as successful, as they are. I think they've been unwilling to give up that edge. It's time it was brought out in the open."

"That, however, isn't why Garan is celebrating, is it?" Sheyna playfully punched her sibling in the arm. It was the first time Malachi had seen her this happy since he'd met her. As an empath, she must have already guessed what was going on.

"You're right." Garan nuzzled Jenna's hair. Her smile lit up the night.

Suddenly Malachi had a flash of precognition, a vision of a lean young man who blended the best of his parents. "Congratulations, Dad." He held his hand out to Garan, who immediately engulfed it in his huge paw.

"You saw our...?"

"I see a young man who looks a lot like a combination of you and Jenna."

"I knew it!" Jenna's laughter bubbled out of her. "I knew our child would be a boy."

Sheyna groaned. "Not another Garan! The world can't handle two."

"He'll have the universe," Garan said, once again wrapping his arms around Jenna. "Once the rebellion has ended and peace established, Jenna and I will be leaving on our StarQuest. I am still a soldier and an Explorer. "

"And I'm just really curious to see what's out there." Jenna smiled at Sheyna. "We have been asked, however, by President Barton, to see if you would stay on Earth, Sheyna. He thinks, and we agree, the future success of the treaty depends on your deft touch. Your work with his son this afternoon has meant a lot to the success of this entire mission. Will you consider it?"

Sheyna bowed her head and closed her eyes. Malachi ached to help her. It was the hardest thing he'd ever done, to keep his thoughts to himself.

After a long moment, Sheyna raised her head and nodded. "I'll stay," she said. "But I'm going to need help." She turned and grabbed both of Malachi's hands in hers. He felt them trembling, realized her palms were ice cold. "I have six young men waiting to be healed. I've been afraid to try again. The president's son needs me. I don't want him exposed to the corruption in my mind. If I am to work with others, I must cleanse myself of the filth that's part of me. It's in my soul—it's fouling my heart."

Malachi thought she had never been more beautiful, more regal, than this moment when she faced her demons.

"I'll link with you, Malachi. You said you could heal me. Well, you're a healer and you know better than anyone here what was done to me. You don't, however, know it all."

315

She took a deep breath. "Even I don't know everything. There are memories I can't touch. I never realized they were so much a part of me until after the assault."

She bowed her head, took a deep breath then squared her shoulders and looked directly into his eyes. Determination and dismay filled her amber eyes. "Bits and pieces of memories I can't explain have infused my dreams since then. Things loathsome and repugnant to me—unbelievable memories I don't understand. You need to know everything if I'm ever to be free of this corruption. We both do! But you must promise me, if what you learn is more than you can bear, you'll walk away without remorse. Can you promise me that?"

"That's all I've wanted since this began." He closed his eyes against the quick sting of tears and gave thanks to the Mother. "Whenever you're ready."

* * * * *

Their rooms were private, comfortably distant from the main compound. Malachi hesitated as he recalled the two other times he'd done comprehensive links, first with Captain Sander as Malachi lay bleeding to death from a serious gunshot wound, the second time with Jenna shortly after she'd arrived at the compound.

Two minds, totally foreign to his, one from another world, the other from another time. He'd traveled intimately through their private databases, learning secrets never before shared, uncovering fears unspoken and dreams not yet dreamed.

Now he stood awkwardly in the doorway behind Sheyna, wondering where they should begin this next journey.

"I was wrong to ask you," she said, stepping into the room, out of Malachi's reach.

No, he telepathed, well aware she was reading him. *If you'll recall, I asked you first. Sheyna, my love…you have never been more right.*

Silently hoping for Jenna's forgiveness for breaching the sanctity of a mindlink, Malachi chuckled aloud. "Did I ever tell you about linking with Jenna?" He stood closely behind Sheyna but didn't touch her.

"Jenna told me. She said General Antoon hoped she would learn how you did your healing and maybe even learn the secrets of precognition."

316

Grinning, Malachi said, "That's part of the story. Did Jenna tell you she linked with Garan first, right before coming to me?"

Sheyna turned and smiled nervously. "She said linking was such an intimate act, she wanted her first time to be with Garan, because she loved him."

Malachi laughed out loud, remembering the awkward first moments of his link with Jenna. "She made it even more intimate without realizing it. She and Garan made love right before we linked. She'll never know, and *you'd better not ever tell her*, that because his scent was on her and the memories of their mutual climax so recent and strong in her thoughts, I spent the entire link with an erection. She absolutely reeked of pheromones and sex and need for the big guy sitting just across the table."

Sheyna laughed, the sound bubbling out of her. "Did Garan know?"

"He was so jealous he was practically breathing green fire...but no, he didn't have a clue what I was picking up from Jenna. He was just very unhappy to see his woman linking with another man. I was scared to death if he got a glimpse of me and what was happening under the table, I'd get my throat ripped out in a heartbeat."

"Garan's very fond of you. There are few people he cares about as friends. You're one of them."

"I care about him as well. Before Jenna, he was someone I admired and occasionally wanted to throttle for his arrogance and attitude, but seeing him through Jenna's love drastically changed my opinion. I had never realized before how caring he could be, or how much he wanted the rebellion to succeed. I had always thought Earth was just a duty for him, one he disliked."

"He did, at first. Jenna's the one who made him see the importance of his job."

"Jenna's made a lot of us see a number of things differently." Malachi stepped closer to Sheyna, pleased when she didn't back away. "Have you thought of how you want to do the link? Sitting at the table, on the couch..."

"On the bed." Sheyna turned her head away as if embarrassed. "Part of my wanting to do this is very selfish, Malachi. I know you admire my body. I want to look at myself once again without shame. If we disrobe and link, I have hope that...I..."

"No need to explain. Let's do it now, before we talk ourselves into trouble."

Malachi led her to the bedroom, lowered the shades to darken the room completely from the security lights along the walls of the compound, and then purposefully turned his back to disrobe.

It took every bit of his control, but Malachi managed to contain his need for the woman undressing behind him. His penis remained totally flaccid when he finally hung up his clothing and sat on the edge of the bed.

Sheyna's eyes glowed in the darkness, reminding him of their differences even as he reveled in their similarities.

She sat next to him, her pounding heartbeat audible in the still night.

Malachi carefully stretched out on the sheets and patted the bed. Sheyna lay stiffly beside him. Malachi heard the catch in her breath, sensed her fear as a tangible thing between them.

He took her hand in his, caressing the fingers, tracing the shape of the fine bones and sharp nails partially sheathed at their tips. "When I first saw you," he said, his voice a quiet whisper, "I remember thinking I finally understood what it meant to be blindsided. You took my breath away. You still do."

A tiny mewling whimper escaped her.

"I know you're afraid. Something tells me you're as frightened of what you'll learn about yourself as what I might see. Don't be. Please. I'm here beside you. I intend to be beside you for a long time to come."

She trembled next to him, then took a deep, ragged breath. "Now, Malachi. Please. Help me."

Her quiet plea ripped his heart to shreds. Malachi had planned to cover her body with his. Instead, he rolled Sheyna over him so that she was on top, in a position of control. He nestled her against him, her legs on either side of his thighs, and then placed her fingertips at his temples.

He did the same to her so they connected along the length of their bodies.

"Are you okay?" He felt her nervous trembling ease as she fought for control. Finally she sighed and relaxed against him.

Yes. I'm fine. What do I do?

I want you to go with me. This won't be anything like the link you did with William. I want to lead you through my memories first. Once you're comfortable with the process...and if you're still willing after you learn everything there is to know about me, we'll reverse the procedure. I don't want you to do any of this alone.

Sheyna felt his mental laughter and it did help ease the nerves she hadn't been able to shake. With more confidence than she'd expected, she followed Malachi as he opened his mind to her.

Amazing! I see the impulses, the activity of your brain. Mal, it's fascinating! So different from that young man.

You need to go deeper, beyond the physical workings of my mind. You need to go into the actual database of information buried there. Here...this way.

Mesmerized, Sheyna followed him through his memories. She witnessed his childhood, his tender healing of wounded birds and other wild things and wondered if he thought of her as just another pet.

Don't be foolish.

Smiling comfortably for the first time since this long, strange journey began, Sheyna once again focused on Malachi's memories. She met his parents, two non-Talented individuals totally confused by their son's odd abilities, felt Malachi's anger and frustration when he predicted their sudden deaths, knowing moments before their car went off the road he would not be able to save them.

She learned how he had come to Daniel Armand as a young man, brash with his power, so sure of himself he'd not realized his pursuit of Mara was not welcome by the young woman. She felt his humiliation at Mara's final dismissal, understood his jealousy and stubbornness when Captain Sander first made his appearance at the Armand Institute.

He showed her everything—his strengths, his weaknesses, and his fears. He even shared the first moments he'd spent with an older neighbor when he was still a teen, so that Sheyna knew where he had first learned how to please a woman.

Awkward at first, unsure and inept, he'd discovered the pleasure of giving pleasure, had taken those lessons and saved them for the one he would someday love. He really had lived like a monk over the years...other than his brief affair with Mara and a short romance with another healer a few years earlier, Malachi had waited patiently for the one true love he believed was his.

Sheyna wept when he shared his deepest desires with her, the pure belief she would one day love him as much as he loved her.

How could she not? He was intelligent, kind, honorable and true. He was beautiful to look upon. There was no darkness in his soul. He carried no secrets in his heart.

Unlike Sheyna.

Could she ever hope?

Slowly they retreated from the link. Malachi held her as she sobbed quietly against his chest, until her breathing steadied. He kissed her face then gazed into the eyes mere inches from his.

"Now, my love. We will face your demons together. Are you ready?"

Chapter 17

She took a deep, ragged breath and nodded her head in agreement. Slowly at first, then with growing confidence, she led Malachi through the depths of her memories.

He struggled to contain his growing dismay when he saw her forcibly taken from her mother as a mere child, removed from the only home she'd known because of tradition, not because the members of the new pride even wanted her.

He witnessed Garan's youthful teasing, then his steadfast support of the growing kit despite Gard's cruelty. Beautiful even as a youngster, she remained quiet and withdrawn, a somber child, more often than not shunned by her peers.

Malachi sensed areas of darkness in her childhood, areas Sheyna deftly bypassed as she led him through her painful adolescence and on into adulthood. Suddenly they faced her recent torment, an area shrouded in black, festering with pain and degradation.

Here the healer in Malachi took charge. Working with Sheyna, he helped her face the terror, understand the courage of her own actions and see herself as Malachi saw her, brave and honorable despite her monstrous treatment.

As they finally withdrew, Malachi was once again attracted to the darkened areas of her childhood. *Wait. Sheyna, what happened here?*

Her body grew very still. *I can't go there. It's not allowed.*

His healer's instincts went on red alert. *I can go there, sweetheart. I'm a healer. Let me in.*

Suddenly her mental touch was that of a child's. Malachi shivered as the frightened little girl Sheyna had once been answered him. *No...even the healer isn't allowed. Only Gard. He says I can't go there and no one else can go there either.*

Why not, Sheyna? It's your mind. Why can't you go there?

Bad things will happen.

Malachi was vaguely aware of Sheyna trembling against him. He wrapped his arms tightly about her. Now they were linked, he only needed to hold her to maintain the connection.

I promise to protect you. Please, Sheyna. You said we could. You promised.

I don't know. I don't want the bad things to happen.

Does Gard make them happen?

I...I don't know. Maybe.

Her entire body shuddered now. Her teeth chattered in his ear. He knew she hovered on the edge of collapse.

Malachi projected his love, his affirmation of her strength, conscious that, on some level she might be aware of his arms holding her and his words loving her, but in essence she was still a little girl, frightened, traumatized by whatever memories remained locked in darkness.

We're going there together, my love. I'm holding you. See? No one can do anything bad to you so long as I hold you.

Sobbing, shivering, she nodded her head against his chest. *Okay.* The word was little more than a mewling whimper.

Carefully Malachi entered the darkened recesses of her memories. He was reminded of the viscous shroud covering the thoughts of the young rebels, the distasteful *wrongness* he'd sensed. Here the evil was more pronounced.

He healed as he entered, repairing the damage of so many years of anguish.

Ah, ah, ah, ah...

Terrified whimpers matched the panicked gasps for air as Sheyna struggled with her fear.

Praise the Mother, Malachi whispered. *Protect her.*

Suddenly, the final shroud fell away.

Sheyna screamed.

Malachi hugged her close and wept.

Gard!

Unspeakable evil, her own father...no wonder.

My god Sheyna, no wonder!

Trembling from both fear and anger, Malachi put his own emotions aside and quickly went about shielding the horror of her childhood. Not removing the memories. No, Sheyna had survived the unimaginable. To take those memories completely away would be a disservice to her strength.

Instead, Malachi blurred them, removed the edge of pain and horror so that Sheyna could look back and still remember the good of her childhood, her mother's love and the wonderful love of her brother.

He left her hatred of Gard, but took away the self-destructive core. She would see, now, the wonder of the woman she had become.

Malachi could give her this.

By the time he finally withdrew from her healing mind, Sheyna was sound asleep in his arms. Malachi kissed her brow and let the reality of what he'd discovered fester in his own mind for a while before he finally took control of his anger and disgust.

Garan must know, eventually, what their father had done to Sheyna. Evil such as Gard's could not go unpunished.

Tonight, though, Malachi wanted nothing more than to sleep, holding Sheyna in his arms.

* * * * *

She awakened slowly, aware of a newfound sense of peace, a tranquility she'd not known before. Malachi stirred beside her, his warmth as reassuring as the slow smile spreading across his face.

He nuzzled the soft hollow of her throat, then looked at her with questioning eyes. "Are you okay?"

How could she tell him she'd never been so okay in her life? *Thank you, my love. You have given me back my self...my childhood.*

Malachi sat up and leaned against the headboard, pulling Sheyna across his lap. He wrapped his arms loosely around her. "I don't understand...when I made love to you, I was certain you were...intact...still virginal. But I saw..."

Amazingly, now she could actually recall what Gard had done to her, she was no longer afraid. "I was. You were my first experience. Gard touched but never penetrated. The abuse centered on forcing me to do things to him. When I refused, he beat me."

"Yet you never told anyone. No one guessed?"

"Abuse of the young is extremely rare among my people. Plus, I realize now he blocked me quite effectively. Until last night I had no idea exactly *what* he had done to me. I feared and hated him, but I was never really certain why. I have buried so much for so long...I think,

323

because the memories were blocked, I blamed myself for the evil I sensed within my own mind."

Malachi shook his head in denial. "There is no evil in you, my love. Remember, I've been wandering through your mind. You have no secrets."

No secrets. Not from Malachi, no longer from herself.

Something dark and brittle shattered within Sheyna's heart. When it broke, the pieces glittered like diamonds and disappeared. She felt whole—complete.

"You, also, are without secrets." Sheyna grinned as awareness consumed her. She was actually flirting—another first.

She turned in Malachi's arms so that she straddled him, her knees pressed tightly to his thighs, holding him in place. "So, an older woman taught you all you know? Do you still remember her?"

His blue eyes were practically violet in the dim, early morning light. A tiny smile tickled at the corner of his mouth. "I certainly recall everything she *taught* me."

Sheyna had never felt so bold. She stroked the side of Malachi's face with the backs of her fingers, then trailed them along the line of his jaw, across his warm chest. She buried her hands in the dark mat of hair swirling about his flat, copper-colored nipples.

"There is much I would learn. Are you willing to teach me, untried though I am?"

Malachi's eyes twinkled with laughter as he solemnly considered her request. "I might," he said, rubbing his jaw between thumb and forefinger. "Is there anything in particular you…"

"Everything. I want to know it all."

* * * * *

Garan held Jenna tightly against his side, thrilling with the familiar warmth of her body along his, the knowledge she carried their child under her heart. This quiet moment before dawn might be the only time they would have alone today.

After seven long years, the rebellion appeared to be nearing a successful conclusion. Mara and Captain Sander were due to arrive late in the afternoon, leaders from all reaches of the planet were already converging on this hidden compound high in the Rocky Mountains.

The evidence was insurmountable. Talent was spreading throughout the human race and it was proving a boon for humanity. Aliens had lived among humans in a peaceful, supportive manner for the past seven years. That contact was also proving to be to humanity's benefit.

The vast numbers of organized rebels wanted essentially the same thing as the leaders of the World Federation and the population as a whole. All things considered, it was difficult for either side to remain hostile.

With nothing more to rebel against, the rebellion was coming to a peaceful end.

All of these thoughts, however, were secondary to Garan's true concern.

"You're worried about Sheyna, aren't you?" Jenna's soft voice tickled Garan's ear.

"She's just about all I can think of," he admitted, holding her close. "So many things right now are outside our control, there is much I need to be concerned with...yet all I can think of is the haunted look in her eyes when we left her with Malachi."

"Malachi is a good man. He loves Sheyna more than life itself. He is a healer. Be patient, my love."

"I am not a patient man." He rolled over on his side and propped himself up on one elbow. "However, if you try, I imagine you can take my mind off my worries." Garan raised an eyebrow and grinned. His fingers traced the line of her waist and settled on the curve of her hip, where he impatiently drummed his fingertips.

Laughing, she turned to him.

Within moments, Garan's only worry was control.

* * * * *

Malachi studied the woman who had suddenly commandeered his life. Never, in all his wildest fantasies, had he imagined anyone as exotic, as erotic, as Sheyna of Pride Imar, in his bed.

Her brilliant mind, a mind he knew most intimately, her feline beauty, her lithe body and small, taut breasts, the gleam in her amber eyes and the touch of her silky coat made him shiver with desire. The fact she wanted him, wanted his love, humbled him. He'd witnessed her power, her strength and her grace under the worst of all circumstances.

Still, she wanted him.

He'd given her access to his most private fears and longings, showed her his weaknesses, his imperfections, his failings...still, praise the Mother, she wanted him.

Praise the Mother. He should be praising Sheyna, not the goddess of her world.

Malachi ran his hands along Sheyna's sleek sides, mesmerized by the creamy, mink-like pelt that covered her. He cupped her small breasts and teased the nipples with his thumbs, grinning when they immediately puckered into tight kernels. Sheyna moaned and leaned into his touch.

Malachi laughed aloud, relishing the sudden wave of confidence her response gave him, the same response he would hope for from a human partner.

His own was sudden and immediate. Her feminine but feline beauty aroused him more than any woman, ever.

Her nails gripped his shoulders. She clamped her knees against his thighs, moaning softly as he plucked slowly at her nipples and massaged the soft swell of her breasts. Her eyes fluttered open and she gazed at him through amber eyes glazed with passion.

Malachi let his fingers trail down her sides to lightly massage her thighs, then he teased her swollen clit with the pads of both thumbs.

She arched her back, opening herself to his touch, then began a slow, rhythmic sweep of her hips, trapping his burgeoning erection in her damp folds without allowing him to penetrate.

He closed his eyes, concentrating entirely on the slick sweep of her labia sliding back and forth along the length of his cock, her tight little clit swelling beneath his thumbs.

Wet. So hot and wet — she branded him with each slow sweep along his cock.

His control near the breaking point, Malachi held her hips, stilled her rocking motion. "Too much. Too good."

She moaned, tilting herself against his gentle grip.

"I want this to last," he said, gasping for breath. "Don't move. Please!"

Sheyna laughed, a carefree sound of pure joy. Before Malachi realized what she was planning, she'd raised herself up on her knees, grabbed his throbbing penis in both hands and slowly impaled herself on his rigid shaft.

"Oh god...really...don't move. Don't even breathe." He gasped and felt the answering spasms around his cock as Sheyna laughed even harder.

Then she raised herself up and slowly rocked her hips against him in blatant disregard for his pleas.

"I thought only the men of my world were so bossy," she said, sliding as far down on him as their bodies would allow. "Now I find human males are just as bad." She raised herself up again, grinning at the audible *sucking* sound as the wet glove of her vagina held tightly to his hard cock.

Maintaining her slow rhythm, she leaned forward and dragged her small breasts across Malachi's chest, chuckling aloud when he moaned and grabbed the bedclothes in both fists. Then, holding her hips perfectly still, Sheyna ran her tongue across his chest, finding the puckered tip of first one sensitized nipple, then the other.

"Ohmygawd, woman..." The abrasive qualities of her tongue heightened the sensation to the point of pain. Malachi held perfectly still as she concentrated on each of them in turn, circling and licking until he thought he might explode.

He knew she learned more of him with each touch and taste, realized, after what she'd endured, she needed this control of their lovemaking for her own pleasure, control he was more than willing to give...so long as he was able.

Her lips suckled his left nipple. As she drew it into her mouth, she flicked her tongue across the sensitive tip. The immediate clenching in his gut, the ache in his balls warned Malachi he couldn't take much more.

Her hips once more began a slow rise and fall, the slick walls of her vagina tightening around his engorged cock in rhythm with the strokes of her tongue.

His breath huffed out in short, sharp pants.

Balancing on the edge of oblivion he fought the multitude of sensations, wanting this to last, wanting this time between them to be perfect, wanting...*Sheyna!*

Suddenly there, joining with him in a sensual mindlink, sharing her pleasure, the fullness, the marvelous stretching sensation of his swollen cock slipping in and out of wet heat, the knobby texture of his own nipple as she tasted him...he knew how it felt to tremble on the brink of climax, felt the pulsings deep in her womb, hovered for an eternity at the edge, the very brink of consciousness...shattering...suddenly, almost painfully shattering, throbbing, a shock of electricity exploding in the center of her universe...

She threw her head back and screamed, a panther's cry of victory as her muscles suddenly clamped around him, pulsing with her climax, rippling and spasming in a powerful rhythm that dragged Malachi with her into the abyss.

He cried out, his own shout of triumph, then...

Darkness. Darkness and light...and love. So much love it made him ache. He welcomed each sensation, each sense of the woman he loved beyond all others. He sighed, his body replete with their loving, his heart filled with joy.

Sated, unbelievably satisfied, Malachi wrapped his arms tightly about Sheyna and held her close against his chest. His cock throbbed deep within her heat in perfect rhythm with the tiny ripples of her vaginal muscles.

Her heart pounded against his chest, her breath was damp and sweet upon his cheek. The lean, muscled body of hers he so admired felt as limp as a washrag. Her arms lay outstretched to either side.

Malachi picked up one finely molded hand, lifted it about six inches off the bed, and then dropped it.

It fell limply back to the rumpled bedding.

"Uhm...was that entirely necessary?" Her voice was muffled against his throat.

He chuckled. Her body bounced against his laughter. "Just checking. Wanted to make sure you were still alive."

"And if I'm not?"

"Then we've got a serious problem." He played with her fingers, the nails more like cat's claws, the hands a slender version of a lion's paw.

Beautiful. Absolutely perfect.

"I love you, Malachi. Is it all right for me to say that?" She raised her head and looked at him, her wide amber eyes steady, the apprehension barely held at bay.

"I hope so," he said. "Because I love you. I think I knew from the beginning..." He nuzzled her cheek, practically wallowing in her sweet cinnamon scent.

"When I decided to come to Earth, I felt my destiny lay here."

"In this bed?" he asked, smiling as he brushed the hair back from her face.

"In your arms," she said, leaning into his palm. "Always and forever in your arms."

Chapter 18

The rebel contingent mingled with the heads of state from across the world, a gathering of close to a hundred of the most powerful political leaders of the planet assembled on the expansive front lawn of the retreat, waiting impatiently for the Miratan ship to appear.

Sipping fine wines, enjoying elaborate hors d'oeuvres and conversing on the issues facing them, the once rag-tag group of rebels proudly held their own against those who had been called *enemy* for so long.

Jenna stood at Garan's side, her arm proudly linked in his. "You realize they're all just dying of curiosity, don't you?" she said.

Garan patted her hand. "No more curious than I, my love."

She smiled at a passing dignitary, then slanted a dark-eyed look at Garan. "I don't understand. You've been among humans for years. There should be nothing special about us at all, anymore. On the other hand, I imagine you're the first Lion of Mirat to grace this well-manicured lawn."

"Possibly." He swept his hand out to encompass the crowd mingling about them. "Let your thoughts flow," he said. He stroked the dark length of her hair. "Open your mind to the myriad questions, the latent Talent, the many Sensitives among us who have no idea the power they posses. I've not been among so many oblivious humans, ever before."

Jenna laughed. "And the punch line is?" she said.

"No punch line, my love. Listen."

Garan watched Jenna's face as she concentrated on the crowd. Suddenly, her eyes widened in amazement. "Oh my. I didn't realize how much I was blocking. There's an entire undercurrent of latent power in this gathering, much more than I suspected."

"That's both a good and a bad thing." Garan gazed across the crowded lawn and tried to put his fears into words. "Members of the rebellion are taught a strong code of ethics and moral behavior. The same with the people of my world. It's part of the very fabric of their growth. That hasn't happened with the Sensitives in this group. Once members of your race realize many of them posses Talent of one form or another, I fear chaos, at least for awhile."

Jenna sighed. "Hopefully, that issue will be addressed during the assembly."

"We can only hope so. I imagine the percentage of Talent is higher among the ones gathered here. Those with Talent naturally assume positions of leadership...their innate knowledge of human nature and unusual abilities give them an edge over the more mundane members of any population."

Jenna merely nodded. Garan hadn't wanted to frighten her, but she had to be forewarned. He noticed she now carefully studied the various emissaries just as they studied Garan. With her strong mental powers, she might pick up even more information.

Barton joined Jenna and Garan. He had a tight grip on the ever-active Tad. "I wanted to let you know, Lieutenant, that as far as any of the folks here are concerned, you're a Miratan diplomat. Thought it would help to distance you from the rebellion for future treaty discussions."

Garan nodded. Diplomacy had not been his strong point. Jenna tightened her grip on his arm and grinned at him. *That's why I'm sticking so close, my love.*

Suddenly Tad ceased his squirming and stared at the sky.

Garan sensed the incoming craft at the same time. Jenna slanted him a knowing glance. *You're right,* he answered. *The boy is definitely Talented.*

There was a collective gasp, then a sigh as the Miratan ship suddenly appeared in the afternoon haze, hovering over the compound in all its silent glory.

President Barton turned to Garan and shook his head. "I've heard stories of your ships, but I never dreamed...it's so quiet. Quiet and beautiful. Is it nuclear powered?"

Garan shook his head. "No, sir. Kinetics. We've learned to harness the power of the mind for space travel. There are no limits to the worlds we can explore, the distance we can travel. If the World Federation is willing to work with us, in peace..."

Barton nodded in agreement. "I think we've all seen enough of war." He gazed, spellbound, at the ship as it slowly settled to earth.

"I've heard of this Captain Sander. He was the first of your kind to reach earth, right?"

"Yes. The first to make contact. Of course, you might want to skip over the fact his actions, along with Mara Armand and the other members of the Armand Institute, planted the seeds of the rebellion."

Barton gave him a knowing glance and grinned.

"Lieutenant Garan." Shing Tamura stepped forward. Garan acknowledged him with a brief nod of his head, continuing the formal relationship they had maintained throughout their visit.

"Your sister is arriving with Dr. Franklin. She looks..." Shing's voice faded out as he grinned in the direction of the couple walking arm in arm toward the gathering.

She looks radiant. Garan stepped forward and took Sheyna in his arms. *It's good to have you back, SheShe.*

It's good to be back, my brother. There is much we need to discuss.

Curious, Garan frowned at the solid block she used to shield her thoughts. There was nothing sinister implied, but she was obviously hiding something from him. He glanced at Malachi, who merely nodded and smiled.

Both minds were shielded.

Later.

The hatch on the ship opened. A slender, dark-haired woman stood at the top of the staircase as it slowly extended to the ground. Suddenly, she was flanked by a huge Lion of Mirat on one side and a beautiful ebony-maned child on the other.

She gazed out over the large group, then grinned broadly. "Malachi! Thom...Shing! There you are!"

Garan stood back and watched the old friends as they greeted one another. Sheyna clung tightly to Malachi's hand. She didn't let go, even when Mara stood on tiptoe and gave Malachi a welcoming kiss.

Sander briefly greeted the president, then came to stand beside Garan, his big paw firmly grasping the little girl's hand.

"Kefira," he said in perfect English, "this is Garan of Pride Imar. Our mothers were littermates."

The child stared solemnly at Garan; her huge eyes a sparkling green, the lines of her face inexplicably beautiful, a perfect blend of Earth and Mirat.

"Hello, Kefira. It is an honor to meet you." Garan squatted down on his haunches to place himself at eye level.

"Hello." She looked up at her father, as if asking for further instructions. Her long tail curled lightly about her slim ankles.

Jenna suddenly appeared at Garan's side. He stood, put his arm around her and drew her forward. "I want you to meet Captain Sander and his daughter, Kefira."

Jenna flashed him a startled look of understanding then smiled at the child. "Kefira? It is so special to meet you." As Garan had before, Jenna knelt in front of the little girl, who solemnly took Jenna's hand in greeting. When Jenna looked up at Garan, there were tears in her eyes.

She is just beautiful…you know I've been worried…

Garan stroked her shiny hair, then helped her stand. "Jenna carries our child," he said. There was understanding in Sander's amber eyes. "Thank you for allowing us this opportunity to meet your daughter."

Garan sensed President Barton's surprise. He'd forgotten the world leader was standing so close by. "Our DNA is much closer than our appearance would suggest," he said.

"Obviously. She's a beautiful child." Barton let go of Tad's hand as he spoke. The youngsters studied each other solemnly, oblivious to the adults around them.

Tad looked up at his father. "Kefira talks in my head like the other cat lady did. She's seven. Can we go play?"

"If it's all right with Kefira's parents. Captain Sander?"

Sander nodded his approval.

President Barton turned to an older woman standing beside Tad. "Gertie?"

Tad's ever-present nanny stepped forward. "Yes, sir."

"Keep an eye on these two for a few minutes, will you?"

"Uh huh…um, yes, sir." Wide eyed, Gertie led the youngsters toward a play area just a few yards away. Thom Antoon, Shing Tamura and Barton continued their conversation.

The rest of the crew began to disembark from the ship and all attention turned to the Lions of Mirat, resplendent in dress uniform, as they joined the gathering. A few of the humans stood apart, obviously uncomfortable with the influx of massive aliens, but most joined the casual discussions.

Garan and Sander stood off to one side, quietly observing. Mara joined them a moment later. *What do you think, my love?*

Sander included Garan in the silent conversation.

I sense curiosity, some apprehension, even fear from a few. There is nothing for us to be afraid of, at least not yet.

Sheyna is a powerful empath as well, Garan added. Silently he called to her. Deep in conversation with Malachi, she raised her head and looked in his direction, turned, said something to Malachi, then quickly joined Garan, Sander and Mara.

At Sander's instruction, Sheyna and Mara linked minds and searched for emotions on an even deeper level than either could manage on their own.

Suddenly, Sheyna broke the link. Mara pulled back as well, a questioning look in her green eyes. "That was…"

"Very unusual," Sheyna said, completing Mara's thought. She took a quick glance around to make sure no one observed too closely. "There is a powerful sense of evil, shielded, which is why it took both of us to find it. Whoever wishes us ill has a strong block."

"Any idea who?" Sander's voice was a soft rumble.

"No, though I…" She shook her head in frustration. "It's vaguely familiar but I can't identify anything specific. I'm not even sure if the individual is actually among this throng or outside the walls. I'll inform Jenna so the three of us can continue to search." Sheyna suddenly trembled as an unfamiliar precognitive sensation flickered across her mind.

"Keep a close eye on Kefira," she said, staring blankly into the crowd.

Sander grabbed her wrist. "What do you see?"

Frustrated, Sheyna shook her head. "I don't know. Nothing…nothing I understand. I'm not pre-cog, I…sense something…I don't know what."

Mara wrapped her arm lightly around Sheyna's waist. "Did you link with Malachi last night?"

Sheyna nodded. Though she wanted to be jealous of this past love of Malachi's, she could only feel grateful to have Mara beside her. "Yes," she said. "We did a comprehensive link."

"I thought so. It probably won't last, but you may have absorbed some of his Talent. Don't fight it. Sander? You'd best find our daughter and keep her close."

* * * * *

"Daddy says you live up there." Tad Barton wrapped his small hand around Sheyna's paw and pointed to the sky with the other. "He said you 'n Kefi come from another planet. Where is it?"

Sheyna sat next to Malachi on a low wall in the Federation compound bordering a garden filled with flowers of every imaginable shade and hue. She pointed in the direction of the setting sun. "It's out there, I think. In your western sky. I come from a world called Mirat but Kefi was born aboard a ship in space. Her mommy is from Earth, her daddy from my world."

Tad nodded as if it all made perfect sense. Sheyna projected an image of her home world to both Malachi and the little boy, showing them the cities built of stone and the twin moons rising on the horizon.

Tad's eyes grew round with delight. "Wow! Mirat has two moons? I gotta tell Kefi."

Sheyna smiled as she watched him race back across the grass to a spot in the shade of an ancient fig tree where Kefira quietly played with Sheyna's stuffed kitten. The little girl had commandeered the toy the moment she spotted it in Sheyna's room.

"It's nice to know you don't need your kitten anymore."

Sheyna smiled at Malachi. "You must be reading my thoughts again."

Always. Mal draped his arm loosely over Sheyna's shoulders. Together they watched the children play. The ever-present Gertie crocheted an afghan, sitting in a lawn chair under a nearby tree.

The afternoon had been filled with meetings among the rebels, the leaders of the World Federation and the two senior Lions of Mirat — Garan and Sander, along with Mara Armand.

They met still, working through the details of the treaty between the rebels and the World Federation, between the WF and Mirat.

Sheyna and Malachi had been drawn to the children.

Their duty lay here, with their senses on full alert to danger. Three of Sander's crewmembers stayed nearby, in the event assistance should be needed.

None of them had been able to triangulate the source of the danger they sensed, even with Mara and Jenna's help. Still, it was out there, a stray wisp of peril, eerily familiar, ever present in their minds.

The children had bonded immediately, their laughter followed by long silences as they communicated telepathically.

"I'm glad your eavesdropping skills are so good," Malachi said. He brushed Sheyna's arm lightly with his fingers, listening to the childish chatter through Sheyna's mind.

"Growing up in a large pride, I learned to keep track of the trouble everyone else was getting into." Sheyna watched as the two children stood up, then began to climb into the tangled, low-hanging branches of the fig tree.

"I always wanted to be well out of the way when the others got caught and punished...Mal, do you think they're safe, climbing so high? I can't even hear them."

"I don't know. The leaves are so thick I can't see them anymore, either. I probably should get them down." Malachi laughed as he stood up and stretched. A tingling along his spine suddenly brought him to full alert. Sheyna leapt to her feet, her eyes wide open and staring.

"It can't be."

"Call the others," Malachi shouted as he raced toward the children, the three attending Lions of Mirat in hot pursuit. "Tell them Merrick White is back."

* * * * *

Jenna leapt to her feet, almost knocking over the ambassador from New Spain. Garan was right behind her. In the space of a heartbeat, Shing, Thom, Mara and Sander had joined the rush to the door.

Sheyna burst into the meeting hall, her breath gone, her mental scream loud and clear.

Merrick White...he's not dead. He's got the children!

Jenna quickly interpreted for the un-Talented as Garan, Mara and Sander, Thom and Shing raced for the back of the compound.

"Merrick White, a madman, a rogue commander for the WF, has kidnapped Tad and Kefira. Call your security forces, quickly. The man's a killer and we believe he has Talent. There's no telling what he's capable of."

Jenna reached Sheyna just as the young lioness crumpled to the floor. Placing her palms at either side of Sheyna's skull, she calmed and steadied her within seconds.

Sheyna blinked and nodded, then quickly stood. "We have to stop him, we…"

"Let's go." Jenna raced out the door. Sheyna followed close behind. Just as they circled the compound, a small aircraft leapt into the sky. Jenna searched for the mental imprint of the pilot and found madness. The children's minds were foggy, as if they'd been drugged.

Or controlled by one of his weird beams, Sheyna projected. *What can we do?*

Jenna grabbed Malachi and Garan's hands. "Join," she screamed. "Link!"

Sheyna grabbed onto Malachi's free hand. Sander, Shing Tamura and Thom Antoon immediately completed the circle.

The tiny craft grew even smaller as Merrick White sped away with his captives.

"What are you doing?" President Barton reached the small circle of Sensitives who stood silently, eyes closed, hands tightly linked. "Go after them! Aren't you going to help them?"

Jenna was only vaguely aware of the soft voice of one of the Miratan security officers. "They are helping, sir. Please. Do not disturb the link."

When Barton persisted, the huge lion gently held him immobile.

Though all the ambassadors and world leaders now milled about the grassy area, not one of them stepped forward to interfere. The president's security forces stayed back, as well, as if all sensed the power of the link.

Suddenly, the aircraft halted its forward motion. Spinning slowly in the air, the distant sound of the straining engine fighting an overwhelming force could easily be heard.

"That's it, baby. That's it sweetheart…work it, baby. Oh, Kefi, Mommy is so proud of you…" Mara's words escaped on a sob as the tiny craft straightened and headed directly back to the compound.

"But, how?" Barton ceased his struggles and the alien set him free with a quick apology. The president waved him off. "No matter," he said, staring intently at the tiny aircraft growing closer with each passing second.

Sander and Garan quietly stepped away from the Sensitives, joining their partners' hands together to maintain the meld. The moment they were clear of the link, Garan shouted "Kinetics," to the president. He and Sander raced toward a small clearing just in front of the fig tree. "Your little guy and Kefira helped us turn the ship!"

The helicopter settled silently on the grass, engine smoking, blades slowly spinning.

Kefira and Tad tumbled out of the back entrance, frightened but unhurt. Kefira grasped Sheyna's toy kitten tightly in her fist. Sander scooped both children up in his powerful arms and turned away from the bloody mess within the aircraft.

Garan's bestial roar echoed from the hillsides as he ripped open the door closest to the pilot...and stood in complete silence, witness to Merrick White's final judgment.

Shing, Thom Antoon and President Barton reached his side. Barton turned his head and was immediately sick. Garan absentmindedly patted the world leader on the back.

Sander carried the children across the lawn to the line held by the security troops, combined forces of both human and Miratan soldiers. He handed the children over to Jenna and Mara. Kefira clung to her mother, the tattered toy kitten clutched tightly in her hands. Tad latched onto Jenna but stared solemnly at Sheyna. Tad's mother broke through the security line and raced to her son. Jenna smiled as she handed the little boy over and followed Sander back to stand beside Garan.

"How? What happened to...?" Shing Tamura's whispered questions barely reached Garan.

Shaking his head in amazement, Garan answered as best he could. "Praise the Mother the children were in a separate compartment in the back...I don't think they have any idea what they did."

"You mean the children did that?"

The horror in President Barton's voice was magnified by the quiet buzz of a yellow wasp as it circled the shattered remnants of what had once been Merrick White.

"I imagine when they tried to turn the aircraft around, they had to work through the coordinates...you know, figure out just what it was we were attempting to do. Something got lost in the translation...it appears they turned their captor inside out before they managed to turn the craft around."

"But...they're children. Tad's just a little boy...he's barely eight years old." Howard Barton's pale face still carried the shock of what lay before them. "The girl, she's...?"

"Kefira is seven," Sander said. He gestured to his soldiers to keep the rest of the crowd far back from the area.

"She is also a powerful kinetic with other Talents we are only beginning to recognize," he added. "It appears she and Tad linked...I think it was purely accidental, but somehow they were able to draw on the power of our link and use it in gestalt to save their lives."

"They didn't see this, did they?" Thom Antoon gestured toward the body. "My gawd, this could..."

"No." Sander sighed aloud. He sounded very tired. "No. Tad just said they stopped the bad man because the bad man was taking them away from their mommies. It appears White stunned them with some sort of force field, but it must have worn off quickly. The children couldn't see him because he'd locked them in the back, so they used the only means they had to save their lives."

"The power of their minds." Garan studied the small craft, considered the mental strength it would take to change its direction in mid-flight, keep it aloft, destroy the pilot and return to a safe landing.

"They weren't alone, my love. Somehow, without any training, Tad and Kefira must have worked in gestalt with our link. There is much power between them, but not enough for this." Jenna stepped closer behind Garan, wrapped her arms around his waist and pressed her cheek to his broad back. The sense of her so close was comforting beyond reason.

As was her explanation.

Sheyna and Malachi joined the small group near the craft. "I'm not so sure this is a good idea," Malachi said.

Sheyna put her hand on his forearm. "I need to see this. Please." Before Garan could react, Sheyna slipped around him and opened the door to the aircraft. She wrinkled her nose at the foul stench then quietly closed the door, hiding the tortured remains from view. "I needed to be sure," she said. "I'll rest much easier, now. He's not coming back."

"I'm sorry, SheShe." Garan shook his head in dismay and sighed. "I thought White was already dead. I was certain I killed him. I thought the risk was behind us."

"It's not your fault, brother. I thought he was dead, too. There was no *sense* of him after you tossed him over the cliff. At the time I was positive he was dead."

Jenna's arms tightened around Garan's waist. "We all did. Please...don't blame yourself. Everyone is fine. The children are okay." She smiled at Sheyna. "Sheyna's tougher than she looks. She'll be fine as well."

"You're right, Jenna." Sheyna stood proudly next to Malachi. "I'm a lot tougher than I look...and definitely a lot tougher than I thought I was."

"Logically I know that. The older brother in me wants to hold you in his arms and Praise the Mother you're okay, the children are okay..." Garan turned slowly and drew Jenna into his embrace instead. He smiled and rested his chin atop her head. "This has been a very long day. I assume, at some point, I'll be able to make sense of it."

"I think we all feel much as you do," President Barton said. He too, sounded exhausted. "Gentlemen, this power of the mind...I had no idea...no idea at all." He held out his hands as if in benediction.

"Thank you," he said to all of them, "for saving my son. For giving him the power he needed to work with Kefira. We will meet again in the morning and figure out where we go from here. For now though, I believe, we all need time with our families. "

Chapter 19

Sheyna leaned against the deck railing and stared out over the sloping lawn behind their bungalow as the day slowly turned to dusk.

Her mental shields were very much in place. Malachi had checked. He'd tried to communicate telepathically but she'd shut him out. Putting medical ethics aside, he'd tried to read her thoughts and failed.

He'd wanted to hold her in his arms. She'd turned away.

He'd told her he loved her.

She'd nodded, smiled and gone outside.

Now he sipped at a glass of wine and watched her from inside the room. She'd been standing there, the sunlight and shadows moving slowly across her silent form, for well over an hour.

Unexpectedly, just as Malachi was beginning to wonder if she was more seriously traumatized than he'd suspected, Sheyna turned and smiled at him. "I'd love a glass of that wine," she said. "Join me?"

Bemused, shaking his head at the unpredictability of females, Malachi poured Sheyna a glass of chilled wine and carried it out to her.

"I didn't mean to worry you," she said, taking the glass from him. "I needed to decide my next step. It is a decision that must be mine and mine alone."

Right now, silence felt like Malachi's best option.

"I finally understood today that every decision I have ever made has been a defensive reaction to something either Gard or, most recently, Merrick White, has done to me. Once your young rebels have all been healed, I have decided to return to Mirat."

Before Malachi could protest, she touched his cheek with the tips of her fingers. He felt the smooth brush of her nails, a reminder of just how different they really were.

"I want you to come with me," she added. "I need to face Gard myself. It is neither Sander's nor Garan's job to bring him to justice. I want to go before the Council of Nine and bring my own charges. I want to look at him and tell him what he did to an innocent child was wrong and will not be tolerated. Nor will it be forgiven. However, I am weak enough to know I want you standing beside me, giving me the strength to carry out this task."

"You are not weak. Never will I think of you as weak. You know I will go wherever you wish, do whatever you ask." Malachi pulled Sheyna into his arms, almost surprised when she leaned into his embrace.

"Today when I saw Merrick White, I discovered something in myself I'm not so sure I like. I was glad he was dead. At the same time, I was angry I'd not had the chance to confront him before he died. I do not intend to miss that opportunity with Gard."

"Revenge is so important to you?" Malachi asked.

"Not revenge. Closure. You've given me what peace you can, my love. Only Gard can give me closure."

"Do you expect an apology?"

At that Sheyna laughed. "Oh no...not from Gard. I do, however, expect his lands will be seized, his good name destroyed and his seat on the Council rescinded and given to one of my siblings, any one of whom is better qualified to govern Mirat than a pedophile."

Her smile suddenly turned very grave. "I also need to do this to protect my younger sisters. There are two, still living under Gard's roof. I want you with me as much for myself as to examine them. One is about the age I was when..."

"We'll go as soon as you're ready to travel."

"We will finish the healing I came here for, first. Your young men have waited long enough. That should only take a day or two."

Mal's arms tightened around her. It was so easy to lose himself in her warmth, her loving spirit, her generous nature. "Whatever you decide, my love."

"Oh Malachi. I do love you so." She brought his head down to hers and kissed him fully on the mouth. His senses reeled with the rich cinnamon scent of her, the sinuous length of her body pressed close to his, the soft purr deep in her throat.

Her fingers slipped inside his shirt and shoved it back over his shoulders. Malachi struggled with the fastening at the top of Sheyna's skinsuit as desire and passion stole his coordination and threatened his control.

Voices sounded just below the deck—the sentries making their evening rounds. Laughing with the joy of her, Malachi walked both of them backwards into the bungalow and quickly drew the shades.

Sheyna looped her foot around his ankle and tumbled him back onto the bed. This time, Malachi rolled her over to her back and raised himself above her, his hips pressed between her strong thighs, his arms supporting him just above her lean body.

Already her eyes had that lazy, glazed look of passion, the need so vividly written in her every move and sound. He wondered if he'd ever get used to the sense of longing, the physical hunger she induced in him with every glance, each small touch.

Her fingers stroked his sides, worked their way across his shoulders. His unbuttoned shirt hung about his waist, partially trapping his arms. He sat up and shrugged out of it, then carefully peeled Sheyna's skinsuit the rest of the way down her body.

He had to roll completely off of her to remove the stretchy fabric, along with her soft boots, then he straddled her. He still wore his denim jeans, but he did manage to kick his shoes off. There was something very powerful about sitting astride this beautiful, naked creature, still partially dressed in his everyday clothes.

She moaned and bucked against him, bringing her crotch into contact with the rough fabric of his pants. Malachi stretched out atop her and pressed himself as close as possible, moving his hips in a slight rhythmic motion that prolonged the contact between the bulge in his pants and Sheyna's hot center.

He felt her heat through the denim. His cock strained against the tight confines of his pants, swelling more with each tiny undulation she made. The sensation practically overwhelmed him. He took a deep breath for control.

"This isn't going to work," he whispered, slowly releasing his zipper. "I feel like I'm going to explode and we haven't even touched."

"Touch me, Mal. I want to explode. I want to feel again…make me feel alive."

"Sheyna, you *are* life." He nuzzled the soft curve of her neck, practically wallowing in the silken pelt he found so tantalizing. He rubbed his cheek along the sleek line of her chest then quickly found her left breast. Her nipple was already turgid and swollen, waiting for his lips. Slowly he drew the flesh into his mouth, circling the hard kernel with his tongue, suckling as if he were a newborn searching for a meal. Her heart beat loud and clear beneath his lips as he concentrated on bringing life to that one part of her body.

He slipped to one side, better to touch her. His swollen cock forced his zipper the rest of the way open. He shoved his pants partially down his legs, just enough to free himself. Still suckling her breast, he pressed his erection hard against her hip.

She moaned and writhed against him. He switched to her other breast as his fingers trailed along her rib cage, found the deep valley of her navel, then slipped into the wet heat between her thighs.

She bucked against his hand. He pressed down on her pubis, holding her still with his palm while his middle finger found her clit. He stroked the distended nubbin, felt it swell even as her nipple swelled between his lips.

He suckled harder, drawing her flesh into his mouth, tonguing the sensitive tip. His finger lightly stroked her needy flesh then dove into her vagina. He found her wet and ready, her muscles clenching frantically at his finger.

He inserted two more fingers, stroking steadily in rhythm with his tongue on her breast. Her tight passage encased him. Teasing, he tickled the inner flesh with his fingertips until she moaned and pressed her hips against his hand.

Mal let his thoughts touch Sheyna's and found desire, white-hot desire without form or name. It fueled his. He burned with wanting until the denim jeans around his thighs were suddenly an impediment he could no longer tolerate.

Slipping them off his legs, he rolled over, turned around so that he lay across her warm belly and put his mouth where his fingers had played. She tasted of cinnamon and brown sugar, sweet and spicy, an aphrodisiac of flavors. He stroked her clit so gently with his tongue, tasting her, testing the boundaries of her control along with his own, then suckled on the sensitive organ.

He felt her hands stroking his thighs, the line of his buttocks, then suddenly she was urging him to lift his legs, turning him so that he stretched the length of her, his legs on either side of her face, his weight balanced on his elbows. He raised himself up on his knees and shuddered when her tongue found him, curling around his cock all sandpapery rough, pulling him down between her soft lips, her sharp teeth, suckling him deep into her throat.

He stabbed into her with his own tongue, forcing himself to concentrate on Sheyna's pleasure, not his own. He tasted her sweet spice and felt the muscles of her vagina contract around his tongue. Fluid, sweet and intoxicating, bathed his chin and lips as he licked and sucked at the tender flesh.

She suckled him deep and hard, then released him so that she could lick the tender folds around his testicles, the soft underside of his penis. Gasping, Malachi forced himself to contain his pleasure, forced his mind away from the exquisite sensations of Sheyna's oral exploration of his cock and balls and...

Ass.

Oh gawd, Sheyna, are you trying to kill me?

She held his thighs steady in her slim but strong hands and ran her tongue oh, so slowly from the underside of his cock to his tailbone. Abrasive as rough sandpaper, gentle yet inquisitive, the raspy surface of her tongue left no part of him untouched.

She repeated the process, slower each time. Malachi tried to concentrate on Sheyna's pleasure, tried to please her, but the sensations were too much. He was lost in a rapturous vortex, every bit of his being concentrated in the spot where Sheyna's tongue connected with his flesh.

He forced himself to focus, to think of Sheyna, to think *with* Sheyna. Gasping, struggling for control, he put his mouth on her, suckling her clit, her labia, tasting the sweet flavors he'd suddenly come to crave. As he tongued her swollen clit, she was there, tonguing him, mimicking his every move, linking with him as she licked and sucked and tasted.

I want to be inside you, he 'pathed, thankful for this silent speech. The only audible sound he felt capable of was an incoherent moan of pleasure.

Not this time. Malachi, my love. Please. I want this.

Suddenly he was engulfed in the sweet recesses of her mouth, the lush promise of her love. Her sandpaper tongue stroked his hard cock; her strong hands clenched his buttocks. He felt the sharp sting of unsheathed claws and she suckled harder, tighter—the sensations, the pressure a combination of sweet pain and unbearable pleasure.

He grasped her thighs, kneading the taut flesh of hip and buttock, pulling her closer to his mouth, suckling her swollen clit in rhythm with Sheyna, a dance of tongues and teeth and lips. Her body stiffened, his mind flooded with sensation, the indescribably lush impressions of touch, taste and smell.

Her clit tightened beneath his lips. He bit her—*oh, so lightly, so hard to control, so sweet, the gush of fluid, your thighs pressed tightly, holding me as if I'd ever leave, as if I'd miss even a drop of your climax, so sweet and pure…*

Cinnamon and sugar, salt and sweet, her tastes and his as the white-hot coil of heat boiled out of him.

Conscious thought ended in a molten spiral of pure lust. He pumped himself between her soft lips. Her nails pierced the flesh of his buttocks as she held him to her mouth, taking all of him, sucking him harder, deeper until the pleasure, the pain, the pure need to empty himself between her suckling lips coalesced into need…need and want, an overpowering, overwhelming desire, until…

Gasping, his weight full upon her, his heart pounding, his lips still resting against her pulsing center, his mind a tangled pile of emotion…*I need, I want, I love…I love. You. Sheyna. Only you. Dear God, Sheyna, you are trying to kill me!*

He felt her lips smile around his flaccid penis. *No, my love. Never that.*

His arms and legs felt like warm wax with all the muscle tone of a two-day-old baby. Slowly, Malachi rolled off of Sheyna and turned around so that he could tuck her head beneath his chin.

She snuggled alongside him, her hands slightly stroking his hip.

Ouch.

She giggled against his throat. *Sorry…I forgot to sheath my claws.*

Malachi groaned and rubbed the shallow pierce marks on his butt. *Isn't that sort of a lovemaking faux pas?*

Can I say I just got carried away?

Suddenly it all came together. This moment, this woman, this future…the road he must take. He kissed the top of her head. *Only because I did as well. I love you, Sheyna. I don't ever want to lose you. You are unique, you are beloved. I don't know all the rules of your people, but in my world I would ask for your hand in marriage.*

She turned her face so that she looked up at him, her amber eyes sparkling in the deep gloom of early evening. *On Mirat I would request a pair-bond, that you be my lifemate.*

Would you?

Would I what? She flashed him a coy smile.

You're laughing at me, aren't you? Malachi brushed the dark hair back from her wide brow. Would he ever grow tired of looking at her exotic beauty?

She smiled. "I'm not laughing, Malachi. Never at you. I am, however, waiting for you to explain why you would only want my hand? Don't humans marry the whole person? I certainly intend to ask you to be my lifemate, but I want all of you."

She grabbed one of his hands in both of hers, studied the long, slim fingers, rubbed his palm against hers. "I must admit, though, your hands are very good."

"We will never grow bored, my love." Malachi sat up and leaned against the headboard, pulling Sheyna across his lap. "Will you marry me? All of me? Hang ups, insecurities, strange sense of humor?"

"I thought I was the one with the self esteem problems." She stroked his cheek with the silky backs of her fingers.

"Not anymore. You strike me as a woman who knows what she wants and won't hesitate to go after it. I like this side of you, Sheyna of Pride Imar."

"I like this side of me, too." She stroked his shoulder, followed the length of his arm, draped her fingers softly over his thigh near the crease of his groin.

Malachi immediately tightened in response. He groaned as her fingers crept closer, teasing, softly tickling. "I'm still waiting for your answer. Will you pledge to me? Marry me? I love you, Sheyna. I want you as my mate for life."

She turned in his arms and growled deep in her throat, nipping at his shoulder as she settled herself over his suddenly rampant erection. "I'm yours," she whispered. "So long as you realize, with me you get claws."

Epilogue

Sheyna of Pride Imar, mate to Malachi Franklin, healer of Earth, stood on the ship's deck and stared through the view port. Soon, the familiar blue green sphere would appear in the black depths of space.

So different from her last trip to Earth.

This time, she was coming home.

Malachi stepped into the small viewing area and wrapped his arms around her. He sighed, his breath warm against her throat. She leaned back; close enough to feel the steady beat of his heart against her back. "It's been a tough few weeks," he said. "Not only did you manage a full healing for all six of my patients, you have stood up to a most powerful adversary. I am so proud of you."

His voice was strained, exhausted.

Triumphant.

"Thank you." What more could she say? Once the young rebels were healed, she and Malachi had immediately headed for Mirat and a heated, emotional confrontation with Gard.

Her mate had stood beside her throughout the entire ordeal. It hadn't been easy, appearing before the Council of Nine and accusing one of their most powerful members of pedophilia, of unspeakable sins against a child, but Malachi had been there, a silent tower of strength, ever supportive.

Supportive and able to help provide the information the Council needed to censure one of their own when Malachi had carefully shared with them the journey he'd taken through Sheyna's terror.

She'd hadn't realized, though he'd blocked so much of the pain from her, he'd taken those terrible memories into his own mind and held on to them, knowing they would one day be needed.

He'd been patient and loving toward her small sisters, relieved to learn Gard had not found them, unlike the exotic Sheyna, to his liking. Now, stripped of his land, his power and his name, the once invincible head of Pride Imar waited for exile to a desolate planet designated for the few criminals of Mirat.

Justice, at least, had been swift and sure. Malachi's steadfast support of Sheyna had removed any vestiges of the fear she'd learned from her sire.

"I'm looking forward to working with Tad Barton," Malachi said. "He's showing amazing Talent for one so young. I like his father's idea for setting up training centers for the Talented...centers that will emphasize honor and integrity."

"Both Tad and Kefira are amazing. It's hard to believe they're mere children—especially Kefira. Mara's going to have her hands full with that one! Between her daughter and her mate...I'm still trying to picture Sander as a diplomat!"

"Mara will keep him in line. I'm glad they'll be spending most of their time on Earth, though. Kefira and Tad are learning much from each other. It would be a shame to separate them at this point."

Sheyna turned, wrapped her arms around Mal and rested her head against his chest. She watched the tiny blue green sphere hanging like a beacon in the darkness, slowly gain definition as their craft sped ever closer.

She thought of her sibling and beloved sister of her heart, heading off into space on their first StarQuest. "I think you're right about Mara. I'll miss Garan and Jenna, though."

"I know." Mal's chin rubbed against the top of her head as he held her. "But now the treaty has been signed and talks are progressing so well, it's time for the diplomats to take over. Garan has wanted to go on his Quest as long as I've known him...plus, he's never been very diplomatic!"

Sheyna laughed, remembering all the times Garan had come to her aid, the love he'd shown her when she was frightened and alone. Even Malachi would never know the true kindness in her brother's heart.

Only Sheyna...and of course, Jenna. *Praise the Mother,* Garan had found his perfect lifemate.

As have I. Malachi kissed the top of her head.

Eavesdropping on my private thoughts, my love? Sheyna smiled, well aware she'd been broadcasting her tumbled memories.

Just checking.

Always worried about me, aren't you Mal? Sheyna turned in his strong, comforting arms and studied his beautiful, alien face. *Praise the*

Mother, would she ever get enough of him? Always so concerned, so aware. He made her feel safe, cherished.

He challenged her.

He loved her.

Mal's dark blue eyes were solemn, but Sheyna knew the humor was never far away. *I worry you hide fears from me, SheShe. I see there are none. Not even regrets?*

Regrets? Regrets for having survived the unthinkable, for coming through pain and tragedy with her soul intact, her body whole, her life filled with more love than she could ever have imagined?

Sheyna slowly shook her head in denial. *No, love of my heart. How can I have regrets when all that has happened has brought you into my life?*

They both felt the shift, the minor adjustment in coordinates that meant the ship prepared for entry into Earth's atmosphere. Malachi helped Sheyna into one of the comfortably padded chairs, tightened her restraints, then quickly found his seat beside her and prepared for landing.

Sheyna held her hand out and grabbed his fingers...hers, covered in the silken pelt of her race, fingers broader with darkly sheathed claws at the tips—his darkly tanned and callused, the nails blunt, some neatly clipped, others bitten. She squeezed his hand, alien to her, more dear than anything she could remember, and watched her home draw near.

The STARQUEST series continues with "Synergy" in the anthology THRESHOLD VOLUME 1.

Transported a hundred years into the future by an absolutely gorgeous young man, Carly Harris quickly turns the tables on the sexy Sensitive who tells her that use of his telekinetic power leaves him impotent.

He's used a lot of power to bring Carly forward in time, but he still has plenty left. Before long, Carly and Tim Riley move beyond their awkward introduction and discover the reason Tim's libido is so active- Carly is a Synergist, a Sensitive with the talent to increase the power of those around her.

Does Tim really love her, or is he using her for the power she gives him? Before Carly can get past that twenty-year age difference, she needs to learn the truth.

About the author:

For over thirty years Kate Douglas has been lucky enough to call writing her profession. She has won three EPPIES, two for Best Contemporary Romance in 2001 and 2002, and a third for Best Romantic Suspense in 2001. Kate also creates cover art and is the winner of EPIC's Quasar Award for outstanding bookcover graphics.

She is multi-published in contemporary romance, both print and electronic formats, as well as her popular futuristic Romantica StarQuest. She and her husband of over thirty years live in the northern California wine country where they find more than enough subject material for their shared passion for photography, though their new grandson is most often in front of the lens. Kate is currently working on the Book 5 of her StarQuest Series, Bold Journey, coming in March, 2004 from Ellora's Cave. Read Book 4, SYNERGY, in Threshold, Volume 1.

Kate Douglas welcomes mail from readers. You can write to her c/o Ellora's Cave Publishing at 1337 Commerce Drive Suite 13, Stow OH 44224.

Also by KATE DOUGLAS:

- More Than a Hunch
- Luck of the Irish – with Jennifer Dunne & Chris Tanglen
- Threshold Volume 1 – with Treva Harte

Why an electronic book?

We live in the Information Age—an exciting time in the history of human civilization in which technology rules supreme and continues to progress in leaps and bounds every minute of every hour of every day. For a multitude of reasons, more and more avid literary fans are opting to purchase e-books instead of paperbacks. The question to those not yet initiated to the world of electronic reading is simply: *why?*

1. *Price.* An electronic title at Ellora's Cave Publishing runs anywhere from 40-75% less than the cover price of the <u>exact same title</u> in paperback format. Why? Cold mathematics. It is less expensive to publish an e-book than it is to publish a paperback, so the savings are passed along to the consumer.

2. *Space.* Running out of room to house your paperback books? That is one worry you will never have with electronic novels. For a low one-time cost, you can purchase a handheld computer designed specifically for e-reading purposes. Many e-readers are larger than the average handheld, giving you plenty of screen room. Better yet, hundreds of titles can be stored within your new library—a single microchip. (Please note that Ellora's Cave does not endorse any specific brands. You can check our website at www.ellorascave.com for customer recommendations we make available to new consumers.)

3. *Mobility.* Because your new library now consists of only a microchip, your entire cache of books can be taken with you wherever you go.

4. *Personal preferences are accounted for.* Are the words you are currently reading too small? Too large? Too...ANNOYING? Paperback books cannot be modified according to personal preferences, but e-books can.

5. *Innovation.* The way you read a book is not the only advancement the Information Age has gifted the literary community with. There is also the factor of what you can read. Ellora's Cave Publishing will be introducing a new line of interactive titles that are available in e-book format only.

6. *Instant gratification.* Is it the middle of the night and all the bookstores are closed? Are you tired of waiting days—sometimes weeks—for online and offline bookstores to ship the novels you bought? Ellora's Cave Publishing sells instantaneous downloads 24 hours a day, 7 days a week, 365 days a year. Our e-book delivery system is 100% automated, meaning your order is filled as soon as you pay for it.

Those are a few of the top reasons why electronic novels are displacing paperbacks for many an avid reader. As always, Ellora's Cave Publishing welcomes your questions and comments. We invite you to email us at service@ellorascave.com or write to us directly at: P.O. Box 787, Hudson, Ohio 44236-0787.

Printed in the United States
22881LVS00001B/43-60